THE DARKEST CHASE

A SMALL TOWN GRUMPY SUNSHINE ROMANCE

NICOLE SNOW

Content copyright © Nicole Snow. All rights reserved.
Published in the United States of America.
First published in July, 2024.

Disclaimer: The following book is a work of fiction. Any resemblance characters in this story may have to real people is only coincidental.

Please respect this author's hard work! No section of this book may be reproduced or copied without permission. Exception for brief quotations used in reviews or promotions. This book is licensed for your personal enjoyment only. Thanks!

Cover Design – CoverLuv.

Proofread by Sisters Get Lit.erary Author Services.

Website: Nicolesnowbooks.com

ABOUT THE BOOK

Life is just full of crazy surprises with teeth.

One day you're the forever single wallflower keeping up the boring family furniture shop.

The next, you're getting mouth-to-mouth from a scary hot stranger who wants to make your life a thriller novel.

Yes, my disaster has a name.

Micah Ainsley.

Everything I'm not. Nothing remotely good for me.

He's all wolf—moody, savage, and ferociously protective.

I'm a human puppy.

He thrives on secrets.

Everybody knows what I had for breakfast.

He's experienced. *So experienced.*

I've never even been kissed.

But when he needs my help to take down a rich creep who just happens to be my new client, I'm game.

I'm ready to live a little.

I'm eager to prove I'm more than a hot mess with a cross-eyed crush on a coldhearted man who's too old for me.

Then another surprise bites me in the face.

The night Micah claims me.

The moment our wrong becomes reality and there's no going back.

The darkest chase is on and it only ends one way—sweet dreams or total devastation.

I: IN THE DARK (TALIA)

I think I've been shut up in the workshop without ventilation for too long.

Varnish. Fumes. Lack of oxygen.

That sort of thing.

That's the only reason why I could possibly be standing here in the open doorway of Grandpa's shop, blinking at the bright sunlight filtering in, drenched in the smell of spring wildflowers and the warm scent of rising bread from the bakery two doors down.

All while a clean-cut, dark-haired man in a full three-piece uniform with a tailcoat and white kid gloves bows.

There's a heavy vellum envelope in his hand with A Touch of Grey written across it, closed with a wax seal.

"I'm sorry," I whisper, staring at the envelope with our shop's name on it. "You must have the wrong place."

"No mistake, Miss Grey. I've been asked to request your grandfather's company," the man says. I guess he's a butler or a valet or something. The way he talks is so formal, polite but stilted and intimidating. He straightens, still holding the envelope, waiting for me to take it. "This invitation provides the time and date."

"But *why?*" I blurt out.

The man only looks at me mildly, waiting for me to take the envelope.

Yeah, I'm not getting any answers here.

This is just too weird.

And I have a funny feeling I know who's behind this, considering the uniform and the fact that there's only one family here in Redhaven who'd do something this dramatic. Any other rich client would send us an email or call.

But the Arrendells just have to make a big production out of everything.

Breathlessly, I take the envelope gently like it'll grow teeth and bite me.

By now, I'm used to the Arrendells being the kind of weird only filthy rich people can be. They've been the backdrop of my town for my entire life and they've always given me the creeps.

Honestly, I'm not sure if I want anything to do with them.

It's not me they want, though.

He asked for my grandfather.

I turn that over as I break the seal. The smooth red wax crumbles against my fingertips, and there's a hand-calligraphed invitation card addressed to Grandpa.

We formally and humbly request Mr. Gerald Grey for a consultation on a custom commission project. Please arrive at the manor tomorrow at precisely 8:00 a.m.

-L, M, and X Arrendell

. . .

L AND M—LUCIA and Montero Arrendell—the Lord and Lady of the house and also the town's First and Second selectmen.

X... that must be Xavier.

The only son left in town after the ugly scandals that left two of his brothers dead recently. I'd say I can't begin to imagine how it feels to lose family that way, but unfortunately, I can.

I glance over my shoulder, through the open door to the workshop. I can just hear the rhythmic sounds of Grandpa working the lathe.

I offer the valet a thin smile.

"Um, this seems less like an invitation and more like a demand."

His lips twitch faintly. A hint of weariness, maybe?

"Please forgive the tone. The young master is rather accustomed to getting his way, yes. May I tell him he can expect Mr. Grey in the morning?"

"Well... let me talk to him first." I flash my politest smile, though I feel like I'm putting on a mask. Especially when this guy keeps standing here like he's waiting for me to go talk to Grandpa *now* and come back with an immediate answer. I take a step back, one hand on the shop door, my smile frozen in place. "We'll be in touch. No need to wait around, dude."

The valet looks like he might protest.

I almost feel bad for him.

Too bad.

If Xavier Arrendell is anything like the rest of his kin— and from the rumors, he's the most short-tempered of them all—then he won't like this minion coming home without an answer.

"Sorry to be so short. It's just a busy day for us," I say,

hastily closing the door in his face before I bustle back into the rear of the shop.

God, I need a minute.

I'm not good with people or unexpected surprises.

And I really do need to talk to Grandpa before we can even think about accepting this invite to hell.

When I step into the workshop, my grandfather stops the lathe. He still uses the old manual kind with a foot pedal, and its whirring grinds to a halt, along with the bassinet leg he's been shaping.

"Serena?" he asks. "Is that you? Would you mind bringing me a glass of water, please? All this sawdust is choking me somethin' fierce."

My heart sinks when he calls me that name.

So it's a bad day.

He thinks I'm my mother again. He's forgotten my parents have been gone for over twenty years, killed in a car wreck caused by a drunk when I was just a toddler.

At twenty-seven, I guess I do look a lot like my mother did when she died, though. Now I know I made the right choice, not letting the Arrendell valet see him.

Gerald Grey is a proud man.

He'll probably work until he dies because he can't stand not being useful. He's been showing more signs of dementia since last year, and we don't like to talk about it.

It's so hard.

But he knows it's there, just like I do.

I won't hurt his pride by letting anybody see him when he's not completely himself.

And I'm not going to upset him by arguing, either.

For now, I'll be Serena, even if it shreds my heart.

"Sure, Dad," I say cheerfully as I walk to the sink and fill a glass, then bring it back to him and press it into his wrinkled hands. "How's work going?"

He takes the glass with a grateful nod, then scratches a hand through his sparse remaining hair. It's tinged grey with a fading touch of the same red as mine.

We have the same eyes, too. His midnight-blue gaze darkens as he looks over the piece mounted on the lathe.

"Slow." He draws the word out thoughtfully and takes a long sip from the glass. When he speaks again, his voice is smoother. "Then again, handcrafted's always slow as molasses. It'll come when it comes."

"Oh, I'm sure it'll be beautiful." I squeeze his shoulder.

"Eh, we'll see."

He looks down at his free hand, flexing it slowly. His knuckles are thick and swollen, his fingertips shaking slightly.

Dementia isn't the only thing on his plate.

I know he'd rather die than admit his rheumatoid arthritis hurts him. God, if he's mentally back in time right now to when my mother was my age, he probably doesn't even understand why his hands hurt, so gnarled and broken.

Keeping my smile right now feels harder than it was with the Arrendell valet.

Seeing him like this, everything he is fading away...

It's a blister on the soul.

Even worse because when he forgets himself, he's still a brilliant craftsman. The bassinet leg on the lathe already looks like art, etched with delicate grooves. It's like the Alzheimer's patients you hear about who forget who they are, yet they can still play a full Mozart piece while swearing they've never touched a piano in their lives.

Even when Grandpa's so far away, his talent still lives in his hands. Muscle memory.

No wonder someone like Xavier Arrendell wants his magic before it's gone.

Like the mind reader he is, Grandpa glances at the thick envelope clutched in my fingers. "What's that?"

"This?" I shrug, tucking it under my arm with a smile. "Invitation to a class reunion. I probably won't go."

He chuckles. "You were always so shy. Talia's taking after you, ya know. I worry about her. The kids at school pick on her too damn much."

Crap, crap.

No, I'm not going to cry.

My eyes sting anyway, but I bolt on my smile like it's the only thing keeping me alive.

"She'll be okay," I say faintly. "Talia, she can hold her own. I promise you she's stronger than she looks."

Right.

I definitely don't feel strong right now.

Not when I'm completely helpless to do anything to set his mind straight today, much less stall the inevitable.

No matter how many custom orders we take in, no matter how much artisan furniture we ship out, we'll never have enough money to buy real treatments for the disease destroying his hands.

Let alone the demon eating his mind.

Not that there's any cure for dementia, but it can be slowed, minimized—if you pay through the nose. There's even a promising new study out of Minnesota that's seen better results than any of the treatments on the market.

But it's funded by big corporate sponsors.

And it costs a lot of money to buy a spot for late-stage human trials.

Money we'll never have.

Still, if the richest family in town wants to hire us, that might help a little. At least we could keep his hands working for a few more months.

Am I in the mood for a deal with the devil?

I bite my lip and tighten my fingers against the invitation, watching Grandpa as he sets the half-empty glass down and bows over the lathe again, already hyperfocused, losing himself in work and forgetting I'm even here.

I don't want to put the burden of this meeting with the Arrendells on him.

But *I* can go, can't I?

I've been working under him my entire life. Learning his trade. One day, this shop and the entire business will be mine.

My stomach churns at the thought. I don't usually do customer-facing things, and dealing with people like them—

No, you can do it.

He's worth it.

And he absolutely is.

Fine, whatever.

If the Arrendells really want us, they'll just have to settle for the lesser Grey.

* * *

My bravado's not holding up as well the following morning.

The very first thing I do is check my purse for my inhaler.

I throw on a smart pink skirt suit—the only nice outfit I really have in my favorite color—and low heels, then pin my hair up before heading out, kissing Grandpa on the cheek as he hovers over his morning coffee in the kitchen of our loft above the shop.

He glances up at me, his eyes bright and clear today. *Present.*

"Look at you," he says cheerfully. "What's with the getup? Big date this early in the morning?"

"Grandpa, no! I'm meeting a potential client." I drop

another kiss on top of his head. "I'll tell you all about the job when I get back."

I leave him blinking after me curiously as I escape before he starts asking any real questions. He might not have been there yesterday, but he's sharp today, and I'm—

I'm not a good liar.

I still feel a little weird not telling Grandpa where I'm going, but I don't want to get his hopes up in case this doesn't work out.

I borrow our only vehicle for the uphill drive, a rickety dark-grey delivery truck.

The Arrendell mansion looms over Redhaven like a twisted castle, perched at the peak of the tallest forested hill overlooking the small valley that cups our little colonial village.

There's only one road leading up, a winding paved lane that passes under bowers of trees bursting with spring growth.

The mansion itself resembles a strange white dragon coiled at the peak, this eerie brooding thing of tall columns and white marble and old Gothic architecture.

My nerves flutter wildly as I pull into the circular roundabout at the foot of the massive, palatial steps leading up to the house. As I park the truck, it coughs out a black cloud of smoke from the tailpipe.

Way to make a good first impression.

I feel like the universe is trying to remind me I don't belong anywhere in spitting distance of this place.

At least I'm a few minutes early, though.

I sling my purse over my shoulder, tuck the shop's project portfolio under my arm, and step out, handing the keys to a valet who looks nearly identical to the man who came to the shop yesterday.

Wait. That *is* him, I think. His nose wrinkles at the bitter smell of exhaust.

"Sorry!" I hate how small my voice sounds. "You, um, you have to pump the clutch a few times. If you don't want to bother, you can just leave it here."

"Miss," he says calmly, sliding behind the driver's seat.

I watch for a moment with a wince as the truck sputters while he fights the clutch. Then I turn—and nearly jump right out of my skin as the man from yesterday materializes at my elbow.

The *actual* man from yesterday, I mean, though with their identical haircuts and nondescript faces I can't be blamed for thinking they're clones. Especially with those uniforms.

I leap back with a little shriek, almost stumbling on the bottom step, but he catches my elbow smoothly and steadies me with a dry look.

"Are you well, Miss Grey?"

"Never been better," I lie.

"Right this way then," he says cordially.

"Thanks," I answer faintly and follow him up the steps.

I'm just killing it today.

Please, shoot me now.

Although I've lived in Redhaven my entire life, I've never been up to the big house. The four Arrendell sons all went to fancy private schools and never really mingled with the little people. They weren't the kind of kids to have playdates with the locals, invite them over for fancy tea parties, that kind of thing. So actually seeing this house up close is... wow.

Intimidating isn't a big enough word.

It's a mountain of a house.

Standing at the top of the stairs and looking up at the looming walls, it's like it takes up the entire sky. The soaring front doors groan as the valet opens them with a grand flourish and leads me into a dim-lit stone foyer draped with red velvet all over the walls.

This is too much house for one family.

And it's all so ostentatious, from the antique velvet furniture to the ornate gold wall sconces, the black-and-white checkered marble flooring, the vaulted ceilings.

Everything echoes here.

My heels chatter like ghosts in the high eaves with every clicking step, amping up my nerves.

I'm sweating as the valet leads me through the manor.

Thankfully, it's not far.

We swing off to the right, mount a short flight of stairs, head down another hallway, and then he stops outside a dark-varnished oak door with carved insets.

It's classical revival, a detail I can't help noticing when it's part of my job to know historic woodwork styles.

That's also what makes Grandpa's brand so unique. He partners old styles and forgotten techniques with modern craftsmanship to create vintage looks bordering on elegantly exotic.

I'm distracted with the details of the insets and varnishing as the valet raps lightly and then pushes the door open to a large office, opulently furnished in oak wood, black, and gold with subtle glassy accents.

A man stands behind the wide, mirror-polished wooden desk.

He's very tall. Lean to the point that if his shoulders weren't so broad, he'd be almost gaunt. There's a dark accent to his saber-sharp features and the deep hollows of his stubble-dusted cheeks.

Handsome enough, but grim.

He's almost posed in front of the window. The light coming through the sheer curtains gilds his razor edges and shines off the corners of a small silver box he holds up, inspecting it with laser focus. His icy-blond hair is short and swept back from his face. His pale jade-green eyes are sunken hollows that glow like embers in their shadowed sockets.

There's also something unsettling about him.

Something heavy that instantly makes me think of a caged animal trapped inside the deep-grey gloss of his finely tailored suit. It ages him, years beyond a man who must not be any older than his thirties.

Xavier Arrendell needs no introduction, though.

"Um." I open my mouth and stop.

I glance at the valet—but he's gone.

Just vanished into thin air, leaving me alone with a man I don't know how to talk to without the buffer of his parents.

But that little sound I gulp out makes him jerk.

He stiffens, his cold eyes cutting toward me, watching me like a snake before he turns slowly, setting the box down on his desk with controlled poise.

"Who are *you*?" he bites off. His voice is full of cultured disdain behind a broken rasp.

I swallow hard.

Do not panic.

Do *not* panic.

I should be grateful, really. In theory, one rich guy seems easier to face down than three, but with the rumors about the Arrendell brothers... I'm not sure I want to be alone with him.

I clutch the portfolio folder so tight my fingers dig in.

"Hi, I'm T-Talia Grey. From A Touch of Grey. Y-you requested an appointment."

"I requested an appointment with Gerald Grey," he retorts. "Not his..." He pauses and those vicious eyes rake me slowly. "Not his apprentice."

That stokes my temper, enough to straighten my spine.

"I'm not his apprentice," I correct sharply. "I'm his partner, and I manage most of the day-to-day operations. Plus, many of our more difficult custom orders. If my expertise isn't good enough, then you're welcome to find another artisan to do your work. But my grandfather is dealing with a work injury, and he won't be attending today."

It's not quite the truth, but I'm trying to salvage Grandpa's pride.

Xavier gives me a long, withering look like he's just waiting for me to crumble.

Honestly, he might get his way if my chest gets any tighter. I force myself to breathe slowly, the way I learned a long time ago.

I'm not having an asthma attack in front of a potential client.

I have my pride to worry about, too.

After holding that look for too long, though, Xavier clicks his tongue dismissively and looks away. "Come inside and shut the door."

I let out an explosive breath and cross the threshold into the lushly furnished office. It's a little overdone, if you ask me. But I hesitate as I turn back to grip the doorknob, glancing at him.

"Does the door have to be closed?"

He meets my eyes again.

Something sharpens in his gaze, and for the first time, he smiles.

I'm sure a lot of people are charmed by that look. It's confident and oddly hungry as he gives me another once-over.

But to me, I just see a hyena.

Unpredictable and wild. Possibly one second away from lunging at my face with snapping teeth.

I shudder as he asks, "Are you afraid to be alone with me, Miss Grey? My family's reputation must precede me."

"No, I…" I stop right there. I feel foolish. This is silly and I'm overreacting. "I just thought I'd be meeting with Mr. and Mrs. Arrendell."

"Ah, yes. My parents are out of town. Vacationing in Sicily. Grieving, I should say." He sobers, that bitter smile falling away with a sigh. "They left me in charge of the estate for a few months while they try to forget the loss of my brothers by burying themselves in palazzos and pasta."

"Oh my God, I'm so sorry. That was rude of me." I flush wildly and shut the door. "I'm sincerely sorry for your loss."

"Yes, well…" He looks away sharply, his eyes glassy as they fix on the window. "That's why I called you here, isn't it?" He's a bit more crisp and businesslike as he turns his back on me, gesturing to one of the chairs opposite his desk before folding his hands behind his back. "Please, Miss Grey. Take a seat."

"I don't understand." Frowning, I sink down into the chair and put my purse on the floor, clutching the portfolio in my lap.

"This manor has been trapped in time for generations," Xavier says. "It hasn't changed a bit since before I was born. Decades of dead lives and dead people entombed in these halls. Shadows and shades haunting the place. Wretched fucking memories. The kind that chased my parents away and make living here a pain I can't describe."

Oof.

Without seeing his hyena face, it's hard not to feel the pain in his voice.

I really should have some compassion.

He's probably a victim of the same nightmare plaguing the family after his brothers turned out to be such monsters.

I'm sure he's struggling with the full horror of what Ulysses and Aleksander did while still grieving them as lost brothers.

"So you'd like to change something in the house?" I venture.

"I want *you* to change the manor," he growls. "Every piece of furniture, every tapestry, every statue, every pedestal, every drape, every fixture—I want them all replaced. A full interior redesign from the ground up."

Holy shit.

For a second, I forget how to breathe.

My vision clouds with black stars before I catch myself with a gasp.

"The whole house?" I whisper, wondering if I even heard him right. My voice sounds tiny. "But we're a small business. My grandfather and I are only two people, and this house—I'm sorry, but it must have like fifty rooms?"

"Sixty-eight when you include servants' quarters, as well as outbuildings like the stables and gardener's cottage," Xavier says sharply. "I want the Grey touch on all of them."

My mind spins.

"That would take *years* for just the two of us. Not to mention the colors, the draperies—we're not interior designers. We bring in consultants for that sort of thing. We're really just furniture people. We don't—"

My throat closes off.

Xavier pivots to face me again, fixing me with a penetrating stare. "Then it takes years, Miss Grey. Consider it a lasting partnership. I'll consult you on every detail. We'll be working very closely together." He arches one sharp, mocking blond brow. "Is that why you're so ruffled? Since being alone with me makes you so uncomfortable."

"What? No, it's not that at all!" Like I said, I'm such a bad liar. It's mostly that for sure. "You just caught me a little off guard. We've never had a project this large before. We'll have to finish out our current client orders, put off any new ones, possibly hire contractors, not to mention the expense…"

"Spare none," he barks back. "I'm prepared to spend seven figures on this, Miss Grey." He smiles his cold, thin jackal's smile. "I know you've grown up in this town. Surely, you know that money is no obstacle for an Arrendell."

Am I dreaming?

That's almost enough money to send me reeling again.

Seven. Flipping. Figures.

But let's not get ahead of ourselves.

I'll need to do a real tour of the mansion. Get a feel for things and what he wants if I'm going to prepare a cost estimate without laughing myself silly.

Seven figures, though—even if it's the lowest end—would leave more than enough to help Grandpa.

Nerves war with dizzy hope until my chest flutters.

"Are you sure you want *us*?" I raise my leatherbound folio. "I brought our project portfolio—"

He waves one long hand—and that's when I notice his fingernails are surprisingly thick and yellow, maybe a bit too long. Is his hand shaking, too?

Grief, maybe?

"I'm familiar with your work," he snaps. "I make it my business to be familiar with everything that happens in Redhaven. You don't need to sell yourself. You only need to tell me if you'll take the job."

He glares at me.

"…can I have a day or two to think it over? I'll bring this back to my grandfather, of course, and we'll see what we can do." My voice sounds like it's coming from down a wind tunnel. "We just need to figure out if we can do this, realistically. If we're only going to let you down, it wouldn't make sense. Ethically, I mean."

Something odd crosses his face when I say *ethically*.

Then he sighs with clear irritation, his nostrils flaring as he pinches the bridge of his nose. "Yes, yes. Take all the time you need. But I'll need an answer soon." He leans over his desk, plucks a business card out of a glossy wooden holder, and passes it over. "My personal number."

I wonder if *my* face is weird now at the way he says *personal*, but I take the card anyway, careful not to touch his fingers.

"Thank you."

"Miss Grey." He nods cordially, and that's when I realize I've been dismissed.

Ouch.

Part of me wants to be offended, but I'm happy to escape.

My skin thrums with goosebumps. The air feels ten degrees colder than it should, and I think it's just my nerves but maybe it's *him*.

Do I really want to deal with this? Spending years working in close collaboration with a man who makes me so uneasy?

But there's big money on the line.

There's Grandpa's health.

I can do it for him. *I think.*

"Thank you again, Mr. Arrendell," I say hollowly, grabbing my purse and speedwalking away.

When I open the door, I almost shriek.

The valet who escorted me before materializes like a phantom. He gives me the same dry look, his dark eyes knowing, right before he reaches past me to close the door.

"Miss Grey," he says politely—a bit shamefaced, and I don't understand why until he continues, "I'm afraid I have some bad news about your truck."

* * *

I stand at the foot of the tall stairs outside the mansion, staring at my truck in dismay.

Yes, it's still in the same spot where I left it. But now the second valet, who looked so offended at having to drive it, just looks apologetic as he offers me my keys.

"I'm afraid I'm not familiar with stick shifts," he says stiffly. "I'll inform the young master, and I'm certain he'll cover all repairs."

"In the meantime," the first valet says, "I'll have a car brought around immediately to return you to your shop."

"What? No," I say too quickly, my stomach sinking. I don't want much to do with anything Arrendell right now. I definitely don't want the looks I'll get for showing up at home in one of their cars.

That'll send the small-town rumor mill spinning, especially when everyone's probably hungry for more salacious gossip about the last Arrendell son left at home. I don't want people thinking I'm his new fling or situationship or whatever.

Groaning, I thank God I wore short, sensible heels today. "It's fine, guys. I'll walk. And I'll send Mort up with a tow truck when I can. Sorry for the inconvenience."

"Miss Grey," they say simultaneously.

This place is so surreal.

And just like that, I'm on my own again.

Sighing, I set out for the road.

It's not a terrible walk since I'm going downhill, even if it strains my calves. I'm huffing and puffing about ten minutes in.

God, I'm not going to have an asthma attack *now*, right?

It's over.

I survived the meeting without melting down. I should be happy I have a lead on a job that will pay our medical bills and then some.

But it's a lot to think about.

It feels insane to think about taking it on alone.

There's no question I'll have to manage the project with Grandpa fading in and out, and there are never any guarantees when the bottom could fall out on his health.

Still, if we get a big enough payment up front, the treatment might buy us time.

Of course, ultimately, I'll be the one who has to draft the concepts, the plans.

I'm the one who has to be responsible.

I'm also the one who'll ruin the shop's reputation if I disappoint one of the richest families on the eastern seaboard.

Ugh.

My heart turns into a knotted ball.

I try to remember my counting exercises, my breathing, as I make it to the bottom of the hill where the wooded lane opens up toward the town square.

I've been dealing with this since childhood. It used to be a lot worse.

When I was a little girl, I couldn't do anything on my own at all. I was homeschooled, and my few attempts to play with other kids usually went horribly wrong. I'd wind up wheezing on the ground while the little jerks just laughed and pointed and called me names. Sometimes they even played keep-away with my little wheeled oxygen tank.

Sometimes, just going up the stairs would drop me on my knees.

I'm managing better now.

But some days—like today—my anxiety short-circuits my lungs.

And I realize I'm about to fall headfirst into an attack when I reach the town square.

No time to scream.

There's just a sunlit glimmer before my vision blurs. The striking bronze statue of the first Arrendell, rearing up in the center of the square.

Coughing, I scramble for my purse, fishing for my inhaler, but it's already too late.

My fingers go numb.

My vision darkens.

My legs disappear under me, and my lungs flap as I gasp helplessly.

Too late, too late.

Everything goes dark as my brain stops working and the ground comes crashing up.

II: DARK HORSE (MICAH)

When the hell did I wind up being coffee boy?

When I first signed on with Redhaven PD, Chief Bowden showed up every morning with coffee for everyone—jolly, welcoming, always swinging into the backroom belly-first with a cupholder in one hand. He'd grin like a Cheshire cat as he handed out everyone's orders on his way to his little corner office.

Black coffee with just a dab of sugar for Captain Grant Faircross.

A half-milk, half-coffee, all sugar diabetic monstrosity for Lieutenant Lucas Graves.

A sweetened vanilla latte for our dispatch officer, Mallory.

Black with Irish crème, no sugar, for me.

Cinnamon chocolate cappuccino for Officer Henri Fontenot, unless he was just on his way out as the chief came in. Then he'd end his nightly on-call shift with a steaming cup of chamomile tea on the chief's dime.

How do I know all this?

Because I'm the poor bastard filling those orders now.

All because our jolly, bumbling chief has turned sullen and withdrawn lately—when he bothers to show up at the office at all.

If we're going by rank or tenure, this should be Henri's job.

I've been here longer and I outrank him by a smidge as a junior sergeant, while he doesn't have any real title besides officer. Even so, that smooth-talking Cajun already wheedled his way out of coffee duty by reminding everyone he got the short end of the stick with night shift in the most boring town in North Carolina.

Nothing usually happens after dark besides the odd coyote running through town or summer kids stirring up misdemeanors.

That's why I'm walking out of Red Grounds and into the morning light, carrying a cardboard cupholder with five steaming paper cups printed with the café's logo.

I'm the last one in to work. I always am.

Technically, it's a medical exemption, though there's nothing in my medical history that requires coming in later in the morning. The excuse lets me use my morning hours as I see fit. Walking my dog. Hiking the woods.

Making a few phone calls.

And what I learned during this morning's phone calls left me pretty fucking pissed.

That brick of cocaine we recovered when we arrested Culver Jacobin for the attempted murder of Delilah Graves—formerly Delilah Clarendon before she went and married Lucas—was a key piece of evidence in an ongoing case.

We'd followed protocol. Turned it over to the FBI to poke at with a few other alphabet agencies. Forensic analysis showed this particular cocaine sample was a dead match for the drugs plaguing the east coast over the last decade, far north of Redhaven.

Proof that the drug epidemic that's been escalating every year—and taking more lives along with it, stealing folks from their families, stealing from *me*—can be traced right back to this nowhere town.

So close.

I was so fucking *close*.

Yet somehow, every last lab sample wound up destroyed in a freak accident.

Coincidentally, right before the forensic analysts verified all their notes.

Then the rest of the entire brick of coke disappeared from evidence lockup.

Clerical error, my ass.

This was a classic cover-up.

A lot like how Culver Jacobin's and Ulysses Arrendell's 'suicides' in prison were a cover-up, too. The wealthiest family in Redhaven—hell, in all of North Carolina—has a vested interest in burying investigations. They also have all the money in the world to make damn sure it happens.

They've also set me right back to square one, putting me in one hell of a mood.

My blood simmers so thick I feel the bright midmorning light turning darker in my vision as I head up the sidewalk toward the station.

My vision hazes and halos around the edges.

I've always been sensitive to light. If I didn't need my nights to myself, I'd trade with Henri for evening on-calls in a heartbeat. The corrective contact lenses I wear don't really help, scattering the sun into starbursts.

So I almost miss it when it happens.

The girl, staggering through the loose streams of morning shoppers out running their errands. She starts fumbling with her purse, wearing a desperate look.

Her skin looks like white ash against her fiery-red hair, her eyes wide, her face an unnatural red that screams panic.

It's her motion that grabs my attention.

Then the dull thump of her purse and leather portfolio hitting cobblestone.

Right before she goes tumbling down, collapsing in a spill of vivid scarlet and delicate limbs.

"Shit," I mutter.

The people milling around her gasp, pulling back with a collective cry.

I don't even realize I'm moving until I'm halfway across the square.

Dropping the coffee with a messy splash, I sprint to the girl's side and fling myself down so hard I bruise my shins.

She's not quite unconscious, not yet.

Her long lashes flutter against her red cheeks, offering glimpses of hazy blue eyes.

A familiar face?

Yeah, she works at the furniture shop down the street. Can't remember her name, but that doesn't matter right now.

I cup her face gently in both hands, stopping her from turning it from side to side in case she has head trauma.

"Miss," I growl firmly, looking down into her eyes. "Focus on me. I'm a police officer. Can you tell me if you hit your head?"

Her lips part, but nothing comes out besides a wheeze. Her chest rises and falls, swift and shallow.

No blood, though.

No contusions that I can see at a glance.

Then I freeze.

She's trying to reach her purse, I realize, her eyes rolling toward it helplessly while her throat clicks with fear.

That's when what's happening really sinks in.

She can't breathe.

Probably an allergic reaction or an asthma attack.

I let go of her head and dive for her purse, ripping it open and spilling the contents. Notepad, phone, pens, receipts, lipstick, comb. Come on, *come on*, where's the goddamn EpiPen or inhaler—

Aha.

An inhaler goes clattering across the stone.

I snatch it up, pull the cap off, and hold it to her lips, fitting it carefully so her soft red mouth wraps around it.

One pump.

Give her a second.

Then another.

My brain whips back to first responder training. Okay, I need to keep calm for her own sake through the adrenaline spike.

My focus narrows to her, and only her.

Tracking her breathing.

The jitter of her eyes.

Watching as she sucks in a deeper breath, then another, her eyes widening, her head tossed back.

Fuck me, I don't think this inhaler is working fast enough.

I also don't have time to wait around for dispatch to send EMTs, even if there's one on the way by now from someone calling it in.

Not when she's struggling and turning redder by the second.

There's no hesitation.

"Sorry, lady," I whisper, right before I bend over and fit my mouth to hers.

She goes stiff.

Her hands come up, clutching at my shoulders almost comically.

I know what this looks like.

What it *feels* like.

But when I gently pinch her nostrils shut, she gets the message.

I only leave a single airway for us to manage.

She relaxes slowly as I exhale into her mouth.

Normally, we use CPR for someone who's unconscious, but right now, what she needs is to get her breathing under control until the inhaler works.

Breathe with me, woman, I'm beaming into her with my lips.

Fucking breathe!

One breath at a time, I take control of her.

In, out. In, out!

Our mouths fuse together so perfectly there's not a single molecule of air lost between us, the heat and friction building with each wet slide like a kiss.

Her lips taste like citrus, sweet and tart.

With every passing second, we slowly taste the same.

Every time I exhale, I force another breath down her throat. We separate for just a minute, our lips parting with a damp sound before I seal them together again.

Over and over, taking my time, razor-focused on her alone.

Slowly, her rhythm matches mine.

Her rapid panicked breathing softens until it turns slow and steady, each breath more measured and controlled than the last.

It's almost weirdly intimate.

The people around us watching silently, the sunlit morning square, all of it falls away.

There's only that rhythm.

That heartbeat.

That push and pull.

Here, there's only her, while her eyes slip shut and she goes slack like she's surrendering to me.

When the fear and tension go out of her, I feel it.

With the next breath, I touch two fingers to her throat, feeling her pulse through her artery. It flutters under my fingers, a little start.

Thankfully, it's acceptable. No longer the panic-rush that was beating frantically against her pale, slender throat.

Now it feels safe to let her go.

So I do, releasing her delicate nose. As I draw back this time, I don't go in for another breath.

My lips hover over hers as I tell her, "Good girl. You're all right. Just keep breathing, nice and steady."

I straighten, slipping an arm under her, coaxing her up until she's resting in the crook of my arm, half-draped across my lap. Her breath turns a little shaky for a second, then evens out.

She swallows hard before letting out a slow, controlled exhale that looks almost practiced.

Like she's dealt with this a lot, but she just wasn't ready for this kind of chaos.

I still need to call dispatch and make sure the EMTs are coming. I'm just not sure if it's safe to let her go yet.

I force myself to give her a once-over, taking in her flush, her paleness—some of which I realize now is just her natural color.

She's so warm in the crook of my arm.

So small, so breakable.

Her bones feel finer than a bird's wings against her wrist, and in the exposed dip of her collarbone just visible past the collar of her soft-pink suit coat and button-up shirt. Her skin shines like moonlight, even in the morning, spattered with cinnamon-colored freckles across her face and throat.

She's got the kind of round, high cheekbones that make

her jawline look like a porcelain sculpture. Her hair is a wild cloud, deep red like embers, long and pouring down her shoulders over my supporting arm.

And those eyes—fuck.

They're the darkest blue I've ever seen. Dangerously close to conjuring up very unprofessional thoughts.

Especially as she looks up while I clear my throat.

"Are you with me now? Are you feeling all right?" I ask.

Her lips part, but she doesn't answer.

Her mouth is cherry red from my CPR kisses, making the bright cobalt-blue of her eyes stand out so much more sharply. They're wet and glimmering, her curling lashes beading with tears.

There's something brutally innocent in her gaze.

I'm fucking arrested. Lost for words.

For what I was trying to do.

For what I should even be thinking in this situation.

Think, Micah. Find your brain and quit fucking staring.

I should be thinking about her safety and nothing else. She's a flushed, disheveled mess and I don't even know her name.

Only, right now, I'm gutted.

An unhinged thought cuts me open.

I'm staring at the most beautiful woman I've ever seen in my life.

III: DARK WHISPERS (TALIA)

I'm being kissed by a vampire.

That's the first thought clouding my foggy mind as the pale man leans over me. Maybe I'm hallucinating from low oxygen, but he looks—

Inhuman.

Imaginary.

Dangerous, with his red, red mouth descending toward mine.

His skin glows like moonstone.

His hair, too, a pale silvery-white like ice teased into side-swept strands. His face is so beautiful, so angular. He's like some dark elven prince from the dirtiest fantasy books, smoldering and strange.

And his eyes—Oh God.

They're somewhere between desert blue sky and arctic grey.

Twin moons on a hollow night, holding me hypnotized.

Yes, in the back of my mind, I know he's a cop. He's wearing a navy-blue police uniform.

I've seen him before.

I even remember when he first moved here a few years ago. Half the town whispered about Junior Sergeant Micah Ainsley because they'd never seen an albino before. The other half whispered because he was from 'the big city'—New York City, I think—and they thought he'd be stuck up as hell and cosmopolitan.

But when he quietly blended into our town, mostly out of sight when he's not walking his dog or doing local patrols, everyone just sort of stopped chewing that bone, and he faded into the scenery.

I've never had a reason to talk to him.

No one bothers us much at A Touch of Grey, not even the odd teenage vandals during tourist season. We don't deal with the police.

So I've never really gotten a look at him up close, just quick glimpses as he heads past the shop some mornings with his hands full of coffee.

But now, he's all I see.

He becomes my whole world as he seals his lips to mine and literally breathes life into me and I blush like I'm dying.

Vaguely, I know what he's doing.

He gave me a few pumps off my inhaler, but it takes a few minutes for the prednisone to really hit, and those excruciating minutes can be life or death.

That's why he's sharing his breath.

A taste of his life, helping me hold on to mine.

But my drowning mind remembers something else, too.

A teenage fantasy. Dark dreams I'd never tell anyone about when they'd just laugh at me for being so excited by a pale, inhumanly beautiful man with a dangerous mouth and eyes drawn like swords.

Christian Dracul.

…okay. Yes. I was one of those freaks growing up.

Totally vampire-obsessed, and the movie version of

Christian could curl my toes with the thought of his lips at my throat, so hungry and seductive.

...and it's not so different from what's happening now, is it?

That's what a vampire man does.

He gives you a piece of himself to make you like him.

He brings you back from the dead, sharing his blood like Officer Ainsley shares his breath now.

I'm trapped in the most surreal place right now.

I should be panicking. My chest caving in. The pain stitching up my lungs until I pass out.

I know this feeling all too well.

Instead, I feel like I'm dreaming.

I must be when all I can feel is this slow, molten warmth as the tightness in my chest slowly eases. It feels like escaping a giant's fist.

His mouth burns so hot against mine. I taste a hint of coffee and something stark and creamy-minty every time he exhales.

His touch feels far too warm for the undead, too.

The graze of his teeth teases my lips.

That's why I think I'm dreaming.

Because I swear his teeth feel sharper than any man's have a right to be.

My heart rabbits, but not because of the asthma attack anymore. Because right now, I am so *confused.*

The logical explanation for what just happened battles the weird fantasy devouring me and making me wonder if this is all a grand delusion from my oxygen-starved brain.

But his eyes are too real. They never leave mine.

That pale, stark color completely swallows my world.

I don't even remember why I had an asthma attack.

But suddenly, it's over.

Suddenly, Officer Ainsley leans away from me and I'm

looking up at him through a haze of tears while the sun forms a burning halo behind his head.

He's suddenly cast in shadows, and all I can make out is his athletic silhouette, tall and strong with an older runner's frame, so sleek inside a crisp dark uniform that seems tailored for the graceful angles of his body.

Then one strong arm slides under me and he lifts me up, cradling me against his wall of a chest. His warmth envelops me.

"Are you with me now? Are you feeling all right?" he whispers.

I don't answer.

I'm too dizzy.

I can't even speak and it has nothing to do with the unwanted audience witnessing my crappiest day ever.

It has everything to do with my gaze locked on his mouth.

It's still so very red.

So wet, too, gleaming and slick.

Like we've been kissing.

Like that's really what I need to be thinking about right now.

He studies me with a searching gaze.

He doesn't smile.

If anything, he looks like he doesn't know *how*, even if that scarlet mouth can be so generous.

"Feeling better, Miss Grey?" he asks. His voice is dry, dispassionate, serious yet somehow reassuring.

I blink slowly.

Yeah, I'm… definitely not reacting very well right now.

Blame it on the attack, though I can feel the medicine now, easing that suffocating, reminding my lungs how to work again.

"H-how…" Talking is hard, my throat constricted so tight,

barely a whisper squeezing past. "...how do you know my n-name?"

"Small town." His lips twitch at the corners, but no... no smile. He tilts his head toward the far edge of the town square, our shop a short ways down the lane. "I remembered you work at the furniture shop approximately thirty seconds after I was sure you weren't going to die on me."

"O-oh. Yeah. Okay." I try to smile, but everything feels so numb and floaty. I'm not sure if my lips are moving. "It's... it's Talia. You d-don't have to call me Miss Grey."

"Got it, Talia." God, the way his sultry voice rolls over my name does something crazy, warming me from head to toe and chasing away the chill of trauma. "You couldn't answer me before, but did you hit your head?"

"No. I'm... I'm used to falling. It's almost instinct to tuck up so my body takes the brunt of it."

"You've probably got some bruises, maybe knocked a few bones around, but no concussion. That's good."

Pale eyes flick over me quickly, taking me in from head to toe.

There's this careful coolness in his voice, completely at odds with the kindness in the way he handles me. Almost like his voice and those gunmetal-blue eyes are a mask, and his touch tells the truth—and maybe it's that neediness after having a bad attack, but I don't want him to let me go.

Not yet.

"So this is a regular thing for you, Talia?" he asks.

I shake my head, wincing as it pulls at my sore shoulders a bit.

"Not anymore. I mean, I used to have bad attacks as a kid, but it doesn't happen much these days."

"I see." A discerning look lingers on me. "Let's get you on your feet. We'll see how steady you are and if I'll be driving you to the medical center or waiting for the ambulance."

"*No!*"

I go stiff with fresh panic. I can't.

I spent half my childhood in that medical center.

I know those depressing institutional walls by heart. A cold, sterile ghost of loneliness.

As if I wasn't already totally humiliated, I see half the town gathered around us in a distant circle, watching me batting my eyes in Officer Ainsley's arms.

Ugh.

I can't stand going back there.

But Officer Ainsley just stares with this cool, intense question in his eyes.

My face heats. I lower my eyes to the point where his long, pale hand curls against my elbow to support me.

Holy hell.

I've never seen anyone with skin paler than mine. I can see the veins snaking along the backs of his hands and through his fingers, huge and powerful, making him seem even more like some strange beast of the night.

The only color is in his fingertips and his knuckles—thick, coarse, red. His hands seem too big and sharp for such an elegant man.

"Talia?" he whispers.

"S-sorry," I stutter. Speech comes easier now as my throat slowly relaxes. "It's just… the prednisone's working. I'm fine. I'm used to this, but I don't want to waste anyone's time at the medical center. I just need a few minutes. I need some water."

I'm expecting him to tell me I have to go to the medical center anyway. For him to completely dismiss me and override my wishes.

It's the same thing the doctors always did, and just about anyone else besides Grandpa, always treating me like this glass doll that has to be locked away in a protective case and never allowed to *live*.

But after a few long seconds, Officer Ainsley nods.

"Compromise," he growls. "If you can get up and walk to Red Grounds with me, we'll sit down, talk, and have something to drink. If you're still feeling okay after that, I'll let you go. If not, I'll give you a ride to the medical center. Fair?"

Too fair, maybe.

I stare at him.

I know he's just looking after me, being responsible, but—

No. That's the wooziness talking.

That, and the fact that he's so captivating that I can't stop looking at him.

He raises both brows. "You're starting to worry me, Miss Grey. Are you processing?"

"Processing?" I squeak.

"Are my words getting through?"

"Yes! Loud and clear. And um, I told you before, it's Talia. None of that Miss Grey business." I'm about to blush myself into passing out again. "Sorry, I'm just—"

"You're asking if you should trust me," he offers.

I freeze.

Holy shit, how?

This is the first time we've ever really spoken.

And in a matter of minutes, he sees right through me.

I look away sharply with a weird flutter in my heart.

"It's not you, I promise. It's habit. But if you can help me up and get me away from this crowd, you've got a deal," I say.

He doesn't reply.

A second later, his strong arms flex around me before he gently sets me down, maneuvering his thighs from under me so he can stand without ever fully letting me go.

Instead, his hand slides down my arm until he catches my

hand. His fingers may be raw—almost brutal—but they're still graceful and warm as they catch mine.

My heart skips again as I see him standing over me at full height, rakish and framed in morning light. A fallen angel.

Dear God.

I've got to stop doing that, letting myself get so swept up in *looking* at him.

It's the damsel in distress shock, I bet. That, plus the fact that I've never kissed anyone. While that wasn't really a kiss, it was the first time I've ever felt a man's mouth on mine.

Something about the liquid push and pull between us brought me back. I don't just mean the oxygen.

I curl my fingers in his, trying not to tremble.

"You don't have to do this, you know," I say. "You must have better things to do than babysitting."

"It's not babysitting." He continues holding my hand firmly. "It's my job. The second you hit the ground, I clocked in."

It's my job.

Right, right, right.

Duty calls.

All the more reason why I need to stop tumbling head over heels into fantasyland and wondering if I should check myself in for brain damage.

"Of course," I say distantly—then I tighten my hand in his and give myself a little bit of a pull.

What I'm not expecting is the way his arm flexes.

The way he lifts me up like I'm weightless.

The whole world spins for a second.

Gasping, I get my feet under me, trying not to waver from the surprise of it, bracing one hand against his chest.

Oops.

I freeze up for the tenth time today.

Yes, with my hand still locked in his while my other hand rests over the beat of his heart.

He's so calm on the outside. So withdrawn, this impenetrable alabaster statue. But under my palm, there's a heartbeat just as wild as mine.

Is he caught up in this strangeness too?

Or is he just wondering what the hell is wrong with me?

He pulls away, just as I tilt my head back to look up at him. His hand untangles from mine and my fingers fall away from his chest, leaving me feeling oddly chilled.

He's not looking at me now. He's looking over my head, toward the crowd still lingering along the sidewalk and the edge of the square.

Or is he looking past them at something else? There's a sudden burst of black crows taking off from a nearby lamppost.

"She'll be fine. Move along now, people," he says with a flash of annoyance. His cool, dry voice projects authority.

I'm grateful.

I really am.

I'm so flipping tired of people gawking like I'm going to die right in front of them.

I'm going to be okay.

Sure, I passed out, but my head feels clearer now. I'm only a little sore from banging my hip and my elbows when I fell.

My legs are steady. I think I can walk.

I test my balance, bending to pick up my purse and my portfolio, gathering my scattered belongings back into my plain leather shoulder bag. I don't get dizzy when I dip down. There's a little head rush when I stand, but that's normal enough.

When I rise, I find Officer Ainsley watching me closely.

Why do I feel like I'm being watched by a hungry animal?

Even after he inclines his head politely, his eyes shuttering over as he gestures toward the café up the street.

"After you, Miss Grey."

"Talia!" I correct again. "You said it before."

He doesn't say anything.

He just moves silently at my back, this pale shadow of a man trailing in my wake, making me feel so warm and haunted as we make our way to Red Grounds.

IV: DARKEST LIGHT (MICAH)

*T*alia damn Grey.

I roll the name on my tongue silently as I follow her back to Red Grounds. I'm watching her closely, making sure she's steady, I tell myself.

Making sure she's not downplaying any injuries worse than she cares to admit.

Seems like her pantyhose took more of a beating than she did, thankfully. There's a long rip in the sheer material, stretching from her ankle to the hem of her skirt, baring a strip of pale freckle-dotted skin.

I shouldn't fucking notice that.

I only glance for medical reasons.

Medical. Reasons.

Good thing she's walking steadily enough, this slender pink slip of a woman who must get off on looking like strawberry shortcake.

The girl has a quick stride like a doe. She almost trips when she gets to the mess of coffee and empty cups I left splattered on the sidewalk.

Her pretty face contorts.

I ignore it like I'm not the clown who put it there.

As we near the café, I step around her and pull out one of the elegant wrought-iron chairs at an outdoor table.

"Have a seat. I'll get you something to drink. Water or iced tea?"

After hesitating, she nods, settling slowly into the chair. "Iced tea works. Of course, I'll pay you back."

"You won't."

She stares at me over her shoulder with those big blue eyes, her teeth sinking into one corner of her mouth to plump it to ripeness.

Fuck me, I shouldn't be noticing.

Still, there's something about the way her body language changes when she's close to me. The way she holds herself away so carefully, not quite touching me and yet seeming so painfully aware of my nearness.

It makes the need to get away from her palpable.

Ideally, before I start *noticing* even more.

Distractions from work are the last thing I need.

Especially not a sweet young diversion who looks like she'd melt at the slightest touch, vulnerable and completely exposed.

Assuming she wouldn't be brutally scandalized by me thinking about her that way, that is.

Once she's settled, I duck inside the café, letting the scent of fresh grounds chase her smell out of my nose.

Vanilla.

Rich vanilla beans with a cinnamon undercurrent. That's what she smells like, airy and sweet with a subtle bite.

There's something seriously wrong with me today.

I swear, I don't normally do this.

A woman collapses on the street with a medical emergency, and my reaction is to want to taste just how breakable she could be.

Maybe I really am my bastard of a father's son after all. The crows always come to remind me, just like the ones I glimpsed a few minutes ago.

My old man just wore his cruelty on the surface while I bury mine deeper.

Just like I bury it now, under the surface of Officer Friendly as I put in a fresh order for the team and grab a sweetened iced tea for Talia Grey. I slip a little extra—*fine, a lot extra*—into the tip jar for the mess I left outside. The barista already gave me an awkward look, but I guess I've earned my place in Redhaven when I don't get a snarky comment to go with it.

When I head back out, Miss Grey's perched in her chair, looking in her compact mirror and wiping at her smudged mascara.

She's managed to pat her mussed-up hair back into place, though it's still a little wild.

The look suits her. She's an ivory candle with a crown of fire.

As I approach the table, she glances up and offers me a worn smile.

"Thanks," she says as I set the tea down in front of her.

"It's nothing." I take the chair across from her, setting the cupholder down and fishing out my own coffee to take a sip. "How are you feeling?"

"Embarrassed, mostly." Biting her lip, she closes her compact and tucks it into her purse. "I can't believe I passed out like that in the middle of town."

"No need to be embarrassed. The crowd was concerned about you."

"Well, yeah, but it's still embarrassing, you know? Like if I'm going to collapse into an asthma attack, I'd prefer to do it in the privacy of my own home." Her lips quirk. "I usually manage them better."

"This is a regular thing for you?" I ask again, sipping my coffee.

"Not as much lately." Miss Grey shrugs, glancing away, her fingers tangling in her hair and twining a lock of it slowly. "I was sick all the time when I was little. I could barely get up a flight of stairs without collapsing, and I was always in and out of the hospital. I've gotten a lot stronger, though. I'm normally pretty good at controlling my breathing before anything severe hits, but this time…"

She trails off.

She looks so uncomfortable I cock my head, studying the way the light falls over her jawline until it's almost transparent. Her skin is so fine.

"This time?"

"I was a little off my game today, I guess." Her eyes fall. She won't look at me. "I should've been able to handle it better."

I'm not sure how to respond.

It's not my job to console her, and it would be crossing a professional line to try—just as much as it would be to give in to the urge to reach out and touch her pale skin, watching the color bloom under my fingers when she's just so delicate.

So frail, and I don't just mean her body, her lungs.

Even if it must have taken incredible willpower to master her asthma, there's something about her.

Something that would be so easy to destroy.

Deep down, I can't decide if I want to shield it or take her in hand and watch her struggle.

Obviously, I can't do either.

I also can't seem to look away, and the longer I watch her, the more she fidgets in her chair, darting quick glances at me. Her cheeks are cherry blossoms now.

She snatches her drink, the ice rattling against the plastic cup and the tea sloshing as she fits the straw between her lips, pursing them like a kiss to take a drink.

Damn.

That gleam on her lips steals my glance before I shift back to her wide, questioning eyes before she looks away.

Why are you staring, Officer?

That's what she's asking.

I can't help answering the unspoken question. "Am I making you uncomfortable, Miss Grey?"

Her shoulders jerk sharply as she sets her cup down. She might as well have said *yes*.

Her brilliant blue eyes shift to me—but not quite.

My mouth.

Is she staring at my mouth?

Right before her eyes drop back to her drink.

"Oh, I— Um, no. You're just the second person to ask me that today."

Her voice fades into this breathy whisper.

Interesting.

Who was the first person?

"Is it because I gave you mouth-to-mouth?" I ask. That must be why she keeps staring at my lips. There's an urge to taunt her, just a little to make that blush deeper, to watch her flutter and tremble, but I hold myself back, remembering my role. "It wasn't personal. I had to make sure you were stabilized."

She doesn't answer, not at first.

Not until she lets out the smallest murmur, still looking down.

"...your teeth are really sharp."

If I was a laughing sort of man, I'd bust a fucking seam.

"Yes. That." I wasn't expecting that answer, though I'm not surprised by it, either. I lean back in my chair with a sigh and take another sip of coffee. "Albinism usually comes with other abnormalities," I say bluntly.

I hate this shit, even if she deserves an answer.

I have too much pride to talk about my condition like I'm ashamed of it.

If I speak about it matter-of-factly, others tend to respond in kind, instead of treating me like I'm a freak or like I'll turn to ash in direct sunlight. I fix my gaze on her intently, tapping my fingers against the side of my cup before I continue.

"Unnaturally long canine teeth. Poor vision. Circulation issues. Skin cancer. Sunburns. General light sensitivity. Bruising. Blood disorders. The list is a mile long." I shrug. "I wound up with vision, teeth, light sensitivity, and bruising on my bingo card." I tap my right eyebrow. "Lasik. Contact lenses. Light therapy. Avoiding coffee tables with sharp corners. Though I've considered filing my teeth down." I quirk a brow. "Biting my tongue hurts like a bitch."

She's been listening intently, watching me with that wide-eyed, curious gaze, and no judgment.

That's new.

No judgment. No pity. No awful sympathy at how bad it must be to be me.

Then again, I suppose she'd know, wouldn't she?

The way people look at you when they think you're just a walking corpse that hasn't figured out it could die at any minute.

But when she blinks and gives me a delayed laugh, it's a whisper. Barely there.

It lights up her face with a flushed sweetness and makes her eyes glitter above the slim hand she brings up to cover her mouth. I cock my head, watching her.

"There you go. Laughter suits you better." I choose my words carefully.

She instantly squeaks, her laughter fading. Her knuckles press against her mouth, her cheeks flushing again.

It's too damn easy to tease reactions out of her.

She's like a musical instrument.

I have to remind myself *not* to and instead refocus on her condition.

"It sounds like your asthma attacks are triggered by stress now. Did something trigger this one, Miss Grey?"

"*Tal-ia*," she corrects sharply.

I expected that.

Then her nervous fingers are in her hair again, separating a lock of crimson like she always needs to keep her hands busy.

"I had a big meeting with a new client. A really wealthy client for a huge long-term project. I made it through the meeting okay, but the whole thing was really unsettling... all the panic came bubbling up, I suppose. The long walk didn't help. I don't even know if we're going to take them on, but I was scared I screwed everything up."

As she speaks, her gaze drifts past me, fixing on something far away. I glance over my shoulder and instantly realize what she's looking at.

That giant house on the hill, casting its long shadow over the town like a phantom.

Now I know the client she means.

Not that it was a big secret when we've only got one wealthy family around these parts.

My interest sharpens. I look back to Talia.

"You met with the Arrendells?"

"Arrendell. Singular," she says. "It was just Xavier. He said his parents are out of town, grieving in Italy or something."

Interesting.

Suddenly, every prickling awareness of her attractiveness, her vulnerability, becomes secondary to a different urgency inside me. It's almost catching a scent that tells me my prey is near, if I'll only follow the lead.

Could this be an opportunity?

And could it end with closing in for the kill? Taking out all the hatred I've nursed for years on Xavier Arrendell's all-too-tender pampered flesh.

I've thought long and hard about killing that fuck.

In my mind, I already know the smell of his blood, the sound of his pain.

Even though I know it's not right—I know I shouldn't *want* it, I know I have to uphold the law—I can't stop.

I can't halt the dreams where I watch the light fade from his eyes like a candle sputtering out.

The same way it did from my brother's.

I keep my composure, though. No point in scaring her now.

"What did he ask you to do?"

"Um, only redecorate the entire huge-ass manor." She blanches and takes another quick sip of her tea. "Really crazy. We're talking new handcrafted furniture in every room and he wants a whole new interior design on top of it. I don't even *do* much interior design. That's not really our thing, but... I guess I'll learn. Whatever I can with a good contractor."

"So you're taking the job?" It comes out too fast.

Something strange passes over her face.

"Well, yeah. I think. We do need the work. I have to throw together a quote, but it's going to be amazing money. It could keep us sitting nice for years."

Then why does her smile look so pained at the windfall?

There's something weird there.

Something odd.

Something hurting her, tied to this job.

"Miss Grey, do you not want to work for Xavier Arrendell?"

No smile now. Her lips crease bitterly, but they're trembling and she won't look at me.

"It's not my business, I know," I tell her. "If I'm getting too nosy, go ahead and tell me to—"

"I'll answer that if you can remember my name." She cuts me off.

"Talia," I say softly, and this time she almost flinches.

Lowering her eyes, she compresses her lips, rubbing the tip of the straw along the crease of her mouth.

"I don't know. Something about *him* makes me uncomfortable. But maybe it's just all the rumors swirling around his family and bad vibes and I'm just overreacting. Being around him makes me feel..." She pauses. "...unsafe, I guess. But we do need the money. Desperately."

I want to reach for her hand. Hold it. Grip it until her fingers stop shaking so much they rattle the ice in her cup.

It's not my place.

And if she knew me—the real me—she might feel less safe with me as she does with Xavier.

"Is your business struggling, Miss—Talia?" I ask, probing carefully.

"No, it's fine." She shakes her head, crimson curls swaying against her jaw and shoulders. "It's just, everything costs so much these days. Sometimes things you really need."

She's being vague.

It's damn sure not my business, and I sense it'd hurt her to pry.

This is the first time we've been more than two strangers passing on the street, not even meriting a second glance. The first time we've ever spoken.

So I'll mind my manners.

But I may need her to help me mind someone else's, too.

Leaning forward, I brace my arms on the table.

"What if I could give you a better reason to take the job?" I ask, dropping my voice to a whisper. "Would that make it easier if it was worth more than money?"

Talia's brows wrinkle.

She throws back such innocent confusion that the guilt punches me, but I started this and now I've got to finish it.

"What... what do you mean?"

Leaning back, I glance around the morning-lit street.

People are scattered around us at the café's little outdoor tables. Others pass by now and then, strolling and not really paying attention as they bustle between shopping and errands. Though there are a few curious glances that make it clear some of the town's gossipier citizens wonder what the oddball cop and the furniture store girl are doing together.

"Not here," I mutter. "Would you be willing to meet me again tonight?"

"Tonight? Uh, what? Officer Ainsley, what *are* you asking?" She stares at me, flushed and stammering.

"Not what you think, I promise." Not that I wouldn't goddamn mind, but I keep my eyes firmly on her face, ignoring how her flustered look heats my blood. "I need to tell you some things about Xavier Arrendell. I'd also like to ask for your help."

"Help? Oh," she whispers, pinching her fingers against her straw. "You mean like... something you can't tell me here?"

"It's not the sort of thing you talk about in public, no. Take that into consideration before you decide if you'll meet with me."

That's my cue to go.

While she goes ash-white, staring at me wordlessly, I push my chair back and stand. Her head tilts back to follow me.

"I've got to get to work," I say, pushing my empty chair

back in. "Try to stay awake for the next twelve hours. If you feel dizzy, suffer any hearing loss, ringing ears, blurred vision, call 9-1-1 immediately." I flick my gaze over her.

She looks fine, like she never even fell.

The only signs are the rips in her pantyhose and a few scuffs on her pink dress, but head injuries can be serious. That seems to jolt her out of her daze.

"I told you I didn't hit my head." Her voice is small yet composed. "I really am an old hand at controlled falls."

"Your phone number?" I ask.

There it is again. That blush that makes her so bright, so vulnerable. Her fingers jerk against her cup, making it shake loudly.

"...number? Why?"

"So I can check on you. Make sure you didn't give yourself a concussion," I say. "And so I can text you where to meet, if you're game."

"Oh. Okay."

It's too long before she moves, before she mumbles something incoherent and thumps her cup down on the table so she can bend over and rummage around in her purse.

She comes up with a business card reading A Touch of Grey. Her name is on it—Talia Grey, Store Manager—plus two phone numbers, one labeled (O) for office and one labeled (C) for cell.

"That's my personal cell," she says quietly, reminding me how small Redhaven really is, where people still have paper business cards and put their personal numbers on them. "Just tell me where. I'm free tonight, so I'll think about it."

"I appreciate you, Miss Grey."

"Dude. Talia," she snaps, almost on autopilot. I bite back a smile.

No, I still don't say it.

I just touch two fingers to my temple, nod, and scoop up my crew's drinks to make the rest of the walk to work.

Her eyes trail after me like a lost puppy, watching me the whole way.

* * *

My house doesn't fit into Redhaven any more than I do.

It's been a long damn day.

The Jacobins' pigs got loose again, and at this point I wonder if they're doing it on purpose just to keep us tied up while they're moving their mobile moonshine stills around, always one step ahead of us.

There were more hogs than usual this time. Took us all evening to round them up.

I'll admit I was distracted and screwed up a few times—and nearly got trampled under several hundred pounds of hooves for my trouble.

I also came about three inches short of letting one of the biggest sows plow right into the A Touch of Grey delivery truck as it trundled past, dragging behind a tow truck from Mort's garage.

If the Houdini pigs are a ruse, they're effective as hell.

I'm almost too exhausted to do my usual stakeouts tonight, watching to see if they're cooking up more than moonshine.

I also have more on my plate than watching the hillfolk and waiting for them to slip up this evening. Looking for a boost, I settle behind the built-in bar in my basement, relaxing while I mix up a cocktail or two.

You can tell the vacation homes built by out-of-towners from the original colonial architecture of a historic town. This house is rustic enough, a rugged sprawling ranch house in raw timber wood. All log cabin on the outside and cosmopolitan black leather, stone, and dark brushed steel on the inside.

I bought it for a song when I first moved here from a wealthy investor who thought Redhaven might be good for some real estate speculation, only to realize it's only interesting to hikers and people who *really* love hand-tapped maple syrup, true crime podcasts, and small-town crafts.

I'm sure it's not the only house with a fancy built-in bar, but it's probably the only one owned by a former bartender.

Whipping up an espresso martini feels strangely comforting.

Not really a martini at all by proper definition. More like a cocktail that involves a lot of vodka.

A little Stoli Elit, some flavored syrup, concentrated espresso, and coffee liqueur.

Then, because I like my martinis the same way I like my coffee, I add some Irish crème.

It's soothing, falling into routine pours, mixing, both hands working with years of practice.

Once upon a time, I paid my way through college slinging drinks.

It's been more than a decade since, but at thirty-five, I can still mix up a pretty mean cocktail.

It honestly doesn't take long enough.

There's too much shit on my mind.

Too much to tame in ninety seconds of mix and pour.

The taste, at least, is enough to chase away a few brooding thoughts as I settle into a deep-set chair next to the crackling fireplace, slouching down against the leather.

Not bad.

It gets better when my massive German Shepherd perks up from his nap in front of the heat and trots over to lie down at my feet, thrusting his muzzle under my hand. He's so old his fur is greying around his face.

"Hey, Rolf," I murmur against the rim of my martini glass, scratching between his ears. He lets out a satisfied grumble, leaning into my touch and thumping his tail hard against the woven wool rug. "Did the big boy have a good day? Not me, I'm afraid. But I might have a better night."

His only answer is a low *whuff*!

I set my drink down on the side table and snag my phone, flicking through the texts until I land on the one I sent Talia as I clocked out of work.

Talia, it's Micah Ainsley. Shore of Still Lake. 9:30 pm. Can you be there? Are you still feeling well enough to meet? Mallory didn't report a call, so I'm hoping you made it through the day.

There's no answer.

How can I blame her?

When a stupid cop you've never spoken to in your life rescues you from a public asthma attack, then asks you to meet him over something clearly related to your job with the Arrendells, you don't jump with joy.

I'd be wary, too.

Only, I'm not the one she should be wary of.

Xavier Arrendell and trust don't mix.

I never gave him the benefit of the doubt, even before it started getting weird with vicious secrets dripping out.

The whole family's rotten to the core, and those boys learned it somewhere.

I'm convinced Lucia and Montero Arrendell are fully aware of their sons' twisted hobbies. There was Ulysses Arrendell first, 'claiming' girls and turning into their stalker-slash-suitor, only to strangle them to death and use Culver Jacobin to help hide their bodies.

Then there was Aleksander Arrendell, knowingly manipulating his own secret half sister into an engagement and then trying to murder her. Thankfully, his other half sister intervened with Captain Faircross before he could get that far.

You want to convince me Xavier Arrendell is innocent?

When he was forged in the same crucible of filth?

Guilt by association won't fly in court, no, but I've been watching Xavier since I moved here.

And I'm pretty damned sure he's got plenty of guilt of his own, no association needed.

Except for his association with the case I've been working.

The plague of cocaine sales and addiction-related deaths spreading like weeds up and down the East Coast over the last decade.

The ugly fact that most of the supply can be traced back to a single source.

The killing fact that I found my own brother dead in his apartment, his nostrils still lined with the dust of the last hit he'd ever taken.

Maybe the bad memories just finally crushed Jet in the end.

The fucked up pain of being beaten every day by a father too drunk to realize what he was doing.

Maybe I shouldn't blame the drug supplier.

Maybe I should blame Jet for his choices alone, the wrong ones he made to escape the hellish way we grew up.

But *someone* tempted him down that path to death.

Someone gave my brother the poison and the habit that killed him.

I can't stand that heartbreak happening to anybody else.

My brother deserves that much.

After the way he'd protect me when we were kids, standing between our father and his furious fists while he snarled at me for being so weak, so scrawny, this bloodless abnormal *freak*.

THE DARKEST CHASE

It took years to stand on my own, to find my inner strength.

Just like Talia Grey.

Maybe that's why I'm actually feeling guilty as I eye that unanswered text. The double check mark says she left me on *Read.*

I do hope she's feeling better.

I checked with dispatch for any new medical emergency calls, just in case. It's more likely she doesn't want to get involved with my mess.

Maybe she can sense I'm trouble, and she's right.

I'm asking to drag her into something she should never make her business.

"Am I fucking this up, Rolf?" I scratch under his furry jaw. "She's a nice girl. So innocent. If I ask her to do this, she might lose that. She might walk away tarnished and bitter."

But if I don't, I could lose my best chance to pin down Xavier Arrendell and destroy his greedy ass.

Rolf doesn't have any answers, but his tail thumps harder.

I can't help but smile.

"You're never much for conversation," I whisper, letting him lick my hand. "But you are a good boy."

I start to swap my phone for my drink, but before I can set it down, it vibrates in my hand.

Talia Grey: I'm okay. No concussion or anything. I'll be there.

Damn, now we're talking.

Tonight, at least I can ask if Talia will hear me out.

So I drop my phone on the accent table, toss back my cocktail in a fuming burn of liquor and strong espresso, and stroke Rolf's fur.

"C'mon, old man." I stand to pull his leash down from its hook by the door. "Let's go meet a girl and try not to scare her."

V: GOING DARK (TALIA)

I don't know what I'm doing here.
Honest to God.

Not after Officer Ainsley texted directions to a secluded spot on Still Lake, over on the far side where it's all trees hugging close to a thin strip of grassy shore.

It's cold for April. The night breeze seeps under the collar of my light jacket and gives me goosebumps everywhere.

The chill. That's all it is.

Not me wondering what Micah Ainsley really wants with me.

Something to do with the job for Xavier Arrendell, I guess. Which makes me as uneasy as Xavier himself, and considering Officer Ainsley is a cop…

I wonder if it's something dangerous.

Something I should run away from before I even find out what it is.

Yet somehow, I can't.

I can't help wanting to see him and find out anyway.

I can't miss a chance to be brave when I grew up afraid of my own shadow.

It's definitely a challenge, considering who I'm meeting with.

Micah Ainsley, with those cold quicksilver eyes and that moonstone skin. Deadly, sharp, and honed.

And soon, all alone with me.

Just a strange, gorgeous man and a thousand wild thoughts I shouldn't have.

Nothing spicy will happen, of course.

Officer Ainsley is an ordinary cop and he honestly seems like a bit of a hardass.

I'm a grown woman who definitely shouldn't be having fantasies fit for a high school diary.

I wonder if that's one of the ways I've never quite grown up, though.

Because I stayed inside, cooped up with my illness, I never made many friends. I never had the young, dumb experiences other kids did.

So did I really grow up at all?

Sighing, I crane my head back, gazing up at the clear night sky. The Milky Way glows overhead, the yawning universe with its necklace of stars framed by tall trees.

It's like an eye opening up to let me look inside its jeweled colors. Breathtakingly beautiful, but a little lonely, too.

I just don't know what I'm pining for.

A life I never had?

Some days, I feel like I only live for work.

It's not that I don't love what I do.

I live for feeling smoothly sanded wood under my fingers, the awl in my hands, the scent of sawdust. Grandpa's workshop was where I first started to learn to control my breathing, so I could savor that scent without the dust triggering an attack.

So I could be with *him*, caught up in his warm approval as he taught me how to shape wood, how to etch, how to engrave, how to know the difference between carved designs and burned, and so much more.

For a child shut-in who spent half her free days at the doctor, he gave me a life.

Grandpa's workshop was pure magic.

He was a sorcerer and I was his happy apprentice.

Still, I feel like I missed out on so much else.

Running and playing with other kids. Sports and band. Going to dances to peek at boys over my fingers.

Stealing young kisses behind the bookshelves in the library.

Even dating in college. I just never learned *how*.

All the little social rituals that turn into flirting and dates and kisses and more still feel like a mystery.

Anytime someone tried the first half of that call with me, I panicked.

Every time, I dropped the ball awkwardly and left the guy fumbling away from me with confusion. Like he thought he'd tried to win over a girl and then realized he was actually chasing some weird, gross bug.

Miss Grey.

Does Officer Ainsley see me the same way?

He calls me *Miss Grey* like he's from another time. That doesn't stop my mind from spinning daydreams about him in a waistcoat, lurking against a window with the moonlight in his eyes and reflecting off his deadly lips.

He almost looked upset when I asked him about his teeth.

But I get it.

For him, it's part of what singles him out and makes him so different.

Just like my asthma.

He probably got picked on as a kid for his teeth and his albino skin, the same way I did because I couldn't run or play or fight.

When I think about him that way—the real man behind the fantasy—it stops being this taboo thrill.

It just makes me hurt for him.

It makes me want to tell him it's okay to be different.

And he's definitely *different* from what I expect tonight when I hear a faint metallic jingle and look up, realizing it's a dog collar.

Officer Ainsley makes his way quietly along the thin strip of grassy shore, his reflection mirrored in Still Lake's glossy surface. He's walking a German Shepherd that looks like a small bear—an older dog, I think.

The dog moves slower and a little unevenly, but Ainsley matches the canine's pace, stopping when the dog wants to stop.

And when I stop and get a good look at him, my breath stalls.

He's so normal tonight.

Almost rugged in dark jeans, dark hiking boots, and a deep blue and black plaid flannel shirt, the sleeves cuffed to his elbows. The open throat shows off stark lines of collarbones.

Instead of the side-parted sweep he wore earlier today, his hair is a little messy.

He might look perfectly ghostly under the moonlight, but the way he's dressed, the way he moves, the way he looks down at his dog with his eyes brimming with clear affection?

It reminds me he's a *man.*

Not some prop for swirling hormones and juvenile fantasies.

It's nice seeing him like this, honestly.

And there's also something else.

Something melancholy about him, like a human echo of Still Lake itself.

I don't realize I'm straight-up staring until our eyes meet.

My heart lurches—and then tries to stop its frantic beating when he smiles.

Yes, he sort of smiled at me a few times this morning. But it was a curt, professional cop smile meant to put me at ease.

This is a small, reserved smile, too. But more honest, more real.

It also suits him better when he's so quiet with his feelings and shows only as much as he needs to.

I try to smile back, but my lips won't work. I can't even remember to blink as he makes his way closer.

"Miss Grey," he says, drawing into earshot.

"Hi!" I'm already mentally kicking myself.

Seriously, *why* am I freezing up?

To distract myself, I look at the dog because it's easier than looking at him.

"I heard you had a dog," I say, offering my fingers for the German Shepherd to sniff. "What's his name?"

"Rolf," he answers. "He's a K-9 retiree from New York. He makes good company."

"Oh, wow. I bet he does." I can't help smiling while Rolf stretches his neck, tongue lolling, and sniffs my hand.

But his ears flip back with a disgruntled sound and he turns his face away, the slow wag of his tail completely stopping.

"I'm sorry?" I pull my hand back.

"Don't worry about it," Ainsley says. "He's old, spoiled, and set in his ways. He doesn't warm up to new people easily. Always takes the guys on the police crew a hundred treats to bribe him into feeling civil."

I smile again, wondering if he's talking about the dog or himself.

With a nervous laugh, I look away and run a hand through my hair.

"It probably doesn't help that I still smell like varnish no matter how much I shower. That stuff's potent, and aren't their noses pretty sensitive? He's a drug dog, right?"

"He was," he says.

Then nothing.

I look him over carefully. He's staring out over the water, his face pensive. Rolf settles at his feet, quietly leaning against his legs.

"So, what did you want to talk about, Officer Ainsley?"

"Micah," he clips, his lips firm. "I'm not on the job right now."

I huff out a breath. "Wait. I'm supposed to call you Micah, but I'm still Miss Grey? I'm not on the clock, either."

"Using a respectful title has nothing to do with your job." He's so still, so quiet, the only motion is his thumb rubbing the leash looped around his cragged knuckles. "You can call me Mr. Ainsley, if you'd like."

"It just feels stiff. I'm fine with calling you Micah if you are. *You're* the one who won't say my name."

"*Talia*," Officer Ainsley—*Micah*—growls.

Oh God.

His voice feels like a cloud of frost. I shiver.

My eyes widen as I hug my arms around myself.

Suddenly, I can't even feel the cool night breeze.

I'm too hot, burning from my scalp all the way to my toes.

Breathe.

I count three breaths in, three breaths out, reminding myself I can't get so flipping worked up over a guy saying my *name*, even if it's with a voice like frozen sin.

"You wanted to talk about Xavier Arrendell?"

"Yes," he answers, suddenly all business. His voice drops from cool to downright frigid. "How much do you know about the Arrendells' scandals?"

"Um…" I bite my lip, racking my brain. There's so much, growing up in this town, let alone the news lately. "I mean, until the last year or two, it was all rumors, right? The kind of stuff where you never really know what's true and what's gossip. I know the oldest son, Vaughn, he left a long time ago and no one knows why. But people think he did something really awful. And Montero, he's a known womanizer. He and Lucia act like they kind of hate each other. I don't know why they stay married."

"Go on." Micah nods.

"...but they know a lot of big celebrities and power broker types, don't they? And people think Lucia's connected, like using her money for dark stuff and not just charity, buying off rich folks for favors. Plus, all the rumors about the missing girls, but that turned out to be Ulysses and that whole rotten business with the new teacher. Then the Faircrosses and their trouble... I heard Aleksander jetted around the world, throwing wild parties with sex and supermodels before he started to settle down—" I stop and clear my throat. "I mean, before he tried to marry his half sister. *Gross.*"

"Nasty as hell," Micah rumbles. "What else? What do you know about Xavier?"

"Xavier... I guess nobody talks about him as much. He's older and not as flashy as the other two. But I thought there were rumors he's been in and out of rehab since he was a teenager? He's kind of standing in everyone else's shadow, but it's more like he's a shadow himself." I let out a rush of breath after tumbling over those words. "Did I miss anything?"

Micah's eyes sharpen.

He lets out this low, rolling laugh like sandstone and grit. It lights up his face in a way I couldn't have imagined, like a glacier catching the sun.

"Glad your lungs are doing better," he says. "I don't think

you even stopped for breath once. When you showed up wearing the same color, I admit you had me worried."

I glance down, blushing at my windbreaker. "This? It's just my coat."

"And the gloves, the purse. Does all that pink give you some special powers with your woodwork?"

"Hey! You can't come at a girl for having a favorite color *and* a sense of fashion." I turn my face up mockingly.

He chuckles like thunder moving in.

God help me, I can feel it in my bones.

"Whatever, Strawberry Shortcake. I really am glad you're doing better, well enough to launch into speeches and all."

With my face on fire, I clear my throat and fiddle with the wrists of my jacket. "It's just a little stream of consciousness. I guess I just got carried away."

"It's fine," he says, though that cryptic smile lingers. "It means I don't have to catch you up on much. I expected you'd know more than I would, growing up here. I'm just a transplant. But I also have sources you don't—and those sources know a hell of a lot more about Xavier Arrendell than any vague rumor mill."

"Like what?" Alarm thumps through me.

"Like the fact that he may be more than a drug fiend. He's in deeper, and I think it's connected to the Jacobins. Linking them together with solid proof, that's the trouble." He shakes his head with a weary sigh. "Those hillfolk have been here for generations. They know how to hide their shit too well, how to make themselves invisible. It doesn't help that Chief Bowden lets them off lightly. He treats it like something harmless, like it's petty crime and a little rotgut moonshine won't hurt anybody."

I shrink back, staring at him.

"You think it's more than moonshine?"

"I do," he snarls without hesitation. "Something uglier

that reaches far beyond the borders of Redhaven, or even North Carolina. I think one reason it's so easy to slip under the radar is the power and influence the Arrendells have to make things magically disappear."

"But... but Chief Bowden, you said? You think he's part of it?" It almost hurts, thinking the kind old chief could join up with something bad. "He's always been so nice."

"Nice folks aren't always good, Talia," Micah replies. His strange, intense eyes lock me in place. "You truly are innocent, aren't you?"

I don't know how to answer that.

I don't know if I *want* to answer, when I've never really thought of myself as innocent.

Just sheltered.

But now, I feel naïve.

I push on, trying to keep my composure.

"I guess I don't get it. What do you want me to do with this information? How am I supposed to help you?"

"Easy. Just do your job for Xavier, and if you can, keep your eyes open."

"For *what*?"

His face hardens, all cold-eyed hunger again. "Anything that might interest a man who wants to destroy everything Xavier Arrendell stands for."

Holy crap.

It's so quiet, yet so forceful it takes my breath away.

And why does it feel *personal*?

Like there's something more driving him to go poking around.

I wonder what Rolf senses radiating from his master that I don't know when the German Shepherd finally moves again. He thrusts his head under Micah's trusting hand with a low, comforting whine.

Micah answers with his fingers, scratching through mottled brown and black fur.

Shivering, I wrap my coat tighter.

"Wouldn't the other guys on the force be better for this? Why aren't you asking them for help?"

"They're not insiders, for one. Even in a town this small, we're stretched thin. Plus, the Arrendells know them—and me—on sight. They keep things tighter than a drum when we show up at the big house. They'd never let their guard down or let anything incriminating slip. A pretty girl, though, one so innocent she's disarming, and who's already there on legitimate business... They'd never see it coming."

Whoa.

Hearing him describe me like that makes my ears burn.

I sputter and pinch the cuffs of my sleeves.

"That's just it!" I protest. "Innocent. As in, I have no guile, no game, and no idea how to hide anything from someone like Xavier, much less an ulterior motive. How can I get away with snooping around? He's pretty smart. He'd see right through me."

"Would he?" His eyes narrow. Skewering. Incisive. "You were so nervous with him that it triggered a panic attack. If he's used to you being nervous and thinks that's just how you are, he won't notice if you're a little on edge."

No.

He might actually enjoy it, judging from the way he acted when we met.

The thought makes me feel slimy. It also makes me feel like a terrible person.

Whatever else he's up to, Xavier Arrendell is busy grieving two huge losses. I was probably misreading his behavior when people tend to get weird with grief.

When I don't say anything, caught up in inner turmoil, Micah steps closer.

"You can always say no," he says gently.

"Wh-what?"

"This isn't a command or a direct order. I'm not telling you to do this because I'm a cop asking for a little help from the public. This is you and me, Talia, and it's completely off the books."

Oof.

That alone should make me wary. It's like it's not just that he doesn't want to burden the other guys at Redhaven PD.

I think he's actively keeping this to himself, for some weird reason.

But it's like he has a magnetic choke hold on me with that unblinking icy stare, stealing my thoughts. Soon, I can only hear the way he speaks, hypnotic and intense.

"You can walk away from me right now if you'd like. Nothing bad will happen to you, I promise," he whispers. "I'm not making demands with my badge. I'm asking you to help me as a human being. And if you feel that what I'm asking you is wrong, or if it scares you, or even if you just don't want to—tell me no. We'll never speak of it again. I'll go back to being that cop you say hello to now and then whenever we pass each other on the street. Not the strange man asking you to help him scale a goddamned mountain."

I don't know why that hurts.

Yes, I've been tossed into Micah's orbit so fast it's left me dizzy. Yet the thought of being cast back down and just being acquaintances leaves an odd tightness in my chest.

He basically saved my life, didn't he?

And I wonder if that's my conscience talking when he's asking me for *help* or if it's that damsel in distress reaction I can't smother, getting emotionally attached to a white knight who came charging to my rescue.

Whatever it is, I can't stop myself from asking, "...and what if I say maybe? What if I say I'll think about it?"

"Then I'll ask you to go camping with me tomorrow night." His eyes are smiling when he says it.

"I... *What?*" He's very good at that, catching me off guard. I can never figure out what goes through this man's head. "I don't follow. What does camping have to do with Xavier Arrendell?"

"Everything," Micah whispers. "You aren't sure because you need proof, you need more info—and I'm going to show you, Miss Grey."

* * *

I'M STILL REELING by the time we part ways.

I take the long way home to give myself time to think, walking alone under the clear night sky without Micah turning me upside down with his nearness.

I'm so confused.

I don't know how I'm supposed to trick Xavier Arrendell into incriminating himself in front of me, or even what incriminating clues would look like. This idea that Xavier's a drug dealer, that he may be behind a major regional drug operation...

This isn't my world.

It's not something I understand, and it's definitely not somewhere I belong.

I can't unknow what I know now, though.

Even if I tell Micah no, I'll still have that awareness in the back of my mind, always watching Xavier like a skittish animal.

God, I don't know what to *do*.

If I listen to Micah and he's wrong, I could wind up hurting a man whose worst crime is struggling with complex grief over his dead brothers. It could be true that Xavier's a drug addict, and honestly, being an Arrendell would probably drive anyone to bad habits.

But if he is, couldn't he be a victim of the drug dealers, too?

And if I tell Micah no and he's dead-on right...

How many people will end up hooked on cocaine and dead? All because I was too scared to do anything?

This feels too big for me, like a gaping hole opening up in the fabric of my reality.

It's not the kind of decision I can make quickly—if I can make it at all.

Right now, I can't even decide if I'll go camping with Micah to find out what he wants to show me.

I'm also nowhere closer to an answer by the time I make it home.

Grandpa's waiting up for me like usual. I can tell before I cross the street to the shop.

The light in the window over the storefront is on, and when I slip into the narrow alley between our shop and the building next door, where the private outside entrance to the upstairs waits, I instantly feel safer.

The light's on over the door, its golden glow filling the dark crevices of night.

The kitchen upstairs is just as warm, too.

I let myself in and climb the narrow stairs behind the workshop to our loft.

My grandfather sits at the raw wood kitchen table, cradling a mug of tea, his eyes almost disappearing under the thick grey bushes of his eyebrows. There's a half-eaten loaf of banana bread in front of him, courtesy of the bakery next door.

Mrs. Brodsky stops in practically every night when I'm not around, bringing him goodies. Last year, when I asked her to check in on him, she jumped at the chance when he reminds her so much of her own deceased father. She didn't even ask about his condition.

As far as she knows, I'm just asking for help to keep an old man company. Not to check in to make sure he hasn't abruptly lost another piece of his mind and started the place on fire—though Grandpa's never been anywhere near that reckless and absent-minded.

I hope—*I pray*—that sort of worry is a long way off.

Still, better safe than sorry.

Coming home instantly brightens my evening.

Everything in this kitchen was handcrafted by him, from the dining set to the wood countertops and giant butcher-block island. It's all white ash, carefully selected and shaped and artificially aged. Every deceptively simple piece is a quiet testament to untold hours of meticulous craftsmanship.

I stop and sigh, hoping I'll be a tenth as good as he is someday.

There's a second mug of tea sitting across from him, still steaming. It's like he can tell when I'm coming back.

I shrug off my jacket and hang it on the peg by the door, then settle in across from him and curl my hands against the ceramic for warmth.

"Hey, Grandpa," I say.

"Hey, yourself. Late night, sweetheart?" He gives me a long, searching look and sips his tea, smacking his lips.

"I was meeting a friend." I shrug flippantly. "Why'd you wait up for me so long? Mrs. Brodsky must've left an hour ago."

"Yeah, well." He stops there.

He worries about me a lot, I think.

But one reason I love him is because he's never tried to tell me how to live my life, even knowing how careful I have to be.

We're partners, and he trusts me to take care of myself.

So it's not like him to be waiting.

But tonight, I'm glad he is.

Because right now the homey warmth of this kitchen, surrounded by the sweet smell of hot herbal tea and the ever-present scent of sawdust, feels like something I didn't know I needed.

It grounds me again.

Makes me feel like I can figure this mess out, if I just sit down and take my time and really think it through.

"Guess I couldn't wait to see my granddaughter. Is that a crime now?" He snorts, but his eyes are shrewd over his mug. "You went up to the big house today."

"Oh, yes. I did. You remember?"

"Took me a minute, but yes." He doesn't dance around his dementia episodes.

After they pass, he's open to talking about them and where he is mentally. The practicality of his generation makes him the kind of man who won't shrink away from facing his reality.

"What was it about again?" he asks. "Help an old fart out."

"Mm." I stare down into my tea, watching the misty curls of smoke rising. "Xavier Arrendell has a job for us. A big one. He wants us to redecorate the entire manor. Top to bottom, every piece of furniture, all the interiors. Half the stuff he wants, I'm going to have to get like a whole new certification to know how to do. An army of subcontractors. Something."

"Damn. But it's something you can do, if you want to," he points out, those blue eyes still holding mine. I seem to be surrounded by men who like to skewer me with heady looks, but Grandpa's gaze is a familiar thing. Very different from the way Micah Ainsley makes me shiver just by staring. "The real question is, do you want the work, Tally-girl?"

"I don't know," I admit. "It's a lot of money, even if we could use it." He knows why. I don't need to say it. "But it's also a lot for us to take on alone, even with some hired help." I bite my lip, watching him. "Do *you* want to do it?"

He laughs roughly.

"You know I'm no stranger to hard work, even if I might have my doubts about the client. Those folks up on the hill always did leave a sour taste in my mouth, but I suppose I wouldn't have to deal with them, if you're already talking to that Xavier boy. Which leaves this in your hands." His gaze softens. "I'll leave it up to you, Tally." There's a softness to the way he says that name that just chokes me up every time. "If you want to take it on, I'll follow your lead. But if you don't want to, there's no shame in turning it down."

But I don't want to!

Instant knee-jerk thought.

I'm not just talking about the job, either.

There's a stubborn, restless part of me that balks at playing it safe, at being careful like I have been for my entire life.

I may tell myself I'm different now—not that frightened little girl locked away behind closed doors anymore—but when do I ever get a chance to prove it?

I've also never been a big fan of people who tell me how *brave* I am just for trying to have a normal life. It feels patronizing. Like I'm this small pathetic thing who can't hope for anything bigger and better.

Maybe sometimes I feel like that's what I actually am, but I don't want to be.

I won't deny I'm afraid.

I'm afraid of Xavier Arrendell.

I'm afraid of what Micah's asking me to do.

But I don't want that, either.

So I offer Grandpa a smile as resolve hardens inside me.

"I need to think a little more," I say. "But it could be interesting."

I need to think, sure.

I also need to meet Micah tomorrow night.

Because if he really has something compelling up his sleeve, then he deserves a chance for me to hear him out.

And I deserve a chance to find out how brave I can be.

VI: DARK DREAMS (MICAH)

*S*he came.
 I won't lie, I didn't expect her to.
Last night, she looked at me like *I* was the danger.

The one she should be afraid of.

Can she see right through me so easily? I wonder.

Does she know that underneath the calm façade, under the mantra to serve and protect, I'm not a good man?

I tried to be once.

I tried to be *better* than my father, but since the day Jet died, there's just this slow, deep-rooted poison swirling with black thoughts.

Horrors I'd like to do to Xavier Arrendell.

To Ephraim Jacobin and his rotten fucking clan.

Also, what I think about doing to Talia Grey—very different, very devastating things—as I watch her now.

She's standing on my doorstep under the bright morning sun.

There's a bulging rucksack piled against her back. Her slender shoulders strain, making her chest thrust forward in curving mounds that threaten to burst through her pink plaid flannel.

Danger tits. She just invented them.

And pink again.

Damn if I don't smile.

The shirt looks brand new, still a little stiff despite the way the fabric clings to her—and there's not a single scuff on the dark-brown leather hiking boots she's wearing, laced up tight over the cuffs of dark jeans molded to her shapely legs and vanishing into her scrunched pink and black argyle socks.

Is she already flushed?

A little breathless, perhaps, her coppery-red hair pulled up in a ponytail, minus a few wild strands that billow against her cheeks.

Her eyes are so bright.

So eager.

Even if I never lay a hand on her, fuck, I'm going to *defile* this young woman's innocence no matter what I do.

One more reason why I'm a terrible person.

The more I think about how wrong it would be, the more I want it.

I screw my mind back in place, though, giving her another once-over.

"Did you buy out the entire sporting goods store?" I ask dryly, and her flush deepens. I can't help wondering if she blushes so easily all the time, or if it's something unique about me—the way I clearly twist her up.

Yeah.

Bad fucking man.

Because that just makes me want to pin her up against a wall and find out how red I can make her, how I can make her tremble, and if that flustered look could ever be something else.

I don't know why vulnerability turns my crank.

Maybe because I was made to feel helpless my entire young life, and now there's something darkly satisfying about turning it back on someone else.

About being the one in charge.

About holding her pleasure and her fate together in the same iron fist.

Fuck, I *definitely* need to get this over with and forget all about wondering if Talia Grey's thighs quiver the same way her lips do.

Those lips move now, reminding me I need to process normal words instead of my own deviant thoughts. Especially with the way she's scuffing her feet and toying with the adjustable sections of her backpack straps, twining the black nylon around her fingers, blissfully unaware of my filthy thoughts.

"Fair warning, I've never been camping," she starts sheepishly. "I thought it'd be better to overpack a bit."

"Never?"

Talia averts her eyes.

"...I know. It's weird, living here and never doing it when it's like the only thing to *do* for fun. But yeah."

There's an awkward silence.

I think I get what she means, but I won't embarrass her more by pushing about it.

"Give me a minute," I say. "Let me grab my gear and put Rolf in his harness, and then we can sort your bag and head out."

"What do we need to sort?"

"Emptying it out, first," I answer. "Even I wouldn't want to haul that around in the hills for hours, and we're going to be climbing for a while. It's just one night, Miss Grey. Considering the weather, we'd be fine with a couple canteens, a sleeping bag, and a fire."

"...oh. Okay. I feel dumb now."

"Don't," I throw back. "Your head was in the right place. Be right back."

I step back and push the door back, leaving it open just enough to not seem rude, but still not inviting entry.

I'm territorial about my space, though it's not just that.

Having a woman here feels too intimate.

Like this is more than me dragging her into my business, if I let her get familiar with my home.

I can't afford that.

Not when I can never predict what might blow my cover and tear the identity of Officer Micah Ainsley into shreds, revealing the truth.

So I leave her standing outside while I snag the smaller backpack I prepped yesterday and sling it over one shoulder, then coax Rolf into his harness. It's designed to make it easier to manage him on steep inclines and help him if he takes a fall.

You don't want to be holding a leash attached to a collar if your dog goes over a ridge. If he were younger, I'd let him just roam free without a harness. But he's fifteen years old now, well past his breed's typical lifespan.

I'm a little overprotective.

For him, I act a little human.

He clings near my leg like he always does as I take his leash and lead him to the door. His tail starts wagging like mad.

He can always tell when we're about to hit the woods for an extended stay, and even as old as he is, he gets all worked up at the thought of chasing squirrels through heaps of dead leaves.

The second I open the door again and see Talia standing there with a confused, slightly hurt look on her face, Rolf's tail stops.

She flashes me an odd look, then looks away, bowing her head and smiling at the dog with one slim hand reaching out.

"Hey, big guy. Ready to give me a second chance?"

Rolf just stares at her, stone-cold and flat.

Talia wilts like the pretty pink flower she is.

"...he really hates me, huh?"

"He hates anyone who steals my attention, Shortcake. It's not personal."

Talia blinks, throwing me a startled look.

I knit my brows.

What?

What did I say?

She looks away again, almost pointedly avoiding eye contact. "So, where should we leave my stuff?"

"Back of my Jeep is fine." I step forward, nudging Rolf with my knee to get him across the threshold. He balks, but then circles around Talia, giving me room to step outside and lock up.

For a second, we're arm to arm, and I can catch her scent—vanilla again. Smells more natural than any lotion, perfume, or other fragrance.

Then she skitters away, stumbling down the concrete front step onto the leaf-littered paved walk. She keeps avoiding eye contact while her thumbs hook in the straps of her rucksack.

I lock the door, then sigh and turn to face her.

"Spill."

"...huh?" Talia's head jerks up. "Spill what?"

"Something's wrong," I say firmly. "You won't look at me. You looked upset when I came back outside."

She winces.

"Oh, no, I—I'm just being a dork..."

"A dork about what?"

"I just wondered if I'm annoying you?" she strains out.

"You just shut the door in my face. I mean, and I know we don't even know each other, but—"

"No, I get it. In a town like this, you're used to being invited in for coffee, chatting a little and making niceties before getting down to business," I finish. "Yeah. I know. Guess I never let go of my New York manners. Or the New York need for privacy." I step down onto the walk, coiling Rolf's leash around my fist. "It's mostly for Rolf's sake. At his age, he gets twitchy if there's anyone else's scent in the house."

It's not an outright lie.

He really is a possessive beast.

The guys have tried like hell to make friends and he's just not having it. Lucas Graves must've fed Rolf his weight in sausage several times over.

I've just never let anyone stick around long enough to find out if he could truly get used to them.

"Oh," Talia says, trailing behind me as I head for my Jeep. It's so old it's a miracle it hasn't fallen apart, but these old machines were made to last. I picked it up at a police auction in New York when I was still a rookie, and it's held up forever even though it's so battered it looks like mud was the original paint color.

With an eager whoof, Rolf leaps up into the open back, bouncing and wagging his tail. I scratch his ruff.

"Get down from there. I need the space today." I hold my hand out to Talia. "Show me what's in that sack."

After hesitating, she shimmies the backpack off.

Can't say I mind the show, considering how she squirms. Her tits press against her flannel shirt so hard the buttons are damned near ready to pop.

I get a glimpse of a very thin undershirt and hints of what looks like black lace showing through the thin white fabric.

Damn.

She's a little too distracted to notice me watching, at least, though I enjoy her breathy exertion. Her noises are somewhere between adorable and fucking erotic.

I need to stop being a dick.

So I offer her a little mercy and step closer, circling around her to take the straps in both hands. "Here. Just slide your arms out."

"Y-yeah!" She flicks a nervous glance over her shoulder, then she goes still. It's hard not to bury my face in that cloud of crimson hair and inhale her vanilla scent like it's the air I need. "Sorry I'm so clumsy."

"It's fine. I'll just have to keep an eye on you when we're on the trail."

With a mortified sound, Talia hands over the backpack and steps away.

"You shouldn't have to babysit me, y'know."

"It's hardly babysitting, Talia. It's common sense with new hikers." I pretend to let my arms dip with the hefty weight of the bag. That earns me an almost grateful smile. "Everyone starts off as a beginner, and it's better if you're out there with an experienced hiker. You'd be surprised what you can stumble over on a calm day."

"Like what? Something dangerous?" She watches me intently.

I heft the rucksack into the back of the Jeep for support. Rolf sniffs it curiously while I unzip it.

The tight-packed supplies explode out like I've just pulled the string on a party popper.

Talia shares an amused look before we start sorting everything, digging out plastic cups and a rappelling harness kit. I toss them freely into the cargo area, ignoring that sudden ache in my cock.

I could think of a few interesting uses for those ropes, but we shouldn't be hitting any trails that need us tied together.

Mind out of the gutter, Ainsley. Right now.

The deprivation must be getting to me.

I haven't had a woman since New York. Carina—some six years ago.

My last serious relationship, broken off years before I packed up for Redhaven. I'm not sure if I loved her.

I know she loved me, but she always said there was something unreachable about me. Something that scared her.

I never understood that, not when I was careful with her —always gentle, always putting her needs first, always holding back that part of me that wanted to leave red marks on her skin, that wanted to hold her down and make her thrash and beg.

I did everything I could to be safe for her—and I *still* frightened her.

No question, I'd scare the shit out of Talia, too.

That's why I've kept myself in check since coming to this little town. With how brutal small-town gossip can be, all it would take is one misplaced hickey and everyone would start whispering.

Worse than when I first moved here and every single woman wanted to find out if my dick was as pale as the rest of me.

Talia's still watching, waiting for me to explain.

I leave a few things like bundled-up snacks in the sack and wrestle with a bulging pack of space blankets, crinkling them noisily the whole time.

Really, woman?

She grins nervously.

I hold it up with a raised brow before tossing it aside. With a self-deprecating giggle, she glances away.

"What? I heard you can make tents out of them if there's a real emergency."

"Except we have tents, so we don't need them."

Shaking my head, I break the pack open and fish out five of the folded blankets, a small concession to their potential usefulness, and tuck them back into her pack.

I immediately pitch a box of cheap-looking hunting knives, still wrapped in the store plastic. They look like the kind of novelty things where the blade would break off the hilt with any pressure and probably leave a nasty cut behind.

"As far as dangerous goes, we won't be taking on any particularly steep trails, but even experienced hikers still slip and fall," I say. "Ravines can pop up out of nowhere when it's this overgrown. You think you're going through a break in the brush, and suddenly the earth is gone and your ass is bouncing down a rocky grade. Gopher holes, tree roots, buried rocks, they're all waiting to snap your ankle. Then there's the wildlife. North Carolina has cottonmouths, diamondbacks, copperheads, and they don't take too kindly to being stepped on if they're hiding under the leaves. Mountain lions. Coyotes. Plus, the simple risk of getting lost. You think you're navigating by the sun and you know the way home. The next thing you know, you're turned around and it's night, it's getting cold faster than you'd like, and you're fatigued and low on water with no damn clue where the closest creek is. And that's just the natural dangers, mind you. You know as well as I do that stumbling on the Jacobins without warning is a good way to get a face full of buckshot."

Her eyes are saucers.

I'm pretty sure she's stopped breathing.

"So hiking alone is always a bad idea, even when you're good at it?" She swallows. "You sure know a lot about the woods for someone who just moved here."

"I've been around long enough, but I guess a few years still counts as being new in a place like this—and what *is* this?" Frowning, I tug on a vacuum-packed bag wrapped tight around something rectangular and heavy as hell. It won't come out, and I wiggle it, giving it another yank.

The clothes she packed underneath it go flying as I yank the bag free.

T-shirts, jeans, a thick parka, and some very interesting lacy things sail through the air while I stare at the label on the bag. It's dense-packed cubes of instant high-protein survival food, the kind of stuff you'd find in a doomsday prepper's bunker—and probably enough to feed five people for a week.

I'm about to ask Talia a smartass question, but she lets out a strangled sound and darts past, grabbing at a pair of panties made of the most translucent, sheer pink net I've ever seen, with delicately embroidered lace edging.

The bra matches. So do the stockings when they vanish into her clutched fists, so flimsy they disappear into nothing past her fingers.

I'm not fucking breathing anymore.

I'm trying not to stare.

But goddamn, you mean to tell me *that's* the underwear she packed for a camping trip?

That's her style?

Makes me wonder what I glimpsed past her flannel and what other little secrets this shy girl keeps locked up. If there's more fire under her fluttering and nervousness than I realized.

Not your business, man. Focus on the mission.

Not on the drumming in my pulse and the reckless throb of my cock taking an interest in things I've got no right to.

Outwardly, I'm a perfect gentleman, averting my eyes from her brilliantly red face while I unzip one of the side pouches on the bag and hold it open for her.

Her fingers brush mine, all warmth and softness, as she

stuffs her garments inside, fumbling my hand aside so she can zip up.

After the soft rasp of the zipper stops, she pulls back, her warmth leaving my side while she mumbles, "...sorry. You didn't have to see that."

"Didn't see a thing," I growl. "Nothing besides this thirty-pack of *D* batteries." I heft the big brick of boxed batteries out of the bottom, followed by a six-pack of flashlights. "You had the right idea. You just overpacked."

"I just kept thinking, what if we lost things? What if we needed backups?"

"Miss Talia, with everything in your pack, if you lost one thing, you'd lose everything, so having this many spares wouldn't do you much good. Better to lighten the load." I toss two of the flashlights back on top of her folded clothes, then steal one of the battery packs from inside the box. I pick up the parka, too, twisting my lips. "You don't have a thinner jacket?"

"At home?" she offers. "I just thought—you know..."

"Hypothermia," I guess. "This time of year, it's not a big concern unless you fall down in a river after dark." I start to toss the parka back down—then stop and hold it out to Rolf, letting him sniff. "Here, boy. Get used to her."

Rolf prods his nose at the parka.

He snorts and shakes his head roughly before backing up to settle on his haunches, giving me a disgusted look.

Talia lets out a disappointed laugh. "He's never going to like me, is he?"

"Give him time. He's more used to guys and cops, not..."

I stop, frowning.

How the fuck do I even describe her without giving away the flame in my blood?

There's a soft twinkle in her eyes as she cocks her head at me.

"Not...?" A little smile plays about her lips. "What am I, Micah?"

"Difficult," I snarl, shaking my head. I drop the parka again and deflect. "Just a second. I'll get you one of my jackets."

I duck inside, leaving her with Rolf, and quickly head to my bedroom to rummage in my closet. I'm not some wide tank like a few of my coworkers, but I'm tall enough that my jackets will hang down to her knees. Even so, it's fine. If she needs protection against the cold, more coverage is better than less, even if a *parka* is a bit much.

I pull down a battered dark-grey military-style jacket with a warm inner lining, drape it over my arm, and head back outside.

Talia leans on the back of the Jeep, offering a hand to Rolf with a piece of beef jerky broken off from one of the snack packs. He delicately sniffs it and I stop, holding still, not wanting to ruin the moment when food softens his defenses.

Unlike with Lieutenant Graves, he's taking a slower interest in her meat offering.

A second later, he rewards her by nipping the bite out of her hand, his tongue flicking lightly against her fingers.

"He took it!"

She pumps her fist, letting out a squeak and turning to look at me.

"The way to a dog's heart and also a man's, or so they say." I step closer, offering her the jacket. "Here. Now take at least half those water bottles out of the bottom of your bag, zip up, and let's get moving. Daylight's wasting."

She takes my jacket and curls it against her chest, just holding it, before she nods and folds it into the bottom of her rucksack. She digs out a half dozen water bottles next—she had almost a half a case in there—and drops them into the Jeep before she hoists it up.

"Oh, wow, that's way lighter now."

"You'll still be feeling it by the time we break for lunch, believe me. Let me know if it gets to be too much." I tighten the straps on my own bag, adjusting the fit around my shoulders. I watch as she tries to fling her bag on, fiddling with the adjustable bits. "Let me."

"You make me feel so helpless." She almost pouts before edging closer.

"You're not helpless." If anything, I'm the asshole who feels helpless right now, unable to stop the sharp tug of *desire* that bolts through me as I pull at the straps. My knuckles graze her arms, her shoulders, almost touching the sides of her breasts before pulling back like she'll set me on fire. "You're learning. There's a difference. And you packed smart. You just overdid it. Notice I didn't toss out the compass, sleeping bag, first aid kit, or spare clothing. Your head was in the right place."

There's also the clear outline of multiple inhalers and the rattle of pills from one of the interior zipper pouches.

I'm not going to point them out. I won't embarrass her.

For some things, there's no such thing as being overprepared.

When I finally step back, I realize she's giving me another odd look.

Not that trembling, scared look. This is more measured, that enigmatic little smile on her lips again.

"What?" I ask.

"Nothing." Talia shakes her head, rolling her shoulders and settling the straps with her thumbs, still smiling. "You're just not like I expected before we met."

"You had expectations? Before I gave you mouth-to-mouth?"

Gasping, she clamps her lips together, then lets out a loud laugh, shaking her head.

"Not like that. It's just... you know. You hear things. Antisocial big-city guy, nice enough but everything slides off you like glass. No one really knows you, and around here that gets people *talking*. Rumors that you're a serial killer or you're in witness protection or something. I guess I was expecting you'd be—I don't know—colder?"

Fuck.

Maybe I haven't been as subtle as I thought in keeping people at a careful distance.

Still.

It's all just dumbass rumors, even if they're brushing the truth.

I shrug and lean over the back of the Jeep to coax Rolf down again. He can make the jump up, but the landing can hurt his joints.

"I don't see how I'm not cold," I mutter.

"I don't mean you're soft. Or warm. Or even approachable—"

"Thanks," I bite off.

"Sorry! This is coming out wrong. Like, it's not about what you say or how you say it," Talia points out. "It's about *what* you do. And what you've done so far is save me from an asthma attack, and now you're saving me from breaking my back with this pack, *and* you're worried about my safety. That's enough to tell me you're a pretty good guy, and that's all that really matters."

I stop cold, looking over my shoulder at her for too long, my heart thumping.

How naïve *is* this girl?

So bright, so sweet, so prone to seeing the best in someone just from a little commonsense preparedness and the fact that the other morning I was doing my job as a cop.

I get the same weird sensation on the back of my neck that I always do before I look up and see them on the tree outside my house. Two of them today, both crows I'm sure I've seen a hundred times.

Do you remember why you ended up in law enforcement, Micah?

Do you remember that once you wanted to be better?

Yeah, once.

Before you died, Jet.

Before I had nothing left in my unhappy life but hunting down the men most responsible for that.

The small-time dealer who sold him his stash is already in jail. I almost lost my job over that bust. Fucker shot at me and missed my throat by inches. I kneecapped him and broke both his legs.

He lived.

He's lucky I let him have that much.

I'm not asshole enough to abuse my authority to murder a small-timer. Not when it was far more satisfying to deliver him into a lengthy prison sentence—and in exchange for reduced sentencing, that small-timer was happy to start blabbing.

Insane stuff at first. Yet as I started tracing leads and following the trail, they all pointed to Redhaven. It all started making sense.

The rot here really does run deep, right to the soil and soul.

I tear my gaze away from Talia's sweet blue eyes.

If I'm not careful, she'll wind up just as blood-soaked as the rest of this accursed place.

The damn crows are still staring with their black button eyes.

You're putting her in harm's way, asshole.

Is that what you want?

I grit my teeth. This isn't the time to bark back at them like I do some days and leave Talia wondering how sane I really am.

I know crows don't really talk. They don't telepathically beam my dead brother's accusations into my mind or whatever.

It's all in my head. My own conscience, plus a dash of natural weirdness when it feels like the birds follow me around.

Too bad my conscience gets annoyingly loud at times. I remind myself that Talia would be interacting with Xavier without my involvement.

Then I tell my conscience to shut the fuck up entirely.

"It's just common sense," I say as I help Rolf down. "C'mon. It's not that long a hike, but we want to be settled before sundown. Let's move."

As I nudge my dog down the walk, Talia scampers to catch up with me, watching me like a small animal that doesn't have the good sense to be afraid of a wolf.

"Why sundown?" she asks.

"Nightfall. That's when the Jacobins swing into gear," I tell her. "We want to be concealed and silent before they show up."

She's suddenly much quieter.

"Oh," she whispers.

Yeah.

Oh.

With nothing else to say, I lead her off the path and into the woods bordering my property. Rolf's collar jingles as he leads the way.

Without Talia noticing, I move a hand behind my back and flip off the crows.

* * *

I WASN'T EXPECTING this to turn into a field trip.

Normally, it's purely tactical when I'm out here alone.

Scout out where the Jacobins have set up shop, find a good vantage point, and settle in out of sight. I enjoy the activity, and Rolf loves the chance to scamper through the leaves before quiet time.

I've gotten so used to our routine that I rarely stop to notice the beauty of the North Carolina forest.

Talia Grey seems determined to notice nothing else.

Breathless and sparkly-eyed, she has as much curiosity as Rolf, wandering off the barely visible trail to gush over a field of peonies buzzing with fat bees. Or stopping to stare at a massive canopy of spiderwebs arching over the path, dozens of spiders building it communally between the trees and filtering the light into misty veils.

Everything leaves this woman endlessly fascinated, from the redheaded woodpecker hammering away, to a tiny spring erupting between stones, to the way the trees form a canopy spinning sunlight into glitter.

Now and then she'll pluck a plant and come tumbling up to me, asking me what it is.

Wood anemones, maidenhair ferns, swamp milkweeds.

She seems as amazed by them as she is by the fact that I know them on sight.

Good thing I made a point of learning the local vegetation in case anything happened to me out here alone and I had to rely on herbs for medicine.

Around noon, I catch her just before she reaches for a patch of leafy doom.

"Not that," I say sharply. She freezes, still reaching for the three-lobed leaves. "Not unless you want rashes for days in places you never want to itch."

"Oops!" She backs away guiltily. "What is it?"

"Poison oak." I point at a break in the trees, just past the poison oak patch. "Head through there. There's a creek coming up on the map. We'll break for lunch."

"Oh, thank God. My calves are *killing* me." But she laughs as she says it.

I wonder if she remembers why we're even out here.

I don't have the heart to remind her.

She nearly dances through the trees, whirling around the poison oak and disappearing from sight.

I speed after her, slipping through the hanging branches with Rolf. We step out into the sunlight on a narrow open valley cut through the forest, right where a creek—barely five feet wide—runs through it with a narrow dirt shore on both sides.

Talia's already halfway down on the shore, following the slow-moving water. She stretches her arms over her head before she turns to me with a sunny smile.

"Here?" she calls up—then stops, clapping her hands over her mouth, dropping her voice to a dramatic whisper. "Wait... do I need to be quiet?"

Damn her.

My mouth twitches.

How is it she takes everything so seriously, yet at the same time never quite seriously enough?

"Not yet. As long as there's daylight, we're ordinary hikers." I make my way down the slope toward her, unclipping Rolf's leash from his harness before lightly slapping his flank. "Go on, big boy. Have some fun."

With a joyful bark, he leaps toward the creek with the energy of a pup half his age and goes splashing into the shallows—to the dismay of several frogs sunning themselves on the stones. They plunge underwater in a croaking panic.

Talia laughs with delight.

"He likes playing in the water, huh?"

"More than a steak." I unsling my pack and set it down on

a large log. "Go ahead and set your stuff down. I'll show you how to make a fire."

With an eager sound, she complies.

She's an attentive pupil, I'll give her that, watching me closely as I show her how to pull up grass to make a safe fire circle and how to find good tinder to keep the fire going.

Before long, we've got ourselves a real fire with a teakettle simmering. A pot with some chili and vegetables boils while flatbread toasts on my small foldout grill.

Talia sits across from me on a log, watching the food cook with hungry anticipation.

I try like hell not to stare.

Her hair is autumn fire in the middle of summer, the color of bright leaves.

"You've really never gone camping in your life?" I ask.

Talia jerks her head up at me before looking down.

"Never," she answers. "I don't think I made it clear how sick I was when I was little. I had an oxygen tank on wheels for a little while that I had to take with me everywhere. I insisted on a pink one and covered it with pony stickers." She smiles weakly, fretting her fingers together. "Some kids grow out of asthma. Some just get better. I got better, but by the time I did… I was already so wrapped up in Grandpa and the shop. I never really caught up on the things I missed out on."

"That's rough," I say sincerely.

"I don't regret it. I love him. I love *making* things with him —and truth be told, he kinda depends on me." She tilts her head back, looking up at the canopy overhead and the sky with sweet wonder. "But it's nice, y'know? To be out here breathing this clean air and smelling how different it is from town. To just run and play and *see* things that were always too far away before."

And if something happens to her because of you, what happens to that old man? I wonder darkly.

"I'm sorry," I say. "If that was an insensitive question."

I mean it, even if that's not really why I'm apologizing.

She looks at me and her smile strengthens as she shakes her head. "It wasn't. I'm really okay with talking about it. I mean, you get it, right?"

I blink, recoiling a little.

"Yeah, I do." I look away then, staring into the small crackling fire. I prod at it with a stick, sending up a shower of sparks. It's almost uncomfortable to share a confession when it feels like admitting weakness, but some part of me feels like I owe it to her after dragging her into my fuckery. "I didn't exactly grow up like other kids, either. Most kids' idea of 'playing' with the albino freak was finding out how easy I bruise. If they wanted to know that bad, they could've just asked my old man. I was his favorite canvas."

I freeze.

What the fuck did I just say?

I never say *that* out loud to anyone.

Not even Carina knew how my dad used to beat me. She only knew I had no interest in introducing her to my family and thought it was a slight against her. I never asked for her sympathy.

I didn't need anyone's useless platitudes.

I don't need Talia's, either.

I definitely don't need her to straighten up and practically yell at my face.

"You're not a freak!" Soft, yet so loud. "You're just *you.*"

I look up sharply to find her watching me across the fire, her blue eyes almost hard with warm determination. Her mouth is a firm line of lush lips trembling with conviction.

Goddamn.

This girl confuses the hell out of me.

One minute, she's looking at me like I'm a monster. The

next, she's running around me like a puppy, pulling me in all directions.

Now, she's looking at me like she *sees* me.

Not my strangeness.

Not my coldness.

Not the shield that keeps people at a distance.

Me.

And I don't know how the hell I feel about being seen.

I have to break that innocent gaze again, deflecting by standing to take the kettle off the fire and pour water over two waiting cups of tea.

"Can't be anyone else, can I?" I say harshly. "Wouldn't even know how."

That's a lie.

My entire identity in Redhaven is a lie, even if it's mostly a lie of omission when all I do is keep my business to myself and let other folks fill in the blanks.

I wonder how betrayed the guys would feel if they knew the truth.

How betrayed would Talia feel if she knew she's out here with a liar?

It doesn't matter.

I'm not here for lasting relationships or friends. Once I take down Xavier Arrendell and the Jacobins, that's it.

I'll probably pack up for New York or New England.

The thought leaves an odd chasm in my chest that's never been there before.

I hold a steaming mug out to Talia. She tilts her head back, looking up at me, her brightness eclipsed in my shadow falling over her.

It feels a little too heavy.

Without a word, she reaches up to take the mug in both hands. Her slender fingers curl against mine.

For an instant, we're connected.

Our fingers are so close, the heat of the mug fusing us together.

Her skin feels like silk on mine, lingering with a tension so thick you can taste it.

Her heart is in her eyes.

I don't know how to read it or what this feeling is stirring inside me.

I wasn't expecting this shit.

Not when I only just tripped over this girl this past week.

Not when I'm so close to kicking down doors that have been sealed off for years.

I'm *this* close to the Arrendells' secrets.

Talia's a distraction.

This pure pink doll, just begging to get her dirty.

If I don't keep my mind on track, I'm going to piss away years of work just to have a taste of her.

So the moment I'm certain she's got a proper grip on the mug, I let go and step back, reclaiming my seat on my log.

"Eat up," I say tersely, rummaging in my pack for the small bag of freeze-dried meat kibble I brought for Rolf. He's heading over the second he hears the bag rustle, still shaking himself dry from the water. "We need to get moving again. The site we're staking is still a few more miles upstream."

Talia only answers with a wordless murmur.

Does this crackling energy between us disturb her as much as it does me?

I fold a large green leaf into a makeshift bowl for Rolf and leave him scarfing his kibble while I tuck into my own lunch.

We use the flatbread as pita pockets, pouring the chili and vegetables inside. Easy, quick, and filling.

Though Talia dribbles down her chin every few bites before catching it and wiping her face off, all delicate manners even out here in the wilderness.

I try to keep myself from laughing.

I don't know how any grown-ass woman can be so adorable.

Once we're done, I douse the fire with creek water, then rub Rolf down with a towel from my pack before packing up, clipping his leash back onto his harness, and setting back out.

Talia's quieter as we hit the trail again.

She doesn't seem upset, just thoughtful, looking around and occasionally smiling as she sees a hawk soaring against the sun or turns her head to track a chipmunk bounding through tree roots.

She doesn't complain, not even when I can tell she's starting to get tired. I admit I'm keeping a close eye on her breathing, too, but I don't ask about her asthma.

I know what it's like having people smother you with concern, and I won't do that.

It doesn't seem like it's triggered too much by physical exertion, though. Mostly by distress.

Which just adds another pebble on the scale of guilt for what I could end up putting her through.

She's clearly flagging by the time we reach the campsite I scoped out a few days ago.

Tracking the Jacobins feels like a second job where I moonlight by learning how to find them even when Chief Bowden gets creative with diverting the crew's attention.

You don't have to catch them skulking around in the dead of night. There are little markers that will tell you where they're planning to migrate next.

They'll find a good, discreet spot in the woods, somewhere they can stay deep and hidden. Usually an old logging site with a lot of new growth, easy saplings they can clear.

They'll cut themselves a road or reopen an old logging trail the forest reclaimed.

Not a big road, not something you can see from a hill. More like the kind of thing that you could walk right past five feet away without knowing it's there on the other side of the dense growth.

Here's where they get clever—the trees they fell for that road, they lay down on the path to create a sort of bumpy paving for their trucks. No wheel ruts people can find later.

Once that's done, they'll come swooping in and set up their portable sheds, supposedly with their moonshine stills inside.

They'll hover around in one spot for about a week and disappear again, leaving behind a ghostly patch of cleared earth—hard for anyone to use as evidence when it could just be an area cleared by one of the Arrendell-owned timber companies, a little storm damage, or somebody's weekend retreat.

They know how to make it look innocent.

They know how to disappear.

And I know how to find them, just like now.

I tell Talia to wait for me in a secluded nook in the trees partly down the slope from one of the hills while I take Rolf and climb up for a look, checking the coordinates on my phone.

Right on the money.

The last time I was here, they'd already cleared the brush and saplings.

Now, there it is.

That subtle path cut through the woods, leading north, just wide enough for their trucks and paved with fallen logs stripped of their limbs.

It'll come out about a mile north, I think, on an old farmer's trail, and then another few miles west to the highway. Home free to wherever they want to go next.

If the logs are there, they'll definitely be here tonight.

I climb back down to Talia.

She's puffing a little, sitting on a large mossy rock and sipping from a water bottle.

When I emerge through the trees, she jumps, squealing and splashing water down her front.

"You okay?"

"Y-yeah, you're just *really* quiet, you know that?" She gives me a wide-eyed look. "I didn't even hear you coming. His collar didn't jingle."

"Force of habit." I unsling my pack and unclip Rolf's leash. "Rest. I'll set up camp."

Talia takes a quick look around the glade.

It's barely ten feet across, an intimate pocket of tall grass and bright sunny buttercups almost walled in on all sides by trees, save for the far side where it ends in a short rock face.

A small spring bubbles out from the rocks in a tiny, clear pool lined with mossy stones. It's the perfect place to set up. Close to the vantage point, yet far enough down the slope and shielded enough so we won't be visible.

"It's pretty here," she says with a small smile. "I like it."

We really are different, aren't we?

I'm thinking purely about the tactical advantage.

Meanwhile, she sees magic everywhere.

Rolf walks over to the tiny pond and plunges his tongue into it, lapping away. I drop to one knee in the center of the clearing and start pulling up grass. Talia stands, coming over and kneeling next to me.

"Let me. You showed me how before." She smiles. "I don't want to be lazy. There's probably other stuff you need to do that I don't know how to help with."

"You sure? You can take a break. I'm used to doing this solo."

"Extra hands make everything faster." She shrugs and starts pulling up brisk handfuls of grass, piling them to the side like I showed her. "I hate being useless, anyway."

You aren't useless, I want to tell her, but I don't think she wants to hear that from me.

So I leave her to it while I work on our tents, pretending I'm not sneaking glances her way.

She's diligent and focused, very serious about her job.

Hell, I feel like I spend half my time around this girl trying not to smile.

I don't want her to think I'm patronizing her.

There's just something about the way she throws herself into the smallest things with an intensity that's too charming.

Now and then, she glances at me like she wonders why I'm watching her.

She probably expects me to avert my eyes and pretend I wasn't.

Most men would.

I hold her gaze while I work, arching a brow.

There's a deep, *deep* pleasure in watching how her eyes widen when she realizes I'm not feigning any secrecy.

Too fucking fun.

Especially when she blushes every time, fumbles, looks like she's about to stammer something out right before she turns away and hides her face. It happens more than I can count, this shy little song and dance that could go on for hours.

Did I mention I'm not a nice man?

When I get the first tent sorted, it pops up into a full-sized camo-colored dome in my hands, and I have her full attention.

She turns back with a gasp, her arms full of dry branches.

"How'd you do that?"

"Magic. Next, I'll pull a scarf a mile long out of my ear." Smirking, I practically toss the lightweight tent to one side and hold up the other. "It's just a popup tent. They're easy."

"Do it again!" She dumps the wood in the middle of the fire circle.

I can't help it.

A chuckle rips out of me and I'm shaking my head.

"All right, all right. Watch."

I find the wire coils and twist them just right. The flat disc balloons out again into a 3D dome in seconds. Talia belts out pure joy.

"That's so *cool*." Then she gives me a shy look through her lashes. "And hey, you laughed."

I snort, moving to set the other tent down with enough space between them for privacy. "Yeah. I do that sometimes."

"Doesn't seem like it happens often," she points out.

"Usually, there's no reason to."

"Why is that?"

I stare at her.

I don't answer.

I don't have one I think she'd want, anyway.

So I just go back to setting up camp.

After another silence, Talia goes back to making those cute sounds of exertion while she works, ripping a few small sap-filled green branches off the trees around us.

I toss her my lighter, and by the time I'm done putting out the rest of our supplies, setting out Rolf's food and water bowls, and spreading my sleeping bag, she's got a good fire going.

When I pull out a long cord strung with over five hundred soda can tabs, though, she looks up from stealing my camp stove and blinks at me.

"What's that for?"

"Security." I start weaving the string through the trees around the clearing at about knee height, a foot out from the inner edge. "If someone gets too close, I'll hear the tabs rattling. It's not so loud that if we accidentally hit it, it'll alert anyone far away to our presence."

She nods briskly, then her face falls.

She's remembered what we're really here for.

And she's much quieter as she finishes setting the fire, putting our dinner on to cook while I line the clearing with the string of tabs.

* * *

SUNSET COMES FAST OUT HERE in the hills, and by the time we're parked around the fire with bowls of soup and warm bread, it's already getting dark.

The circle of sky over us blooms in pink and purple layers. When was the last time I let myself enjoy a sunset?

Hell, enjoy anything, honestly.

Between police work and private grievances with the Arrendells and looking after Rolf, there hasn't been much time for a life.

Have I become obsessed?

Is there nothing left besides destroying Xavier Arrendell?

I remember having friends in my twenties.

I remember learning how to mix drinks, whipping them up with a flourish and enjoying people's reactions to my concoctions. I was younger then, more innocent, high on escaping from my father and being my own man.

I still had Jet. Not in the way I have him now, watching me from the trees on black wings and driving me madder than Edgar Allan Poe's fictional tortured lover.

So why are you the one who's still alive, Mikey, when you're not really livin' at all?

"Are you okay, Micah?"

I blink, focusing on Talia again.

She's holding her little bowl in both hands, cupping it

close to her face and sipping from it. Her eyes are dark with concern.

"Just thinking. Why?" I pin on an artificial smile that feels more like showing the teeth she's so fascinated with.

"I can't explain it. You just seemed kinda sad."

I don't answer.

I just stand and start kicking dirt over the fire, banking it down until it's just embers, low coals glimmering against the darkness, casting us in shadow. There's enough light left to see Talia frowning as she watches me.

"Won't we get cold tonight?"

"That's why we have the tents and sleeping bags."

With the mood I'm in, the reminder that she'll be wrapped up in *my* jacket doesn't send my mind vaulting down those dark, possessive paths it could easily follow.

She still looks confused, so I clarify, "We don't want any light drawing attention. The trees are good cover, but not perfect. If the Jacobins happen to come through from this direction, the firelight and the scent of smoke could give us away."

Her expression clears.

"*Ohhh*." She takes another sip of her soup. "When do they typically show up?"

"Usually around midnight. They like to do their business when the town's asleep." I sink back down on my log and reach for my own soup. "Finish your food and get some sleep until then."

"Fine. But how will we know when to wake up?"

"Trust me, we'll *know*."

We finish dinner silently. Every now and then, Talia looks over her shoulder like she's expecting one of the hillfolk to come bursting through the trees, swinging an axe.

I don't blame her.

The locals grew up with all sorts of weird stories about

the Jacobins. To half of Redhaven, they're this chainsaw massacre family who love wearing human skin and can be summoned by dark rituals. They make a few bucks off their crops and baked goodies at the farmers' market whenever they're not turning kidnapped children into pies.

The townsfolk don't see them from the outside the way I do.

Really, they're an insular people who keep a low profile.

They believe in stark tradition over modern law and social conventions. Hillfolk keep to themselves and do their own thing first, second, and third.

They don't like to hurt anybody else if they can avoid it.

However, they also don't care if a few outsiders are collateral damage.

Once we're done eating, she crawls into the tent set aside for her, peeking around on hands and knees before she crawls back out and promptly spreads her sleeping bag over the floor.

Wiggling back inside, she sticks her feet out, kicks her boots off—giving me a glimpse of her toes in those pink and black argyle socks that match her flannel shirt—before disappearing inside again.

There's a whisper of cloth on nylon, her silhouette squirming against the camo siding, and then her head pokes out again.

She's all bundled up, snug inside her sleeping bag, and she watches me for a minute before murmuring an uncertain, "Good night."

"Good night, Miss Grey. Might want to zip up. Keeps the bugs out and keeps you warm."

"R-right," she says, then she zips the flap of the tent shut.

I shake my head, refusing to smile again.

Little pink hellion.

Another half hour passes before I tuck into my own tent.

I sit with Rolf at my feet, watching the last glimmering embers from the fire, alone with my thoughts. A second helping of soup goes down before I put the rest away in a thermos for morning.

Before I settle in, I risk peeking into Talia's tent, easing the zipper open slowly and silently.

I'm expecting to see nervous blue eyes looking back at me, too anxious to sleep.

Instead, she's a peaceful little ball of woman tucked up inside her bag. Her red hair spills all over the built-in pillow like scarlet paint.

She really is too innocent.

Trusting that she's safe, as long as she's out here with me.

I settle into my own sleeping bag but leave my tent flap open.

I don't mind being a little cold, and it's actually a pleasant early spring evening.

Rolf beds down outside.

I'd let him sleep in my tent, but he's still an old police dog at heart and always takes a wary position. He lays his head over the bottom edge of the opening of my tent, resting against the pillow of my sleeping bag.

We both doze lightly with my arm draped over his shoulders and his jaw pillowing my head.

I've learned to sleep sporadically. There's always some part of me always on alert.

The wake-up call comes a few hours later, right on cue.

I'm up when Rolf stiffens, his ears pricking, his head going up.

He's a better alarm than anything I could ever buy.

Slowly, I sit up without making a sound. His head points toward the site I marked earlier and I listen hard, straining to hear.

There.

Muffled engines.

Several engines by the sound of it, coming from that direction.

It's go time.

Whether or not Talia will believe what she sees remains to be seen.

Before I wake her, I slip out of my tent and stuff my feet into my boots, lacing them up while I dig around for my binoculars.

Creeping into the trees, I step over the pop tab warning system.

Rolf slinks under it, too, following me quietly as I inch toward the subtle sound of tires on noise-absorbing dirt.

At the crest of the hill, I hide behind a tree and look through a gap in the branches, using my binoculars.

I can just make out the Jacobins' trucks.

If you expected rickety pickups with raised slats around their beds for big loads, you're dead wrong. These are more like retired military surplus vehicles, big and blocky with their cargo areas covered, painted in muted greens, greys, and browns. Whatever helps them blend into nature unseen. Even their license plates are completely covered by black cloth they can move in seconds.

Now, why would any backwooded farmers cranking out moonshine go through all this trouble?

I race back to the campsite and drop to one knee next to Talia's tent.

When I reach in and gently shake her, she gasps awake, blinking at me. She starts to open her mouth but freezes when I rest my finger over my lips and shake my head.

The sleep clears from her eyes and she pushes herself up swiftly, looking past me and then mouthing,

"They're here?"

I nod, pulling out of her way and beckoning her. *Come on. Hurry.*

She scrambles up. Inwardly, I cringe at the noise of denim and flannel on nylon and the soft thuds as she pulls her boots on.

She can't help herself, though, and it's probably me being paranoid.

Still, the smallest crack of a twig can sound like a gunshot when it carries over these hills.

Once she's ready, all wrapped up in my jacket and looking at me nervously, I turn to lead her back through the woods, guiding her over the string trap.

We take the easiest path, praying the entire time she won't trip or step on a dry branch or a loud heap of leaves.

She manages well enough, keeping up with me in careful steps. Her red hair nearly glows in the dark.

I really fucking hope the Jacobins don't look up.

There's a thin sheen of sweat making her throat gleam by the time I stop her with a hand on her arm, showing her where to hunker down and kneel.

We're clustered close together in a small group of bushes flanked by trees, at the peak of a very steep drop down to the site.

By now, the trucks are parked in a metal ring. Small figures in dark clothes scurry around, hauling equipment.

Not all of them are Jacobins by blood, I'm sure.

Some are hired thugs from out of town, brought here to do grunt work, faceless and untraceable behind masks and head coverings that conceal everything but their eyes.

Their eyes, plus the gleam of the automatic rifles slung to their backs, each muzzle a third eye staring back into the night.

Without a word, I hand her my binoculars.

Talia takes them with an audible gulp, pressing them to her eyes as she leans down over the drop to watch.

I can make out well enough from a distance.

I'm familiar with this process.

Our targets are lightning fast as they set up portable sheds with just a few posts dug in the ground between corrugated aluminum walls. When they start off-loading the trucks, I see confusion sparking in Talia as she watches them pull down bales of green leaves bundled into tight sheaves.

"Is that corn?" she whispers. She's good enough that it's almost subvocal. I'm glad I have to strain to hear. "They make moonshine with corn, right?"

"Corn kernels. Not the leaves. Those are the wrong color and shape." I watch her closely as I say, "Those are coca leaves, Miss Grey."

She sucks her lower lip into her mouth and bites down. Her eyebrows knit together above the binoculars.

"It smells," she whispers.

"Gasoline. It's part of the process, rendering coca mash."

Her distressed sound is almost too quiet, but it's there.

She's nearly mangling her bottom lip now, turning it a succulent red.

"I thought there was gasoline in moonshine? That's why they say it's bad to drink..."

"You can make gasoline out of moonshine if you want to ruin your car. You can't make moonshine from gasoline. Also..." I gesture toward the two men who are busy off-loading several large sacks, clearly marked *cement*. "You want to tell me what you think happens with cement in the moonshine process?"

"No clue." She shakes her head.

"Nothing. Because cement powder binds cocaine, but it doesn't have a damned thing to do with brewing rotgut booze." I can't help how my whisper turns fierce. "I'm telling you the truth, Talia. All that equipment, those ingredients, they're brewing coke out here. I've tried following them back to their farm to find out where they hide the equipment and raw materials between batches, but they're too fucking crafty. They know how to pull a disappearing act before I catch them with real evidence. If I tried a bust out here like this, it'd be me and the guys—and they'd mow us down before we ever flashed a warrant. No one's going to send in SWAT for one crazy albino dude stalking the hillfolk over what everyone thinks is just bad whiskey."

I'm expecting another protest. Another denial.

Instead, I get a low, almost betrayed whimper.

Not at me, though.

Her fingers clench the binoculars as she lets out an almost heartbroken whisper. "Oh my God. Is that… the chief?"

I turn my head, looking down at the almost mechanical assembly line getting everything in working order with terrifying speed.

Sure enough, there's a familiar figure there, portly belly in plainclothes, standing with Ephraim Jacobin and another figure I don't see too often. An older woman, who stands there like a witch in a black shroud, her face like death.

"Yeah. I told you he's part of it," I whisper.

"Holy shit! But I didn't know you meant—"

"I know. Keep it down. I'm the only one who knows. He's someone you've always thought was safe, right? Someone who's part of your everyday life. But even the people you think you know can lie their asses off."

I can't take my eyes off Bowden. There's something different about the way he carries himself tonight. The hardness of his face is so at odds with his usual jowly smiles and bumbling pleasantry.

"This is where lies are born. Lies people tell themselves, that maybe if they take this powder, they can be superhuman.

They can feel amazing. They can forget their worries, and they'll never stop feeling that way; the consequences will never catch up to them... *their* bodies won't eat themselves alive for another hit." I trail off, hatred bubbling on my tongue. "But karma always comes around. The lie always has empty promises. And thousands of people on the East Coast alone *die* every year thanks to those assholes down there, who think it's all fine and dandy just as long as the plague they unleash doesn't touch their little town too much." That hatred turns into a lump in my throat. "Like the people they never see suffering don't matter. Like my brother didn't matter."

I can hear the moment it clicks for her.

The shudder of her breath, the noise in the back of her throat.

I can't look at her—but I know she's looking at me.

Her big blue eyes pull on me like she wants to help me when I don't *want* to fucking feel better.

I want to hate.

I want raw and ugly and real.

I want this bloodlust fresh on my tongue until the day I demolish them.

"Micah," she whispers, her voice full of a hurting sympathy I can't stand when it tempts me to be weak, to fall into the comforting distractions of her softness and scent.

"Don't," I bite back bitterly. Rolf lets out a low whine and presses himself against my calf. "I don't want to hear it. It won't bring him back. All I want to hear is whether or not you'll help me after seeing this. I *know* Xavier Arrendell is the final key. He's what makes this possible. I just need to prove it."

"We," she answers with firm conviction. It rips through my grim focus, my fury, and forces me back to her. "*We* need to prove it."

I stare at her.

She looks back at me with glassy eyes that seem like they could swallow the whole sky.

No matter what an anxious little thing she is, she has heart.

She has a spine.

More importantly, she has the strength to stare at me, determined and firm in her decision, even though she's shaking and I don't think it's the cold.

This woman might be the key to *everything*.

And if I'm not careful, she could be my undoing.

VII: DARK DAYS COMING (TALIA)

I am a secret agent.
I am a smart, sexy secret agent who is totally ready for this.

I am a smart, sexy secret agent who is so totally ready to blindside Xavier Arrendell. Dazzle him. Completely bamboozle him.

I am—

I'm staring at myself in the mirror with my hair a frizzy mess around my face, my skirt seam ripped up one side, and my pantyhose completely ruined.

I'm supposed to meet Xavier to tell him we'll take the job, discuss details, and finalize the contract proposal in forty-five minutes.

And I look like I just tumbled out of an industrial dryer.

I've been a mess since last night.

Too many things whirling through my head.

Memories of the feral way Micah moved in the dark, like a snow leopard prowling through the trees, pure animal.

The shock at seeing Chief Bowden in the woods, helping the Jacobins hide their dirty laundry. Impossibly more sinister than the man who used to play Santa Claus for the kids a few Christmases ago.

It's changed everything, knowing that our seedy little underbelly involves more than bad whiskey that could fry your gut bacteria.

Then there's the skepticism at myself. I just took Micah's word for everything, his explanations about what I saw.

And the uneasy feeling that it really is believable.

Because there's something off about Xavier.

There's something off about Redhaven, too, and everyone who's lived here for more than a few years knows it. They've learned to live with it the way people near a factory learn to live with industrial smells and noise.

You know it's always there, but eventually you get desensitized. You stop asking questions if it doesn't affect you directly. You shrug when you read articles about groundwater getting tainted with cancer-causing chemicals.

Maybe we should wake up.

Maybe we should start asking *more* questions around here.

My only question now, though, is how I'm going to make myself presentable enough to get away with this fraud.

Originally, I had this idea of going in all sleek and sexy, rocking the femme fatale look. Xavier did look at me with—you know, the way men do—so I thought maybe if I made myself pretty it'd be easier to distract him and get him to slip up.

I'm *bad* at this, okay?

Right now, I'm less worried about making myself pretty and more concerned with looking human and professional.

I barely slept a wink last night.

That's why I wound up steaming my hair into a coppery-red Brillo cloud. Trying to tame it with a flat-iron just heat-crackled it into something that looks like the fiber stuffing inside a duvet, and then I went and made it worse by going out in the early morning dew to fetch the repaired truck from Mort's garage. With all this fumbling around, now my whole outfit sucks.

Yeah, I'm so not ready for this.

Not sure I'll ever be.

I sink down on my bed with a groan, fumbling for my phone and staring down at Micah's contact. He's listed under *V* for Vampire Man.

Seriously, I don't want to disappoint him.

But I'm clearly not cut out for this, and if I screw up, there's no denying the risks.

I could get him hurt or worse, if Xavier and the Jacobins figure out Micah's watching them so closely.

Hey, I send. ***I think I'm getting cold feet. I'm sorry. Please don't hate me?***

I'm not expecting a quick answer.

He's probably on his way to work or there already—if he's not still out walking Rolf. So I'm surprised when my phone buzzes in my hand.

I yelp and almost drop it before I clutch it to my chest.

Calm down, girl.

Micah: Are you all right?

Just that.

No demand for explanations, no condemnation, no scorn. Just a simple question, and it's a question a lot of people wouldn't ask when they'd be razor-focused on their own selfish goals.

I tease my lower lip with my teeth as I text back.

No, I answer. ***My nerves are shot. I'm such a mess I can't get out the door. I look like a circus clown someone tossed in the dryer for three hours. I'm scared, Micah. So scared I'll screw this up and Xavier will figure it out, and then he'll come after you.***

THE DARKEST CHASE

There's a long silence before my phone pings again.

Micah: That's why you're nervous? You're worried about me?

Yes! I answer hesitantly. ***Please don't hate me?***

It's true.

So maybe I'm a little worried about what Xavier could do to me or my grandfather, but it's my job to take care of myself. Of *us*.

I'd panic, sure, but I could figure out what to do if it was just me and Grandpa at stake. But knowing there's so much more riding on this...

No, I won't stand it if my clumsiness gets Micah hurt when all he wants is justice for his brother, for so many victims.

I don't know the whole story there.

Still, the look on his face spoke volumes last night, when he told me his brother was dead.

It cut me to the bone.

A few moments later, he replies.

I'm not afraid of Xavier goddamned Arrendell. He won't hurt me. I won't let him hurt you. But if you're that afraid, no. I won't hate you if you back out. Don't push yourself too hard, Talia. It's okay. The choice is always yours.

I actually believe him.

I believe he won't hold a grudge if I quit. If I chicken out.

Trouble is, I'd hate myself plenty to make up for it.

I've spent my entire life trying to be *more* than the weak, sickly girl, haven't I?

Now, the second I'm put to the test, I want to hide?

Hell no.

It's not pushing, I answer, then take a selfie, cringing at the camera and wincing as I tap Send. ***But look at me. Like I said, circus clown. I'm in no shape to dazzle anyone, much less pull anything over on him.***

111

Micah: Tell me one thing, woman.

I wait while he types with my breath stalled.

Micah: Why the hell are you trying to be anything besides your own gorgeous self?

I gasp.

The man knows how to hit *hard,* not mincing words. He's also annoyingly right.

...I guess I'm trying to be the type of girl Xavier would find appealing.

Micah: Talia Grey is appealing as hell. Just be comfortable. Be you. The more real you are, the more natural you'll be around him.

He's right again, but I'm stuck on one thing, trying not to grin like an idiot.

Talia Grey is appealing as hell.

I stare down at my phone, biting my lower lip so hard it hurts, but I hardly notice.

He can't mean that the way it sounds, can he?

Before I can figure out what to say back, he texts again.

Micah: Besides, you're less Ronald McDonald and more Raggedy Ann.

Oh, thanks. Such an upgrade*,* I text back, but I can't help laughing, the tension relaxing a little.

Micah just has this way.

Somehow, he makes me feel better with the smallest things, and I don't think he realizes it. He's such a quiet man, but he speaks with certainty—and when he really unsheathes himself, there's this steady, unwavering conviction in every word.

Micah: Raggedy Ann's cuter. You feel better now?

I am. I'm going to be a little late to meet Xavier, but I think I can get myself together and out the door.

Micah: No need. That's not why I was asking.

I smile, running my thumb along the edge of my phone. ***I*** *know. But I want to do this anyway. I'll text you when I get there.*

Micah: If I don't hear from you in three hours, I'm coming after you.

My eyes widen.

Three hours? What if I'm working there all day?
Micah: Check in. Let me know you're safe.

There it is again.

He's so adamant, despite the fact that he's a silent sentinel. It's all part of what makes him so—

So *Micah*.

I will, I promise. Then I put my phone down and try to make myself as presentable as possible.

It's easier to think with Micah's concern and protective fierceness buoying me. I take another quick shower, washing my hair again and scrubbing my botched makeup off, then towel dry my hair.

I redo my makeup—forgetting the foundation this time and just going for natural accents. A soft-pink lip gloss and subtle touches of rose along the creases of my eyelids, accented by a little liner and mascara, should do the trick.

Since there's no salvaging my skirt and I don't have another pair of pantyhose, I go for my nicest jeans and strappy sandals, paired with a loose, fluttery blouse in pale shell pink. Depending how I move it, I can skew it to one side and turn it into an off-the-shoulder blouse or rise up enough to become a crop top, even if it only shows an inch of flesh. I finish off the look with a patterned scarf in light-rose shades, knotted loosely against my neck so that the ends trail to one side and fall down my chest and back.

Casual. A little flirty, but not too much.

Stylish enough to pass for casual-professional chic even if it doesn't dress up enough for real business casual.

Since Xavier's giving me a tour today, I can say I dressed

for the job. That house is fricking enormous, and I'd be ready to collapse trying to handle that hike in a pencil skirt and pumps.

I look cute, though.

And I kind of wish it wasn't Xavier I was getting dressed up for.

No.

No way.

I'm still riding that high, romanticizing Micah as my very own vampire man.

Really, I'm just a useful tool to him. An unlikely partner, if I'm being generous.

All of that growly business by text about protecting me, coming for me, that's just him guarding his investment in this weird little spy mission.

So I take a deep breath, check myself over one more time, and peek inside my folio to make sure I've got my work stuff before tumbling out of my room with my damp hair swaying against my shoulders. It'll finish drying on the walk up the hill.

I'm not risking the truck stalling out at the big house again, and the walk will help clear my head.

When I step into the kitchen, my grandfather's sitting at the kitchen table, lingering over an almost empty mug of tea. He glances up and offers me a smile.

"Heading up to the Arrendell place?"

"Mm-hmm." I bend and kiss his wrinkled cheek. "Going to take the tour, get some photos, discuss what Xavier needs, and start sketching."

I start to pull away, but he catches my wrist gently.

His fingers are long and tough despite the arthritis. His touch always makes me think of home when those hands have guided mine as he taught me over so many patient hours and months and years how to work miracles with wood.

They're careful, sensitive hands, full of love. But the way he holds my wrist so delicately captivates me as he looks at me with blue eyes full of that same love—and concern.

"Tally," he whispers. "You're not pushing yourself too hard?"

One reason I love Grandpa is that he always lets me set my own limits.

He always *asks* what I can handle, instead of telling me.

Smiling, I gently pull my wrist free so I can lean over him and hug him tight, resting my chin on his head.

"I'm not," I promise. "I'll let you know if I am or if I need help. We're going to have to hire some outsiders for this project anyway. It wouldn't be so bad to have a few apprentices around."

He curls his hand against my arm and leans against me, his bristly grey hair scratching my cheek.

"Think you're ready to teach some young'uns?" He chuckles. "You've got a good eye for it."

His praise brightens my spirits. By the time I snag a muffin and a bottled coffee from the fridge and head out, I'm feeling much lighter.

Also, far more ready to stare down Xavier Arrendell with a smile, never giving away that underneath the grin I'm actually Talia Grey, sexy spy girl extraordinaire.

I have a vivid imagination.

My brain dreams up several scenarios with Xavier as I make my way uphill, enjoying the brisk morning walk while nibbling my muffin.

Hopefully, this will just be a normal client consultation. I'll follow him through the house, take notes on everything, write down his ideas, take photos, and make a few sketches if anything strikes me on the spot.

It'll give me a chance to really see the place and keep an eye out for anything useful to Micah. I mean, I doubt Xavier leaves bricks of cocaine lying around, but there might be something.

Trays with leftover residue.

Paperwork related to illegal shipments.

Even something coded and scribbled in a calendar—or like a diazepam kit.

I Googled that last night, and I'm a little proud of myself for it. Diazepam treats a cocaine overdose, so if Xavier's got himself a habit, he'd probably keep some around just in case he went a little too wild and needed treatment without anyone else finding out.

Who knows, I might just turn out to be good at this spy thing.

I'm feeling awkward again when I climb the steps to the mansion and realize I've still got my crumpled muffin wrapper and an empty coffee bottle.

I hold them tightly as the valet from before greets me with a muted "Miss Grey" and opens the doors for me. I look around for a trash can, but there's nothing.

Jeeves lets out a patient sigh and holds out his hands for my trash.

"Sorry!" I mutter. I hand them over and follow the stone-faced man to Xavier's office.

The mansion's a little less intimidating the second time around, but I get that same feeling of unease when the valet brings me into Xavier's space. He's settled behind his desk, seemingly engrossed in a thick leatherbound hardcover book, but as I step inside he lifts his head with a charming, surface-level smile that doesn't reach his lidded green eyes.

"Talia Grey," he says.

I fight a shudder.

I haven't asked him to call me anything besides Miss

Grey, and he makes my name sound oily and oddly possessive.

But I force a smile, trying to keep it natural, though I can't stop how my hands clench on the strap of my bag.

"Mr. Arrendell," I say. "Good morning. I hope I'm not late for our walk-through?"

"Not late enough to matter." He rises smoothly and sets the book down with a decisive *thump*, closing it without marking his page.

What kind of weirdo *does* that?

He rounds the desk, reaching for me with both hands—but I slip out of the way, trying to make it look like I'm just moving to keep from blocking the doorway as we step into the hall.

Xavier gives me a long look and smiles again, showing just a hint of teeth.

"You look eager today," he rumbles.

"I've never taken on a project this large before," I deflect. "I'm a bit excited, yes. I love to really flex my imagination."

"That's what I like to hear. I hope you'll give me the full benefit of your... *creativity*."

It's an innocuous statement, yet the way he purrs the last word... Ick.

A lump rises in my throat, but I ignore it and keep smiling. "So where did you want to start?"

There's a long, lingering look, one that dips over my bare collarbones.

It's like he's actually touching me, and it feels unclean—but it also feels like he's *testing* me, too. Trying to see how easily he can make me react.

I fight to keep my bright smile even if it feels completely vapid now. I'd rather let him think I'm stupid than figure out how uncomfortable he truly makes me. I have a funny feeling knowing it would just make him do it more.

He seems to like getting me flustered.

And I remember Micah said it would be easier for Xavier not to suspect me if he thinks I'm a fluttery mess all the time, but I don't want to be that person right now.

I want to be someone Micah can rely on.

So I just look at Xavier, blinking like I have no idea why he's just staring at me and not saying anything, until he finally looks away with a grim smile.

"This way. We'll start with the first floor and work our way up." He glances down at my feet. "I hope those shoes are comfortable?"

"Very, thank you," I say brightly, moving to follow him at a slight distance as he leads me down the hall.

From that point on, it's all business.

I'm too blissfully absorbed in my notes to notice if Xavier gets creepy-eyed again, writing down details about the Ionic columns in the grand hall, how the first floor uses oak for doors and accents while the second, third, and fourth floors rely on mahogany and ash wood. He tells me parts of them were built over generations, noting the number of bedrooms and suites and how each room seems designed to let in gobs of natural light from the gaping windows.

I quickly sketch the black-and-white pattern of the floor tiles in the main hall, taking down notes on the colors of the walls, the draperies, dimensions. I snap photos like mad to supplement.

I'm listening to Xavier, too, as he tells me how the place always felt like the Winchester House, to him—a living beast that just grew over decades in this rambling sprawl.

I get the feeling.

I studied the Winchester House during my architectural courses. Sarah Winchester, heiress to a rifle fortune, went kind of house crazy because she thought the ghosts of everyone killed by their guns were after her for revenge.

So she just kept building to confuse the ghosts and made the place as unnavigable as possible. Staircases that ended on empty air, rooms with no doors, hallways to nowhere, winding passageways and switchbacks.

The end result was a living Escher painting, baffling and sometimes dangerous.

Now, the Arrendell house isn't that surreal and unstructured, but somehow, it's got a similar eerie vibe.

This odd, disjointed thing that doesn't quite fit together and doesn't feel like a home, but more like a museum where people live.

It just feels like a twisted collection of ghosts and dead dreams.

"I think," Xavier says as we stop on the very top floor, standing against the railing, looking down over the main hall with a close-up view of the giant crystal chandelier, "I would like this house to somehow feel smaller. Look at that." He gestures to a pair of wingback chairs in the corner of the main hall, ivory-upholstered and gold-accented. "From up here, those chairs look tiny, don't they?"

"Like they belong in a dollhouse," I agree, pausing my furious scribbling.

"The backs of those chairs stand head and shoulders above my height," he says. "This house was built to be imposing and grand, but all it does is make the people inside it feel small."

I stop, looking away from the chairs to Xavier.

There's kind of a Jekyll and Hyde thing with him sometimes.

Like there might actually be a human being buried deep under the smarmy rich creep. You see it in the little changes with how he talks, in his expressions. That change settles over him now as he looks thoughtfully over the enormous main hall.

There's something distant in his eyes, something haunted. Like maybe not all of the ghosts in this house are dead.

"Is that what you want us to do?" I ask. "Make the house feel warmer? Less austere and cold?"

"I'm not sure if that's possible as long as a single Arrendell lives under this roof," he mutters. I think it's the first honest thing he's ever said in my presence. "However, if you could make it feel more like a home—a stylish one, admittedly—and less like a human display case, that would be appreciated."

"I can try," I say firmly. "Do you have any ideas for what you want to start with? Any particular styles you love?"

"I admit this isn't my area of expertise, so no. I'm open to suggestions." He glances at his watch, pulling the sleeve of his expensive suit back before sweeping a hand out, gesturing toward the stairs. Just like that, with an almost mocking bow, the smug asshole returns. "If you'll allow me—we're pressed for time. You should see the outbuildings."

Pressed for time? Why?

But I keep the question to myself as I follow him downstairs.

He leads me through a complex maze of corridors, sections that look mostly like servants' areas, the kind of behind-the-scenes halls that let them get around easily—until one opens to the midday sun and pathways leading out into expansive grounds.

Much larger than I expected, honestly.

The massive labyrinthine grounds feel like they must have their own dimension apart from Redhaven to be able to fit on the backside of the hill where the mansion perches.

Xavier shows me stables, gardeners' sheds, the pool and pool house, a hedge maze, storage buildings, and long fields for riding around and playing cricket.

I keep snapping photos, partly with an eye for work and partly looking for anything that could help Micah.

So far, I haven't spotted anything useful. But maybe Micah's experienced eye will catch something in the photos I overlooked as mundane.

What's definitely *not* mundane, though, is the sudden shift in tone as Xavier leads me between two hedgerows into a quiet clearing in the middle of a grove of willows. There's a flower-lined pond on one side and a small table in the center, draped in white fabric and set up for two.

A man in Arrendell livery stands at attention beside a cart piled high with covered dishes, right next to an ice bucket and a gleaming champagne bottle.

My brain stops cold.

I blink at the table, then at Xavier.

He smiles indulgently, like he's expecting me to be impressed.

"I thought we could discuss the contract and quotes over lunch," he says. "I had it prepared in advance."

"O-oh. Oh, wow. Very thoughtful."

That's why he was checking his watch?

So he could spring this on me?

I try not to frown.

Now this entire consultation feels like a ruse to get me into this date-like situation, but no. I can't flatter myself that way.

No one—not even an Arrendell—would go through this much trouble to get a girl like me in an uncomfortable situation for very little payout besides getting to watch me squirm. Right?

So I just brush it off with a smile.

"Thanks," I clip. "I had a light breakfast, so I'm starving."

He almost looks disappointed I'm not gushing all over him.

But he moves to pull my chair out.

Yes, it takes all my willpower to grit my teeth and keep smiling as I settle down and set my folio and bag against the chair.

I hate the creepy-crawly feeling that darts through me as he leans over, pushing my chair in.

His body heat, yikes.

I catch a whiff of an odd smell wafting off him—like burning rubber mixed with nail polish remover? If that's his aftershave, he should really look into changing it, and there goes my appetite, too.

So when the servant sets plates in front of us with everything from egg salad sandwiches to shrimp cocktails, custard cups, and some sort of savory thin-sliced beef dish drizzled in gravy, I'm ready to gag.

Across from me, Xavier looks at me mildly.

"Are you well, Talia? You look a little pale."

"I—oh. I sat down too fast, that's all. It's a side effect of my asthma, orthostatic hypotension. Sometimes if I move too fast, my blood pressure drops." I'm babbling now. There goes the cool, calm spy lady with her smile etched in stone. But I'd rather reveal that little vulnerability about myself than tell him that his body odor or cologne or whatever nauseated me that much. I force a shaky smile. "Just give me a second and it'll simmer down."

"Miss, this may help," the valet standing by says, pouring a glass of ice water before setting it close to my plates.

There's something almost knowing about the way he says it, deferential but understanding. I flash him a grateful smile and pick up the glass in both hands, taking a deep sip.

"Thank you," I say over the rim.

He's right, the cold water helps settle my nausea pretty fast.

Xavier looks weirdly displeased, and he flicks his fingers at the servant.

"You may go," he snaps.

The man bows briefly, and I don't think I'm imagining that he bows a little deeper to me than he does to Xavier before he excuses himself without a word, disappearing between the tall hedge paths.

Leaving me alone with Xavier Arrendell.

Crud.

I can't help looking for exits, trying to remember the way we came through.

The man just watches me, that cold, canny look back in his eyes. I feel like he's trying to figure out how to—how to break me?

I don't even know, but it's nothing good.

"Talia," he rumbles, getting his voice all over my name again like a stain. "Is something bothering you?"

"Mmm," I demur, stalling for a second with another sip of my water. "It really was just a little dizzy spell. It always passes quickly. I'm fine."

"Are you?" Steepling his fingers, Xavier props his elbows on the table and leans closer. The sunlight shines off his blond hair until he looks like Lucifer's son, striking and intimidating and damned. "You're certain that's all that's making you uncomfortable? Surely, you aren't intimidated by the Arrendell name. I promise you we're fool's gold. Worthless glitz and glamor."

I blink in surprise.

"I, no, not at all. Mr. Arrendell, forgive me, but do you hate your family?"

"Not hate, no." He smiles humorlessly. "At least, not my family itself. Our name, our legacy… I can't say I'm fond of those."

"Is that what you're trying to erase with this renovation?"

His eyebrows shoot up. "What the hell makes you think I'm trying to *erase* anything?"

Oh, crap.

Me and my big mouth, just tripping off my tongue.

Swallowing thickly, I look around, taking in the looming house, the trees, the hedges.

"Well, it's not hard to tell this house is a legacy. Many generations layered on top of each other. Everyone keeps adding to it, and while it all sort of fits, it doesn't fit together *well*. And it feels like instead of trying to make it fit, you just want to erase it all and start over from scratch. Wipe all the history and the personal touches that went into it."

Xavier remains silent.

His jade-green eyes are arctic, unchanging, and he looks at me for so long I start to squirm, looking away, biting my lip and lowering my eyes to my plate.

Just to give my restless hands something to do, I pluck at my scarf, picking at the knot and unwinding it from around my neck, then fretting it between my hands in my lap.

"...I'm sorry," I murmur into the silence. "That was presumptuous of me."

"No," he says softly. "That was dead accurate. Are you really paying that much attention to me, Talia?"

Panic knifes through me.

Does he realize I'm watching him, listening to every word, hoping for something Micah can use against him? Does he know I'm playing him—or trying to, at least?

When I peek up at him again, he's not looking me in the eye.

His gaze rolls over my shoulders, dipping down, and I know before he even says another word that I won't be eating anything. Not when pure revulsion fills up my stomach.

"Do you want to know more about me?" Xavier smiles

slowly.

There's an unclean edge to those words.

An unwanted suggestion.

That's when I know I shouldn't stay here another minute.

"I wouldn't dream of violating your privacy, sir." I stand hastily, snatching up my folio and bag. "Gosh, I'm sorry! I just remembered I have another consultation in the next hour and you said you're pressed for time. So, how about I email you the quotes and potential sp-specifications once I've done a full workup? Thank you for your t-time, Mr. Arrendell. Honestly."

He only watches me with that predatory gaze as I turn and scurry toward the closest path. I don't even know if it leads out of this labyrinthine hellscape.

I don't care. I just want to be away from Xavier Arrendell.

When he speaks again, I almost flinch—but he's not speaking to me.

"Joseph!" he commands, imperious and sharp enough to cut, followed by a clap of his hands. "Show Miss Grey to the exit, please."

The man who'd served us materializes from the hedges nearly right in front of me.

I jump back with a small squeak.

He gives me an understanding, patient look.

"This way, Miss Grey."

"Thank you." I take a shaky breath, my heart fluttering like a captured sparrow, and nod.

I feel safer with the servant—Joseph—than I did with Xavier, and safer still when Joseph escorts me through the hedges out of Xavier's sight. We're almost back to the house before he speaks.

"Are you all right, Miss Grey?" he asks in a low voice, and with a certain *knowing* that tells me he's asked many women the same question in this house.

I smile gratefully.

"Better now," I say. "Sorry. I had a little panic attack thinking I'd be late for my appointment, but I'm fine now."

I can't bring myself to tell the truth. Not even to a man who seems sympathetic and who's probably dealt with much worse than Xavier being a little smarmy.

And he seems to know it, too, giving me a long look before he nods and pulls the back door open for me. "Follow me, please."

The massive gargoyle of a house feels less oppressive without Xavier hovering over me with every move. There are things I want to ask this Joseph guy, things that make me nervous and afraid.

You know how it goes—servants see everything. And if there's anything that Micah really wants to know, I'll bet the people who work here are the ones who could tell him. Didn't some ex-butler blow open the whole case with Aleksander and the Faircrosses? And wasn't there a dead maid involved? I think I remember reading that.

The help are way more useful.

Not me.

I'm not a good spy.

I'm not good at anything but making pretty furniture.

He's going to be so disappointed.

I don't even know how to bring up the topic with Joseph.

I keep my eyes fixed on the trim line of his shoulders in his perfectly starched tailcoat as I follow him through the house. Maybe money makes the people at the Arrendell manor too loyal to ever turn on their employers, though.

There's an entire cult of secrecy around this place.

We rarely see the servants in town shopping for things the 'royalty' might need; everything gets delivered or brought in from out of town.

But with everything that's happened here lately, no

amount of money can buy those servants' loyalty, or their silence. Killing them, on the other hand, just might.

…or so I've heard from, like, mystery novels and such.

I feel so naïve right now.

I'm just working up the nerve to ask Joseph a few leading questions when we cross into the main foyer and he pulls the massive double doors open, standing expectantly and watching me.

I stop on the threshold. It feels a million times warmer on the other side, like I'm caught between two completely different worlds.

I look at him as he raises his brows mildly.

"Is there something else you need, Miss Grey?"

"N-no." I can't do it. I can't trust that anything I'd ask would be innocuous enough not to give the game away. So instead, I just smile. "Do you mind if I ask your last name? It feels too informal, calling you Joseph."

He gives me a curious look, unreadable. I wonder if he can see right through me.

"Peters," he says after a moment.

My smile brightens.

"Thank you for showing me the way out, Mr. Peters." I file that away. "Have a nice day."

I can at least tell Micah his name and that he seemed concerned about me—worried enough to possibly be sympathetic to Micah's cause, and possibly willing to disclose a few Arrendell secrets.

I feel a bit better. Like I finally did something useful.

There's a spring in my step, chasing away the unclean feeling Xavier left behind, as I slip back into the sun and grab my phone to shoot a quick text to Mr. Vampire Man himself.

Are you busy right now? I send. ***I'm leaving the mansion, and I really need to see you.***

VIII: DARKEST BEFORE THE DAWN (MICAH)

I really need to see you.

I frown down at that message on my phone, propping my elbow up on the wheel of my patrol car and raking a hand through my hair.

I really need to see you.

That shit worries me a hell of a lot more than it should.

Talia's a grown woman.

She's leaving the big house, clearly safe and under her own willpower. Still, my mind whipsaws with a hundred dark scenarios.

Talia, backed into a corner in Xavier Arrendell's office.

Talia, trying to fight him off while he rips at her clothes.

Talia, with her long red hair tangled in his brutish fingers, innocent prey being dragged into his spiderhole—

Fucking stop. Answer her.

Are you safe? I send back. **How urgent? I'm on patrol for a few more hours.**

While I wait for an answer, I gaze over the street.

I'm parked down one of the cobblestone lanes of the

THE DARKEST CHASE

shopping district that branches off the central square like spokes from a wheel.

It's quiet this time of day.

The morning rush has come and gone. Everyone's got their kids bundled up and off to school. The stay-at-home moms are already back home doing the morning cleaning and won't be out running errands until afternoon, squeezing them in between Pilates and grabbing their rug rats. Their working spouses are in their offices and workshops, busy hands filling the hours until they can come home.

Redhaven has a predictable rhythm, patterns people always follow.

Anything that breaks that rhythm always catches my eye.

This morning, though, the only thing out of sync is me.

I shouldn't be this worried over Talia Grey when she's talking to me. If she was truly in danger, she'd come out and say it.

You'd almost think I'm obsessed.

Or worse, growing a conscience. Thankfully, no crows yet today.

But I look down instantly as my phone vibrates with a new text.

Talia: I'm safe. He didn't do anything but leer at me. I didn't get much intel out of him, but I might have another lead you can follow. And I took some photos for the project, if you want to look through them for anything interesting. But it can wait until you're off shift! <3

Intel. I almost smile.

Isn't she picking up the lingo fast.

Red Grounds at 4:30? I send back.

Talia: Your treat?

You think I'd dream of asking my informant to pay for herself? Get over yourself, Shortcake.

She just sends back a laughing emoji and a bubbling cluster of hearts.

Goddamn.

I can almost see the way she smiles—shyly at first, then slow, before it spreads big and bright while laughter glitters in her eyes and she ducks her head, tucking her fiery hair behind one ear.

I really need to stop that shit and focus on the job.

Not that there's much to focus on.

The afternoon passes normally enough. I recognize every face that passes, pushing a stroller or lugging a reusable tote bag.

There's Ophelia Faircross, stepping out for lunch on the arm of our captain, Grant. I almost never see the captain smile, but he's got this slow, content grin shining out of his thick beard as he offers her his arm.

Past the closing door of the Sanderson family shop, Nobody's Bees-ness, I can just glimpse her sister Rosalind behind the counter. She's looking much healthier after her stint in rehab to shake the bad habits Aleksander Arrendell encouraged.

Was Xavier the family supplier, too? I really wonder.

Fuck, *everyone* in this town looks happy.

I watch as Grant and Ophelia stroll down the sidewalk, completely absorbed in each other on their way to the little deli on the corner.

What must that feel like?

To be so content.

To have your life sorted, feeling like you're free to *build* something rather than dedicating everything you have to tearing shit down.

I don't like these thoughts.

For me, they're not normal.

On any other day, I'd have stolen one of Lucas Graves'

cheesy paperbacks and skimmed a few chapters to pass the time. Now, I don't even pick up the one sitting on my dash.

I'm so fucking restless it hurts. Every minute crawls by like a drunken snail.

What's Talia's lead?

And why do I care less about that than seeing her again and making sure she's truly safe?

My mind spins in circles as the minutes and hours tick by.

At 4:19 p.m., I step out of my cruiser, leaving it parked on the curb—it'll be fine there—and lock up before I make my way down the street toward the coffee shop.

I'm expecting to arrive early and wait for her.

When I get there, she's already there waiting for me.

Looking pretty as a picture in a pair of close-fit jeans, cute heeled sandals, and a loose, breezy blouse that threatens to be translucent but flirts enough to suggest pure sin.

Her hair ripples in red waves tumbling everywhere, fire and copper all burnt together into shiny gloss, bringing out the pink in her cheeks, her lips, her skin.

She's so goddamned beautiful I forget to breathe.

Knowing Xavier Arrendell saw her that way makes me taste blood.

I shove it away.

I don't fucking own her.

It's not my business how she dresses or who looks at her. It's only my business that she's not distressed.

I just don't like it.

Don't like the idea that the slimiest motherfucker in town probably made her feel disgusting, all because she looks damnably sexy today.

I'm glad she doesn't look traumatized—and as I make my way up the street, she turns her head, sees me, and brightens.

She raises her hand in a shy wave, smiling. I answer her with a brief nod as I draw into earshot.

"Miss Grey."

"*Talia*. I'll even settle for that 'shortcake' business," she says playfully. My lips twitch. I'll admit I said it just so she'd give me crap. "Sorry I'm early. I finished the sketches I was doing at the shop and I was bored."

"Nothing to apologize for." I ease past her and catch the door of the café, pulling it open. "After you."

She flashes me a grateful smile and slips inside.

We're quick to the counter. I order my usual black coffee, no sugar, Irish crème and a sugary mocha slushy thing for her.

I offer to buy her something to eat from the pastry case, but she declines, shaking her head and wrapping her soft pink mouth provocatively around the bright green straw, her lips pursed happily as she takes a sip.

"I ate at home," she says. "Grandpa was baking and I can never turn down his muffins. He loves to try out new recipes from the bakery next door."

"Your grandfather likes to bake?" I ask as we make our way to a secluded corner booth. The café is mostly empty by now, just a few people with their laptops, and it's easy to stake out a spot where we can talk privately.

We settle into the leather seats across from each other under the string lights above.

"I'm not sure if he likes it so much as he got used to it when he was stuck with me. Cooking in general, I mean," she says wryly. "He just turned out to be pretty good at it. We mostly take turns, unless it's crunch time on an important order, and then we live off takeout and frozen pizzas."

"The life of the creative." I lean back in my seat, loosening the neck of my uniform shirt and watching her. "You care about him more than anything, don't you?"

She starts, then smiles and ducks her head. "Is it that obvious? He's always been there for me. He taught me everything I know about the woodworking trade…"

"No wonder you're willing to do anything for him."

That's enough to wipe the smile off her face.

"…am I doing anything, though?" Her brows wrinkle together. "I didn't find anything, Micah. He didn't say anything strange, except when he was being weird at me and thinking I was, like, interested in him. I'm sorry I'm useless."

"You're not useless," I growl. "This is a long game, Talia. You have to have patience. He won't let anything slip in front of you, not immediately, but give it time and—"

"How would I know, though?" she asks firmly. "For all I know, something he said today *was* important, and I'm just too clueless to follow the trail."

"Trust your instincts. You start to get a feel for things. If you have doubts, tell me."

"I guess." Her straw whistles softly as she pokes it in and out of the lid of her drink, her eyes downcast. "Today was mostly business. He gave me a tour of the house and talked about what he wants. He said the mansion feels like a human display case, and he wants it to feel more like a home. He wants it to feel *smaller*. Whatever else is going on, I think he's struggling with his brothers being gone."

"People are complex creatures." I sip my coffee, turning my thoughts over, then continue. "The worst person on earth can fall in love. Save a life. Change the world. The biggest saints can be vile. Selfish as hell. Give them the wrong crusade and they'll destroy thousands. They may have the best intentions, but who they are or what they stand for doesn't matter. All that matters is the end result."

"And the end result for Xavier is that he kills people… even while he's killing himself," she whispers.

"Exactly." I can't stand that look on her face, the quiet

realization of the ugly harshness of life, so I divert. "You mentioned a lead? And pictures?"

"Oh! Um, maybe. Just someone who might be sympathetic." Talia brightens a bit and takes another sip of her drink before she fishes out her phone. She swipes to the photo album and passes it over without hesitation. "Joseph Peters. He's a valet at the house. He just seemed worried about me being alone with Xavier, and he was nice about getting me out of there fast when I got uncomfortable and left. The servants see everything, I'm sure. Especially when we're talking rich people who treat the hired help like they're invisible."

"Yeah." I rub my chin, looking down and swiping through the photos. Just interior shots, nothing jumping out at me. I scroll through them quickly. "I think I remember who you're talking about. I interviewed him after the maid's death—Cora Lafayette—after all the bullshit with Aleksander and the truth came out."

Her face falls. "Oh, yeah. I thought about that. But I dunno. I don't think money would keep everyone loyal or their lips sealed. But I guess you have to be careful, because if I'm wrong, then Mr. Peters might screw us over."

"Leave that part to me. I'm used to handling investigations delicately." I pause to find a gentle smile for her, even if I can't hold it very long. "Like I said, you're far from useless. You've already found something on the first day."

"Yay?" Talia glances away, then laughs. "I tried to convince myself this morning that I was a sexy superspy. But I think I'm more Velma than Kim Possible."

I snort loudly. "No clue who Kim is, but Velma was sexy enough. Short skirt, cute glasses, plus that repressed look that said she was probably a frigging demon in the sheets."

Talia freezes mid-reach for her drink, watching me with wide eyes. Her cheeks flush and I realize what I just said.

Fuck.

Now she knows I might have a thing for repressed girls who go wild when you tease them out of their shell.

Clearing my throat sharply, I avoid eye contact, focusing on my cooling mug of coffee and her phone—though I'm not really seeing the pictures now, other than a subconscious alertness for anything out of the ordinary.

"When are you meeting Xavier again?"

"I haven't set a date yet. I kind of ran out of there and promised to email him once I had more comps ready."

Sobering, I shoot her a frown. "He made you *that* uncomfortable?"

"It was kind of a lot." Wincing, she frets her straw up and down, a grating squeaky noise. "He set up a private lunch in the garden. He kept staring at me. Asking if I want to know more about him and the way he *said* it…"

She winces and I grind my teeth together.

If he touched her, he's dead.

"You don't have to keep doing this," I growl, the words tumbling out without thinking. "I can work with the staff angle. If he's being that big of a prick, you don't have to keep exposing yourself. Especially if he makes you feel unsafe."

"I'm not sure I have a choice. Not because of you!" she says quickly. Her hands wrap around her plastic cup, squeezing until it crinkles while she looks anywhere but at me. "So, did I tell you why my grandfather and I need the Arrendell cash?"

"No," I answer—then stop as my swiping moves past the photos of the Arrendell mansion and lands on a shot of an older man with Talia's blue eyes. He's bowed over a thick cedar log, shaving away, intensely focused and lost in something that looks like love. I linger on it, wondering if she looks the same way when she's working. I pass her phone back to her. "You were fairly evasive when the subject came up before."

"Yeah, I'm sorry."

She goes silent, glancing back over her shoulder to see if anyone's eavesdropping. She ignores the phone sitting between us.

"He's losing himself," she says, her voice low with hurt. "Who he really is, I mean. He's got rheumatoid arthritis and it's destroying his hands. Of course, our crappy insurance won't cover surgery. But it's not just that, he..." Her lips curl up in a pained wince, trembling. "He's suffering from early-onset dementia. There's an experimental treatment, but it's *expensive*, and we don't have the funds. So I've decided I'll deal with Xavier Arrendell being a creep if it means I can use that money to help my grandfather."

Fuck *me*.

I'm a louse.

This means so much to her.

And I'm going to destroy everything this girl loves to have my revenge.

"Miss Grey," I say slowly. "You know that if I arrest Xavier—"

"*I know*," she says quickly, her voice thick. There's a wet gleam in her eyes and a strange smile on her lips and she won't quite look at me. "But that won't happen for a while, right? Going after his money?"

"Right," I say flatly.

"And he'll pay something up front." Her fingers knot together against the table, going still. She stares at her hands. "It'll be enough. It *has* to be enough."

"Talia." Shit. Fuck. I can't do this. "Listen, I'll find another way. I won't—"

"*No*." A sharp look whips toward me, almost a glare, and I understand it more than I wish I really did.

She doesn't want my pity.

She doesn't want me to go easy on her or on Xavier.

"We started this, so we'll finish it," she whispers. "I trust you to make sure everything turns out okay."

"You shouldn't," I snarl, and her smile strengthens, melancholy yet so sweet.

"I think I'm going to anyway."

"Why?"

I don't like the way those blue eyes watch me, beaming back an innocence I shouldn't risk for anything.

"Maybe," she murmurs, "I think you're a better man than you give yourself credit for."

Everything in me wants to shut down.

Shove her away.

Close off so she won't depend on me, won't expect shit from me. I couldn't protect my brother and I couldn't protect myself.

How the hell can I ever protect her?

I tear my gaze away, staring across the café instead.

"That makes one of us," I mutter tightly.

"Fine," she answers with absolute conviction, picking up her phone, and when she swipes the screen and smiles down at it softly, I know exactly what picture she's looking at. "I'll just have to believe in you hard enough for both of us, Micah."

Fine is fucking right.

Let her believe whatever she wants.

Nothing Talia Grey does will make me a better man than the twisted creature I truly am.

IX: DARKEST HOUR (TALIA)

Nothing else in the world calms me more than the scent of the workshop and the sound of Grandpa hard at work.

I'm at my drafting table, with a perfect view of the shop front so I can head out if a customer comes in. But I'm not really thinking about sales right now.

Papers scatter across the angled wooden tabletop and my pencils are strewn everywhere. I've filled pages with sketches until my hand hurts, using my photos of the Arrendell manor as a reference, trying to tame that strange beast into something livable.

Behind me, Grandpa works over his lathe, humming softly to himself as he fills the workshop with the scent of hot sawdust, slowly bringing another masterpiece to life.

I feel like half my drawings are a tribute to him, to what I know he's capable of. I've always designed with Grandpa's style in mind, but also with a touch of my own.

No matter how I might feel about the Arrendells, there's something exciting about taking on the challenge of transforming a luxe dungeon into something warm and alive. The interior is mostly black and white with wood accents and tacky splashes of red. It makes me think of a chessboard strewn with the blood of kings and queens and pawns.

Then there's the garden out back.

Even if it was mazelike, there's natural beauty there.

Trees and flowers growing wild, a touch of lightness, like those grounds could somehow purify the darkness of the family's history. The idea stuck with me while I sketched and bled into concepts focused on light wood tones with a soft gloss meant to capture the natural light that could permeate the place if we replaced those heavy velvet drapes with modern fabrics and hand-carved wooden shutters.

My concepts turn the bedrooms into bowers, complete with flowered trellises of climbing vines. Others get more technical, but there's an organic look to it I like.

With a little grunt work, we'll make the interior of the manor look like it's sprouting up from the surrounding forest.

Yes, it's going to take years of hard work.

But as long as my grandfather's here, I don't care.

I'll work with Xavier Arrendell indefinitely if it helps Grandpa hold on to what he cherishes.

Right now, though, if I don't hurry, I'll be late for a meeting with the man in question.

I get up, shuffle my papers together, and slide them into a portfolio folder before slipping over to kiss Grandpa's cheek.

"Heading up to the big house," I say, while he slows the lathe and smiles at me. "Did you want to see my sketches before I go?"

"Show me when you get back." His smile brightens. "I trust you, Serena dear."

Only practice stops me from gasping with distress.

It hits me so hard, every time he calls me by my mother's name.

He must be in some strange liminal space between past and present, if he's not asking me why I'm going to the Arrendell manor.

I take a shaky breath, wondering if I should leave him unsupervised. No matter what happens to his mind, he never forgets his skills with his tools.

And in less than half an hour, Mrs. Brodsky will pop by to check on him and bring him his usual lunch.

"Okay." I force the words past my closing throat. "I'll do that. Are you okay with the backlog? We're up to our necks in orders lately."

"Oh, don't you worry about me. These old hands love keeping busy." He smiles so cheerfully his eyes crease into little crescent slits of blue.

Still, I'm hesitant.

But if I don't go, there'll be no job and no hope.

My feelings can wait.

I kiss his cheek and smile. "Be back soon. Have fun!"

His only answer is an affectionate nudge, his attention already back on the lathe and the bedpost he's working on. It was supposed to be my project, but when we discussed the Arrendell job the last time he was lucid, he agreed to take on all of my client work so I could sort out the logistics to prep for the big job.

I know it's necessary, but guilt still swamps me as I linger, watching him before taking a deep breath, shouldering my bag, and heading out with the portfolio of sketches under my arm.

I can't help craving distractions as I stroll down the street under the bright noon sun toward the lane leading up the hill.

Too bad my favorite distraction is parked in a patrol car down the street.

His tall, lean frame is slouched in the driver's seat, his

uniform sitting so crisp and trim on his rapier-like frame. There's one angular cheek propped against his knuckles and a paperback open against the wheel.

He's on the opposite side of the street. I have to stop myself from crossing traffic to stare at him.

So I make myself look away, pretending not to notice when he's busy working. But I can't help watching Micah from the corner of my eye as I head down the sidewalk.

The second I do, I glimpse movement.

His head comes up.

Those silver-blue eyes hit me like a gunshot.

I'm an instant ball of fire.

But I can't let myself look at him, not directly, not when I'm too embarrassed to admit I've been watching him with the weirdest butterflies storming away in the pit of my stomach.

They only intensify when my phone goes off in my bag.

It couldn't be him.

It wouldn't be him, not when he doesn't need anything from me right now.

But when I fish out my phone, there he is on my screen.

Vampire Man.

Even if it feels a little weird calling him that right now when he's out here in broad daylight and clearly not disintegrating under the sun.

Micah: Person of interest spotted on 4th. Baseball cap, oversized sweater, sneakers, jeans, red ponytail. Pink everything. Very suspicious.

I stop at the corner of 4th and Main, looking back at Micah's patrol car.

He's stone-faced, looking down at his phone—until a sly glance slips toward me from under his arched brows.

I smile as I send back, **Am I really that suspicious just for liking pink?**

Micah: You're never supposed to trust pretty women in pink. So that makes you trouble, yeah.

My eyes widen.

I don't know if I want to giggle or hide.

He thinks I'm pretty? He's not just teasing? I—

No, stop it.

I'm not feeling that pretty today, I counter. ***I want to be as unpretty as possible. This outfit is defensive.***

Micah: Uh-huh. You'll need more than that to look ugly, Shortcake.

God.

This man is trying to kill me.

My heart beats faster.

I step back, letting a mom with a stroller move past, stepping under the overhang of the bagel shop and leaning against the wall. I watch him as I try to figure out what to say back.

This feels almost like a strange secret, the two of us pretending we don't see each other while the whole world looks on.

But just as I'm trying to figure out what to say, he texts again.

Micah: Are you heading up to see him?

I don't like the way he phrases it.

I mean, I'm not going to see Xavier specifically. He's the last person alive I care to see.

I'm going for work, for my Grandpa's sake, for Micah's little mission.

I'm showing some sketches. I nibble at my lower lip. ***After the way he acted last time...***

Micah: Got it. You don't want to give him a chance to sexualize you.

It's nice that he understands.

He just *gets* it without needing to be told.

I nod, glancing up at him with a small smile. He cocks his head curiously, studying me, then texts again.

Micah: I'm going to send you a link to an app. Would you install it for me, then set me as your emergency contact?

What app?

Micah: It's an emergency alert. Instead of having to call or type in a number, you tap the button and it alerts your emergency contact if you're in trouble. It's faster and more discreet. A second text follows immediately. ***If he makes you feel unsafe, if you feel threatened or like you can't leave voluntarily, hit the button. I'll come.***

I swallow roughly.

Part of me still can't believe Xavier Arrendell is so dangerous that something like that seems necessary. He's been creepy, for sure, but not overly threatening.

Not yet.

The rest of me feels completely dumbstruck that Micah would go to those lengths, when that's a little more personal than a police officer responding to an emergency call as part of his duty.

I don't feel like I'm worth that.

Mousy little me.

I've always felt like background noise to other people's lives. The sick girl, almost invisible, always left out and left behind.

But Micah makes me feel *seen*.

For the first time in my life, he makes me feel important.

And right now, the way he's looking at me across the street blows my heart up.

It's almost like he can't see the real Talia Grey, the annoying runt everybody else knows.

I can't hold eye contact or I'll start thinking things I absolutely shouldn't. So I look down at my screen, taking a deep breath and texting.

And you wonder why I trust you're a good man.
Micah: You shouldn't. I'm fucking not.

My lips twitch. *You're going to figure out pretty fast that I'm more stubborn than I look. You're not going to change my mind about that, Micah.*

Micah: You think I want to?

I look up again, watching him from under the brim of my baseball cap.

I can't read his expression, not from this far, but the look on his face is so strange, so intense. The way he watches makes me feel like he's right next to me.

Feeling that strange, overpowering body heat that makes him seem more inhuman, that vivid presence that makes me shiver.

There's a loud pulse in my ears as I think about sharp teeth and fire in his dusky blue eyes, what that man could do with one kiss if he—

Oh my God, no.

No.

We're not going there.

It's not fair to Micah, seeing him as this fantasy instead of a real person—and honestly, I don't want to go see Xavier Arrendell with those kinds of thoughts rattling around in my head.

A weak smile flicks over my lips.

I'd better get moving. I'll be late.

Micah: Good luck.

His lips curl faintly and he looks away, out the other window of his patrol car.

It's like being released from a spell.

Thanks. I'll update you when I get back, I send, right before I force myself to turn away and cross the town square, only glancing at my phone again to install the app Micah sends with his next text.

THE DARKEST CHASE

The sun glints brightly off the bronze statue in the center of town, the rearing horse with the noble figure of the first Arrendell, briefly blinding me before I move past it and take the road leading up the hill.

This trek is getting familiar.

The trees overhead, the bright morning sky, the call of hunting hawks piercing the day. It would almost be a pleasant spring walk, if only I didn't feel like I was heading toward a brooding smudge of darkness waiting at the peak of the hill.

But there's a pleasure here, too.

Once, I wouldn't have been able to climb this hill without collapsing in a wheezing heap.

As I hit the steepest portion, there's a tightness in my chest, but nothing to be concerned about. I just measure my breaths carefully until it levels out in the huge roundabout courtyard at the front of the manor.

I really have come a long way from that girl I used to be.

That girl would never smile first at Joseph Peters when the valet greets me at the door with a solemn look.

"Miss Grey," he says, almost dubiously—eyeing me like he's wondering what I'm even doing back here after I scurried off days ago. "He's waiting for you in his office."

"Thank you, Mr. Peters," I answer brightly. "Have you been well since the last time we spoke?"

"I cannot complain, miss," he answers neutrally and turns to lead me into the house.

I follow him down now-familiar halls, working through my thoughts. What could I possibly ask him to probe for clues?

"There's a lot of history in these walls. I feel like I'm being hired to overwrite it, but I suppose it can't be all bad," I say. "Rumors, you know. People love to spread the dark stuff around, but what about the happy memories in this house? I just wonder if I'll be erasing them."

Joseph doesn't look at me, but his back stiffens.

I almost think he won't answer until he mutters, almost under his breath, "I'm not sure happiness can ever thrive in this house, Miss Grey. Frankly, I am not certain that even extensive redecorating will banish the ghosts in these halls."

My breath catches.

"Wait, do you mean... do you mean the maid?" I ask. "Did you know her?"

"*Cora*," he says sharply, as if *her* is an insult.

"Sorry," I answer. "I totally meant no disrespect."

Joseph Peters stops in the middle of the hall, turning to face me with a long, thoughtful look. He's younger than some of the other servants I've seen around, probably under forty. He has a neat crop of brown hair parted down one side and kind, but wary brown eyes.

"Cora Lafayette was like an aunt to me," he says slowly. Carefully. Like he's choosing every word. "Perhaps even a second mother, better than the one who never wanted me. I came here for work, but Cora, she made me feel like I belonged. Not a day passes that I do not miss her, Miss Grey." He swallows tightly. "And I do not know what you mean to accomplish by asking me this."

"I'm sorry!" I hiss. "Really. I didn't mean to be rude or poke at any open wounds."

Joseph gives me another lingering look, almost unreadable. "This house is an open wound, Miss Grey," he says.

Then he pivots sharply on his heel. The forbidding line of his back tells me this conversation is over.

Well, crap.

I think I just hurt a man who doesn't deserve it, and possibly closed a door for Micah.

I want to apologize again, but I keep my mouth shut.

Sometimes, it's better to just stop digging.

We're not far from Xavier's office anyway, and I'm surprised to look past Joseph and see Xavier's usually closed office door hanging open. A hint of sunlight from the windows spills into the lamplit halls.

Joseph moves to the doorway, then goes stiff, whipping around like he's about to stop me, stretching out one hand. "Miss Grey—"

Too late.

I'm too close on his heels and I stop behind him, staring into the room.

Xavier Arrendell stands behind his desk with—

My scarf?

What?

It's pressed to his face, right over his nose and mouth. His eyes are closed almost blissfully as he inhales deeply.

Holy shit!

I nearly barf on the spot.

I didn't know I left my scarf here, though now I remember setting it in my lap at lunch. It must have fallen in the garden when I fled.

Now, here's Xavier, sniffing it like a curious dog.

He doesn't even notice Joseph and I are standing there.

For a second, there's a flash of abject disgust on Joseph's face. It feels like he's expressing what I can't.

But the valet abruptly wipes the look away as Xavier slowly lowers my scarf from his face and opens his eyes with a deliberation that stops my heart.

He knows.

He effing knows.

He's aware we caught him.

And he also doesn't care how we feel about it, either.

In fact, his gaze slides lazily to me, his catlike green eyes lidded with sick satisfaction, like he's *enjoying* the shock that must be written all over my face.

"Miss Grey," he drawls slowly. "Excellent timing."

I make a choked sound, trying to find impossible words. But Joseph speaks up first.

"I'll take my leave, sir," he says. "Do call if you need anything else."

He's clearly speaking to Xavier, only his eyes cut to me briefly. There's a sympathetic look, like he doesn't want to leave me alone with this man, but to keep up appearances he has no choice.

Is that a warning in his eyes? Is he telling me to play along?

My heart shrinks.

And I remember that app Micah had me install. Maybe his instincts were right after all.

I'm starting to get just how serious this is.

Joseph bows and turns to march away, leaving me frozen in the doorway and trying not to hyperventilate while Xavier watches me like the cat that got the cream.

Honestly, it pisses me off that he thinks it's so cute, that it *had* to be intentional, staging this scene so I'd catch him.

Anger loosens my tongue and pins a hard smile on my lips, one that doesn't feel like me. My fingers dig into the strap of my bag.

"Mr. Arrendell," I bite off. "I didn't realize I forgot my scarf. Thanks for returning it."

The glint in Xavier's eye says I'm not fooling him, but we're keeping up appearances, aren't we?

"Naturally." He beckons me forward. "Come in. I apologize for being so unseemly. I caught a whiff of your perfume, and I was hoping to identify the scent. It's a lovely floral, almost vanilla. It reminded me we really should keep more flowers around this godforsaken house."

THE DARKEST CHASE

Double yikes.

Stepping into this room feels like sticking my head through a noose.

Especially when I tear my eyes away from his smug face and glance down at the desk. There's a small silver tray there, a business card lying at an odd angle, and—

Oh. Is that a few grains of white scattered there?

My breath stalls.

If that's what I think it is…

There's too much spinning around me to process. My voice sounds so distant when I say, "Actually, I don't wear much perfume."

"What a shame," he replies smoothly. "It must be natural, then." His lips curl in an oily smile, and he offers me my scarf. "Here, Miss Grey."

Yeah.

I think I'd rather eat my own hand than get closer to him right now. I've never felt so filthy in my *life* from a compliment.

I edge a few inches deeper into his office, snatch my scarf from his hand without touching him, then move closer to the door with a dead-eyed "Thanks."

All while he watches me with pleasure.

I swear, if I didn't need this man's money, I might just punch someone for the first time in my life.

Keep it together. For Grandpa.

This is for him, even more than Micah.

I have to remember that.

I just need to keep him on track, keep this professional, and keep my stuff the hell away from Sniffy the Clown.

So I peel my bag open and fish out the sketches while stuffing my scarf inside.

"I brought some fresh concepts." I push them onto the desk hastily. "You can review them at your convenience and get back to me with any revisions. Or if nothing catches your eye, just let me know and we'll work up something else."

"Sit. I'll have a look now." He gestures flippantly to the seats opposite his desk. "It shouldn't take long."

Well, crap.

I was hoping to just drop off the sketches, make my escape, and maybe do the review over email. After that creepy lunch, I should've just tried to keep this remote to begin with.

But that's never easy in a town this small for a client this big.

Plus, if I make excuses and run, it'll be too obvious. I hate that so much rides on not alienating this maniac.

And there's a stiff, proud part of me that hates backing down and letting him intimidate me when that's what he's clearly trying to do.

Deep down, I imagine Micah over my shoulder, silent and strong and encouraging.

Stay strong, Shortcake. Show me how brave you can be.

He's just a tap of a button away.

He could stare down Xavier without a second's hesitation.

So I sink down in the chair, holding my bag in my lap like a shield while Xavier settles behind his desk and flips the folio open. Under the guise of looking for something in my bag, I find my phone and silently tap the app open so the emergency button is right there.

I sincerely hope I won't need it.

But it helps me feel calmer to have it ready.

Feeling calmer doesn't stop how awkward this is, though.

Dead silence, while Xavier slowly flips through the sketch folio. His expression gives away nothing.

I don't know if I should explain my ideas or just shut up and let him think, so I say nothing and just look around the

THE DARKEST CHASE

office slowly, skimming the spines of books. They're just old encyclopedias and other reference sets. Maybe a set of Great Western literary classics.

Hmph.

There's something soulless about a man who doesn't keep any other kinds of books around, especially when these are probably just background décor. But I remind myself that I don't know Xavier, much less his reading tastes.

Even if that nagging core of sympathy over his dead brothers makes me feel a little guilty, I also don't *want* to know Xavier that way.

Not when his presence feels so smothering my chest wants to seize up.

I refuse to have another asthma attack over the stiff silence in the office, broken only by rustling pages as he looks the sketches over, taking his sweet time. It's only when I glance at him and realize he's locked eyes on me over the top of the folio that the panic hits.

He's doing it again.

Making me squirm on purpose.

Jesus. I am *definitely* not wasting an inhaler hit on this asshole today.

So I start counting, timing each breath. Old trick, calming and soothing.

As I wind down, my brain refocuses. Just enough to notice things about Xavier that hadn't filtered in before.

He's not the cleanest man for such a pampered existence.

There's dirt under his nails.

His eyes are too dilated for the sunlight coming through the office windows. They're jittery, too, and the pupils aren't just scanning across the page.

No, they're leaping, like restless marbles he has to grab and drag back into place.

There's a clammy film of sweat making his stubble look

greasy, even though it's actually chilly in the office—and his dark-grey tailored suit isn't heavy enough to warrant it.

Micah would probably know what he's looking at. He'd be able to identify it with razor precision and insight. I can only guess.

Still, between that and the little tray, I wonder.

Is Xavier coming off a high right now?

For a second, I wonder who he might be, if he'd been born into a different life.

If he had a chance even now to get into rehab and start over—would it matter?—but I'm being naïve again. Because he's not just a drug addict.

He's involved in distribution, and that's a choice.

That's not an illness.

I feel queasy, sitting across from a man who would make a choice like that and shamelessly being willing to take his money.

"Interesting." He finally breaks the silence, loudly stroking his chin. "An arboreal theme? Are we dryads, Miss Grey, flying around the branches naked?"

I swallow hard, suppressing a shudder.

"It's just a concept. If you don't like it, I could come up with something else—"

"No," he says sharply. I clamp my lips shut. "But I wonder, what would it take to add water installations in the great rooms to complete the look?"

"Contractors," I answer immediately. "Lots of them. That's architecture, plumbing. We'd need to hire consultants. I'm not sure it'll work, not without ripping up the entire floor in some places. It depends on the room. Some of them have marble flooring, and that's going to be hard to work around."

Not to mention, I'm not sure how well it would integrate

with the general structure and design of the rooms. I mean, random water fountains and falls indoors?

I guess the customer is always right, but that's stretching it here.

"Show me," Xavier says imperiously. "Adjust the sketches and let me see what you come up with. Add the extra costs into your estimate." His gaze scans over two pages that he holds apart again. He frowns. "I see a few notes here about materials and costs, but not an overall quote for everything, including labor."

I swallow hard. Talking money makes me nervous, and quoting this price tag feels like death.

"Well, with a few architects involved, it would probably put the estimate at about four million dollars—and that's lowballing it." Just saying that amount makes me dizzy. "Also, we're looking at a minimum timeline of three years. Possibly longer. It all depends on changes through the process, the usual delays, material backorders, staff availability, and time needed to relocate people and functional areas temporarily while large sections of the house are being worked on."

If anyone told me they were about to send me a bill for over four million dollars, I'd faint.

Xavier doesn't even blink.

In fact, he smiles faintly, a strange ghostly curl that makes me uneasy.

"Let's make it easy and round up to five million. Why skimp? I like round numbers and this is a big undertaking."

I get dizzier. "Five million? But this—"

"It's not charity," he replies sharply. "Frankly, I'll be rather demanding with this project. Consider this advance compensation."

The way he says *demanding* feels so slimy that it's a miracle I don't grab my phone and hit that button right now.

Instead, I just nod slowly, feeling broken.

"All right. Five million. Very fair. I'll get the contract drafted and sent over, along with scans of the revised sketches. Typically, for larger long-term projects like these, we break up the payments into a downpayment and then installments. Does every six months and project milestones work for you?"

"Yes. I'll leave the logistics to you." He narrows his eyes. "You look pale, Miss Grey. Are you—"

"I'm fine," I lie.

"Are you about to have an asthma attack?"

I tense, recoiling. "How did you know about my asthma?"

"I'm as much a resident of Redhaven as you are. What ever stays secret in this town? Maybe I'm not as close to the daily gossip as the townsfolk." His smile is self-deprecating. "I hear things more like a thief holding his ear to the door, yes. But I *do* hear them." His brows lift mockingly. "Or did you think I was fishing for information about you?"

Of course I did.

I'm not sure I'm wrong, either, despite his explanation. I flush with mortification anyway and hold out my hand.

"If I can have those back, I'll get out of your hair..."

"So hasty to get away from me?" he mocks softly as he slips the pages back into the folio and passes it to me before rising. "I'll escort you out since Mr. Peters has disappeared."

Ugh.

Xavier has this way of talking that makes everything sound ominously significant. I can't tell if it's just the way he is, if he overheard any of my conversation with Joseph, or even if he already suspects his money may not buy the loyalty he thinks from his underlings.

There's a fresh chill in that green stone stare.

I feel numb as I back out into the hall, keeping precious space between us as he rounds the desk and approaches me.

That distance remains as he turns to lead me down the hall.

Xavier doesn't comment on it, thankfully.

I hate how I feel like a servant shuffling along in his wake, a few steps behind and to his right, but I'm more interested in escaping without any more weird moments.

Can I really spend years working here?

Well, it won't be all on-site.

Most of it will be in the workshop, I remind myself.

And with five million bucks, even with most of it going to cover materials and labor, Grandpa has time.

That gives me a thrill as we exit the hall and step into the foyer. But that feeling vanishes when I realize we're not alone.

I almost don't see her at first.

She's standing in a niche behind the huge double doors, like a statue tucked out of the way just to occupy space in an alcove.

Her severe all-black clothing doesn't help. She's dressed in an old-fashioned gown that covers her from neck to toe, severely fitted in the torso and loose in the skirt.

Her hair is iron grey, bound back in a prim knot.

The only pale points are her hands and her square face. She almost looks like a ghost, and as my eyes lock on hers, I nearly scream, clutching at my bag, my heart rabbiting in a panicked thump.

She stares back at me, totally expressionless.

Still, there's something so vile, so cold, so hateful in her black eyes, and my mouth goes dry.

I've seen her before.

That night we went camping.

She was *there*, standing back and watching like a black queen on a chessboard—and the way she looks at me right now hurts.

Like she's marking me.

Like she *knows* me.

But she couldn't know I was there that night with Micah... could she?

I can't think that.

It's not possible, and when Xavier breezes past her to open the doors without even glancing at her, pretending she's not there, I take my cue and look away without acknowledging her.

But I can still feel her watching as I step over the threshold.

It leaves me frozen, sweat breaking down my spine in beads.

Not even the afternoon sun feels warm enough as I venture out, down the soaring stairs. Xavier lingers in the doorway like a ghoul who can't cross into the light.

"Until next time, Miss Grey," he says with a strange formality.

"S-sure," I say. "I'll email you!"

"See that you do."

Everything feels wrong right now. Like I've just stepped out of a nightmare and back into the real world, yet I don't like it.

I breathe, shallow and swift, my lungs burning as I lunge downstairs to get away from here.

I wait until I'm on the path and in the trees before I stop, bending over and bracing my hands on my knees, just letting myself *heave* a little before I regain control.

Holy shit.

That was a Jacobin, wasn't it? That woman.

Micah was right.

They're connected.

And I need to get back to town and tell him ASAP.

* * *

When I text Micah and tell him ***I'm out, and I think I have something***, I'm not expecting the text I get back nearly instantly.

Micah: My place. 8 p.m.

Blinking, I shiver for different reasons as I make my way into town, taking the long way to stretch my legs and calm down. The last time I went to Micah's place, he very conspicuously kept me from going inside.

Is he actually going to let me into his man cave this time?

…I hope so.

Just because suddenly, desperately, I want to be near him. He makes me feel safe. He makes me feel *clean*.

Everything I need to scrub away the taint of Xavier's company.

I'm on edge the rest of the day.

By the time evening rolls around, I'm a nervous wreck.

It's just another business meeting.

Nothing personal.

I drop things, mess up sketches, send my pencils rolling across the drafting table. Luckily, when I got back to the shop, Grandpa was back to his old lucid self.

The whole afternoon, I can feel him watching with a thoughtful eye, though he keeps his observations to himself.

I don't know what I'd do with him teasing me about my jitters.

Have I mentioned I have near zero experience with men?

I need to remember that.

The fact that I'm not used to men who aren't family means I'm overly sensitive and likely to read more than I should into things.

So I need to stop thinking about how even though Micah almost never smiles, it always feels like he's laughing over text. How he tries to pass himself off as this human icicle, but he's so gentle with me, so sweet, and even funny in his own dry way. How he's a good man for caring about stopping the harm the Jacobins' drug business causes so many.

How it's not hard to tell the death of his brother broke him.

I definitely have no business wanting to cradle those small pieces of him in my hands and soothe their sharp edges.

After we close up shop for the day, I have an early dinner with Grandpa, then bounce to my feet and head for my room.

"Don't wait up," I tell him. "I'm going out this evening. Should be back by ten."

He watches me from the kitchen table with his thick brows raised, working at a bit of whittling. That's how he fell in love with woodwork a lifetime ago, starting with these small things.

The piece he's shaping now looks like a sparrow.

He's so good that he doesn't even have to look at the knife in his hand while he asks, "Date tonight, Tally?"

I nearly trip over empty air and catch myself on the doorframe to my room.

"N-no!" I sputter. "Just meeting a friend. To hang out."

"Mm-hmm. You're blushing," Grandpa points out. "So it's a friend you wish you were dating."

I stare into his twinkling eyes with abject horror.

"What? No, I—I..." I groan, hanging my head. "Am I that freaking obvious?"

"Only because I love you."

"I'm lucky you do." I smile faintly.

"And any man you've got your eye on would be lucky to have you." He cocks his head. "Tell me, when do I get to meet this young man?"

Never!

"Um, for real, it's not that kind of thing, Grandpa." I shrug. I'm a daydreamer, but I'm not completely unrealistic. "He's not interested in me."

"Bah. Then he's not someone worth meeting, if he's that big a damn fool."

I want to say he's wrong.

But I don't know how to make Grandpa understand, so I just smile and blow him a kiss.

"He's a good friend and that's all he is," I say before ducking into my room. "I'll be back before I turn into a pumpkin, don't worry."

His loud chuckle follows me.

I dig around in my closet to figure out what to wear.

So, yeah, maybe it's not a date.

Maybe I'll be at Micah's for twenty minutes before he puts me out with Rolf nipping at my heels.

Maybe I'm being silly.

But I feel like looking pretty tonight when I cross the threshold into Micah's domain.

I flick through my closet, eyeballing outfits before I settle on a layered sundress.

It's gauzy, pink-and-white stripes with a shirred bodice and spaghetti straps. The skirt flares out like a daffodil's bell from the high empress waistline, skimming down to mid-thigh.

I take a quick shower, then shimmy into the dress and touch on a little lipstick and a hint of pink eyeshadow.

Pink again.

It's like I want him to tease me into a smoking hole in the ground.

Yes, I'm doing the whole 'trying hard to not try too hard' thing.

My sandals match the dress, at least. My bag doesn't, too big and bulky, but I don't care.

Since dresses tend to not have pockets, I'm a bottomless handbag kind of girl.

Once I make sure my phone is charged and in its pocket, I shoulder my bottomless handbag, kiss Grandpa's head, and slip out into the night.

Redhaven is a weird town.

You never know when you'll find out that the son of the town's wealthiest family is a notorious serial killer, but it's also safe enough that a young woman can walk alone after dark without feeling threatened.

Micah would laugh at me for that with his big-city ways. I'm sure New York girls are a hundred times smarter and savvier, more experienced in everything from avoiding danger to attracting men.

They'd know how to make the man they want look at them with hungry eyes.

Me, I only seem to attract the one I *don't* want.

Isn't that usually how it goes?

I try to make my brain shut up.

Self-awareness sucks.

I tell myself not to think about it.

Not to get all giddy as I make my way through a night drenched in the scent of azaleas and just warm enough to feel pleasant. Until I turn down the lane where Micah's house sits in its own little glade.

It's shaded by old trees, settled on a neat lawn with a small pond glimmering to one side. The modern timber-frame house looks so cosmopolitan against Redhaven's classic colonials, all sharp angles and clean edges.

Just like Micah Ainsley himself.

The porch light's on, casting gold everywhere, but the tall windows fronting the house look dark, only faint glimmers inside. Even if I tell my heart to settle down, it's thumping by the time I knock on his door.

It thumps even harder when he answers.

He's still in his uniform slacks, crisp and blue and pressed just right, highlighting the angle of his hips. But he's stripped down to a black short-sleeved undershirt that clings to his body like paint, hugging his chest and nearly snapping at the seams over sculpted biceps.

His silvery-white hair looks disarrayed tonight, falling into his eyes.

And those silvery eyes seem dilated behind a pair of thin rimless glasses.

A glass tumbler filled with gold liquid surrounding large ice cubes dangles from one hand.

Oh, my.

No wonder he wanted to meet here instead of in public. It would probably look sketchy for an upstanding officer of Redhaven PD to be tipsy among the people, even if he's not on duty.

Micah leans against the doorframe with a long, brooding look.

He's so unreadable I feel naked, every inch of me prickling as he takes me in. I want to say *hello*, but I can't look away from him until Rolf thrusts his head past Micah's leg.

The dog looks up at me with guarded curiosity, laying his ears back.

"Still hates me, huh?" I manage a smile, clutching the strap of my bag.

"I told you, he's stubborn." Micah stares, then takes a step back. "Come on in."

I follow him inside.

It really does feel like stepping into a wild animal's den.

The entire house is *dark*, paneled in mocha shades of wood in interlocking accent patterns to create a subtle motif.

Black stone makes up the rough-tiled floor, the massive fireplace, and the lower wall accents. The furniture is all black leather, too, with hints of glinting steel here and there.

It's almost too classy for small-town North Carolina.

"I feel like I just stepped through a portal. Right into your fancy New York condo."

Micah stops mid-stride, looking over his shoulder.

I can only make out one blue-grey eye past the gleam of his glasses, but it's hard, *bitter*.

Oof.

Maybe I shouldn't have said that, even if I'm not sure why it upsets him.

I feel like I've earned the wary looks from Rolf as the dog pads along in our wake, his nails clicking on the tile. We head for the basement.

But Micah only shakes his head and moves on, nodding at the seating arrangement around the crackling fireplace.

"Pick a spot and make yourself comfortable," he says. There's a grittier edge to his voice, like the alcohol just scoured his throat. And it turns huskier, even more burned, as he takes a deep sip from the tumbler, making his way over to the long wet bar in glossy black lacquer along the room's back wall. "What's your poison?"

I blink, drifting toward an overstuffed leather chair.

"Uh, good question. I don't drink much to be honest. Just the occasional beer now and then with Grandpa."

"Hmm." He sets his tumbler down on the bartop with a *clink* and slips behind the bar. "Do you like sweet or tart?"

"Depends on the mood." I sink down in the chair, holding my bag in my lap. "I think tart sounds good right now."

"I can work with that."

Whatever I'm expecting, it's not the way he moves—graceful, efficient, slinging bottles onto the counter and whipping out a cocktail glass with practiced ease.

His big hands move like magic as he pours.

I don't even see the labels except for the lime juice.

In under a minute, he's whipped up something green and translucent with sugar around the rim and a fresh lime crescent wedged onto the cocktail glass. I think there's a sprig of mint in the concoction, too.

"Wow." I can smell it from here, breathing deeply. "That was *so cool*."

Micah blinks like he's snapping awake from a trance.

He glances over almost sheepishly as he stuffs the bottles back under the bar, closing a concealed fridge with a faint thump.

"Hardly," he says. "I just paid my way through college slinging drinks. Let's see if you hate yours." He picks up my drink and his tumbler, angling around the bar on sinful strides, offering the glass. "Bottom's up."

I take the cool glass and inhale.

It's tart, all right, but nothing overwhelming.

"What is it?"

"Mint lime mojito with a splash of strawberry to take the edge off—and because pink is your middle name." He flops down in the easy chair next to me, propping his whiskey tumbler on his knee, his knuckles bulging around his glass.

Smiling, I take a careful sip, watching him over the rim.

The taste hits in layers.

First the sugar, then a delicate sting of sour lime, right before the strawberry sweetness and crisp mint floods taste buds primed by the lime.

My eyes widen.

"Oh, man, that's *good!*" I sound like such a dork.

But that wins me a weary smile, still bitter and dark. "Maybe I should've stuck with bartending instead of chasing phantoms here. I could've saved us a lot of trouble."

Concern whips through me.

"Micah? Are you okay?" I hold my glass close in both hands.

He looks away with forced detachment before he speaks again.

"I don't come from a high-class background. I'm from a hole in the wall in Queens. My mother died giving birth to me. My father drank every waking moment and beat me and my brother raw. I was his favorite. White skin. The perfect canvas for blood and bruises." His voice is so empty, so cold, so much emotion buried soul-deep. That fierce, chilling smile resurfaces. "I'm not asking for your sympathy. Isn't it ironic that I escaped alcoholic hell as a bartender?"

I don't know what to say.

My heart aches for him, and I don't want to say a single word to hurt him more than he's already suffered.

If he wasn't a little drunk himself, I doubt he'd be saying this stuff.

But I'm frozen, torn between the ache of wanting to comfort him and this feeling like I should keep my distance.

Rolf breaks away from his spot near Micah's chair and trots over with a little whine, his ears perking. I'm half expecting him to snarl at me for upsetting his master, but instead, he grumbles and lays his head on my knee, looking up at me.

Like he's asking me to fix this.

To help Micah when he can't.

I pry one hand away from my glass and scratch between his ears. "*Now* you like me, huh?"

Micah glances back at me, his mouth a humorless line. "He's a better mind reader than me. What are you thinking right now, Shortcake?"

I hesitate, too focused on scratching Rolf, who leans against my leg.

I don't just want to say the right words. I want the honest ones.

"Mostly that I don't want you to regret telling me any of that," I whisper.

"Interesting answer." Micah's heavy gaze weighs on me before he leans forward to scratch Rolf's ruff. "Guess he likes it."

And you? I wonder. *What do you think?*

But I don't ask him.

I just go still as my hand strays down Rolf's head while Micah's hand moves up.

Our fingers brush.

We both stop moving.

Our eyes lock.

There's an electric charge that feels like static.

My stomach twists, my heart pounding as Micah holds my eyes.

God, I still don't understand what I'm seeing there.

But I feel like those eyes could swallow me up, this hypnotic gaze watching me above the lenses of his glasses, drawing me in until I'm willing prey to this wild creature.

For a moment, we lean toward each other.

Then Rolf lets out a curious sound, shoving his head between us and knocking us away from each other.

Inhaling sharply, I pull back.

Micah looks away, still scratching the dog but no longer looking at me.

"What did you find today? Anything useful?" he asks gruffly.

Right.

Business.

That comes first and apparently last.

I try to calm my fluttery insides but it's like my pulse is on fire. I take a sip of the cool drink just to focus on something else before I speak again.

"A lot of things. I talked to Joseph Peters alone, very briefly. He knew the woman who died there last year. Cora Lafayette, right? He said she treated him like family, and he's clearly still bitter about it."

"He might be open to turning the tables on the people responsible for her death, then. And since Aleksander isn't around, Xavier could be the next best thing."

"Maybe," I say with a shrug. "I don't know. I feel like I upset him. He might not want anything to do with us."

"You'd be surprised what revenge will push you to do, Talia."

Micah would know, wouldn't he?

I lick my lips, catching a few stray grains of sugar.

"There's something else. When I got to Xavier's office, he was sniffing my scarf—the one I forgot there the other day." Micah's head whips toward me, his eyes narrowing as I rush on. "And, um, he had a little silver tray with a business card on it. I swear there were a few streaks of white powder. I think he was high. His eyes were odd and really jittery."

"Rewind," Micah snaps. "He was *sniffing* your scarf? What the fuck?"

I wince. "...y-yeah. He said my perfume smelled like flowers and he was trying to figure out which ones so he could keep them in the house. I told him I don't wear perfume."

"Go on." Micah's brows twitch dangerously. "What else did he say?"

I swallow thickly.

"That it must be my own natural scent. Gross, I know. I kind of zoned out because I was a little freaked."

"That fucking man is lucky I don't slit his throat."

I do a double take.

He says it so calmly, so matter-of-factly, like it's just an everyday thing to contemplate brutally killing a man over insulting a girl he barely knows.

I stare at him and he stares back, fierce and sharp as a blade. Then he lets out a ragged sigh and looks away.

"Relax. I'm not looking for prison time."

"Oh, I wasn't— I didn't—" Oh God. I'm dizzy, and I take a quick gulp of my drink just to steady myself. "You know that woman we saw camping? The one with the Jacobins?"

"What about her?" Micah immediately sharpens.

"She was there." It's easier to focus on hard facts and not how I suddenly feel very vulnerable in the gold-tinted darkness of Micah's den in this pretty little dress with him so close. It's not a bad feeling. I kinda *like* the strange thrill of it, but it still makes me nervous so I just ramble to distract myself. "The tall one in the old-fashioned dress? The mean-looking one? When Xavier walked me out, I saw her hanging around the front foyer behind the door. She stared at me the entire time. It was really creepy. Like she was mad at me."

"More like marking you," Micah growls. "That's something, all right. I've never seen Xavier Arrendell and the Jacobins together with my own eyes. You just did. She's probably relying on the fact that you won't recognize her, but hell…"

"I'm a witness to the link." I swallow. "But I *don't* recognize her, besides seeing her that night. I don't even know her."

"Eustace," Micah answers grimly. "Eustace Jacobin, Ephraim Jacobin's wife. Mother of the late Culver Jacobin and a mess of other kids. I've long suspected she's the real brains behind their entire operation."

"Huh?" I stare. "I didn't even know Ephraim had a wife. I've seen the Jacobins lurking around my whole life and I've never seen her."

"For good reason," he replies. His expression is a cold mask, dark with loathing. "You can't arrest her if you barely know she exists. She hides in the shadows, pulling strings with clever fingers. A black widow."

He leans close to me until our knees bump with Rolf trapped between us, so intensely *near* that I squeak.

Embarrassing.

But I'm caught up in those stormy eyes again and the harsh, almost desperate way he stares at me, his lips pulling back from his teeth.

"Never go out alone after dark again," he bites off. "I'll take you home tonight. Be careful. Always stay in plain sight of others. If you see the Jacobins in town, ignore them. Don't acknowledge them, don't glance in their direction. If Eustace Jacobin thinks you're a threat, or even just a loose end…"

He doesn't have to finish that thought.

The horrid danger hangs in the air between us, heavy and frightening, making my heart hammer.

Or maybe it's not the threat of the Jacobins hanging over my head.

It's more that Micah is so close I can feel his breath, just barely teasing my lips. And I can't escape how he is when he's this fired up.

His skin flushes in beautiful hints of red against white skin, making his red mouth stand out more starkly, so unintentionally sensuous it's obscene.

The man is mystery and moonlight, an arctic fox, and the firelight licks gold along his cheekbones and swims in his eyes.

When his gaze drops to my mouth, I shiver.

And I realize he's staring at me as intently as I'm staring at him.

There's something there.

Something I've never experienced in my life, and it pulls me closer.

This dangerous thing, so dark and hot it makes the air vibrate as he sways closer, too.

His teeth gleam white, just past his parted lips—hungry, so hungry, just like the stars in his eyes.

This is pure want.

The kind I know too well.

Wanting the anticipation building between us.

Wanting the way my lips tingle as he tilts his head, bending over me, so close, deliciously oppressive as I rise to meet him and—

Rolf shoves his big furry head between us, panting cheerfully and nosing for attention.

I pull back with a muffled sound.

Micah slumps back too, giving me an almost guilty look before he turns his head away, looking through the tall windows to the pond at night.

He adjusts his glasses and strokes a soothing hand between Rolf's ears, taking another sip of his whiskey, but he says nothing.

Holy hell.

I don't even know what to do with this much tension.

So I just look down into my drink. I'm tempted to throw the rest down to ease this feeling inside me, but when I get too drunk, I get even *more* jittery. So I just take a delicate sip, filling the silent, strained seconds.

Maybe I should let myself out.

I said what I came to say, after all.

He knows he can hit up Joseph Peters, and he knows I saw Eustace Jacobin at the manor. Just like he knows I probably caught Xavier when he was high as a kite.

This is a business meeting. Nothing more.

So I really should go and stop flipping daydreaming.

"Listen to me, Talia. If Xavier Arrendell ever lays a hand on you, you tell me," Micah says, still staring out the window. "I will break every last one of that man's fingers into pebbles."

I blink. "He... he didn't try. I promise. And I won't let him!"

"What makes you think he'll give you a choice?" Micah growls. Then he tosses back his drink and clunks the tumbler onto the black glass coffee table. He stands, hooking his fingers in Rolf's collar and gently helping him to his feet. "Take your time with your drink. There's water under the bar too if you need it. It's time for his walk. When you're done, wait for me and I'll walk you home."

What, he's leaving?

He doesn't wait for me to answer, to find my words.

To ask him why the hell he almost kissed me and what we're going to do about it.

There's only the angry line of his back and the unbreachable distance of a man I can't begin to comprehend. He leaves me staring after him as he walks away, fetching Rolf's leash from a hook by the sliding door before he leads the dog out into the night.

Leaving me alone, with more questions than answers and the lingering scent of his smoky whiskey breath still clinging to my skin.

X: DARK TIMES (MICAH)

That man is definitely dead.

I sink down on one knee at the edge of a sharp drop-off, deep in the woods in the hills past the outskirts of town.

Grant, Lucas, and Henri lean over me, peering down the rocky cliff to the bottom.

There, the body of a man in his late twenties wearing jeans and hiking boots sprawls, broken on the rocks. His blood spatters the fallen leaves and dirt from where his head appears to have struck one of the larger boulders.

"Well," Grant drawls at my back. "This looks pretty open and shut. Just gotta get down there and get the poor guy into a bag."

"Does it?" That's all I say.

Lucas and Grant both let out exasperated sounds. They know that one simple question means this case will be more work than it's worth.

"Someone want to explain?" Henri looks confused.

I turn my head to the left, toward the peak of the high ground where we're clustered. We've kept ourselves to a very small area, stepping carefully so there's no disturbing the possible crime scene—like the uneven earth and blades of grass right where the cliff juts out to a little point.

Several overgrown tufts of grass look snapped in half by a boot. There's a chunk of dirt kicked away, exposing fresh soil and threads of grassy roots.

Also, more broken grass leading up to the edge.

Footsteps.

If I'm right, those footsteps belong to more than one person.

"The obvious answer is that he was hiking," I start slowly. "He didn't know the area or else he got too close to the edge and it broke off under his weight. He fell, and the rest is history."

"Don't, Micah. Don't even." Lucas groans. "Look, man, we know you think something else is up. C'mon, what's that bloodhound nose of yours telling you?"

"That if any of you boys move another inch, you might fuck up a crime scene."

I peer over my shoulder.

The crew freezes while Lucas gives me a dirty look, his green eyes piercing over his black beard. He's wearing it thicker these days with married life and all.

I smirk.

"Just stay away from the path leading up to the ledge," I say, bracing my hands against my thighs and pushing to my feet. "Doesn't look like there's anything else, though we should have a thorough look just in case. Someone might have dropped something."

Grant gives me a solemn look—his ordinary look, really—always so grave. "Stop going around in goddamn circles. Fill us in."

I circle around the team and stop just shy of a little divot in the earth, this churned-up grass in the shape of a heel.

"For starters, this wasn't made by a hiking boot," I tell them, pointing.

Suddenly, I've got a crowd gathered around me.

Three grown men the size of bears, practically tiptoeing like ballerinas to see what I'm looking at without stomping on anything crucial.

Henri frowns, crouching next to me, looking at the footprint.

"Don't quote me on this, *mes amis*," he drawls in that thick Cajun accent. He's so bad we've started calling him Gambit lately. "Need to get a good look at the vic's shoe size, but I'd say this was a smaller foot. A loafer, maybe. No treads on the sole, half-moon heel."

"There's a pattern of steps overlapping his. Here, see the larger sections of crushed grass? That says more weight, deeper heel divots, then smaller steps, smaller feet, different shoe," I point out. "Somebody followed him. Their heel imprints don't fit inside his, so they weren't tracing his steps. But they were right on his ass. Their steps overlap, sometimes blur his. The second set of steps goes both ways—right to the ledge before they turn around and come back. The victim's, they don't."

Grant heaves out a long, rough sigh, dragging a hand over his bearish brown eyes. "Really? Do we really need *another* murder case?"

"We've got to earn our pay somehow, Captain," I answer dryly, though this isn't fucking funny at all.

It reeks to high heaven.

"You know, guys," Lucas says, "it's possible he was just here with someone. What if he fell, and the other person panicked and ran without reporting it? Might've been scared they'd be blamed for his death. People turn into idiots all the time."

"Maybe," Henri says. "But if someone was out hiking with

him, they'd be wearing boots. This looks more like... dress shoes?"

Yeah, I think he's right.

There's a nagging suspicion teasing at me.

Dress shoes or loafers—or the severe church-style shoes of someone who dresses like she just stepped out of the year 1800.

Grant grunts. "We'll sort that out by working the scene. Let's start off by seeing if he's got any ID on him. He's definitely not a townie or anyone I recognize. So we'll find out who he is, where he came from, and see if we can track down anyone connected." He rubs a finger to the side of his nose, giving us all that baleful, stern Captain Faircross look. "Let's keep a lid on the murder talk for now until we can dig up more information."

Henri frowns, tapping a hand against his knee. "I dunno, Cap. I trust Micah's instincts on this. Man's got a nose like a wolf. Feral instincts, tracks like an animal."

"I don't know if that's a compliment," I mutter before Grant cuts us off with a sharp sound.

"Split up, you bozos. Work the scene, document evidence," he says. "Micah and Henri, head down the hill. I'll call in the paramedic team to get the body lifted, but do what you can to find the evidence. Photograph everything. Lucas and I will photograph the footprints up here."

"Yes, sir, Captain." I snap off a sardonic salute.

That just gets me an eyeroll. Henri grins, straightening and tossing his head, sending his long shag of brown hair flopping.

"C'mon, *renard arctique*." *Arctic fox*. "Let's go find out who this guy is."

Shaking my head, I turn to follow Henri.

We pick our way around the main path up the slope and into the trees, toward where the ground slopes more gently to the bottom and we can skid through without too much effort. The guys always tease me for the way I analyze crime scenes, but right now it's really sticking with me.

Maybe because it's how Talia sees me, too.

The way she reacts like I'm an animal, dangerous and feral.

Last night, I almost fucking kissed her.

Blame it on the whiskey, sure.

But like hell I'll be my father, blaming every bad move on booze alone.

I know full well it wasn't the bottle.

Truth is, it took everything in my power not to fucking eat her whole when she showed up on my doorstep in that gauzy little dress that let me see the freckles on her shoulders, strewn around the soft curves of her tits. Every last dot made me want to bite her.

To taste her.

To sink my teeth in until she screams.

She looked so innocent. My own Little Red Riding Hood.

And I've never felt more like the big bad wolf.

I need to keep my hands to myself—because she *is* innocent, and the only thing I can do is taint her.

I'm terrible with fragile things.

Right now, I also need to keep my mind on the job, instead of thinking about this ache in the pit of my stomach that makes me want to go find her for no other reason than the fact that I can.

I *know* I can, and she'd just look at me with those wide blue eyes, like she sees something in me I can't see myself.

As we reach the bottom of the slope and break through the trees, we nearly trip over the victim's bag.

Looks like it went tumbling free as he fell and landed several feet away. I put down an evidence marker and leave it where it is until I can photograph it later.

We make our way to the fallen man, flanking him and avoiding the blood as we bend for a better look. Henri pulls several nitrile gloves from the breast pocket of his uniform, shakes them out, and offers me a pair.

"Thanks." I snap the gloves on and then carefully grip the man's chin. He's got sandy-brown hair and a scruffy hipster beard.

His eyes are wide open, pale brown.

There's a sort of quiet shock etched on his dead face. Like he was startled right before the lights went out.

I gently turn his head left and right.

There's a little stiffness.

"Rigor. He's been dead for a few hours, at least. No other signs of trauma. So the impact is definitely the cause of death."

I carefully settle his head back in the exact position where I found it, then fish my phone from my pocket and start snapping photos. Henri frowns.

"No bloating, not seeing any discoloration," he says quietly. "Damn, so when? Maybe this morning?"

"Late last night," I answer, carefully capturing his position and the blood spread with my phone. "There's dew on his skin. It hasn't rained, but there's liquid pooled in the corners of his eyelids and under his neck. Plus, the blood looks like it's been congealing for at least six hours."

"I will never get over how you notice things like that, *mon ami*." Henri stares at me in awe.

"Check his clothes. If they're damp, you'll see I'm right."

Henri carefully pushes up the flap on the breast pocket of the man's red and black plaid flannel shirt. "Yep. Just a lil' wet, but there. Oh—" He whistles softly as he fishes a soft black leather billfold out of the victim's pocket. "What do we have here?"

He flips open the billfold. In the small laminated window,

an ID peers out at us. He arches both brows and offers it to me.

I snag it with two fingers.

"Brian Newcomb of California," I rattle off. "Time to find out what Brian was doing in Redhaven so far from home."

* * *

It doesn't take long to track down Mr. Newcomb.

Within a couple hours, we've marked, photographed, and packed up the crime scene, transferring the body over to Raleigh's morgue and a proper workover by the Raleigh PD forensics team.

We don't have much bagged and tagged to enter into evidence except the backpack and billfold, and when we break everything down to catalogue what's inside, we just find a canteen, a change of clothes, a pop-up tent, emergency knife and rope, flashlight—the usual camping supplies, along with his phone.

It's his phone that leads us to pay dirt.

It takes our dispatch officer, Mallory, two seconds to get past his lockscreen, revealing a history of texts as recent as last night with a contact named Ariana Lewis. Girlfriend, judging from the conversation.

Looks like she's staying at The Rookery.

Janelle Bowden greets me warmly when I stop by the bed and breakfast.

I can't help being reserved with her, wondering if she's oblivious to Chief Bowden's side hustle or an accomplice, as hard as it seems to imagine. I flash my professional smile and lean against the counter.

"Afternoon, Mrs. Bowden," I say. "Came by to see one of your guests. Ariana Lewis? Here with her boyfriend?"

"Oh, yes—those two." She flutters a little over the

keyboard of her computer. "They're staying in the Statesman suite on the third floor, second door from the right. I've been bringing the poor girl hot water bottles all day. She's having a terrible time with—oh." She drops her voice as primly as any proper lady of a small colonial town. "You know. That time of the month."

"Sounds rough," I say dryly, pushing away from the counter. "Thanks. I won't be long."

"Is something wrong?" She gives me a worried look.

"Yes, but let me talk to her first," I call back, already heading for the polished oak stairs leading up to the walkway ringing the upper floors.

I can feel Janelle's eyes following me as I make my way up to the third-floor landing—but I don't look back.

Maybe she's completely out of the loop with all this.

But with most murders in this town tied to the Arrendells and the Arrendells tied to the Jacobins and the Jacobins tied to her husband?

I'm not about to trust her with anything related to a pending investigation.

Even if, technically, I should be reporting those details to my boss.

Hell, I haven't seen Chief Bowden in the office for days. There's a sort of mutual understanding with the guys now.

We don't tell him anything if we don't have to.

We can all do our jobs just fine without him, running on autopilot.

When I knock on the right door, a soft, feminine voice calls through it, "Coming, just a minute!"

I hear a faint shuffling from inside before the door pulls open on a small, thin blonde girl with a wispy layered cut and sad brown eyes. She can't be older than twenty-five.

She's very obviously just thrown on the fluffy sky-blue

bathrobe wrapped around her. She'd started to smile—but when she sees my uniform, that fades.

She frowns as her eyes flick down to the shield on my chest and then back to my face.

"Can I help you?"

"Ariana Lewis? Officer Micah Ainsley, Redhaven PD." I offer my hand. "Mind if I come in to talk?"

"What's this about?" She eyes my hand suspiciously but doesn't take it.

I hold in my sigh.

I'm not the best person for this.

I can be a little too clipped, too blunt. Then again, there's never an easy way to tell someone their partner is dead.

Even so, I try to soften my voice as I say, "It's about your boyfriend. Brian Newcomb?"

"Oh, no." Her eyes widen. She clutches harder at her bathrobe like it can protect her. "Is he in jail?"

"No, Miss Lewis." I shake my head. "It's a little more complicated than that. I think we should talk alone."

She goes pale—but I think she's starting to get the idea, and at least I've gently eased her into considering the possibility before slapping her in the face with the ugly truth.

"Um, okay." Eventually, she nods, swallowing thickly and stepping back. "Come on in."

I follow her into the suite.

It's a two-room unit in the usual rustic antebellum style Janelle favors, all lace curtains and wood furniture. I recognize the woodwork from A Touch of Grey.

Ariana and Brian seem to have settled in for a little while. There's none of the usual disarray of people living out of suitcases, just a little camping equipment against the wall of the combination living room and kitchen.

Ariana flutters her hands a little, standing between the kitchenette and the dining table. "Can I get you tea or…?"

"Would tea make you feel better?" I ask. "And do you mind if I sit?"

"No, go ahead, I—" She stares at me for a few moments longer. She *knows*. As I sink down into one of the ladderback chairs at the table, she whirls away from me, picking at cabinet doors and an electric kettle.

"...he didn't text me back this morning," she says miserably, looking at her hands.

I fold my hands on the table.

"When was the last time you heard from him, Miss Lewis?"

"Last night." Her voice gets smaller with every word, and she's holding the electric kettle under the faucet without turning the water on, just staring at it in her hands. "Around nine o'clock, I think? I said I was turning in early because I didn't feel well, and... I sent him kisses. He sent kisses back and said he was going to stay up late to do some wildlife photography." She lifts her head, turning a wistful smile over her shoulder. Her eyes are pleading. "That's what he does, you know? He wants to work for the big magazines, the ones still in print, but he's sold some really gorgeous pieces to nature magazines while he builds his portfolio. So, when he didn't text back, I figured he just got wrapped up in his shoot and stayed up all night, then crawled into his tent and crashed." Her laugh is brittle. She abruptly snaps the faucet on with a jerky movement, filling the kettle. "He'd never sleep if I didn't remind him, but I didn't go with him this time."

Interesting.

We didn't find a camera with his body.

We circled the whole area in a broad sweep and found a burned-out campfire. The ashes were old enough that he likely set up camp there before his death, then moved on and hadn't put down stakes that night before his mishap.

If he had a camera on him, we'd have found it nearby, even if it wasn't in his bag. It's possible he lost it somewhere else on the trip, though it doesn't seem likely.

"Janelle said you weren't feeling well?" I ask.

"Yeah, I—sorry for the TMI—but I have PCOS. Sometimes I get cramps so bad I can't walk. I have to stay in bed." She shrugs stiffly. "He offered to stay with me, of course, but I didn't want him to miss out on this when it's why we came out here. I told him to go have fun."

It's not hard to tell what she's thinking.

That I'm about to say her boyfriend's dead, and he might not be if she'd just asked him to stay.

"Miss Lewis," I say gently. "I want you to know that what I'm about to tell you isn't your fault."

She closes her eyes.

What I can see of her face over her shoulder crumples.

"…no. No, it's not, he can't be… Jesus, tell me he's not?"

"I can't tell you that, ma'am." I choose my words very carefully. I let her piece it together, holding back a blunt statement of fact.

Not optimal, but kinder than dropping a ten-ton sledgehammer on her head.

The kettle falls from her fingers and bangs in the steel sink.

She clutches her hands against the edge of the counter, her shoulders hunching.

She just stands there for more than a minute, her eyes closing, the only sound between us the rush of water from the faucet.

I know I should say something here.

I don't know how.

What would Talia do? I remember her first thought when I got my stupid ass drunk and spilled my shit all over her.

How she didn't want me to regret trusting her with that

information. That told me more than anything how much she cared about never using that to hurt me.

Is it any wonder I wanted to kiss her?

I think I know what Talia Grey would say if she were here right now.

"I'm sorry, Miss Lewis." I've always thought apologies were empty, weak platitudes that can't bring the dead back or unfuck wrongs. It sure wouldn't bring my dead brother back.

But that's not what I'm apologizing for.

I'm apologizing for having to hurt her, for having to shatter her life this way.

That's fucking genuine, and the one thing I can give her right now is real honesty.

"I wish I could tell you it would be all right, Miss Lewis. I'm afraid I can't. Do you want me to tell you what we found?"

She opens her eyes, staring into the sink.

I catch a tear sliding down her cheek, visible from my angle.

"Y-yes! Tell me," she whispers.

"He fell. From a rather steep cliff," I say. "The drop was massive. His skull struck the rocks at the base of the cliff. It's very likely he felt nothing; it would have been quick."

"Quick doesn't make him less… less dead," she stammers, sobbing.

That sob turns heavy fast—and I move quickly to rest my hands on her shoulders, giving her a gentle push toward the table.

"Sit," I urge. "I'll make your tea."

Crying herself hoarse, she staggers over to the chair I just left abandoned, drops down, and buries her face in her hands.

Fuck, I hate this.

I give her a moment to cry it out, without forcing her to think about me at all, and retrieve her kettle from the sink to finish what she started.

While the water heats, I fish out a mug and a teabag, grab the kettle just before it screams, and fill the mug.

By the time I slide the tea in front of her, she's starting to calm down, violent heartbreak dying into sniffles.

I settle in the chair across from her, trying not to be obvious about watching her.

She's small enough that the footprints in the grass could have belonged to her, but I don't think she's faking this reaction.

Some people can cry on demand, but not like this.

This is real.

Full-body, racking grief that speaks of true pain.

The kind of howl from the heart I knew when I stepped into the morgue to identify my brother's body.

Miss Lewis takes a shaking breath and wipes at her eyes. "I'm... I'm sorry..."

"Don't be." I shake my head. "You're allowed to be upset. Take all the time you need."

She curls her hands around the steaming mug, staring into it.

"I just can't believe it," she whispers. "He's been hiking his whole life. And now he just, what? Slipped in the dark? He was that careless?"

Damn.

Now comes the hard part.

"Miss Lewis, judging from the footprints at the scene, we suspect Brian wasn't alone last night."

"What?" Her eyes fly to me. "What are you saying? Did... did someone push him? *Who?*"

I don't say anything, watching her carefully.

She goes pale, recoiling.

"Wait. Am I... am I a suspect?"

"Highly unlikely," I answer quickly. "However, it would help if you had an alibi so I don't have to trouble you any further."

"Mrs. Bowden," she rushes out. "She's been checking on me. She knows I didn't leave my room at all last night, or even today."

"I'll talk to Janelle and make sure that's in the police report." I lean in closer, watching her. "Can you think of anyone who wanted to hurt Brian?"

"God, no! We don't even know anyone here," she flares. "We're from Sacramento. It's... we've been together since high school. We do everything together. We love going on these trips, but like, anyone who doesn't like us would be back in California."

"And the locals? You haven't had any trouble with them? No drunken bar altercations or road rage?"

"No. Absolutely nothing." She smiles sadly. "We never went to the bars. We'd go shopping together, but everyone here has been so nice. I can't imagine anyone wanting to hurt him."

"Of course." I lean back in the chair, tapping my fingers on the table. "It may have been a crime of opportunity. It's also possible it was still an accident and someone else stumbled on the scene and fled after the fact."

I doubt it.

The depth of the impressions and the dryness of the earth made it clear they happened not long after each other. Moist, exposed dirt from the first set of boot prints would have dried enough in the open air that if someone had stepped over those prints later, the ground would have crumbled differently under their heels.

Still, I don't want to say anything conclusive to a grieving girl when I can't confirm anything yet.

She looks skeptical, though.

She looks at me like she *wants* something from me, something more, and I'm suddenly wishing for Talia again. She'd understand what this hurt, confused young woman truly needs when she stares at me that way.

But then Miss Lewis looks away, staring at the wall.

No, at the camping equipment stacked there, I realize.

She's playing through her regrets, wondering what would have happened if she'd been with him.

"What now?" she asks hollowly. "What will you do? What do *I* do?"

"I'm going to pursue an active investigation. We'll try to get an idea what happened out in the woods. Narrow down possible suspects. Can you stay in town for a few more days? Just in case I need to ask you questions about the investigation or anyone else you've spoken to here."

"S-sure." Her eyes well up again and she presses her lips together. "I don't know how to go home and tell his parents, *my* parents. God, they… they really loved him. But I have to stay in this room by myself?"

"Is there anyone you can call?" I ask softly. "Someone who could come out and be with you?"

"My sister," she says. "She'd drop everything for me."

There's warmth in her ragged voice, and I smile slightly. "I know that feeling."

"You have siblings?"

"A brother. I lost him just as unexpectedly. So believe me when I say I *do* understand what you're feeling right now."

Until this past month, before Talia, I wouldn't be able to tell a complete stranger something so personal.

Something about that girl changes the way I think.

The decisions I make.

It's like I don't want to ruin the misguided faith she has in me.

Miss Lewis' sorrowful eyes search mine.

"How did you get over it? How do you move on?"

"I don't know. That's the hard part," I say softly. "It's different for everyone. Some days, I wonder if I'll ever move on at all."

Her lips curl in a bitter, understanding smile, and she looks away, rubbing at her nose. "You probably need to go, don't you?"

"That depends," I say, even as I ask myself what the hell I'm doing. "Do you need me to stay?"

It's like that one question shatters her.

Suddenly, she's crying again, curling over her untouched tea mug and bawling herself out with a broken, "...p-please. Please d-don't leave me alone just yet..."

"Okay, Miss Lewis." I reach across the table and cover her hand with mine. "I'm here, as long as you need me."

* * *

I'M STARTING to wonder if I'm getting tunnel vision.

If I've gotten so wrapped up in this long, slow game with Xavier Arrendell and the Jacobins, in maintaining my cover in Redhaven, that I've forgotten what's really important.

The human factor.

Sitting there for nearly half an hour, holding this stranger's hand while she cries herself into an exhausted sleep.

For the first time in ages, I feel like a *person*. Not a hard, cold automaton stuffed into a uniform with a quiet rage.

Shit.

What happens if I *do* take down the Jacobins? If I get my justice for Jet?

What will I be after that?

What can I be?

It feels like the same question Ariana Lewis has been asking herself since the moment I told her Brian Newcomb was dead.

That grim realization that her life has a different purpose now, and she doesn't know who she'll be once her grieving is all said and done.

That weighs heavy on my mind as I politely excuse myself and head back into the expansive sunlit lobby later.

Janelle looks up from the front desk, pulling at her bobbed hair.

"You were up there for a while," she says. "Is everything all right?"

"No." I stop, leaning one arm against the desk. "We found her boyfriend dead at the bottom of a cliff. Looks like he fell. She's in shock, but if you've got the time to go check on her, I'm sure she'd appreciate it. Probably shouldn't be alone right now. Bring her a meal, something light. Open a tab in my name."

Janelle goes pale, fretting her hands together and looking up toward the room, then back to me.

"Oh dear—oh my God, that poor girl! He was such a nice boy, too. So polite. Lord, that's *terrible*! Don't tell me it's happening here again?"

I wish I didn't have to.

"It is," I agree. "I've asked her to stay in town for a few days while I investigate. She's calling her sister to fly in and stay with her tonight."

"Of course. I'll keep an eye on her until then, don't you worry. And forget about the tab, it's the slow season. I don't need to be down here all evening. I'll go talk to her immediately."

I nod with a brief salute, touching my fingers to my brow. "Much appreciated, Mrs. Bowden. I'll be heading back in to work now."

She switches her gaze to me with a weak smile. "Of course. It just never ends around here. Take care, Officer Ainsley."

I only nod and turn to walk away—but then her voice drifts after me.

"Oh, and could you stop keeping my husband so late?" she calls, her voice brittle, a weak attempt at forced humor. "Honestly, you're all such workaholics. He hasn't been home before midnight in ages."

I stop, turning back to her.

She's just looking at me.

Her eyes are almost desperate.

Like she's begging me for answers.

I should probably lie to her. Say something comforting. Make a goofy joke. Mind my own business.

Not open a huge fucking can of worms.

Too bad I've never been one for lying.

And I'll admit, I want to know if she's really as innocent and sweet as she seems. Wouldn't be the first time appearances were wrong here in Redhaven.

"Mrs. Bowden, you must be mistaken?" I ask slowly. "Chief Bowden's called out sick for the past two weeks. We haven't seen hide nor hair of him at the office."

"O-oh." It's less shocked and more resigned. Even so, she shakes her head with swift denial. "Wow. Okay. That... that doesn't make sense, though. Where does he go every day?"

I stare at her pointedly.

"You tell me, ma'am. Surely, you must have some idea?"

Janelle Bowden's a smart woman. She'll put two and two together.

For now, she's apparently committed to sticking her head in the sand, because she shakes her head fiercely, pressing her lips together.

"I don't. But there must be a logical explanation, I'm sure."

"Sure. You'll just have to ask yourself if you're okay with what that explanation means."

She doesn't say anything, only stares with a stricken look.

I've done enough damage for today.

I turn and walk out into the bright-red glow of the evening sun.

I'm fucking crushed as I make my way back to the station on foot.

The question of who killed Brian Newcomb and why.

The heaviness of Miss Lewis' grief and my weird reaction to it.

The shock etched on Janelle's face and just what her denial might be hiding.

What the chief might be *doing* every day when it's not feasible that he's hanging around the Jacobins all day.

My intuition tells me there's something deeper going on, something goddamned disturbing.

Bowden's always been off.

The man smiles a little too easy, a little too bright, and he laughs at the oddest times. It's like he puts a lot of effort into being disarming and harmless.

As I head down the street toward the station, I pass A Touch of Grey.

I can't help glancing in the shop window, but Talia's nowhere in sight. She's probably holed up in the workshop in the back.

Move on, I tell myself, but I stop when a faint jingle across the street and a flash of sunlight off glass catch my attention.

Out of habit, I scan that direction.

Then stop.

Ephraim Jacobin steps out of the butcher's shop on the other side of the lane.

He's a lean specter cut in black, dressed in their archaic-looking handmade clothes with a buttoned shirt and neat pants and suspenders. His wide-brimmed hat lays low over his face and his thick black and grey beard bells out over his chest.

There's nothing inherently wrong about Ephraim stopping at the butcher's. The Jacobins sell pig meat and blood to the shop all the time.

Still, I don't like how he stops one bit.

How his head turns toward me.

No—not me.

He's looking at Talia's shop.

The man stares at the window for too long, his scarecrow expression unreadable—right before his eyes snap to me with a sharpness that says he knows I'm watching.

He knows why.

I see it in the slimy, overly polite way he tips his hat at me.

Yeah, I don't fucking like it. Don't like him being within a hundred yards of Talia.

My teeth are clenched as I hold his eyes.

Then I turn and walk pointedly inside her shop.

XI: DARK DESIRES (TALIA)

I barely register the bell over the shop door jingling.

Not when Grandpa and I practically have our heads knocked together, poring over a sample book of wood grains and finishes and fabrics, debating color, texture, and etching methods.

We've been at it all morning, ever since I showed him my revised sketches and asked his opinion on adding Xavier's indoor water installations without making everything too awkward.

He just lit up.

I love when he's like this, how he still sparks alive with a creative challenge.

Honestly, his energy feels contagious, and I've been buzzing all day.

We've just settled on wall fountains with trickling basins embedded in tiled alcoves and framed in leaf carvings when I notice there's something else grabbing my attention.

I lift my head, squinting against the light like a mole person coming out of the cave.

It takes a few seconds more to realize the bell jolted me from my trance.

"Oh, customer!" I glance back at Grandpa. "I'll be right back."

"Mm-hmm. Thanks, Tally," he murmurs, bent over his sketchbook and scribbling away.

I smile.

He won't even notice I'm gone.

I straighten my babydoll-pink baseball tee and wipe a little sawdust off my jeans, then put on my best customer service smile and step into the front. "Welcome to A Touch of—oh!"

My heart leaps up my throat.

Micah.

As always, he looks a little out of place in the daylight, this inverted shadow man cast in permanent moonlight. Yes, he's still staggeringly handsome, especially in the sleek trim of his uniform.

Something about his stance makes me think of a gunslinger from the Wild West translated to modern times. His hips slouch forward and his heavy belt rides low, giving him this lazy swagger. He's got his thumbs hooked in his belt loops, and his attention snaps to me when I gasp.

"Miss Grey," he greets me, his lips twitching in that subtle way that says this is a *thing* now.

He knows better. I don't even hesitate.

"*Talia.*" But I stop, giving him a closer look, frowning. Even if he's giving me that not-smile I crave so much, there's something heavier and darker there today.

Worry furrows his brows and my frown deepens.

"Micah? What's wrong...?"

He purses his lips, then glances over his shoulder, though I can't make out what he's looking at. "Is there somewhere we can talk? Alone?"

Hello, alarm bells.

But I nod, taking a step back. "This way—our loft is right above the store."

"Let's go."

I turn to lead him into the workshop, although there's a part of me shriveling up as I remember Grandpa grilling me about the 'date' I never had. Hopefully, he's still too caught up in work to notice I'm not alone.

Ha, good luck.

The instant Micah steps into the workshop, his silvery eyes scanning curiously, Grandpa lifts his head and looks at him with a slow, knowing smile.

"Who's this fine young man?" he asks. "You a friend of my Tally-girl? Or are you just here on business?"

Micah doesn't miss a beat.

He steps forward, offering his hand.

"Officer Micah Ainsley. Only Talia can tell you if we're friends. You must be Gerald Grey. I've always admired your work when I've seen it around town."

Grandpa chuckles loudly.

"The boy starts with flattery. Smart." He shakes Micah's hand firmly—then stops, still clasping his hand, giving him a long look. "Strong handshake."

"The only respectful kind." Micah inclines his head.

"Yes, yes, it is."

Whoa.

There's some secret man ritual passing between them, something I don't get. Their hands clasp together almost like warriors meeting off the battlefield.

But I remember now.

A long time ago, before I was born, Grandpa left Redhaven. He doesn't talk about it much, his old combat memories from Vietnam. But upstairs in the albums there are photos where he's young and dapper. Decked out in his uniform, even if his eyes are haunted by war.

That's the way he and Micah look at each other now.

Like soldiers.

Like two men who share a certain strength that makes them kin, even though they've never truly met before.

Soon, Grandpa pats Micah's hand with his other hand, then lets go, smiling brightly. "It's good to see you, young man. Well, up close, I should say, since you didn't come in last night."

Oh. My. God.

"Grandpa, no. He was just walking me home." I drop my face into my hand.

"All I'm saying," Grandpa says innocently, "is that he could've popped in to say hello."

Micah smiles blankly. "Truth be told, I wasn't entirely sober, sir. I wouldn't have made the best first impression."

"Hmph. Not all sober yet he still thinks to walk a girl home after dark, huh?" Grandpa's eyes twinkle. "Tally-girl, you've found a good one."

Oh *no*.

No, no, no, I do not want Micah knowing about my silly little crush.

I definitely don't want to think about how he almost kissed me last night or how maybe he didn't and I just misread the signals.

I don't want *any* of this and I step forward quickly, breathlessly catching Micah's wrist in my fingertips.

"We need to talk about something for work," I say quickly. The man in question stares at me with the most startled look I've ever seen, blinking down at my hand around his wrist and then up at me. He even stumbles a step as I tug him desperately toward the stairs. *Please just go along with it.* "We're heading up."

"Don't forget to make tea!" Grandpa calls after us as I try to drag Micah upstairs. "I'll be going out, so behave yourselves!"

I stop a few steps up, eyeing him past Micah's shoulder. "Where are you going?"

"Errands, girl." He's still feigning innocence. "Don't worry. I'll be fine."

Even if he's feigning innocence... there's a real worry there.

He knows it, too.

He knows I worry when he goes out alone, wondering if he'll have a bad spell and wander off, but he really does seem okay today.

So I nod slowly while he gives me a heavy look.

"Go on," he says.

Sighing, we go before Grandpa has another chance to embarrass me forever.

Once we're up in the loft, I release his hand and stumble away from him.

I feel like I'm going to pass out if I blush any harder. I groan, scrubbing my hands over my face.

"Sorry about that," I say. "He's terrible with me making friends. You know, the sheltered childhood thing and all. I was never much good at it."

"Didn't mind. He seems pretty charming." Micah glances back at the stairs with a discerning look. "He's doing well today?"

"...yeah. Well enough. He's lucid and living in the present." I smile slightly. "The good days really are good." But if I think about that too hard, my emotions will turn me into a wreck, and then I'll end up blubbering all over Micah without even finding out why he's here. So I gesture to the kitchen table, breezing past it to put the kettle on. "What did you come to talk about? I haven't been back to see Xavier yet. We're finalizing some concepts before there's any need to stop by the house again."

"It's not about Xavier. Not exactly," Micah says cryptically. He settles down at the raw wood table, lacing his hands together, his posture perfect. "I caught Ephraim Jacobin lurking around outside your shop."

I blink at him.

His words don't compute.

"...what?" I feel faint, dropping the kettle and moving to the window, looking out on the street. I tweak the pale-yellow curtains aside, trying not to be obvious.

I immediately bounce back with a strangled sound.

There's no mistaking that lean scarecrow figure across the street.

Jesus, he's *right there.*

Just staring up at the window from under the wide brim of his hat, plain as day.

I don't think he saw me. *I hope not.*

But my slamming heart can't be sure.

"Why?" I whisper. "Why's he staring at the shop?"

"So you know they're watching," Micah says, his voice heavy. "Nothing good ever happens when the Jacobins get interested in a girl involved with the Arrendells. Before Ulysses and Culver were arrested, Ephraim and Culver weren't shy about stalking Delilah Graves."

I can feel my chest caving in.

So quick my fingers go numb.

I don't even think to reach for my inhaler.

All I can do is stare at the closed curtains, feeling doom descending like a cloud.

No matter where I hide, that freaky beanstalk man is *looking.*

I remember reading the news about what Ulysses and Culver did before they were stopped, when they caught another man who tried to get in the way of their creepy business.

…could that be me?

Gutted like a farm animal?

"Grandpa—" It hits me so hard it almost knocks me over.

No, he can't go out on errands today. He can't go where Ephraim Jacobin can find him and hurt him.

"Talia, breathe." Suddenly, there's a tall body in my way and strong arms holding me in place. "Your grandfather's going to be all right. They wouldn't dare do anything in the middle of town. It's safer to pretend you don't notice them. If you or your grandfather start acting suspicious, they might wonder. If you react, they'll know you know something."

"But they might—" I fight Micah weakly, but I'm about to hyperventilate. My limbs are noodles, and all I can do is sag against him with a miserable sound that feels like I just had my heart torn out. I drop my head on his shoulder, struggling to breathe. "If they hurt him and it's my fault…"

"They won't. I won't fucking let them."

I can feel his vow rumbling through me, the closeness of his body making his voice a physical force.

His hand curls against the back of my neck, gently roaming my hair.

His other hand slides down my back, and I tremble.

A nervous rush goes through me—until I realize he's slipping his fingers into my pocket, delving in so close to my skin to find my inhaler.

A few seconds later, the cap pops off and he's pressing it between my lips.

There's something oddly intimate about letting him slide this slick plastic thing into my mouth.

"Breathe," he growls. "Breathe until you're okay."

I'm so not okay.

But for him, I'll try.

I close my eyes and let the mist open my lungs. I have to remember Micah Ainsley is as good as his word.

He'll never let anything happen.

With him, I'm truly safe.

And I've never felt safer than now, wrapped in his arms.

Slowly, I steady my breaths and the terror in my chest eases.

That's when I realize he's holding me so close, resting his chin to the top of my head, fully enveloping me.

I can feel his heartbeat.

His chest under my palms, and a heartbeat so strong it makes me dizzy.

His scent screams cool, raw masculinity, just as sharp as Micah himself.

"Do you need more?" His voice is heavy.

"N-no." I shake my head, keeping my eyes lowered. I don't know if I can look up at him when we're this freaking close. "I'm better. I just... I had a moment. Thanks for helping bring me out of it."

"Wasn't my smartest move when I don't know your dosage, but I'm glad I didn't guess wrong." Instead of letting go, his grip tightens, gathering me closer. "Talia, fuck."

The way he says my name.

My heart races even faster than his.

"Yes?" I curl my fingers against his shirt.

"You don't have to keep eavesdropping on Xavier. Not for me, not for anyone. If you back out now, they'll decide you aren't a threat and they'll leave you alone. You're not bound to this shit. Fuck, I can't stand putting you in danger. Just do your work. Keep as much distance as you can. Take care of your grandfather. That's all that matters."

"What?" I blink, pressing my palms to his chest and pushing back to look up at him. "You can't be serious. What about your brother? What about the drugs, the people they've hurt?"

Micah's eyes are impenetrable grey clouds as he looks down at me with his brows like thunderheads. "I'll figure out another way that doesn't involve you."

Anger flares, quicker than an asthma attack.

"Because you think I'm fragile?" My eyes slit. "You think I can't handle this."

"What? No, I—"

"I don't want to hear it!" I snap. I can't stand it. I can't stand that even Micah Ainsley sees me as this broken little girl who can't do anything, who has to be sheltered for her own good. I shove at him, scowling. "I can handle the Jacobins. I can handle Xavier flipping Arrendell. What I can't handle is you patronizing me—"

The only warning I get is Micah's lips thinning.

His eyes flashing.

His feral grip on my arms.

Then he seizes my mouth and shuts me up with one brutal kiss.

For a single breath, I freeze.

I don't know how to process what's happening.

I remember his lips on mine that day in the square, remember how my mouth tingled, but it was nothing like this.

Nothing like this *force* of a man's naked desire, all fire, his mouth hot and firm on mine, coaxing my lips apart.

The heat sears me in the space of one breath.

I'm melting.

My entire body turns into hot honey, leaving me clutching him to keep standing as I stretch on my toes and lean into him.

I'm so greedy it scares me, taking that kiss I've wanted for what feels like a lifetime, as his tongue flicks against my mouth.

Holy shit!

When I was a girl, I used to daydream about falling in love. In those dreams, kissing was always this nebulous thing with a vague sense of forbidden pleasure, but the reality?

Pure inferno.

And Micah baptizes me with flames, dragging me in roughly, growling heat into my mouth.

I'm deliciously crushed against his body until I feel every inch of him.

I'm too *aware* of him, from the hot texture of his lips to the wetness of our mouths gliding together to the roughness of his tongue.

His powerful height.

His arm, as hard as steel across my back.

His fingers, strong and controlling as they fist my hair.

My head falls back in surrender.

There's a demand in the way he seeks deep inside me with slow taunts, sweet plunging caresses, searching strokes.

God.

I'm about to spontaneously combust.

"Micah," I moan against his lips, and he groans.

There's a faint clatter past the haze of my perception—my inhaler hitting the floor, I think—and suddenly Micah's fingers touch the small of my back with nothing between us.

His palm feels so hot it's like I'm already naked. Even my shirt can't buffer the burn of his touch.

"Say it again. Say my name again, Talia, and I can't turn back," he breathes raggedly.

The thought of what *can't turn back* means hits like a lightning bolt.

I curl my hands against his arms, pulling back enough to look up at him, breathing so hard I'm shaking.

Yet instead of my lungs hurting, it feels *good*, this sweet rush electrifying nerves I never knew I had.

"So don't?" I whisper. "Do whatever you want with me."

He stares at me with his eyes boiling, all liquid mercury. "Talia, you don't want to be with me."

"You don't get to decide what I want." I don't even know what I'm doing. I'm being reckless, being wild, and I don't care.

I lean into him, pressing my body to his, shivering as I savor his hard muscle molding against me.

"Talia—fuck!" His cock grazes my leg through his pants.

I almost die right there.

"You… you only get to tell me what *you* want," I whisper. "Do you want to be with me? Would you regret it?"

Micah searches my face.

I wish I could read him more easily.

There's something *there*.

Something vulnerable behind the wolfish hunger.

Something almost afraid yet so brave and certain.

"I thought you were shy," he rasps.

"I am." I smile shakily but don't pull away. "Honestly, I'm scared out of my wits, but I still *want* it. I want you. Even if it means getting hurt when you say no."

"I don't fucking want to say no." His voice comes even rougher than his touch when he presses the pad of his thumb to my lower lip, his gaze fused to my mouth. "But, woman, I don't want you to regret saying yes. I'm no good for you—no fucking good for anybody—and I don't want you figuring that out after I've hurt you."

I swallow thickly.

"You've been nothing *but* good. Micah. I wish you could see it…"

He strokes his thumb to the corner of my mouth and his lips curl faintly. "And how do you see me?"

No words.

I don't have words to tell him how every time I see him, my world gets just a little bit brighter.

How I feel alive.

How protected I feel, how I trust him to watch over me, to shelter me.

How I know that no matter how he struggles, he's guided by a moral compass made of steel, a righteous sense of justice so strong it could drive him to do terrible things for the innocent.

For me.

I also think he's been told so often that he's a freak of nature that he started believing it.

His father's ugliness crawled down inside him and still whispers in his ear, telling him he's no good. He doesn't know he's so right for me, it's actually insane.

So no, there's no telling him, not with words.

Only another way.

Stepping back, I break his hold and reach for his hand, lacing our fingers together. I tug his hand lightly as I walk to my bedroom, an open invitation.

To *be* with me.

To destroy me, if he must.

He could pull free so easily and storm away when we're barely touching.

But he doesn't.

With a rough breath, he follows, never releasing my hand.

My heart leaps, thunder building with a power that feels too great for my small body.

The power to make this man undone.

When I meet his eyes and realize it, I'm almost giddy.

He's almost helpless with thirst.

That's the strangeness I saw before.

This man is so lonely, so disciplined, that when someone

reaches out and offers to break down his walls, how can he resist?

I hurt for him as much as I want him.

And as I step backward into my bedroom, crossing the threshold, I stop and tug on his hand to draw him in closer, then rise up on my toes and press my lips to his.

"Close the door," I whisper before retreating deeper into the room.

There's no turning back now.

Before I can second-guess, I catch the hem of my babydoll tee and pull it over my head, baring the cups of my bra in pink lace rosettes.

"Fucking pink all over," he growls with amusement. "You're a born tease, Shortcake."

Blushing, I shake my hair loose from the shirt and toss it aside. I bite my lip, watching him and praying he'll like what he sees.

There's a trembling silence.

A dead moment where I worry Micah will turn his back and walk out the door, and in that moment, I love and hate the nerves eating me alive.

This impulse, this *risk*, taking a leap of faith instead of playing it safe—it could come crashing down right here.

I could find out the hard way that risks are never worth it.

But then he steps closer, prowling toward me.

His eyes are barely even human.

"*Talia,*" he rumbles, taking me into his arms and kissing me so hard my vision blurs.

He pulls me up until my feet aren't on the floor.

Then I'm devoured.

His hands on my bare skin.

His lips claiming mine.

Everything—*everything!*—about his touch feels so possessive, and it's all so raw and new that I'm ready to scream just from feeling his uniform shirt scraping my bare flesh.

Just from feeling my breasts against his chest as he pulls me closer and sucks my bottom lip until I'm delirious.

He's got the devil's own tongue.

I can barely kiss him back when he's turning me inside out with slow, wet thrusts that leave my lips so tender.

So sensitive that when he nips at them with those sharp teeth, I gasp. My thighs shake as I fall against him with a moan.

There's a dark, raspy laugh when he does it again, catching me with rough hands on my hips as my entire weight collapses against him.

"Did you come already, girl? All from a kiss?"

"No!" I gasp, then stop. "At least, I don't think I did... What does it feel like?"

Sad.

But how do you describe an ocean sunset to the blind?

Does it feel like this wet sugary sensation inside me, clenching up tight, hot and molten and quaking between my thighs until my whole flesh simmers?

Does it feel like the way my whole body comes alive?

Every sensation stronger than before, stronger than ever, throbbing in my fingers and toes and nipples, and the heavy, full sensation in my breasts?

Micah's eyes flash with awe as he stares at me.

"Have you never?" he asks softly.

Part of me wants to crawl away and die.

God, he'll mock me for this.

He'll laugh and tell me to take my little girl self somewhere else and leave him to find a real woman with experience. The kind of worldly woman he probably knew back in New York.

"Never," I admit, lowering my eyes.

I'm expecting a snort.

A startled chuckle.

Pure derision.

Rejection, however polite.

What I don't expect is the reverence in his voice as he sighs my name like a prayer and curses.

"Talia, fuck."

Then he kisses me again.

This time, it's different.

Slower and softer and tender, caressing my mouth in gentle strokes.

I feel like he's trying to tell me something, but my brain is so hazed up right now I don't understand. I can't.

Nothing except for how good he feels.

Everything about him feels *divine.*

His weight, his kiss, the careful way he handles me as rough palms slide down my waist. He hefts me up with an easy strength that scrambles my senses.

Suddenly, I'm weightless again, my body floating as he raises me up.

I instinctively wrap my legs around his waist—then let out a startled sound as my jeans, my panties, press against me.

I'm aching with wet heat, firmly pressed against the ridge of something hard and thick against his slacks.

And harder still as his hands slip down to my ass.

His fingers dig into my flesh, leaving no mistake.

He wants this.

He wants *me*.

I don't know what to do, even if I know what I want—and even as he bites my mouth, I can't help squirming, grinding against him.

Wanting more of that sensation that feels like flint on steel, striking sparks every time his friction sweeps my skin.

Oh, it's glorious.

This needy pleasure pulsing inside me.

Every time I do it, I feel his hardness more.

His hands tighten while his chest heaves against mine, his shallow breath rushing over my lips, soft growls in the back of his throat.

"Hold *still*, Talia. Before I lose my fucking mind," he grinds out in a tortured snarl—then snaps his head down and strikes.

Protector.

Beast.

Vampire.

His teeth sink into my throat, catching the tender skin and holding me prisoner.

I arch against him, crying out.

Terror and pleasure bolt through me until my entire body sings, but there's no pain here.

He's rough, yet so gentle, too, biting down softly.

His tongue traces my captured flesh in devilish caresses as he sucks my neck with a pulling rhythm that reaches down inside me. He tugs at something so tight and hot I feel like I'll go up in cinders.

Wrapping my arms around his neck, I curl forward, gasping as he teases me, barely aware that he's carrying me to my bed.

Barely aware of anything but his ravenous red mouth fastened on my throat, making me feel every sucking lick.

It's the daydream of yesterday and the better reality of now.

Micah Ainsley isn't a night-creature who can pierce my flesh smoothly with razor teeth and make me love the pain.

He's a real man, holding tight and trembling in a way that feels so powerful.

I love how just touching me makes him react—and he's

touching me like a real man, kissing me like a real man, delivering pleasure with his teeth the way only a real man can.

Still, I don't expect it when he bites me again, this time a little harder.

Again and again, he's covering my neck with hot rings, only for gravity to upend itself as he tumbles me down on my bed.

I fall on my back, gasping, but he's already covering me with his body.

He fits between my legs, weighing me down with hard muscle.

His hands grasp my thighs and his hips rock down hard into mine, stroking between my thighs with the full pressure of his body.

A fire burst washes through me.

And just as he twists his hips to grind, to tease, to ruin me, he bites me again.

Lust imprinting my skin.

A fever burning us both down.

I dig my fingers into his hair and toss my head back, writhing under him, completely trapped and yet *God, I don't want to escape.*

Not now.

Not ever.

If Micah is a monster, I'm his willing captive.

But as his teeth hold on, I scream, hugging my thighs against his hips and digging my fingers into his shoulders.

He pulls back, leaving my neck throbbing.

He breathes harshly, staring at my throat, his thumb grazing over the pulsing spot on my skin before those feral eyes flick to my face.

"Too much?" he asks, husky and gritty. "Did I scare you?"

"No." I shake my head quickly, reaching up to touch my trembling fingers to his lips.

It's hard to speak.

Not because I'm afraid, but because I'm overwhelmed.

"I couldn't be scared of you, Micah. Never. It just startled me, but... it felt good." It takes all my courage to say that out loud.

His lips curl faintly under my touch.

"So, there really is a little wild thing under all the pink," he whispers.

"Show me how wild I can be," I whisper back. "And then, next time, show me more."

Next time.

Part of me wants reassurance that there'll *be* a next time.

That he's as caught up in this as I am, this madness that feels like a spell. But that small, eager smile is all he gives as he kisses my fingertips.

"Next time, yeah."

He lowers himself over me to claim my mouth again.

It hits deeper this time with his hips rocking in slow, dragging thrusts between my legs, grating against my jeans.

His hands stroke my belly, my ribs, cupping my breasts.

I whimper as his huge, strong hands cover my flesh, bathing me in this creeping pleasure as he makes me so *aware* of his touch.

His tongue delves deeper, stealing my breath, silencing me as his thumbs tease my nipples through my bra, working them in circles.

Every last one sends an arrow to that hot, wet place inside me, hungrier than ever.

With every stroke, he inches my bra down until it's skin on skin.

Then I feel the roughness of his work-weathered fingers, teasing my flesh until I'm tender.

Until I'm breathing in whimpers.

Until I'm clutching his hair each time his tongue thrusts *deep* in matching rhythm to the sway of his hips.

Until my entire mind sears to ash while my body ignites with wanting.

I *want* him.

I don't need experience to know that, to crave our bodies crashing together in a demonic rhythm until I'm a wrecked mess.

I want to feel him thrust.

And when he pinches my nipple between his forefinger and thumb, a sensation so raw arcs through me that it's like he's given me exactly what I'm craving.

I jerk up until my back arches, rubbing against him, grinding my hips against his, raking my nails over his uniform shirt.

I'm so desperate.

Quivering.

"Micah," I gasp against his lips. "Don't treat me like I'm fragile…"

"Hush." The word itself a kiss, even as he gives my nipple an electrifying tug. I dig my knees into his sides. "I'm not treating you like glass, Talia. I'm treating you like you're one of a kind."

Oh.

Oh, wow.

Butterflies swirl as I open my eyes, looking up at him—and a wicked smile bares those teeth that make me go wild.

It's the only warning before he dips down.

Then it's not his hands on my breasts, it's his lips, kissing and turning those teeth loose.

He makes my skin sting with shocks of pleasure, even as his hands stray lower.

Lower.

And there's a harsh uncertainty as he unzips my jeans before I make myself relax as much as I can when he's teasing and tormenting me with every bite and every play of his fingers over my belly.

Lower still.

I forget how to breathe as he slides those long, strong fingers inside my panties—just as he closes his mouth around my nipple, between his teeth, and sucks *hard*.

No words.

I don't have words for how it lances deep like a sword thrust, cutting me in places never touched before.

A single finger roams outside my drenched, tingling pussy lips before he finds my clit.

It's like being bathed in raw pleasure.

This raw, erotic hellfire erupts from that finger toying with my clit.

I'm—oh God, oh *fuck*, I'm tossing and jerking under him and I don't know how to do anything else.

I just know I'm shaking as I strain toward him, fighting not to flinch away.

It's too much—too much—but it's also everything and I want more, more, *more*—

"Micah!"

I've stopped clenching my thighs.

They're flung open now, wanting and shameless.

I'm ready to scream.

His tongue laves over my nipple, his roughness tormenting me, making my flesh draw tighter and tighter.

He works my clit in circles every time he sucks, and the rhythm takes me over.

My entire body becomes one hot throb of madness.

Then he slips two fingers inside me, his thumb still flicking and teasing my clit while those long, white, searching fingers turn me inside out.

I'm gone.

Hot, storming, as quick as a whiplash and as powerful as a hurricane.

It hits me so hard it pins me to the bed with the weight of pure feeling.

Oh, my pleasure has *teeth*, taking and taking and *taking* but giving back ecstasy.

I'd give anything to hold on to it forever.

I almost don't even realize I've come until it's over, leaving me dazed, gasping.

I open my eyes, staring hazily at Micah with my blood running slow as molasses.

He watches me intently, his fingers slowly sliding out of my aching flesh.

My eyes go wide.

"Oh!" I manage to pry one clenched hand free from his shoulder to cover my mouth. "I didn't... I didn't mean to—"

"I wanted you to." Micah's smile is almost dangerous as he leans down, brushing his lips over mine. "It'll feel that much better when you come for me again."

Holy hell.

That kiss melts me into the bed, sighing.

My eyes close as his lips trace mine, before opening again as he pulls away.

"How do you know my own body better than me?"

"Experience," he answers, and that dangerous smile widens into wicked teeth. "Enough questions. I don't want to get kicked out before I have the chance to taste you."

Taste me?

Every question about how many people he's been with before, his past relationships, what those women were like fall away as I realize what he means.

I just watch, stunned as he lifts his glistening fingers to

his lips and licks them clean, running his tongue over each digit with such shameless hunger I freeze.

But I'm wrong.

I *still* don't truly understand.

Not until he's licked his fingers clean, holding me hypnotized the whole time, only to catch the belt loops of my jeans and tug them down.

I'm paralyzed, realizing how in over my head I am with this man.

But I certainly don't resist as he strips them away from me.

My panties, too, leaving me naked except for my bra pulled down around my ribs, the straps hanging loose against my upper arms.

My legs feel like velvet and raw sex as Micah strokes my thighs.

There's something so alluring about this, him kneeling with his uniform dark against the pale-pink sheets of my bed and my own pale skin.

Yet he's whiter still, all winter enchantment.

In the back of my mind, I still think of him as a little more than human. And what he does to me next definitely feels like black magic.

That crown of snowy hair dips down.

He uses his shoulders to nudge my legs apart, and then— oh *God*, it really hits me what he meant by *taste me*.

His tongue traces every fold of my pussy with a knowing touch, alternating so randomly I never know if I'll be holding my breath or gasping in a rush every time he thrusts.

He paints mad, hypnotic circles on my skin, probing me until there's no part of me he hasn't licked completely.

I barely last a couple minutes.

Not when I'm so sensitive, so hot, and so starved.

Not when I'm still wrung out from the first time.

And it's almost painful to come again this soon, but the pain is the sweetest kind.

I hardly realize I've got handfuls of his hair, tugging roughly.

I hardly realize I'm crushing my thighs around his head, digging my feet into his spine.

I hardly realize I'm barely even still on the bed, arched so taut my shoulders hardly touch the mattress, head thrown back, broken cries escaping my throat.

I can't *think*.

I can only feel.

And Micah Ainsley makes me feel everything.

The second orgasm comes on harder than the first.

If the first O was a whiplash, the second is an avalanche, burying me until I'm a thrashing mess.

I can feel him in my depths, vibrating through me, turning my vision white.

For an instant, I'm pretty sure I'm *gone*—because when I come back, I'm struggling to breathe on a bed so hot it feels like a furnace.

Micah lifts his head, dragging his thumb across his gleaming red mouth with a satisfied smirk, so tense he looks like he's about to snap.

"You good?" His voice could set the world on fire with the heat in it. "Not pushing too far?"

I shake my head quickly, if only because I can't speak when I can't breathe.

But it's so different from an asthma attack.

It's not my body failing me, but lifting me up.

For once, this tight ache in my chest feels *just right* instead of heralding panic.

After I catch my breath, I manage to talk.

"Not too far," I whisper, even if the throbbing between my

legs might disagree after two climaxes so close together. "What about you?" I ask.

And I can't help how my eyes dip down.

There's no missing the hard ridge of his cock against his blue slacks, tenting the fabric.

I don't even need to see it to tell he's huge.

Of course, he is.

And if I didn't know better, I'd think there was a wet spot against the fabric.

Is he really that turned on? By *me*?

I've never felt more desirable as his slow, dark smile returns and carnivorous eyes rove over me.

I must look wrung out, shivering under him, already so well used.

"We're getting there," he growls. "Just want to make sure you're keeping up."

"Hey, I'm not that delicate." I pout at him.

"Talia."

And he's hovering over me again—shrugging out of his shirt and the tight-stretched undershirt beneath, all dense muscle under white velvet.

His body cages mine, his hands cradling my face.

His fingers weave through my hair as he gazes down with skin-stripping silver eyes that could leave me in white-hot flames forever.

"Stop," he growls. "Stop being defensive. Stop thinking I see you as something small and weak. I'm not coddling you, woman. I'm not sheltering you. I want you to feel good, and I want your body." His lips press against my brow, a tenderness at odds with the blaze between us. "I couldn't live with myself if I lost my mind in you and found out you didn't enjoy it."

I shiver.

There's something searing in his voice, this subtle hint of real emotion. I'm so starved for it.

"It's new," I admit, leaning into him. His closeness is a comfort and a sweet, sexy torment. "But it's a good new. I feel kinda wrecked, but I like it."

"Just wait, sweet girl." Another kiss brushes my forehead, then down the bridge of my nose before feathering over my lips. "I'm not even close to done with you yet." He stops, though, going tense. He drops his head to rest his brow to mine, eyes closing as he curses. "…fuck. I don't have any condoms."

"Oh. I don't either." Disappointment sweeps through me —but then I catch a breath, biting my lip, touching his stark cheekbone. "Micah, I'm on the pill."

It was just a formality when I never really dated.

My doctor said it would help with the steroids in my inhaler and the effect they have on my hormones, but it never really felt necessary before.

Now, as hope blooms in my chest, I've never been more glad.

Micah pushes himself up sharply, staring down at me.

"Yeah? No shit?" His gaze is almost *greedy*, a wild question flicking in his eyes.

It takes all my courage to answer.

"I want to," I whisper.

God, if I wasn't already sweltering, I'd probably detonate with the blush ripping through me.

Micah's smile returns, but there's more—a warmth in his eyes, melting their glacial ice. He leans down and kisses me, then nips my upper lip.

"Dirty girl."

I shudder, leaning into him. "I just want to feel everything my first time. Nothing between us."

"Happy to oblige." His body settles on mine, his fingers

skimming down, tracing fresh warmth over my skin before I hear the jingle of his belt buckle.

The rasp of his zipper.

And his mouth comes down on mine as the rest of his clothes fall away.

I crumble at the sensation of his heat and my own words given back against my lips.

"...nothing between us. Are you ready for this dick?"

I'm lost.

Lost for speech.

Lost for thought.

Lost for breath.

Lost for anything but the feeling of my body tangled with Micah's, the way his kiss guides me, shows me how to arch, how to spread my legs so we fit together.

His cock presses against me, totally ravenous.

The tremor of anticipation tears me apart before he's even in me.

Our tongues twine together.

My body goes liquid.

Another split second of hesitation right before his entire muscular frame tenses under my palms, barely held in check like a beast straining on its leash.

"Yes?" he whispers, all animal. "Shortcake, fucking tell me."

"Yes!" I hiss back, giving him permission.

Giving him me.

Groaning roughly, his hands tighten on my hips as he moves.

As he *takes*.

It's like nothing I've ever felt before.

Like being pierced with steel wrapped in silk, filling and stretching, pure intimacy and obscenity, wonderful and terrible, leaving me in flames.

He strokes so deep inside me.

My cry becomes a shrill purr as I rise up against him, wrapping my arms tight around his neck, digging my nails into his shoulder blades.

I'm being fucked by a ghost and I think I like it.

It feels like it never *stops*, inch after brutal inch sliding deeper, caressing me in places I didn't know any man could reach.

With every inch, Micah kisses me deeper, not just taking me but taking me *with* him.

"Micah!" I whimper against his lips, over and over again as we flow into each other, deeper with every movement, coming together in vicious rhythm.

I don't know how I fell into this but I don't ever want it to *stop*.

There's no sound except our racing breath and rubbing skin and the wet slick murmur of our mating lips.

We're like one animal, moving to the same heat, the same tempo, rising and falling together until this thing between us shreds time.

Holy hell.

An endless crescendo.

My body sings with every thrust that makes me hold on to him tighter still.

I don't know how Micah managed to get so deep inside me, so fast, but he makes me feel the full majesty of every thrust.

Wild.

Tender.

Lust.

Fear.

Desperation.

It's like flinging open a Pandora's box that's been sealed for my entire life.

Now it's wide open and everything floods out, washing us away, ripping my breath from my lungs.

Right now, I don't care if I never breathe again.

Not when all I need is *him*.

Micah, and this sticky sweet madness we find together.

Urgency, tumbling, faster, falling, *falling*.

Coming!

"Let it fucking go, girl," he whispers with a firm hand pressed against my throat. "Give me your fireworks."

He doesn't stop as I thrash under him, a punished mess, drunk on his ecstasy.

And my eyes slip open as I realize he's watching me.

He's *been* watching me this whole time, looking at me like there's nothing else in the world.

For just a moment, that look catches me off guard, strikes my heart, and it's that moment of distraction that's his undoing.

He bares his teeth and pours his gaze into mine.

There's one final thrust, plunging to my depths, where it's impossible to go further.

His back stiffens like a human hammer slamming into me, a reverberating strike.

"Fuuuck!" He's roaring when his cock swells.

His eyes pinch shut, his head whips back, his fingers bite my skin, and his hips bruise mine.

I feel like shattered crystal, thrown back into a full force of a new orgasm before the first one ever finishes.

I dissolve into bliss, clenching and shuddering and fighting to breathe, alive with one thought as I experience the greatest high of my life.

Somehow, I fell in love with Micah Ainsley.

And this mistake is going to tear me apart.

* * *

THE DARKEST CHASE

MICAH FEELS good wrapped around me.

I snuggle deeper into the sheets with him pressed to my back, his arm tight around my waist.

The sweat on my skin should be chilling, but all I can feel is warmth from the place where his palm imprints against me to the lingering burn of the bite marks on my throat and shoulders.

I'm honestly not sure what to say right now.

I never thought he could even *see* me that way, no matter how close he came when he was drunk.

This was Micah sober.

This was heart and soul.

I'm not even sure how to ask what this means.

After a lazy, quiet moment, he kisses my shoulder. "I suppose I should stop arguing with you about being my femme fatale spy."

"That's what it takes to convince you? Sex?" I giggle.

He lets out a low growl and lightly bites the back of my shoulder. "That may have had some influence."

"Oh, good. Now I know how to get you to do what I want."

"Yeah?" I feel his smile curving against my shoulder. "Is there something else you want from me, Miss Grey?"

"*Talia.*" I laugh, snuggling in closer. "And no, I think right now, I have everything a girl could want."

"You'd better." He nips me again, then settles, leaning his sleek chest against my back a little harder. "I actually wanted to thank you."

If I was warm before, my face nearly combusts now. "For having sex with you?"

"*No.*" His laughter vibrates against my back. "Not to say I'm not grateful for that, but it's more." His laughter fades and his voice sobers. "I was in a situation today. Had to tell a girl that her boyfriend was dead." He pauses before his voice deepens. "...possibly murdered."

I stiffen.

I think I get why Micah was so worried for my safety now.

Another Redhaven murder.

But he's not done.

"I don't know how to deal with things like that. Not on a human level. Never figured out how to be as gentle as I should be with the victim's kin. I've been so focused on finding who was responsible for Jet's death for so long that I forgot how to care. How to connect." Yet he's connecting with me now. Every word makes my heart wrench, warming my soul. "Today, I managed, thanks to you. I managed not to hurt her any more than necessary. I managed to show her comfort because I kept asking what you would do." He hesitates. "...and what you would want me to do, to be the kind of man you think I am."

Oh, Micah.

Soft emotions rush through me. I shift in his arms to face him.

There's something I've never seen on his face before.

Openness.

That impenetrable shield gone from arctic blue-grey eyes, leaving them the color of a winter sky, unguarded and almost lost as he meets my eyes.

"The man you are," I whisper.

"I still don't believe that."

"I do," I answer, pressing my palm to his cheek as I lean in to kiss him.

It's so wonderful to be *allowed*.

To be free to kiss this man who's been in my thoughts nonstop from the moment we met and to have him kiss me back without reservation.

His mouth feels gentle against mine, yet it still stings delightfully with lips he bruised as he'd taken me.

It just reminds me how sore I am everywhere else and how I've never felt *anything* like that moment when he held me down and claimed every molecule of my flesh.

And with his hands against my back, I'm ready to find that feeling again—but we barely kiss for a minute before a new sound startles me.

The side door opening.

The jingle of Grandpa's keys.

And his voice drifting up the stairs. "Tally?"

Micah never got around to closing the door.

We break apart like a lightning strike, staring at each other for a second before I break away and go vaulting out of bed so fast I tumble to the floor on my knees.

I scrabble along with my butt in the air and my hands pulling across the floorboards, then launch to my feet and slam the bedroom door shut before he sees us naked.

"Just a minute, Grandpa!" I yell through the door, wheezing—only to stiffen at a stifled snicker behind me.

I whirl around and glower.

There he is, standing there shamelessly naked, his gorgeous body gleaming like ivory in the pale sunlight streaming through my curtains. He looks like Michelangelo's *David* in every place but one—the hard-on jutting toward me.

"Nice view," he says.

I sputter.

"Dude, I *tripped*!" I snag his uniform pants and throw them at him before snatching my panties and hopping into them one clumsy foot at a time. "Hurry and get dressed. Right now!"

"Working on it."

Liar.

Still smirking like Sex Lucifer, he fishes around on the floor until he finds his boxers and steps into them.

"Shame to put all this back on when all I want to do is rip it off you again."

"...yeah?" I freeze with one leg in my jeans, just staring at him.

God help me, I smile, shimmying my jeans up around my hips before I reach for my bra. "I wouldn't mind doing this again. Just don't get too crazy about it."

Oh, but that smirk turns cockier.

"Later then? After you've convinced the old man we were just having tea?"

I sigh, hating and loving the giddiness bubbling up inside me.

"Definitely later," I whisper.

XII: DARK SIDE (MICAH)

I don't recognize the man in the mirror.

It's supposedly me, staring at myself as I shave after a shower, foaming my face up and slowly dragging the razor over my skin as I clean up for work.

But Micah Ainsley doesn't kiss a woman like she's something to cherish rather than break.

Neither is being gentle because as much as I want to mark her and make her scream, I want her to *want* that even more.

Neither is actually caring at all, instead of having a quick hookup and then parting ways.

The man who made love to Talia yesterday isn't me.

Today, I don't know who the fuck I am, when all I can see is a broken predator.

How does Talia Grey see a man capable of kindness?

And is it possible for someone else to believe something so hard that you start believing it, too?

No.

That old darkness is still there, hungry and ready to shatter her.

Ruin her.

Yet maybe I'm hoping there's a part of her that can accept me for what I truly am, instead of the vampire lover from her dreams.

I swear, I can still taste her and feel her skin on my fingers.

It's fucking distracting.

So much that as I'm shaving off the last bit of foam, I nick my jaw, raising a blood stripe on my skin like a carnelian flower against snow.

I stop, holding the blade against my face, staring at the scarlet drop sliding down my jaw to my neck.

Doesn't that bring back memories?

Blood on my skin in esoteric patterns.

Daddy's little work of art.

Snarling, I shake myself free from my thoughts, get dressed, and check on my dog.

"Morning, old man. How'd we sleep?" I stop to scratch Rolf's head before clipping his leash on and leading him into a morning too bright for my bitter thoughts.

He's cheerful and eager to go, at least.

Every now and then I bring him into the office just for the hell of it.

It's not hard to tell he knows he's about to get spoiled completely.

Sometimes, I think he misses his days as a police dog. Being around the guys seems to liven him up until he's as spry as a pup again, even if he'll never be the world's friendliest ball of woof.

He practically drags me down the street on the walk to work—though he's well-behaved when we stop at Red Grounds to pick up the usual order.

I'm not surprised when the barista slips him a strip of bacon from the breakfast griddle. Everyone loves Rolf.

I usually enjoy their reactions more.

Maybe because I'm realizing how much people project onto the blank canvas I present, and Rolf is part of that image. That fakery, even if I like sharing my life with him.

I really do love this giant furry goofball, but it feels so cynical sometimes, holding together this false identity that makes people smile as I pass by with my fun, yet standoffish German Shepherd.

It never bothered me before.

I came to Redhaven with a purpose.

It's been slow, this grinding game, but someday when it ends, I'll be gone and so will Rolf, leaving this town behind.

Before, I never considered the fact that the people around me might feel betrayed.

The guys on the team. The folks in this town who accept me like one of their own.

Hell, Talia.

She's all I can think about as I coax a tail-wagging Rolf out of the café with his leash looped around my wrist, leaving my hands free for the double load of coffee cups in their carrier.

When the barista waves me off cheerfully, I almost forget to flash my usual polite smile.

How long can a man keep wearing a mask before it becomes his face?

But that mask will get me through this day, dammit.

As I elbow my way into the precinct and everyone—from Mallory to big grumpy Grant—lights up at Rolf.

I let him off leash and he dives through the forest of happy hands reaching out, letting me slip into the background.

I drop off coffee cups on respective desks and cruise by Grant's desk to snag the topmost folder labeled 'Newcomb, Brian' before dropping down at my own desk with my coffee pressed to my lips.

"Hey," I call over my shoulder. "Is Raleigh forensics doing a full workup on this, or are we handling it on our own?"

Grant looks up from sneaking Rolf the deer jerky he thinks I don't know he keeps in his desk. "We're on our own for now, since homicide is possible but not confirmed. They'll get us the autopsy data, but the crime scene's on us. We good on photos? Storm's coming in by this afternoon and any evidence is gonna get washed out by evening."

"Damn." I thumb through the photos in the folder, then lean forward and jiggle the mouse to wake my computer. I pull up the digital case record, scanning through the additional photographs. I also have the images I took and need to finish uploading to our system. "Think we're good, but I'll take my lunch to head back up there and take another look. Might help to see it with fresh eyes."

Lucas hasn't stopped scratching under Rolf's chin since the moment we walked in, leaving the dog's tongue lolling out.

He pauses now, frowning. "You really think we're looking at a homicide?"

"Only other person who could've been with him had an alibi. The girlfriend." Even as I talk, I'm digging my phone out and transferring the notes and witness statement I took into the Redhaven PD system. "They came here from California for a vacation. Hiking and photography. He went out the day before, she didn't. Janelle Bowden vouches she was in their suite sick all day. So, finding the second set of footsteps without a police report about discovering a body?" I turn to Mallory. "Not one 9-1-1 call all day?"

Mallory sighs. "Nothing but people complaining about their neighbors' music. I was so bored I even unlocked Ray, and I can't *stand* that little twerp."

"Still have no clue what any of that means," Grant rumbles.

"Liar!" Henri teases, leaning over Grant's chair and propping his elbows on top of Grant's head. "You just don't like thinking about our sweet Mallory playin' her dirty little games with her sexy anime boys, eh?" He glances over his shoulder at Mallory and winks. "Ain't nothin' slowing you down, gorgeous. Keep at it."

Mallory giggles, blushing and tucking a spiral of her silver-grey hair back into its bun. "You're always such a flirt, Henri."

Grant rolls his eyes, then shrugs Henri off. "I'm not a goddamned armrest, Frenchie. *Move.*"

"Okay, peanut gallery." I swivel my chair back to my screen. "I'm going to actually work the case while you spoil my dog."

"I thought spoiling your dog was part of the job? He's a police vet, after all." Lucas grins shamelessly.

"Pretty sure that's *my* job, but Rolf doesn't mind, so I'll allow it," I mutter, already focused on the photos on my screen.

Grant hefts himself up from his chair and makes his way over to my desk with his slow, bearish stride. He braces his hands on my desk, leaning over next to me and frowning at my screen.

"Besides the footprints, what else do we have? Motive? Suspects?"

"Nothing yet," I grind out, but I'm lying. I very much have a murdering fuck in mind as I squint at the heel prints and indentation measurements. "No one in Redhaven even knew them, no recent altercations. *But.*"

That *but* has everyone in the room listening in.

Even Rolf pricks his ears up, swinging his head toward me.

"The girlfriend said he went out there to take photos," I say. "She last heard from him the night before. So, the night before he had his camera. What did we not find in his bag or on his person?"

A few breaths suck in.

"Mother*fucker*," Lucas growls.

Henri rubs his chin, his friendly air fading into quiet focus. "Perhaps he saw something he wasn't supposed to out there. He photographed something that wasn't meant for prying eyes, and the person who pushed him took the evidence."

"Must've been all they cared about," Grant adds, his brows lowering until his entire face is a thunderhead. "Didn't take his ID or his phone. No attempt to conceal the body or hide who it belonged to. The Jacobins?"

"Only folks out there, usually," I answer vaguely. I don't want them mucking up my leads, and I inwardly apologize for the misdirection. "Of course, besides Culver, we've never seen them stoop to murder. Sure, they'll light up your ass with buckshot for getting in their way, but generally that's it. It's the Arrendells who do the real killing around here."

The entire room goes silent, turning that over.

I trace my thumb along the curve of that clearly defined half-moon heel print. From the soil firmness, imprint depth, stride length, and the narrowness of the foot, I have a good idea.

I'd say a woman, about five-seven to five-nine.

Average weight, roughly.

And I can already imagine one woman who fits that description perfectly, and who'd wear shoes that would leave just this kind of print.

Eustace Jacobin.

The crime scene also isn't far from where Talia and I staked them out.

Yeah.

That's food for fucking thought, all right. A lot to chew on.

Just what did poor Brian Newcomb see that he wasn't supposed to?

Why would she kill him?

I swing my chair to look at Grant.

"Let me take this," I say. "I know the hills around here pretty well. I can get in and out without being noticed. I'll keep you guys posted if I find anything new."

With a dubious grunt, Grant rubs the silver-shot brown scruff of his beard. "You always work alone. Dunno if this is a one-man job."

"It is for now, Captain. We need stealth, not force." And *I* need them out of my hair. One wrong move, and they could undo everything I've been working for when I feel like I'm on the verge of something big. "The second I need backup, I'll loop you right in."

"Gonna hold you to it." Grant eyes me like he knows damned well I'll probably try to manage everything on my own anyway.

He's right.

But we don't need to say it out loud.

I flash him that quick, practiced smile. "Okay. I'll head out and have another look at the crime scene. My witness notes are in the system if you want to check them out. The girlfriend's staying a few days in case we need her. Her sister should be coming in to be with her."

"Got it," Grant says and trudges back to his desk, letting Rolf sniff his hand in passing.

I take another minute to enter more notes.

I'm a little on edge, and I feel like I'm racing not just against the impending storm, but something else.

Something big and mean and unnamed, looming on the horizon.

Maybe I'm imagining things.

Making connections that aren't there because I need to believe all these years of work, of patience, of lying in wait will actually pay off.

But I can't shake this feeling that something big is coming.

And when it breaks, it could take Redhaven down with it.

I finish up my notes and stand, summoning Rolf with a click of my tongue.

Even though he's languishing in all the treats and attention he pretends not to enjoy, he doesn't hesitate to go bounding up, breaking free from Mallory, who's abandoned her post at the 911 dispatch station for a belly rub.

As I'm attaching Rolf's leash, though, the creak of old hinges makes me look up—only to blink as the door to Chief Bowden's office drags open.

Damn.

I didn't realize he was here, considering he's been calling out for days on end.

He's clearly been in his office since last night.

From the looks of it, he slept in there.

He's bleary, his face dotted with stubble and his uniform shirt hanging open over a thin white undershirt that barely covers his ample belly. His hair sticks up everywhere.

Looks like he slept rough, and he's got a hand behind him on the small of his back. It's probably aching when the leather chair in that office isn't too comfortable to sit in, let alone sleep on.

Yawning, scratching at his face, he hobbles toward the bathroom.

When he notices all of us are staring at him, he freezes.

"Uh," Henri says. "Chief? Everything okay? Lookin' a touch rough there, sir."

For a second, tired irritation flashes over Bowden's face before he gives us his familiar 'aw, shucks' smile.

"Had a bit of a tiff with the missus," he says. "Forgot one of our anniversaries. Worst thing is, I don't even know which one. First date, getting married, six months? I dunno." His grin feels a little too fake. "Janelle put me out and told me I could find somewhere else to sleep until I wised up, so I did."

Lucas grimaces. "Damn, man. I'd say you shoulda checked into a hotel, but…"

"Yeah. I wasn't too welcome in my own establishment." Bowden slaps his thigh and lets out a little guffaw. "No worries. She'll forgive me by dinner, and I'll be back in my own bed by midnight. Ain't the first time. My lady's one hell of a spitfire when she wants to be."

Janelle Bowden.

Our version of Martha Stewart Lite.

She's got a backbone, sure, but I'd never call her a spitfire.

And considering our conversation yesterday, I don't believe the chief's story about why he got put out for a hot minute.

Still, I hold my tongue, just watching him.

I don't miss how Rolf tenses under my hand, and how intently he's watching the chief, too.

Maybe he's just picking up my own nerves. Or maybe he senses something more in that mind reader way dogs have.

Because there's something off about the chief.

I can see it in how his gaze sweeps the room, looking flat above his goofy smile, checking to make sure we're buying his load of crap.

How he stops as he meets my eyes—and his own harden before he moves on.

The edge of his mask is starting to peel.

The kindly old chief he pretends to be, well on his way to retirement, who wouldn't hurt a fly.

I can't quite see what's under that mask just yet.

But as he shrugs with another self-deprecating laugh and shuffles into the bathroom, I can't shake it.

I need to have another heart-to-heart with Janelle Bowden.

* * *

Before I have that talk, I need to have one last look at our crime scene before the rain hits.

The once-bright morning sky has turned into a brooding wall of clouds. I walk Rolf back home so I can change. Standard-issue uniform shoes aren't the best for hiking the hills.

Half an hour later, we're setting out again, slipping through trees that have the cool smell of an oncoming storm. The leaves turn up, showing their silvery undersides in the wind.

Rolf throws back a curious look for about the tenth time.

"What? I'm not thinking about her *that* much." His ears perk and I sigh. "Okay, dammit. Only *a little*—and you're taking that secret to the grave, old man."

We make good time, despite my mind drifting back to the hottest sex of my life with Talia Grey.

Soon, we break off the trail, about where the guys left police tape tied to a few trees as a marker. We spill out across the grassy slope leading up to the edge of the cliff.

Evidence markers are everywhere, the footsteps the same.

Nothing's been disturbed.

Slowly, I make my way to the spot where Brian Newcomb would have fallen and look down at the cliff while Rolf leans against my leg.

There's nothing left of him but evidence markers and a dark stain on the rocks.

Even that will be gone after the storm.

I wish I could say the same about the crows. There are three of the little black-winged bastards today, staring intently from an overhanging branch.

Reminding me I'll never stop thinking about Jet.

About how I found my brother, this shell of a man who was nothing like I remembered. No longer the big brother who'd step up and take the blows from our father's fists so they wouldn't touch me.

Sometimes our old man got to me first anyway, his little ghost-white mutant of a child, but not if Jet could help it.

Mikey, get out of the way! Let me. I'm stronger.

I used to beg him to stop, pulling on his arms.

If Dad was going to hit me no matter what Jet did, he should spare my big brother, so only one of us had to take the pain.

Jet wasn't having that shit.

He'd just grin at me, crooked and confident, even with his face busted and covered in bruises and ugly red split skin.

Jet, stop! He'll kill you! I'd scream.

Nah, Bro. If you go down, I'm going too.

I'm good. You're good. It's all good.

It wasn't all good.

It wasn't all good at fucking *all*.

I was the one who found him after the beatings were just bad memories.

This emaciated shell of a man in a dirty one-room apartment, slouched against the wall in his boxers and an undershirt stained down the front with vomit.

I hadn't talked to him for days, and too many missed calls had me worried. I found out fast I had good reason.

My loyal brother died ugly, and I hate the world that let him.

I hate that he was so gaunt, so hollow, I barely recognized him.

I hate that his skin was like one giant bruise.

I hate that it became my final, lasting memory.

Seeing my brother bruised, broken, and this time, not getting up again to face another ass-kicking from life.

Somehow, that was worse in the end than anything our father did.

I blame our old man as much as I blame the Arrendells and the Jacobins.

Maybe they gave him the drugs, but our father gave him the itch.

And now, just like Brian Newcomb, there's nothing left of Jet but a killing memory and someone else living in his shitty rathole of an apartment with no clue that a man died in the same place where they sleep each night.

"Go on! Get the hell out of here." I swear at the crows as they take flight, done with torturing me.

At least it's one of those days where they leave, period.

Rolf lets out a soft whine and lays his head on my knee, just like he did with Talia the other night. I smile faintly, scratching between his ears.

"It's funny, old man," I murmur. "I never minded being alone with these thoughts before. Before her, I mean."

I should not be missing Talia right now.

How the hell have I gotten this attached?

No clue, but there's no denying she's under my skin with her soft ways hiding a free spirit, with her shyness, with her determination and her creative fire.

And I'll only ruin her in the end.

I can't help myself.

Can't help wanting to touch her again and again until she's infected with my darkness, a pale and beautiful thing tarnished like ancient copper.

Get your head back in the game, you miserable fuck.

I lead Rolf on another quick circuit of the crime scene,

letting him sniff around in case anything pricks his interest, considering he was a drug dog once.

There are days when I wish I had Rolf's senses.

Everyone teases me about how I track like a wild animal, but an animal can do what I can't with scents. They can tell what came first, what came second, what came last, and piece together a more complete story than I ever could.

All Rolf tells me is that there's nothing too interesting around here. He takes a few sniffs and then immediately loses interest.

I take him down the hill then and do another slow walk where we found the body, expanding out in circles while I scan for his camera—just on the off chance this really was an accident and the camera just fell and wedged itself somewhere we overlooked.

I check every crevice, every pile of leaves, every rock heap.

Nothing.

I even look up into the trees, just in case the camera's dangling from a branch by its strap, waiting to spill its secrets.

No such luck.

Which tells me the victim definitely caught something on film that someone else didn't want him seeing.

By the time I hike through the woods with Rolf to where the cook site had been during my stakeout with Talia, I'm fairly certain who those someones are.

The site's been completely cleared out, well before the Jacobins usually pack up and move on.

I can piece together a scenario in my head.

Brian Newcomb wanders out into the woods, looking for a little wildlife to shoot. While he's camped out for the night, a noise alerts him that he's not alone.

He slips out and starts taking photos of the Jacobins at

work, thinking he's found some hillbilly moonshine operation or a backwooded cult, something worth documenting.

He doesn't realize he's been spotted by Eustace Jacobin, this tall shadow sailing up to him in the dark of night, her footsteps silent.

Not until it's too late.

Not until she's already pushed him and stolen his camera and left him for dead, right before screeching at her little brood of minions to pack it up and relocate.

They'll be more careful now.

Craftier. Harder to track down.

One more problem Redhaven doesn't need.

Fuck.

Thunder cracks overhead, underscoring my thoughts. The rain smells sharp on the cool ground. I crouch down in the clearing, running my fingers through the loose earth where a post was pulled up. Rolf sets his nose to the ground —then lets out a *yip*, his ears pricking.

He knows what they've been doing here.

He can smell it, and so can I.

"If dogs could talk, eh, old man?" I drape an arm over him. "What would you tell me, Rolf? What the hell should I *do*?"

XIII: DARK SHADOWS (TALIA)

I think I might be pissing Xavier Arrendell off.

In his office, I lean over his desk, flipping through the Post-its I put in the sample books I brought along for our meeting today.

He listens quietly as I talk about all things material, pointing out which colors would complement each other and asking his opinion on anything he doesn't like or would like to switch with something else.

He's noncommittal, occasionally letting out a half-interested grunt, though he doesn't argue back at anything I propose.

Weird. It's almost like he's losing interest in the project.

Whatever. Honestly, as long as he's still willing to sign the contract, make the payment, and go through with it, I don't care how he feels.

I'd actually prefer if he was more hands-off, considering how he's tried to be too hands-on with *me*.

This would be a lot easier if he'd just stand back and let us do our thing.

Maybe it's the possibility of exercising a little creative freedom that actually has me excited today. Even if he's not enthused, I still enjoy explaining color palettes, texture contrasts between wood and upholstery, all the little things that go into making a finished piece.

If I'm being honest, it's not just work-related excitement.

Because right before I headed out to meet Xavier this morning, there was a little buzz in my pocket.

Micah: When can I see you again?

With one little text, he lit my whole world.

Tonight? I answered. ***Your place? I don't want to wake Grandpa.***

I felt so dangerous saying that, knowing what it implied. And I half expected Micah to laugh and tell me he only wanted to hang out and talk about the case he was working, and how it might be connected to the Jacobins.

Micah: My place. I'll cook. Don't wear anything too nice. It won't be on long.

Ahhhh!

But I've been on cloud nine since that text.

Especially when I can still feel that sore, wonderful imprint of him. I can't help remembering his shape, his size, the slow, deep glide as he claimed me in ways I had no idea I could ever be taken. I'm still in disbelief a man like him could—

Rude, rough fingers grasp my chin.

So cold it feels like being touched by the dead.

That kills my sexy thoughts, throwing me back into reality.

I've been talking this entire time, but I was so caught up in my thoughts that I hadn't noticed Xavier's attention shifting, moving from the sample book to me.

Maybe if I was more focused, I could've moved away before he caught me.

But now, as my vision steadies, he's—he's too *close*, right in front of me, leaning across the desk until our noses almost touch.

His hand grips my chin too hard.

This is where I should scream bloody murder.

Instead, I'm turned to stone, completely caught off guard.

Why the hell is he touching me?

He smiles, slow and dark and baring too many teeth, staring right into my eyes. I think I see why he's been so deflated today.

He's sober, his eyes no longer dilated and jittering.

Somehow, a sober Xavier scares me more than one who's high.

He's also laser focused, and when I try to jerk back, his fingers tighten, digging into the hinge of my jaw and locking me in place.

"Now tell me," he purrs. His breath on my face feels foul. "You're looking flushed, Miss Grey." His gaze dips down, and I realize—oh God. My nipples are pressing hard against my shirt, roused by thoughts of seeing Micah. His hateful green eyes drift back to my face. "Is there something on your mind besides work, Miss Grey?"

Sweet Jesus, no.

Not anymore.

Also, it's bizarre how they both call me *Miss Grey*, but it feels so different.

With Xavier, it's revolting.

Hissing, I jerk back, wrenching free from his grip.

My cheeks throb where his fingers dug in.

"Don't touch me again," I whisper as firmly as I can, but my chest is starting to seize up. My voice comes out weak from not enough air.

He eyeballs me with a face like stone.

I want to say so much worse. I want to scream and rake

my nails across his eyes. But I'm alone here, and there's no telling what he might do if I actually put up a fight.

I swallow hard, reaching deep for diplomatic words he doesn't deserve.

"Since you seem so distracted, Mr. Arrendell, we can continue this discussion l-later," I whisper.

I don't look at him as I gather up my books, hugging them against my chest as a shield and backing away.

I still want to scream obscenities for what he did and quit on the spot, but I think about Grandpa and how much he needs this money.

"I'll email you my thoughts," I bite off, my voice arctic.

Xavier watches with a sort of sick amusement, sinking back in his power chair. He smirks, and I feel like he's looking right through my clothes, stripping me naked with his eyes.

"You're sure you don't want to stay, Miss Grey?"

I'm going to vomit, if I don't kill him first.

I need to get the hell out of here.

I need to go *now*, before I either puke or have an asthma attack, and I turn quickly on my heel.

"Definitely not," I wheeze out.

Then I pull his office door open and bolt into the hall.

I know I shouldn't be running with this tightness in my lungs, but I can't stop it.

I know the way now.

I don't need Joseph or any hired help showing me out. I dash down the lurid red carpet and weave through the shadows, diving into the foyer with every breath coming thinner and thinner.

My head throbs, blurring my vision.

Oh no, oh no, I can't.

Not here. Not with him.

I manage to wrench the massive doors open and go tumbling outside.

Bright sunlight.

Open air.

Safety.

I suck in a few rattling breaths, trying to make my lungs work.

Staggering forward, I drop down on the top step. My sample books go clattering across stone. I thunk my bag into my lap, pawing frantically for my inhaler.

There—there it is—and I rip the cap off, push it into my mouth, depress the plunger, and *breathe*.

Mist floods my lungs.

I inhale in the practiced way I learned so many years ago. My vision keeps swimming while I wait for improvement.

I can't believe I almost lost it because this creeper grabbed my face.

No—it's more than that. It's everything tied up in this mess with Xavier, Micah, the Jacobins, the dead man.

Whenever I'm around Xavier, I'm reminded how dangerous he can be. That it's not just a man creeping on a woman with hideously inappropriate advances.

It's a man who might hurt me with no qualms about it.

No matter how I try this subterfuge thing, I can't pretend I don't know what I do.

Worse, he seems to *enjoy* how uncomfortable he makes me, even if he doesn't know all the reasons why.

The help from my inhaler nearly fails me the instant the doors bang open at my back, smashing against the stone like a gunshot.

My eyes snap open.

With a small scream, I'm clutching at my chest.

"Miss Grey!" Xavier yells at my back.

Oh God.

I'm too busy pumping my inhaler to turn around.

Fuck, fuck, *fuck*, why did he follow me?

His footsteps draw closer.

"Please," he says urgently. "If you need medical assistance—"

I cut him off, holding up a hand as I gasp.

I take several breaths, slow and measured, before I speak again.

"No, I'm... I'm f-fine."

"Are you?" When my eyes can focus and I look up, he's bent over me—and shocker of shockers, the concern in his eyes seems genuine.

"Forgive me. I didn't dare mean to trigger your condition. I never meant to cross that line."

That line?

That flipping line?

I'm one second away from gouging out his eyes after all, asthma or not.

There's no mistaking what just happened.

He meant to cross *every* line.

I guess he just thought I'd jump at the chance to ride him like every poor girl who's hooked up with him for his drugs or for his money or both. Ugh.

The fact that I'm desperate enough to work for a scumbag like him probably made him think I'd do anything to close the deal.

This prick.

This slimy, disgusting *prick*, and I'm ready to throw everything away—the contract, the money, hope for Grandpa—until we're both interrupted by someone's throat clearing.

Xavier's face changes in the strangest way.

I almost think it's a look of dread.

Something I understand as Xavier straightens, turns, and I look past him.

Eustace Jacobin stands beneath the open arched door, half in the shadows, as if this is her domain and *we're* the ones intruding.

Her chin is lifted proudly. Her black eyes are cold and fixed on Xavier with an impatient look, her pale hands clasped in front of a gown as black as a funeral.

Her eyes flick to me, skewering and angry.

Oh God, it's a miracle I don't need another hit from my inhaler.

She's like a gorgon. Her eyes turn my heart to stone in under a second.

I feel cursed.

Of course, her gaze lingers a little too long. A little too deliberately. Then it shifts back to Xavier, watching him coolly.

I can't read what passes between them.

But Xavier seems to forget I exist.

That should make me happy, but it doesn't.

He smooths down his suit jacket and drags a hand through his icy-blond hair before stepping closer to Eustace. It's like she summons him without a single word.

That tells me who has the real power here.

I might as well not be here.

As he draws closer, they lean in, speaking in whispers.

I don't catch what they're saying as they step inside—and as they do, Eustace pulls something out of her skirts, shielded by their movements.

…a camera?

Eustace must have realized I was watching them. She pauses, and while the camera vanishes into Xavier's coat, she throws another terrible look over her shoulder.

Then she turns back, watching me like a hungry lizard

the entire time, and pulls the double doors shut with an ominous *thump*!

I'm left alone in the silence of day with nothing but the cries of hunting hawks wheeling overhead.

XIV: DARK FOREST (MICAH)

I hate crossing guard duty like hell.

No, not because I'm always risking getting cooked under the sun like an egg on a griddle.

I just feel like an absolute dumbass, standing in the middle of the street with my Officer Friendly smile plastered on while I wave kids through the crossing.

It always feels so out of character, even though it's a comfortable façade. More of the act that lets me exist here, embedded in Redhaven like I truly belong.

I'd bribe Lucas Graves into taking my shift, but he's got his hands full as a new dad, so here I am. Grinning like an idiot at a gaggle of elementary school kids at the light, their faces sticky with the ice cream pops they just bought from the truck on the corner.

"Skelly man's so cool," one boy whispers under his breath to his little co-conspirator.

That goofy grin on my face gets a little more genuine. After a lifetime of shitty nicknames and whispers, I don't mind this one so much.

I'd rather look like a bone-white skeleton man to these kids than something repulsive.

Hell, maybe I'd mind it even less if I had kids of my own.

If I could look at these little rug rats and think, *Yeah. That. I want that in my future, my own little mini-mes scampering around, making messes everywhere and looking up at me with those big, trusting googly eyes and calling me Daddy, believing there's nothing in the world I can't fix.*

If I'm being honest, I've never given much thought to settling down.

I'm not sure what I'll do once this case gets settled.

The idea of a wife, kids—am I too hollow for that?

Will I have enough soul left to spare after I've made Xavier and the Jacobins pay? And what woman would want an empty shell of a man?

I don't know why I'm thinking this shit.

Only, I do.

I know every goddamned reason why.

Talia's coming over tonight, and I'm already itching to get my hands on her.

It's like thinking about her summons her when my phone vibrates.

I glance at the foot traffic, the few cars coming through, and retreat to the curb, watching the light the entire time even though my shift's over in four minutes anyway. I still wait for every munchkin to get across before I read my screen.

Talia: Just left Xavier's. He was a total asshole creep. But get this! Eustace Jacobin showed up. She gave him a camera. Does that mean anything to you?

My blood becomes ice water.

The street fades into nothing.

A camera.

A fucking camera.

This is it. The missing link.

I'll bet my life that's Brian Newcomb's camera, and not only does it have incriminating evidence on it, it *is* incriminating evidence in and of itself.

If Eustace had it, I was right all along.

I just need to nail down proof, and they're all going to hell.

It means everything, I send back quickly. ***I'm off work in a few minutes. How soon can you meet me?***

There's a pause as she types.

Talia: I need to wrap up a few things with Grandpa, but I can be at your place in an hour.

Bring your camping gear, I reply.

Talia: We're going out again?

I'll explain when you get here.

Looks like we'll be having dinner on the go tonight.

She just sends back a quick heart emoji and a face making the OK symbol.

I glance up, looking around the street one more time to make sure it's clear and I'm good to leave my post. The time it takes me to walk back to the station, drop off a quick report, and clock out early—with Grant watching me the entire time—feels like a goddamned year.

Soon, I'm in my patrol car, heading home.

My head spins fucking faster than the tires.

I can smell what's coming. Something big.

And leave it to Talia to deliver the goods. Getting her involved was the right move, after all.

She's done plenty, though. It's high time to let her step back, before she winds up endangered.

Bringing her along with me tonight?

Whatever.

That's only because—if I have to admit it—I want her company.

I'm home, changed, and almost done packing my own gear for a one-night hike when my doorbell rings.

There's a little déjà vu when I answer and find her there in a cute flannel shirt and jeans again. This time, it's faded pink and black plaid. Her backpack looks smaller and sensible. She's a quick learner, and she smiles so bright it's blinding.

"Hey." She leans up to kiss my cheek. "Ready to go?"

I'm not used to people being happy to see me.

I frown.

Something's off.

I reach down to brush back a strand of fiery-red hair that slipped free from her messy knot.

"You're upset."

"I dunno." Talia's eyes flicker as she glances away. "Upset, that's a pretty strong word—"

"What happened?"

"I..." She sighs, glancing away. "How about I'll tell you while we walk?"

That worries me.

I nod, though, whistling for Rolf and reaching for his leash.

"Let me get my stuff and we'll head out."

* * *

I'll tell you while we walk turns into *I'll keep changing the subject*.

I can't begrudge her when she's still the same slice of strawberry shortcake she's always been. The way she lights up as we make our way through the trees is alluring as hell.

I don't have the heart to kill her enjoyment.

Not when this seems new for her, an outing she practically revels in, darting between plants, startling squirrels, and sometimes Rolf, too.

By the time they end up falling together in a pile of fallen leaves, Rolf's tongue hanging out happily, I've given up on getting anything out of her until we settle in for the evening.

If we settle in at all.

This is a scouting job.

I'm familiar with the Jacobins' usual patterns, but now I wonder if they'd do something new to shake off any extra scrutiny after Newcomb's body was found.

Makes me wonder why they didn't just dispose of it. Then again, they can't risk feeding their victims to the pigs anymore. That's old hat.

Guess they decided it was best to just let it look like a clumsy out-of-towner had a terrible accident on the cliffs.

I lead Talia down a spiraling path through the hills surrounding town. I can't always explain what I'm looking for when I start trying to sniff the Jacobins out.

It's not like they leave any markers or trash in the trees when they're so careful.

It's just a feeling I get.

A scent.

As we head northeast of the big hill where the Arrendell mansion looms, ice crawls down my spine.

Call it a premonition.

Someone's been through here recently.

Could've been hikers, yeah, but I don't think so.

They don't wear farm boots, and farm boots leave a certain imprint when they bend and break the grass.

While Talia skips on ahead to look up at a giant cobweb stretched between several tall trees, I bend down and study the broken grass clumped together.

Rolf crouches next to me, cocking his head like he sees something significant.

From the hint of yellowing on the blades, I'd say this happened last night.

Lifting my head, I scan around slowly until I find what I'm looking for.

A few leaves, torn free from a low-hanging branch about shoulder height. A perfectly good height for a grown man to fit.

Someone shoved their way through while the branches and twigs caught on their clothes and then snapped back with some ripped foliage. Half-torn bits still cling to the stem while the rest fluttered to the ground.

That way.

I slip two fingers between my lips and whistle.

"Talia, through here." I toss my head toward the small opening in the trees.

Breathless, flushed, and lovely with her blue eyes sky-bright, she comes bounding over. Every step makes her chest sway and strain against the pink plaid.

"You found something?"

"Maybe." I loop Rolf's leash around my hand and duck under the branches. "Follow me. Stay close."

She's more subdued as we slip under the canopy. The sunlight filtering through the trees forms a strange mosaic around us.

I let silence reign, keeping my attention on the trail, looking for those little telltale markers that say someone's been here—a snapped twig, a single homespun thread on a bit of flaky bark.

Eventually, I can't stand it.

"So are you going to tell me what happened?"

"Ah?" She sounds startled. I glance back to make sure she didn't trip, but she's just looking at me guiltily. "Oh. Right. Um..."

I stop, turning back to face her. She stumbles and pulls up

short in front of me but doesn't resist when I reach for her hands.

Rolf shifts between us, looking up at her with soft eyes.

"Talia," I whisper. "Whatever's wrong, you can tell me."

"Can I?" She stares at our clasped hands, her fingers curled loosely in mine. "Xavier came on to me pretty hard today. I was thinking about you during a creative meeting and I guess I spaced, and he thought… he thought I was mooning over him or something. He grabbed my face and was leering at me—"

"He grabbed you? That fuck touched you?"

Violence flares in my blood.

My hands burn like I can already feel his throat.

It's settled. If I ever get the chance, I'll tear it right out.

"I kinda ran away. I almost had an asthma attack," she continues. "That's when I saw Eustace give him the camera. She was waiting for him, I guess, and he followed me outside. I think he was trying to explain it away and make what happened feel less creepy. I don't know."

Goddamn.

If we were any closer to the Arrendell mansion, I'm not sure Xavier would be alive tonight.

My hands clench tighter.

I barely stop myself before I crush her hand.

My jaw tightens until there's an audible pop from the joint.

I have to hold still, or the rage boiling over will turn ugly and I don't know what I might do.

Not to Talia, no. Never to her.

But the urge to leave her and storm that hill, straight to the house of horrors, is almost too strong.

She won't quite look at me now.

Her guilt seems to intensify as the silence yawns between us.

"You're not telling me everything," I say tightly. "What else did he do?"

"What?" There's a panicked flutter of her pulse against her throat as she shakes her head quickly. "Nothing!"

"Then why do you look guilty?"

"Because it's my fault, Micah!" she hisses. "I let my guard down. I was so caught up in you, I gave him an opening—"

"*No.*" I drop her hands and cup my palms against her cheeks, leaning in to firmly look into her eyes. Her hair tangles over my fingers like a siren's coils.

Her wide blue eyes lock on mine, startled.

"Listen and listen good. You are *not* fucking responsible for what he does. I'm not angry at you, Talia. I'm furious at *him*. I want to dismember that disgusting fucking creep for thinking he has any right to you. But you? You didn't do anything wrong. I won't stand here and let you blame yourself for one ounce of his bullshit."

She just looks at me, the confusion clear on her delicate features.

"You're sure? You're not mad at me?"

Again, I'm reminded how fragile she is.

For all her iron backbone, for all that she's fought to find her way and make her own life after a childhood plagued with asthma, she's so inexperienced with this world.

So young.

So unsure of herself, even with me.

And it makes me painfully aware of how easily I can hurt her.

That's why I do my best to stamp my anger down, shoving it into those dark awful places where I keep the worst parts of myself.

Closing my eyes, I lean in and press my lips to her forehead, lingering to murmur against her skin.

"I'm sure," I say. "I'm not mad at you. I could kill Xavier

about fifty different ways, all of them torturous, but I don't blame you. Not in the slightest."

I'm not prepared for the way she hugs me, pressing her soft, yielding body into me. She buries her face in my shoulder.

"I was so scared. That freak, he just… I didn't know what to do. I just knew I couldn't be alone with him, and I had to get out of there."

"Good move." I curl my hand against the back of her head, stroking gently. "I don't like the idea of you going back there. Can you take your grandfather with you?"

"Probably not a good idea," she mumbles against my shoulder. "But I can try talking to Mr. Peters again. Ask him to just stay in earshot when I'm there?"

"You think he will?"

"Yes, I think so." Her fingers dig into my shirt. "He seems like he cares."

"You're selling me more on reaching out to him."

"You haven't yet?"

"No." I shake my head, settling in to just hold her. "With this kind of investigation, you have to be delicate. Find the right moment. Considering how rarely the staff leave the big house, if he slipped out for a secret meeting, it would draw attention. I'll have to catch him when he's out running errands."

"Don't they come down for groceries and stuff sometimes?" she asks.

"The shops mostly deliver to the house, but every now and then you'll see a maid or valet at the store."

"Next time I'm there, I could do it." Her voice quivers, and that anger simmering inside me burns that much deeper. "I could—you know—drop a hint. That the next time someone needs to run an errand in town, it should be him."

"Only if you can do it without drawing suspicion. Be

careful." I kiss the top of her head, then pull back enough to look down at her. "You feeling up to more walking?"

Talia lifts her head, looking around, taking in the trees around us and the sunlight through the leaves.

It's not hard to tell her previous enjoyment of the beauty around us is dulled, diminished.

I fucking hate Xavier even more for that, for taking the shine out of her.

"Sure," she says, straightening her clothes and stepping back. "What are we doing out here, anyway?"

"Looking for the Jacobins' next cook site. I caught a trail about a hundred yards back, and we've been following it." Impulsively, I reach over to catch her hand, holding it tight as I turn to lead her toward a break in the trees—another bit of crushed grass and scuffed leaves showing me the way.

Rolf pants as he settles into a steady pace at my side.

"I need hard evidence I can use to get a search warrant for the Arrendell mansion. Unfortunately, your word isn't enough, especially when we can't confirm the camera Eustace gave Xavier is the one I'm looking for."

Talia stays close as we squeeze through the trees. "Why are you looking for a camera? I thought it might be important, but I didn't know you already knew there'd be one."

"The dead hiker. Brian Newcomb." I pause to push a lowhanging branch up so she can duck under it. "His girlfriend said he was out taking photographs, but we didn't find a camera on his body or anywhere near where he camped. Though we retrieved his phone, there's nothing on the camera roll that hints he uses it for his photography much. Mallory found a few selfies and did a deep dive on the data, and nothing's been deleted recently. So I think the camera might have incriminating evidence."

In the pocket of shadow under the boughs, her eyes

almost give off their own cerulean light, wild with comprehension.

"Which means the murderer probably took it..."

"Yeah," I confirm, leading her deeper into the trees.

We're quiet as we walk and our hands stay locked.

It should be awkward, uncomfortable.

I'm not used to being with a woman who needs me this *close* when we're together, who always wants to touch me.

Hell, you'd think I'd find it clingy and annoying, considering the women I used to date back in NYC—icy, withdrawn types who were distant by nature.

Exactly how I liked it then, their bodies freely accessible and their hearts walled away.

Not Talia.

She practically hands me her heart like it's a kitten and begs me to be gentle.

How do I keep something so soft without breaking it?

I'm still pondering that as we break into a clearing near the crest of the hill we're on.

Rolf's ears perk as he turns his face up to the sun.

Even my breath catches as we turn back to look down at the splendor of the valley below.

Redhaven really is goddamned gorgeous, sitting pretty as a painting cupped in the palm of these woods.

All red gabled rooftops and steeples, its cobbled streets laid out like the spokes of a wheel. Still Lake glimmers, this shining mirror throwing back the sky's liquid gold.

I slide my phone out and take a picture.

Something to remember this town if I leave.

When I leave.

Yeah, that's coming.

It's starting to get dark by the time we move on.

I start to get that tingle down the back of my neck again.

It tells me we're close, and I slow down, creeping through the trees and holding my finger to my lips to keep quiet.

Sinking lower, I conceal myself more among the trunks, and she mimics me. Her footsteps are painfully loud as she follows, but she's moving as quiet as she can, barely raising a whisper of noise.

There.

A break in the trees. More disturbed earth up ahead.

I motion for Talia to stay put as I slip closer, hiding behind a thick tree trunk and peering through the gap.

Right on target.

The ground slopes down to a small valley.

There are dozens of pockets like these through the hills, some densely wooded, some filled with ponds or creeks, and some clear. This one was clear-cut by logging ages ago, and it's been untouched for so long that some of the saplings have started taking root.

Except those saplings are pulled up, piled along one side, stripped of their branches and waiting to be laid out to pave a makeshift road.

The usual cover of dead leaves has been swept aside, leaving bare earth.

The old logging trail looks reopened, too, the overgrowth trimmed back for a path just wide enough for a truck.

There's no one there now, but just in case, I edge back silently and make my way to Talia. She's tucked between two tree trunks, making herself small.

She watches me like a nervous deer as I draw closer.

"They've been here recently," I whisper. "Cleared the area for setup. They'll probably roll in and put down stakes tonight. We should find a good spot to camp and wait."

Talia nods slowly. "Will this be different from last time, though? What kind of proof will give you a warrant?"

"Not sure yet."

THE DARKEST CHASE

I take her hand, twining my fingers in hers and pulling her up before I lead her deeper into the woods.

We need to scout out a good camping spot.

Rolf's paws whisper against the fallen leaves as he patters at our heels.

"Frankly, I could've taken down the Jacobins alone a while ago. Clue the guys in and set up a raid when they're at one of these sites. Bring in Raleigh PD to surround them before they pull their disappearing act. Only, that would leave Xavier flapping in the wind, wild and free, and he'd just find someone else to take their place eventually. In all these years they've never given me any concrete evidence linking them to each other. All I can do is wait for my moment."

Talia goes silent behind me, her steps dragging.

I stop, glancing back.

"What is it?"

She stops and stares down at her feet. "Cocaine. That's how Xavier makes his money, isn't it?"

"One of many ways. He's also involved in some shady foreign real estate investments and a few failing private capital ventures. Though I suspect they're fronts for other dark money."

"Wait, that means…" She pulls at her lower lip, her delicate face so crestfallen it looks like she's about to cry. "The money for Grandpa's treatment. It's coming from the same crap that killed your brother."

"Maybe," I admit slowly. "You can't beat yourself up over that."

"But it's filthy, Micah. Blood money."

Goddamn, I hate the tears in her eyes with a vengeance.

I also don't know where this urge to *comfort* her comes from.

I haven't had a nurturing bone in my entire life. Think I

used it all up bandaging my brother's wounds at an early age, along with my own.

Somehow, Talia just brings it out in me. She's huddled in my arms again.

"I see it differently. By doing something good with that money, you're making it clean. We can't undo what's already done. You not taking his money won't change where it came from. At the very least, it can help save your grandfather."

Yes, I know. The more I talk, the more ethically grey it sounds.

No, I don't fucking care.

Truthfully, I don't know how Talia lives like she does.

Taking so many things to heart, *feeling* everything so much.

She's practically vibrating with emotion as she leans into me, her small fingers curling against my arms.

There's something about the weight of her, her softness, her curves, the way she fits into me. It's more than just gritty desire for her flesh.

The way she quivers when I touch her.

The way she *smells*, vanilla-sweet and heady.

The way she feels so damn right.

I don't mind holding her as long as she needs, but after a couple minutes she pulls away and flashes me a brave smile, wiping one eye.

"Let's keep moving. We need a place to crash before the mosquitos come out," she says.

* * *

OUR CAMPSITE GOES UP NEXT to a small creek running through a break in the trees.

There's just enough room to build a fire and lay down our sleeping bags. No tents tonight.

Working together—while Rolf hops around in the creek like the big mess he is—it doesn't take long to dig a fire pit and start working on a quick dinner.

We've got time to kill before the Jacobins' usual late-night work starts. I want the fire banked by then, no fresh smoke or cooking smells to give us away or scare them off.

So we toast flatbread with cheese over the fire, talking casually while we eat.

As Talia finishes licking a bit of melted cheese off her finger, she looks at me. "Hey, do you think you could send me that pic you took of Still Lake? It was really good."

"Sure."

I dig out my phone and text the photo to her.

When her breast pocket lights up and jitters, she pulls her phone out—and I catch a glimpse of the new text notification on her lockscreen.

Vampire Man sent img.png

I raise both brows. "You saved me in your phone as *Vampire Man*?"

"Um." Talia freezes, looking at me sheepishly with her phone clutched in both hands. "…guilty," she whispers with an embarrassed smile. "Sorry?"

"Uh-huh." I lean back on my hands, just watching her. "Why did you do that?"

"I just… you know, the first time we met—"

"You mean when I gave you mouth-to-mouth in the middle of town," I growl.

Her face flashes pink.

She swallows loudly, nodding.

"Yeah. That time. It sorta felt like waking up from a dream. This beautiful man with sharp teeth and a red mouth hovering over me… I used to be a huge Anne Rice nerd. And Grandpa had me watching old *Dark Shadows* reruns from the time I was five."

"Uh-huh." I never take my eyes off her. She's squirming now, and there's a predatory pulse in my cock that loves every bit of it. "Have you thought about me biting you, Talia? Harder than last time? Do you want to be marked?"

"Marked? O-oh." Breathy, soft, and she's already saying *yes* without really saying a single word. She can't look away as her lips gleam and her little tongue slips over them. "Maybe. I mean, you bit me before, but you were being gentle."

"That's not a yes or a no," I tease.

Leaning forward, I prowl toward her.

Every last little vulnerable thing about her jumps out at me in the fire's glow.

One minute, she's this innocent angel who warms me with a light I can't describe, who makes me feel like if I wanted, I might learn how to have a *life* again.

The next minute, she's prey, plain and simple.

Her nostrils flare.

Her breathing quickens.

It's like I can see her pulse thudding against the fragile skin of her throat as her eyes dilate, locking on me with wonder.

When she trembles again, I'm fucking gone.

Forever drunk on this woman.

My inner beast inhales deeply, intoxicated by her scent.

Fuck, her scent.

Vanilla heaven, mine for the taking.

My lips burn, aching to show her what being marked truly feels like.

Closer. *Closer*, every slow movement makes her tremble more until I'm right on top of her.

She whimpers as I stop, almost nose to nose with her, our eyes locked.

There's more than rich vanilla rising off her now. This

aromatic sweetness like pheromones, heady and stinging sharp.

"Yes or no, Talia," I breathe. "Do you want me to fucking mark you?"

"*Ohgod.*"

One word. It comes out in this small, shaky rush.

Then her eyes close and she slumps toward me like her bones forgot how to hold her up.

She's shaking like a leaf.

Her hands knot together in her lap, her lashes trembling against her freckled cheeks.

I'm waiting.

Impatiently, I'm waiting for this fragile, inexperienced girl to tell me no.

To tell me to stop frightening her and talking like a weirdo.

To push me away and ask why I can't be normal, why I even *want* to bruise her just to leave a jealous mark of ownership.

To know why I need something else, something darker than last time, something lasting.

Only, it never happens.

Instead, Talia rolls her head to the side, this soft jerk of quivering submission.

My blood goes electric.

She reaches up to pull her hair free from its loose tail, shaking it down in a waterfall of cinnamon red fire, drawing it over her shoulder to one side to fully bare the long, smooth expanse of her throat.

"*Yes.*" It's such a faint whisper I can barely hear it, yet so husky with desire.

Everything about her feels intensely erotic. Painfully inviting.

I don't think she has the slightest idea what she's doing to me.

I crave her.

I fucking *need* her like the storybook vampires that make her wet, but it's not her blood I'm after.

It's breaking her.

I need her to break for me, beg me to claim her in the sweetest ways.

My mouth dips to her neck.

Her vulnerable, slender throat waits, but some last thread of restraint holds me back. Slowly, I trace my lips over her ear, listening to her rough, uneven breaths.

"If I bite you," I snarl into her ear, "I won't be able to stop myself from marking you all over."

She lets out another soft whimper, completely overwhelmed before she sways toward me.

"Then mark me. Even if it hurts. Cover every inch of me."

Fuck. Me. Senseless.

I have to close my eyes for restraint.

Otherwise, I'll pin her to the dirt and rip her clothes to shreds right now.

Just one minute.

Just a few precious seconds to remember I don't want her to regret this.

Then I open my eyes again, fixating on the wild beat of her pulse, leaping like it's fighting to break past her skin.

My tongue traces my lips in furious anticipation.

My entire body throbs, my cock swelling with vicious desire until it's almost angry, straining against my jeans.

I want her under me, screaming and pleading, torn between delicious agony and sheer ecstasy.

I want to be her living fantasy.

I want to taste her.

I want to ruin her for every other man.

Bowing my head, I graze her throat with my lips, breathing in her scent.

Then I part my lips and sink my teeth in.

My teeth aren't sharp enough to pierce, of course.

But they're just sharp enough that her cry is instant, and it makes my cock rage.

"Micah!" Her voice cracks on my name.

Her back arches, her head falling back.

Her skin is smooth cream against my lips, my teeth, my tongue.

Now I can *feel* her pulse, stampeding against my mouth.

Her body betrays her. She loves it.

I half expect her to push me away as the reality sinks in.

As she realizes this might hurt.

Instead, her arms slip around my neck and her fingers tangle in my hair.

She pulls me closer in abject surrender, begging with her big blue eyes.

Mark me.

Make it hurt.

The last thread of self-control snaps.

Catching her wrists, I pull her hands from my hair, then shove her down against her sleeping bag, forcing her on her back.

My teeth only leave her throat for a second.

Just long enough to catch her startled look.

Long enough to see how flushed she is, her nipples hard against the thin undershirt under her open flannel shirt.

Snarling, I pin her to the ground by her wrists, my body weighing her down.

As she arches, sliding against me from head to toe, teasing my cock with her leg, I fucking do it.

I strike.

I find the pink red mark where I bit down before and

suck hard, pulling tender flesh between my teeth, thrusting my knee between her thighs to spread her open.

There's nothing gentle this time.

Not when I'm greedy as hell.

Nothing tender in the brute way I seize that mouthful of her flesh and bite down harder, *harder*, all while she writhes.

I drag my body against hers roughly, urging her to lift her hips, to rub herself against me, to spread herself open and find her pleasure.

The sounds she makes are pure sex.

They put a spell on my cock, and when I feel her skin stretching to its limit, her mouth opens.

Talia screams.

Pure, sinful pleasure.

I should silence her.

We're out in the open, stalking the Jacobins, and if they show up early and wander off their path for some odd reason, they'll figure out we're here real goddamned quick.

Still, I want to *hear* her.

I want to know how she cries out for more, the way she whimpers my name, the way her voice hitches and breaks as she crashes against me with breathy heat between fear and pleasure.

Yes, I'm fucked up to love this so much. No question.

To be so turned on by painting her skin.

But what if my sickness is also hers?

She's not fighting me, not pulling away, not telling me to stop with her voice dripping with horror.

Instead, she clings to me, her nipples so hard and her breath coming in ravenous gasps as I lick at the bite mark, trailing my teeth over her skin.

Rasping, I push the collar of her flannel aside and leave another imprint.

It's feral and hot and needy, and suddenly I can't get enough of her.

I rip at her clothing, tossing it aside into the leaves, exposing more skin to mark. She's just as frantic with her fingers digging at my shirt and then at my naked flesh as I fling my top and jeans and boots aside until we're nothing but wild animals in the raw.

I barely even register the delicate, pale violet-pink lace of her panties, her bra.

Even the sinful sheen of matching stockings, the wicked side this timid girl hides under her clothing like a secret gift just for me.

Not when I need her creamy skin so much.

Not when I'm this fucking *hungry*.

Today, she's my canvas.

And it feels like I'm undoing every terrible thing my father did, the things I hated, the pain I never asked for.

Ugly pain and hatred, that's not this.

The way I mark her?

The way she begs for it?

There's no hate whatsoever here.

No abuse.

Nothing but absolute desire boiling over as I bite her shoulders, her breasts, her stomach, her thighs, savoring her reaction.

She tosses her head and pleads, "More, more," while I defile her with bruises.

She's too fucking beautiful.

This pure woman, welcoming me wholeheartedly, when all I know how to do is *hurt* to show my love.

It's like she understands, though.

She knows and she isn't just tolerating this like it's the price of being with me.

No, she wants it.

She wants me.

She wants everything I give, and as that realization sinks in, I lick a hot trail up her inner thigh and bite down *hard* at the soft crease where her thigh meets her pussy.

I find wet, clenching folds and slip my fingers inside.

Of course, she's ready.

So *ready*, gripping like a girl possessed.

Her inner walls suck my fingers while her whimpers make me frantic.

"Micah," she begs. "Micah, *please*!"

One more goddamned minute.

I let her suffer just a moment longer.

I'm torturing myself too when I'm so hard I could fucking die, and the feel of her silky skin against me is torture.

Still, I hold off on biting down harder, *harder*, even as I plunge my fingers in and out, feeling her tighten and grip me so desperately, chasing that shivering rush of her breaths that means she's so close to—

There!

I stop right before she unravels, right as she gives me the roughest whimper, begging to let go.

"Not yet, woman," I growl. "Hold the fuck on."

I slip my fingers out of her with one last sweep of my thumb over her clit, then replace my fingers with my cock.

Hands under her thighs, spreading her open, I lift her up.

Then I plunge down, mounting her with a single hard thrust, wild and rough and holding nothing back.

I kiss her just as brutally until our lips taste like bruises and our bodies crash together.

Fuck, I can't hold back.

Clutching her closer, I take her hard, plunging into tight depths that envelop me in the burning pleasure of her flesh.

Pain slices down my back—her nails.

She claws at me, just as wild as I am, rising up to meet me.

This frantic pace turns us bestial, two animals fighting to find out who comes first.

We clutch our bodies, rolling, thrusting, building to a tortured frenzy.

The movement feels like sword thrusts, and I only crave more violence.

More!

My hips slam hers faster, harder, chasing something always out of reach, pulling her with me, taking us both higher—no.

Taking us low.

Down into the nameless darkness, the strangest heat, the thrill that shouldn't be right, yet can't be wrong when we're in this together.

She's flushed scarlet with passion.

Her eyes are dazed and nearly closed, yet there's no doubt there. No fear.

Only raw pleasure and sheer surrender to the end.

And when the end comes, it's a fucking cataclysm.

Volcanic.

A finish made from vicious lashes, dragging me down in jolting rushes as I bury my cock so deep, so *deep*, and fucking fill her.

I come so hard my vision blurs.

I mark her inside the same way I did to her skin, making sure she *feels* me pouring into her and painting her with come.

Her greedy pussy wrings every drop from my balls.

She takes it with a moan, wrapped around me, still begging even as I see that beautiful instant when she collapses.

I feel it as her legs lock around me, milking every last shiver from my body, torturing me and dragging a groan from my throat.

Together, we're two monsters in heat, hell-bent on sating our lusts.

Lust.

Is that still what this is?

The thought barely has a chance to settle before she pulls me down with another needy kiss.

Then the last screaming wave of pleasure roars over me and robs my senses blind.

* * *

"So, I've made a decision," Talia says as she sprawls on top of me lazily. "I'm going to need more high-necked shirts."

I've barely left the haze of animalistic sex and I'm laughing. What the hell is going on?

I don't know what I expected after that.

Tension.

Silence.

Regret.

Maybe for her to be horrified that we were capable of being so crazy, so violent. It wouldn't be the first time.

Usually, when it happens, I gladly take the blame—like I brought out something in her that she couldn't believe was actually part of her, the ability to enjoy being hurt that way, so it must be something I did to corrupt her.

With Talia, who's barely just lost her virginity, I should have taken more time.

Should've built up to this and eased her into it.

It would've served me right if she'd called me an animal and pushed me away from her.

Instead of flopping bonelessly against me, rubbing her cheek to my chest like a contented cat, teasing me about high-necked shirts.

In the firelight, she's all amber and cream. The flickering

flames wash over her naked body and make her skin glow in soft contours before plunging down into gold-lit shadows that accent her like a piece of fine art.

The marks I've left behind, they're dark reddish-purple bruises. Mostly in the shape of my teeth where I branded her.

She shivers in my arms.

I maneuver us so we're lying on her sleeping bag, then stretch one arm out to grab my own and drag it over us like a makeshift blanket. I feel like I should fish out the little first aid kit and swab over her bites with a little antibiotic salve just to be safe.

Soon.

Let me savor this first.

Talia makes a happy sound, nosing at my shoulder.

"Better?" I ask.

"Mm, yeah. Just cold," she answers, folding her arms on my chest and propping her chin on them, watching me with her eyes twinkling.

"Because you're naked and sweaty," I point out.

"And how did I get that way?" She grins, tapping her fingers on my chest.

"By showing me your throat, calling me a vampire, and asking me to ruin you," I growl. I give her ass a crisp smack that makes her squeak. The first time I saw her collapse against the town square, I never would've imagined she could be such a brat. "You're okay?"

Talia blinks at me.

"Yeah. Why wouldn't I be?"

Damn. I guess I'll have to be blunt.

"Woman, I just pinned you down, bit you to hell and back, fucked you hard enough to make you scream. I wouldn't let you up until you were begging for more." I arch a brow. "Most people talk about safe words before doing that shit."

"Oh, y-yeah. Good point." She gives me that cute little

stammer when she's startled and nervous. It gets to me, almost as much as the way she tongues her upper lip in thought. "But it was fun. I liked it. It was *exciting*. I never get to do exciting stuff that scares me. In the good ways, I mean. I never have, I mean."

I frown. "You're saying I scare you?"

"Well, yeah! But, like, it's not the kind of scared you're thinking." She's so serious, giving this her utmost attention, those pretty blue eyes focused. "I'm not scared of you hurting me, not for real. I'm scared of my body falling short. I'm scared of taking a risk with you and no matter how much I want it, my lungs give out and tell me I'm not allowed to just jump and see where we might land. I'm scared, yes. But I'm doing it anyway because I've spent my whole life avoiding living." She smiles, soft and heartfelt. "I won't be scared of being with you."

The way she says it sounds like she means more than just sex.

That she's not just risking her body with me and satisfying my need to hurt beautiful things.

She's risking her heart and challenging my need to shut down. Anything that demands I be real, be *present*, be part of someone else's life instead of an actor moving through their scenery, never intending to stay.

I don't know what to do with that, what the hell to say.

I just know I'm going to break this girl's heart.

Because I don't know how to be with someone who looks at me the way she does.

Because being damaged makes me *exciting*, but not enough to be good for her.

So I reach up to brush her tangled hair back. It runs over my fingers like copper silk, reminding me of blood.

Silent, searching for words, I tuck her hair behind her ear.

I have to say something. *Anything*.

I part my lips, and—

Rolf's head jerks up.

While we were going at it, he'd dozed off on the other side of the fire, the most tactful wingman ever.

Now his ears are up. His gaze snaps toward the site I scouted earlier.

He's got that old tension that strips the years away from him until he looks like a police dog again.

I go stiff. Talia does, too, blinking at me harshly.

"What?" she asks, a note of hurt in her voice before she follows my line of sight toward Rolf. Then that hurt turns into understanding. "*Oh*," she gasps. "Do you think…?"

"Only one way to find out, and it requires clothes."

We glance at each other for a few more seconds—and despite the heaviness when I didn't say the right words to shelter her heart, we can't help how our lips twitch.

There's a small snicker before we kiss and then scramble apart to grab our clothes from the near-wreckage of our campsite.

Her flannel shirt landed half an inch away from becoming kindling. She rescues it and wiggles into her jeans while I get dressed.

By the time we're done, I hear what Rolf must've noticed first—the faint rumble of engines.

Multiple engines.

With a long look, we slip into the trees with Rolf trotting after us.

To her credit, she's gotten better at stealth, crouching behind me as we speed toward a small break in the trees to look down over the new cook site.

It's déjà vu as we hunker down, watching the old, grungy military trucks and pickups come rolling in.

No headlights tonight.

Their license plates are covered in black cloth or removed completely.

There are six of them this time, and they file into the clearing and circle around, forming a perimeter. Swarming like locusts, the Jacobin clan pours out and starts unloading, rolling out sheets of aluminum and tall wooden stakes and crates of equipment.

It's almost impressive how fluid they are.

In minutes, their little stand of sheds start popping up like weeds.

But they don't have my attention right now.

Because there's one more car tonight.

A long black town car, glossy and clearly expensive.

I'd bet my bottom dollar that car belongs to the Arrendells.

No one else in town keeps luxury cars like that, though now and then when the part-time retirees hit town they come in their high-end SUVs.

That's definitely Arrendell style.

The front plates are also covered.

Damn.

Fucking please, I think. *Please let him be in that car.*

The car parks at the entrance to the clearing.

The headlights flash briefly, then cut out. I can't quite see who's behind the wheel, but the back passenger side door swings open.

My heart stops, expecting Xavier Arrendell to step out.

No luck.

It's Eustace Jacobin and—Chief Bowden?

"Holy shit," Talia curses softly at my side. "I still can't believe it." Her whisper sounds tiny.

Too bad I can.

I reach over to grip her wrist lightly, reassuringly, but say nothing.

Focused, I unfold my compact binoculars from my pocket and press them to my eyes, trying to peek inside the car before the back door closes.

There's no one else in there.

Fuck.

I scan over their crew.

Looks like business as usual—hefty barrels of liquid chemicals, large pallets, and metal cisterns are rolled into another shed under halogen lights strung along cords and hooked to freestanding car batteries.

Everything unmarked, of course.

Nothing incriminating from a distance.

Even if I took photos of the bushels of coca plants, any small-time lawyer could pass it off as moonshine materials.

Eustace Jacobin and Chief Bowden have their heads together, talking while they watch the setup, but I can't read their lips enough to work out what they're saying.

Crap.

Looks like this is going to be another useless stakeout.

Nothing incriminating, not without revealing myself.

More than once, I've been tempted to steal a brick of their product, but that won't do anything useful.

I wouldn't be able to prove where the coke came from.

Too bad doing everything aboveboard with proper chains of evidence makes it damnably hard to catch the fucking rats.

Sighing, I lower the binoculars. "No Xavier. I—"

"Hang on a sec." Talia grabs the binoculars.

Blinking, I watch as she strains forward, staring at something.

She's tense now, her body rigid, and she jerks her head up, staring at me with wide eyes.

"It's him, look!" she whispers, thrusting the binoculars back at me. "Joseph Peters. He's the one driving the car."

The car's pulling away as we speak.

I've only got a few seconds before the view through the front windshield vanishes through the trees.

I snatch the binoculars and look, squinting at the driver's seat. Sure enough, there's a man. Trim, neat, with short brown hair and a tired look on his face.

"You're sure? You're positive it's him?"

She nods quickly. "We've talked several times. I know his face."

"Jackpot," I whisper, lowering the binoculars with a grim realization. I'm about to blow Redhaven apart, and possibly Talia's life, too.

"Micah? What now?"

"Now, I need to have a good, long talk with Mr. Peters."

XV: DARKER DAYS (TALIA)

I can't help wondering what I did wrong.

I watch Micah sleep, white as moonlight against the dark sheets. His glasses are on the nightstand.

I know now if he opens his eyes, I'll be nothing but a blur of color until he fumbles the lenses onto his face. The lack of pigment in his eyes means he's almost blind without assistance—and a little sensitive about it.

After the first time he told me while I watched him poke those little lenses into his eyes, I've never mentioned it again.

I've found myself avoiding a lot of things lately.

His bed is enormous and increasingly familiar. I've spent almost every night here since our last stakeout in the woods.

I thought we were starting something, I guess.

Maybe I was just being naïve.

This starry-eyed girl who's never been in love before.

So wrapped up in my fantasies that I didn't realize he wasn't really there with me, thinking about the future.

Still, as long as I'm naked with Micah's teeth on my skin and his cock inside me, there's no shortage of intimacy.

Raw, vulnerable, he lets me see this wild thing inside him, lets me see how there's some wounded part of him that needs to take it out on someone else.

It doesn't scare me.

Not at all.

It feels divine.

The burn of his teeth, the feeling of being willingly powerless while this beast devours my body, mind, and soul. It really is like having my own vampire, ready to play the darkest fantasy.

But as soon as we're sweaty and tangled up and done, he goes quiet.

Yes, he holds me close, kissing my hair and checking to make sure he hasn't done any lasting damage. Sometimes, he pulls me into a steaming shower and cleans me with a reverent touch.

He caresses me with a tenderness that makes me feel cherished.

Loved.

Like he'll leave the hottest bruises on my skin just to kiss them later, growling that he'll always keep me safe.

But he just won't *talk* to me.

He locks up, and when I try to talk to him, he says he's tired.

I'm not buying it.

Because more than once, I've woken up and caught him pacing, brooding around the house with a tumbler of whiskey. Even Rolf watches him, occasionally glancing at me like he knows I'm awake and he wants me to fix this.

God, but I don't know *how*.

Because I don't know where Micah goes when he gets like this.

I just know it has everything to do with Xavier Arrendell, the Jacobins, and Micah's dead brother.

I also know he hasn't confronted Joseph Peters yet. I'm the one who's supposed to make that happen.

I just haven't been back to the house yet, not when I've been putting it off.

This quiet glow I get with Micah, when he's kissed me until my mouth tastes swollen and hot and my body feels so well used, it's everything.

And I don't want to destroy that with Xavier's bullcrap.

He emailed me the other day.

Just a brief, stiff apology, explaining that he was drunk and not fully himself. He didn't mean to make me uncomfortable, he says.

B.S.

It feels like a pretense to get me up there again so he can back me into a corner and watch me squirm. There's a horrible difference between a man who makes me hurt so good and a man who truly wants to *hurt* me for his own selfish delight.

It's darkly funny and twisted, yes.

But it's so much different when I want it.

And Micah always makes *sure* I want it every time.

Xavier Arrendell doesn't care about what I want at all.

Only about scaring me.

I'll go tomorrow, though.

I'm done being chicken.

We'll set up a meeting with new fabrics and fresh concepts. I'll get Joseph Peters alone and ask him to hang close—and I'll do whatever I can to hint that he needs to meet with Micah soon.

If he'll roll on Xavier—if I get how police stuff works—he can avoid being charged as an accessory.

Plus, I kinda want to ask him a few things myself.

Like how dirty our kindly old police chief Bowden really gets.

But I'd probably make a mess of things.

So I'll just be as subtle as I can and hope that Micah will take it from there.

"You stare loudly," he groans, turning his face into his pillow.

He's just a messy tuft of hair, half-buried in the lushly thick king-sized pillow.

He tends to sleep on his stomach with one arm draped over me, the hard ridges of his back visible above the covers. A few old faded scars mapping his history linger across his shoulders and spine.

"Sorry." I smile and snuggle into the crook of his arm. "How often do I get to watch the vampire man, sound asleep in his lair?"

"Very funny, Shortcake." Yawning, he bares those teeth that tease me all the time. Then he rolls on his side to face me, his eyes opening into sleepy silvery-blue slits. He stretches one arm back in a lazy flex, grabs his glasses, and slides them on his nose. It's hard not to tell him how *cute* he is when he does that. "Everything okay?"

"Yeah, I—yeah, it is." I'm not a good liar, but I try. "I was just thinking about going up to the big house tomorrow. I can't avoid him forever, and I'm the only link between you and Joseph Peters, right?"

"Yeah, but that doesn't mean—" He stops, sighs, and caresses my cheek. "This is fucked up, Talia. You don't have to pretend you're not afraid to be there."

"I'm not pretending. I *am* afraid, but I'd be there even if you weren't involved, Micah. I just wouldn't know how to watch my back." I smile weakly. "And we'd still be strangers while I worked on the renovation."

Something in his eyes shutters over.

As always, I can't get a good read on him. He's so free with his touch and so guarded with his emotions.

"Do you wish we were still strangers sometimes? Would that make it easier to deal with Xavier?"

"What? No!" I push myself up on one elbow, clutching the sheets against my naked chest. "Micah, this time with you…" I bite my lip.

"What are you trying to say, Talia?"

It feels like a stranger asking me that.

Like Officer Ainsley, probing at a suspect.

That stabs hard, and I look away sharply.

"Nothing," I say. "It's fine. We should sleep. We both have work in the morning."

"Don't do that." He pushes himself up, tilting his head to try to catch my eye. His fingers trail over my shoulder. "It's just going to fester if you don't let it out."

"But what if letting it out makes things worse? With us, I mean?"

"Is there something wrong with us?"

Yes.

No.

Maybe?

"I don't know." I press my face into my palm and shake my head. There I go, making a bigger mess when I didn't mean to start anything at all. "I'm just wondering what we are, I guess. Because I'm not your girlfriend, am I?"

I don't want to look at him.

But his silence demands it.

When I glance back, he's watching me calmly.

Almost *too* calmly.

Like any part of him that might be affected is totally walled away.

I meet his eyes, then drop my gaze.

"Say something," I whisper.

But he doesn't.

I feel him shifting.

Every silent second twists my heart into knots.

But when Micah sits up and pulls me in close, I can't resist.

His warmth is so familiar. I still throb all over with the way he's used me, touched me, made me feel wrecked and loved all at once.

He pulls me into his arms, so close until we're skin to skin, intimate yet so very distant.

Warm lips press into my hair, hot breaths curling over my skin.

"Don't get too attached," he breathes. "I'm bad for you, Talia. Look at the shit I make you do."

"Things I *want*," I throw back. Part of me feels angry enough to shove him, but I don't want to break away, so I just hide my face in his shoulder. "Look, I know I'm not like you. I'm young and naïve but I'm not clueless, Micah Ainsley. Sometimes people like getting kinky. You like biting me, and I like being bitten. That's not corrupting me somehow. I like this mouth."

I reach up, touching a finger to his lips.

He goes quiet again. I pull back to look up at him, searching his gorgeous, icy face.

"That's what you've been thinking all this time, isn't it?" I ask. "That you're tainting me somehow just by sleeping with me."

"No. Not by sleeping with you."

"Then how?" I'm almost demanding an answer, my voice breaking. "What do you think is so awful about you that you're nothing but trouble?"

I look at him and I realize that cold façade hides something else.

Emotion, raw and ugly and almost startled as he looks at me with those stark silver-blue eyes.

"I'm not a real man, dammit. I'm not *whole*. I'm a black pit, full of hate and violence, pretending to be decent. I didn't come here to arrest Xavier Arrendell, Talia. I came here to *kill* him. And once I do that, after it's done…"

"What? What else will you do?" My heart forms a lump in my throat.

"I won't be anything at all. Once that's out of me, there's not enough left to make a complete person." He smiles bitterly. "I'll probably be in jail, anyway."

Oh my God.

It stings knowing Micah really can't see himself.

He doesn't see all the things I see in him: his pride, his bravery, his dedication. That grumpy chip on his shoulder from being belittled his entire life and fighting like mad to prove he's better than everyone who ever put him down.

That dry, self-deprecating humor.

That heart so full of grief from losing his brother, still weighing as heavily as if it only happened yesterday. Not because he's empty, but because he feels *too much*.

The way he's so gentle with me, even when he's marking me.

The way he always does the right thing, even when I can tell he doesn't want to.

And I think he'll do the right thing in the end when it comes to Xavier, too.

Because even if Micah has a secret darkness, I know who and what he is.

He's not a killer.

Deep down, I'm sure of that.

I touch his cheek lightly, tracing his cheekbone. It's so stark, like someone took a piece of white quartz and shattered it into these faceted edges.

"You're more than that," I whisper. "I know you'll probably tell me I'm projecting. That it's just my fantasy. That I'm seeing you as what I want and not a real person." I smile wryly. "But if you were my fantasy man, it wouldn't be so irritating that you use up all the hot water in the morning before I'm awake. If you were all fantasy, I wouldn't live for the times when you forget to brood and actually laugh. I wouldn't love your terrible sense of humor or how flipping *grumpy* you are."

"*Hey.*" He lets out a tired laugh. "I'm not grumpy. Just don't have much time for people's bullshit."

"Sometimes you are." I grin, stroking my thumb over his cheek. "And sometimes you're just an awkward grumpy-grump who's been alone for so long you forgot how to be around other people. But I think there's some part of you trying to remember."

"C'mon, that's enough." His eyes soften, and he presses his cheek to my palm, a hint of stubble teasing against my skin. "You aren't supposed to be the observant one, Miss Grey."

"I guess I learned a thing or two from the man who keeps pinning me on my back every night and making me scream."

"Yeah? Now who has a terrible sense of humor?" But his lips quirk and he holds me closer, leaning in to rest his brow on my temple. "You're right. I am fucking awkward and bad-tempered at times. There are also things you don't know about me, Talia, and I don't know how to tell you. Until I figure it out, can we let this be what it is? Does it need a name? A label?"

For a second, I mull it over.

"No. No, it doesn't." It still hurts a bit to say that, but it's better than him saying there's nothing between us at all, instead of something nameless.

Nameless, I can deal with, I think.

Even if it leaves a small hole inside me that feels like it

could widen if I feed my doubts into it. But I make myself smile and brush my lips over his.

"Nameless or not, you still get to answer Grandpa's uncomfortable questions when I go limping home in the morning," I tell him.

Micah lets out a half growl, half groan. "...will you let me off the hook if I give you one more reason to limp?"

The mere suggestion ignites my blood.

Sex was always this flowery thing in my head, before I knew what it could really be like. Before I knew it could be slow and raw and deep, or wild and rough and deliciously intense.

Honestly, if we don't last, I don't know how anyone else will ever measure up.

I feel like I have to hold on to this for as long as I can.

Take every chance.

So I slip my arms around his neck, leaning into him.

I'm already sore and well used, but I desperately want to know how it will feel for him to take me when my flesh is already so tender I almost can't stand it.

So I push him back, watching the way his eyes flash with desire, turning smoky and dark as I nudge him onto his back.

I slip across him, straddling his waist.

And I can already feel his cock pressing against me, hot against my naked flesh and harder than steel.

There's a powerful throb against me as I rock my hips, grinding against him. I stop with a shudder as my breath catches and my entire body goes hot, friction pulsing inside me until I feel myself growing slick.

Sighing, I slide my fingers over his chest, following the pale contours of his skin. He's so sculpted he could be made of marble.

"Don't just make me limp," I whisper. "Make me *scream*."

Micah's eyes sharpen.

There it is—that predatory light that thrills me.

This thing almost like fear but not quite when I trust him so much.

He's like a carnivore that's caught the scent of blood, his lips parting, his princely face turning feral.

"You may regret saying that," he warns. His hands curl hard around my hips.

His fingers bite, giving my flesh that wonderful sting.

"*Ah!*"

Holy hell, this is bad.

I'm falling so fast, so hard.

All it takes with Micah is two seconds of going dizzy.

Then the wild animal moves in for the kill.

He lifts me up by my hips, slides me over him, and in a single greedy stroke pulls me down on his cock, burying himself inside me.

Without warning, I'm *full*, spread open and straddling him.

I toss my head back with a cry, bracing my hands on his chiseled abs to keep from collapsing with the shocking pleasure.

He's so hard inside me.

This position opens me in ways that let him go deeper still.

With one vicious thrust, he takes me over, trapping me in white-hot pleasure.

Gasping.

Paralyzed.

Whimpering.

I try to rock my hips, try to twist, but there's no escaping who's really in control. Especially when he freaking *stops* and just grabs my hips, holding me impaled on his cock.

His eyes spill into mine, furious and glinting.

He stares up at me with that cunning smile wilder than ever, dark and brimming with lust.

"Don't think you'll get off that easy, Shortcake," he whispers. "I think I'll keep you like this until I'm good and ready."

I freeze—as much as I can with my body still trying to move, this wild thing beyond my control.

I'm desperate, starving for his hot strokes.

"Wh-what?" I dart my tongue over my lips. "You want me to stay like this?"

"Yeah. Let a man enjoy the view." His smile widens as he sits up in a controlled flex that makes every muscle in his body stand out—and makes his cock shift inside me slowly, pulling gasps from my throat. "Maybe I want to play with you a little first."

"Play?"

He's killing me.

With him, *play* could mean hours of this delicious torture before he lets me come. Or he could make me come so fast and furious I can't stand it anymore.

Either way, I know he won't let me go until dawn.

Yet even with that menace in his smile, there's a sweetness there, too.

And it's there when he kisses me, when he lets go of my hips to slowly move his hands up my back. His mouth caresses mine so gently with a promise.

I'm only here as long as I want to be.

If it's ever too much, I know he'll stop.

And it's that belief, that faith, that lets me melt against him, sinking into his sultry kiss with a sigh.

God, this feels *good*.

Micah spreads my thighs, his cock so hot inside me, this slow inferno slipping deeper, deeper with each moment his mouth teases over mine.

His tongue probes inside my mouth, his hands so sure and firm on my naked skin.

If it were just this, I could stay this way until dawn, languishing in his glory.

But I know better.

I know, and just as I let my guard down, kissing him with pure reverence, he moves.

His hand swats my ass, an open-palmed *smack!* that stings just enough to make me gasp and jerk my hips forward.

I let out a broken moan as his cock plunges up, prodding that sensitive spot that makes every nerve ending a shrieking ball of sweet agony.

My back arches as I break his kiss, digging my nails into his shoulders and tossing my head back.

Big mistake.

Because all I'm doing is baring myself to him—and before I can hope to recover, his mouth latches on to the upper curve of my breast.

He's kissing and sucking and *biting* with a fierceness he's trained me to love.

And it's only the first move of that lethal mouth before his lips work on my nipples and then dart away with the lightest sparking tease.

All while his worn hands dig into my ass, slowly flinging me up and down on his cock.

"Woman, you're flushed. I want you *red*," he spits.

Oh God.

There's no escaping him.

No matter how I twist, how I tense, how I shudder, I can't help *feeling* him turning me inside out.

He wrecks me even with the slowest thrusts.

And there's no stopping the soft sounds pouring out of me, whimpers and cries rushing out.

I can't help the sounds rising between my thighs, either.

Each time I jerk in response to his taunting, I'm wetter than before. Our flesh goes damp with sweet, sucking sounds.

His mouth roams my chest, my shoulders, my throat.

Like a true vampire, he's always so drawn to it, and my pulse flutters as his mouth ghosts vulnerable skin.

Teasing, making me wait for it, the anticipation coiling in a tight, ragged knot in the pit of my stomach.

I'm ready to scream myself hoarse by the time he stops on my neck.

And I *do* scream as he sucks my skin.

My nails bite his shoulders—then pull away as he catches my hands, forces them behind my back, holds them there in one hand.

His free hand cups my breast, rolling, squeezing, digging his fingers in, flicking my nipple with his tongue.

As his teeth play with my flesh, he crushes me against him until I'm helpless and convulsing around his cock, completely losing my mind.

It's too much.

Twin points of heat against my throat, my back curling into this vulnerable position by his bruising grip, my arms trapped, my nipples throbbing as he pinches and rolls and teases.

My clit grinds against the base of his cock.

His thick shaft moves inside me, kissing me from the inside, imprinting him on me like clay.

I'm so gone, tightening around his girth like a glove.

I can't handle it.

Not another thrust.

Finally, I *snap*, breaking like someone split me in half, shaking as my O rockets through me.

It feels like getting fucked raw and deep, my inner walls

clenched around his cock, pressing down tight and then relaxing.

Over and over, a rhythm that leaves me struggling to breathe.

To whisper.

To do anything besides dissolve into a shattered mess.

"Little rocket," he groans softly, thrumming against the skin of my throat.

It tells me how much he loves it when I come on him.

Just how much he feels it when I'm so sensitive I can feel him swelling inside me, thickening, his pulse beating violently.

It's so close.

So intimate I want to hide.

Curling forward into him, I whimper as I bury my face against his neck like I'm mimicking my mock-vampire lover.

That's it.

I'm so completely *ruined.*

"Talia." He kisses my jaw, the corner of my mouth. His voice is husky, raw. His fingers tighten on my wrists. "Talia, fucking move for me."

Oh, I try—but the second my body tightens even a fraction, sensitive pain stabs up inside me, this hyper-aroused aftermath where the slightest touch can make me scream.

I whimper, shaking my head and burying my face deeper in his throat.

"I... I *can't...*"

His palm cups my cheek as he looks at me, coaxing my head to rise.

He helps me find his lips in a sticky kiss that slips into me and opens me in the most sinful way, leaving me helpless.

Slow, so slow, yet always in control.

Always stripping my will until I'm his.

Truly, completely, irrevocably.

And when I open my eyes as our lips part, I see him.

I meet his glacial eyes, and I realize he knows.

He knows exactly what he does to me and he's *enjoying* it.

Relishing the fact that he can make me beg for pain, for relief, for pleasure, for *anything*.

Knowing that I'll push past my physical limits and give myself up in the sweetest ways, just to feel him come.

"You can," he whispers, stroking his thumb along my cheek. There's a moment when his cock jerks inside me, and I suck in a breath, thighs tensing.

"Move for me, Talia. Let me see you suffer for your pleasure."

A low, keening sound rips from my throat.

I tremble, fear clutching up in my stomach and chest.

But it's that fear of something you want, if only you're brave enough to risk it.

I know it won't hurt. I know I'll love the pain.

And after meeting his eyes for a few shivering moments, I move.

Just the slightest switch of my hips at first—only to freeze, tensing with a cry as his cock slips against my inner walls and sensation screams through me.

I feel like a raw nerve, too much stimulation, too swollen and sore already and now this, now *this*.

Yet stopping makes it worse, the flare of his cock head presses against that brutally sensitive spot deep inside me that feels like a trigger.

I'm afraid to move.

But I can't *not* when I'm vibrating like a plucked violin string.

I've never had a clit this swollen in my life.

Teeth clenched, I shift again, rocking back, easing some of the pressure inside me but only making the other feelings worse as his friction hits.

Every imprint of his shape teases me while he stretches me out, carving the ridges of his veins into me, his pubic bone grazing my clit with vicious shocks.

I'm so ready.

So ready to break.

Again, a little thrust.

A small rock of my hips before I have to stop.

Again, *again*!

Each time wrenching a whimper from my throat and a boiling curse from his.

"Fuck, Talia. I'm going to fill that pussy up."

The promise destroys me.

I have to squeeze my eyes shut because the way he's looking at me on the edge feels like being devoured.

Yet even closing my eyes can't hide me from the reality.

Micah's gaze touches me everywhere, his long fingers holding me captive, his other hand sliding down to seize my ass.

The next time I move, he's going faster.

He jerks me against him roughly, turning those tiny, controlled movements into a sudden rolling thrust.

I scream.

He catches my mouth and steals my breath, pushing his tongue in, dominating my lips in an instant.

Ruling my body as he moves with me, his powerful thighs flex under me as he pushes himself up to meet me and drags me down with him.

I'm nearly sobbing with the heat of it.

There's a trembling moment when I could fall apart if my lungs give out, but I won't let them when I need this.

I need him.

I need more while we're writhing together, faster and desperate and chaotic as wild animals.

His teeth turn cruel against my mouth, biting me until my lips are as sensitive as my pussy.

He's so bad, but so good to me, erasing the thin line between pain and pleasure.

Until I can't stand it.

Until I short-circuit, becoming a bundle of live wires and coursing energy.

I'm thrashing and panting and losing the rhythm as the blinding pleasure takes control.

Tearing me apart.

Leaving me lost in this riptide lashing my body and this beautiful monster growling in my ear.

I'm fused to him so tight I'm nearly crushing him, my body somehow finding a way to take him deeper. *Deeper* than he's ever been before, marking me inside in the worst and best ways, and then—

I feel it.

That moment he comes undone, his grip suddenly so much harsher.

His lips part with a guttural sound, half curse and all animal.

His dick surges, raw and rough and overflowing.

Everything I am mixes with Micah until we're both a dripping mess.

Until we find each other where the waters meet.

Until we're drowning together.

God, I really am drowning in him.

I'm in so deep I don't mind his vast darkness or the nameless thing we've become.

I just know that after loving Micah Ainsley, there's no earthly way I'll ever be the same.

* * *

I can't remember falling asleep.

I think I blacked out toward the end as I came down from my high.

Micah must have untangled our bodies and put me to bed because when I wake up with the morning sun stabbing through the window while my feet are numb from Rolf sleeping on them, I'm still with him.

Safely cradled in his arms and tucked under the covers with absolutely no recollection of how I got here.

Though my body remembers what he did to me last night.

...and the fact that I still have to walk up that hill today on *foot*.

Ugh.

Groaning, I burrow into Micah.

Just a little longer.

Just another minute before I have to go face Xavier Arrendell and pretend I don't know the awful truth and hope that this time he'll keep his grubby hands to himself. At least until after the first check clears.

"Stay put. My alarm still has about six minutes." Micah's voice drifts into my hair, gritty with sleep.

"I don't think six more minutes will make us any less tired," I whisper into his chest.

"Whose fault is that?"

"*Yours. Totally*," I bite off.

His chest shakes against me in a muted chuckle.

"Good answer." He pauses and yawns into my hair. "You're going to make me get up, aren't you?"

"Mm-hmm," I mumble into his chest, still burrowed in and not moving at all. "Now I have to go home and get dressed *and* hope Grandpa doesn't notice I look like I've been attacked by vampire bats."

"I'll lend you a jacket to cover up." He sounds too smug as

he kisses my jaw. "Shit. In what world am I lucky enough to land a girl with a vampire kink?"

"I don't have a vampire kink!" I shove at his chest. "I just have a very active imagination, thank you very much. And you just happen to tick a few of my boxes."

"A few?" He stares at me with his eyes narrowed. "So, you're telling me you wouldn't like me if I wasn't an albino fuck with a twisted appetite?"

He says it lightly, teasingly, but I wonder how much he's really asking.

If he really thinks I only want him as this unicorn thing who fits my fantasy, this rare freak who turns my crank and nothing else.

I pull back enough to really look at him.

He's perfection incarnate in the morning light.

Not that I'd ever tell him that when he'd just start scowling, killing that soft, sleepy expression.

He's described himself as a canvas for his father's violence in the past, but I don't think he realizes his skin can hold so many other colors.

Like the dawn light, casting gold and pink and even a little violet into his hair, his skin, his eyes, until he's not so pale at all.

He's wearing the morning, my very own fallen angel with an aura too beautiful for life.

I smile, touching my fingertips to his lips.

"Dye your hair black," I say. "Get a spray tan. File your teeth down. Gain fifty pounds. Micah, I won't care. It's not about how you look. It's about how you make me feel. And as far as the pain thing…" My smile widens. "I liked you before I even knew I liked it or knew you liked doing those kinds of things. So, yeah. Sorry, you're stuck with me."

I'm not sorry at all.

There's a ghost of last night's conversation there, too. That question of what we are, haunting us in every glance.

I can see it in his eyes, wondering if I'll push him again after he diverted me last night.

I don't have the heart for that right now.

So when he just smiles and kisses my forehead, I lean into him and let it go.

"I don't think I'll be dolling myself up like an extra from *Jersey Shore* anytime soon," he says. Then he nudges my hip. "C'mon. You can shower here so you don't have to go home a mess."

Oh, he *definitely* sounds smug.

I almost hate him for how easy it is to flex his lithe body and roll out of bed when I *know* I'll be limping the instant I stand up.

I watch him in pure disgust, eyeing him as he pads toward the bathroom, before I sit up with the sheets clutched against my chest.

I look at Rolf and snort.

"Can you believe your dad?"

The dog cocks his head at me, his ears up.

"Murf?" Rolf answers.

I snort again.

"Murf, indeed."

Even with work looming over our heads, it's an easy morning.

Separate showers this time—or else I won't be walking out of here under my own power—before he puts his uniform on and I shrug into the summery pink dress he ripped off of me last night.

I feed Rolf and give him a good brushing while Micah whips together coffee and breakfast. It's so smooth it's hard to believe we've fallen into this thing together so fast, but I can't complain.

It makes me feel like I'm really a part of Micah's life.

Not just a tourist, passing through his long, dark night.

Yet that wall remains, like I'm reaching for him through impenetrable glass. And that feeling hangs over me as he drops me off outside the shop with a new problem.

I can feel Grandpa watching from the window, but that doesn't stop Micah from kissing me before leaning over to unlock the passenger door.

Then that brazen jerk actually *waves* at Grandpa.

Oh my God.

"Are you kidding?" Spluttering, I shove his arm and duck out of the car.

The bell jingling above the shop door doesn't even fully stop before Grandpa looks up from pretending to check the price tag on a hand-carved rocking chair in the front window and beams at me brightly.

"So things must be going well with Mr. Ainsley?" His eyes glitter with mischief. "I'm starting to get lonely, eating breakfast all by myself."

Ouch, nice reality check.

Guilt swamps me as I kiss his wrinkled cheek.

What if something happened while I was out enjoying myself? Sure, he has Mrs. Brodsky checking and bringing him a few meals, but still.

What if he had one of his *moments*, and I came home with no idea where he might be or if he was even alive?

"I'm sorry, Grandpa. I'll stay home and we'll catch up tonight. I'll make your favorite, cranberry sugar crumble muffins."

"Oh, nonsense, girl." He swats my arm. "I don't need a damn nurse yet. Besides, you know I'm at my best in the mornings."

I smile.

It catches me off guard every time he talks about it openly.

I'm the one dancing around it, I guess, dreading the day when mornings won't be so kind to him anymore.

Maybe I got too used to people treating me that way, like something flawed that could break down any second.

Whispers behind hands, worried glances, long conversations behind closed doors I was never supposed to hear. A thousand things about my illness that never actually involved me.

I meet Grandpa's twinkling blue eyes.

No wonder we understand each other so well.

I think his gaze softens as the silence stretches between us. Then he catches my hand.

"Tally, I know you're doing what you're doing at the big house for me," he says. "Believe me, I'm grateful. Don't think I'm not just because I'm clinging to my independence with my fingernails. But I don't want you leashed to me, either. Do you know how happy it makes me to see you living for yourself?"

My heart hurts so sweetly.

Tightening my hold on his hand, I pull him into a hug, pressing my cheek into the grey and white wisps of his hair.

"They're not mutually exclusive, Grandpa. I can do both," I promise. "I can live for me—and do my best for you."

"I know you can, Tally-girl."

I nearly choke into a sob.

But I pull back before I let myself get too overwhelmed and take a shaky breath, smiling. "I'd better get moving. I need to change, and I'm due up at the big house soon."

"Go on, girl. Shoo! Wouldn't want to keep Mr. Arrendickhead waiting."

I snort, laughing and darting into the back of the shop,

then upstairs. When I step into the bathroom in my bedroom, I'm suddenly grateful Grandpa is so tactful.

I'm human chaos.

Marked from neck to toe with the hickeys.

I hastily wash myself off, dabbing a few spots with a little salve because I know Micah worries about me. After that, I throw on new jeans and a nice turtleneck.

It's a little more formfitting than anything I'd want to wear around Xavier, but it's better than letting him see my neck and getting any new bizarre ideas.

This body only belongs to one man.

The strange, possessive thought makes me flustered as I do my makeup.

I'm going for the 'Oh this? I'm not wearing any makeup at all, I woke up this way' look—secret: no girl ever wakes up like this.

Last, I grab my folio case before darting out with one last parting kiss for Grandpa.

Yep, I'm limping a tiny bit after all, still feeling Micah with every step. But at least I had the good sense to wear thick-soled boots.

They help soften the walk as I head up the hill with a confidence I don't deserve.

Or maybe I do.

Even if I loathe Xavier Arrendell, I'm feeling good about the final sketches and samples.

We've exchanged several terse emails ironing out the details since the last disaster of a meeting.

While he's been a little particular like the stuck-up jackwagon he is, I feel like I've captured the pulse of what he's going for.

Hopefully enough for him to sign off on it and start paying.

We're one signature away from the deposit check and speedrunning our options for Grandpa's care.

I already have a few good medical centers in Raleigh bookmarked on my phone.

The cognitive treatment will be a long-term thing and might even require visits to specialists out of state, but we can at least get him in for surgery to restore his hands. He'll be stubborn about missing out on work for recovery time, sure, but hey.

It's better than losing what he loves.

When I arrive at the Arrendell house, the day feels darker.

I still find a smile for Joseph Peters when he answers the door, swinging one of the big double doors open for me and offering me a polite, almost wary smile.

"Miss Grey," he says smoothly. His eyes are guarded. "My apologies, however, Mr. Arrendell was pulled into a snap meeting. I'll be happy to let you into his office to wait. He shouldn't be long."

I feel like my ears go up.

Alone in Xavier's office? Plus, a few minutes to feel Joseph out?

How did I get so lucky?

"That would be great, thanks!" I step into the house, turning to watch him as he shuts the door behind me. I even manage not to stammer.

I might be getting better at this whole spy thing.

"How have you been, Mr. Peters? Is everything okay?"

His brows knit together as he smooths his white gloves, then turns to lead me into the familiar red-carpeted hall to Xavier's office.

"Certainly, miss. All is well."

Is it?

"I'm not trying to pry," I say quickly, lurching forward to walk next to him. "I just feel a little like I upset you when I asked about Cora Lafayette. You're obviously still grieving and that's okay. It must be hard working in the house where she died."

Where this rotten family killed her, I want to say, but I don't dare.

There's a subtle stiffness to Joseph's posture as he glances at me, folding his hands behind his back.

"I appreciate your concern, Miss Grey," he says neutrally. "Fortunately, I am managing as well as I can."

Dang.

He's a tough nut to crack.

I guess he'd have to be, working here.

The things he sees, the secrets he keeps—like those late-night drives into the woods—I almost shudder to imagine.

He'd have to be a human fortress just to stay sane.

Rather than push him and make it too obvious, I just smile silently, letting him lead me along. Right next door to the office, there's another door slightly cracked.

I can just make out a long, glossy conference table and a large monitor with someone's face on it. There's a shadow passing back and forth through the slit, a hint of Xavier's tall silhouette, the shoulder of his well-tailored suit and the glint of his blond hair.

"—don't care if you have to build a fucking bridge across the Atlantic. Just get the damn ship into port!" I can hear him snarling—cold, furious words so different from the icy calm way he speaks to me. "When did I start paying you to make excuses?"

Joseph clears his throat pointedly.

"Miss Grey." He pushes the door to Xavier's office open.

Crap.

I shouldn't be so obvious with my eavesdropping.

"Thanks," I murmur, ducking past Joseph and into the empty room.

It doesn't feel as stifling without Xavier inside.

The golden light through the curtains actually feels a little welcoming as the sun pours over smooth varnished wood like honey.

"Would you care for a refreshment while you wait?" Joseph asks. "Tea, soda, water, coffee. We also have a small selection of pastries on hand. I could potentially scare the kitchen into putting together a light brunch, if you're feeling hungry."

"Oh, wow. I ate before I left, but thanks. A bottled water would be lovely," I say. He's starting to leave, and I take another chance, turning to face him. "Mr. Peters! Um, are you *sure* you're all right?" Time to be direct. I need him to know this is important. "You just seem tired. Too many late-night drives?"

Joseph freezes in the doorway.

His face goes pale.

He looks over his shoulder sharply, then steps inside and shuts the door quickly behind him. I've never seen his eyes so unsettled.

Ouch.

Even with the door closed, I can still hear Xavier's angry voice, though I can't make out what he's saying when it's muffled by the walls.

But it's Joseph who steals my focus as he hisses, "What do you know?"

Shit. Shit. Shit!

Okay.

So, that worked, but it doesn't mean I know how to handle this. I haven't leveled up my spy points that much.

I fumble for a moment, licking my lips.

"I know it must be hell cleaning the mud out of the town car's tires in the morning. It's not really made for old logging trails, is it?"

His eyes widen, glinting with fear.

His hands are still clutched on the doorknob behind him, and now they tighten until his gloves squeak as they rub the brass.

"Miss Grey," he says gruffly. "I need you to be very clear what you're implying right now."

"I can't be. You know I can't. Not any more than you can be open about what we're discussing," I say. "But if you want to get out of this and not be implicated as an accomplice, I know someone you should talk to."

His jaw juts out. "Respectfully, you *know* exactly what happens to people with loose lips in this household, Miss Grey."

"That's exactly why you should. Because of what happened to *her*."

Cora, I mean. There's no need to say her name to his face.

I step closer.

I've never seen a man his height flinch back from someone as small as I am, but he winces like he thinks I could hurt him.

"Mr. Peters… Joseph, doesn't it ever eat you up inside, doing their dirty work and staying quiet for the folks who killed someone you cared so much about?"

"…that was Aleksander. And frankly, the little bastard got what was coming." His voice turns bitter, hard with sorrow. He averts his eyes. "Miss Grey, please don't press this matter. I've made peace with my demons. I suggest you work on yours before you wind up involved with something over your head. I'm warning you for your own good."

Fear knifes through me.

"I…" I lose it, feeling like a door's just been slammed in my face. I hope Micah won't be disappointed that I possibly screwed this up. I look away, fretting my hands against the strap of my bag. "Mr. Peters, I'm sorry. Please just don't mention this to the Arrendells?"

"Considering I couldn't bear to see you suffer the consequences, you have my word I won't," he bites off. "Never speak of it again."

"I won't if you won't!" I throw back. "But if you ever want help, the offer stands. Come find me. I'll point you in the right direction."

I take a bigger risk then.

Digging around in my bag, I find a small notepad with a pen clipped to it.

I quickly jot down Micah's number.

No name, nothing incriminating, then I rip the page off and offer it to Joseph.

He stares at it like it's active plutonium, making no move to take it.

Sighing, I fold it in half and slip it in the breast pocket of his tailcoat.

I don't know what I'm expecting him to say or do.

But he doesn't say anything.

He just looks down, then up at me again, his lips thinning.

There's the slow creak of the door opening. The click of the latch, a bit too hard and final.

And I'm alone, except for the agitated sound of Xavier's muffled voice filtering through the walls.

Despair curdles my stomach.

God, I'm *never* going to find what Micah really needs.

That means he'll have to keep plunging along, heading deeper into the danger zone. Whatever it takes to get close enough to the Jacobins for something more than circumstantial. Enough to hold up in court or at least get the Redhaven PD a legal warrant.

Ugh.

Something about that nags me, remembering how Micah

never seems to mention any of the other guys on the force knowing about this or helping him.

It just seems *off*.

Especially when I've known Lucas Graves and Grant Faircross my whole life—or at least, known *of* them. I wasn't part of their older friend groups growing up, but they always seemed like this shiny thing, always out of reach. People I observed from the outside in my sickly little bubble and desperately wished I could be like when I got older.

But everyone knows the story of Lucas' sister, Celeste Graves.

How she was possibly having an affair with Montero Arrendell, only to disappear the same night Grant's best friend Ethan vanished too.

It turns out, Ethan Sanderson was in love with Celeste and determined to save her from the Arrendell sickness.

Rumors plagued both cops their entire lives, especially when Grant had to defend his friend's honor after people started whispering that maybe a jealous Ethan killed Celeste and then skipped town.

When the truth came out, first as a trickle and then as gushing horror, it never felt like it would stop.

And knowing what we do now, you'd think both Grant and Lucas would be ready to chew their own arms off for a chance to take down the last standing Arrendell brother left in town, and maybe the entire Jacobin clan with him.

So, yeah. It's odd that they're not in the thick of this.

Or maybe I'm making too much of it.

Micah doesn't talk shop with me much.

It's very possible the rest of the force are working other angles and he just hasn't told me. I'm definitely not his police peer, spy girl or not.

More than anything, I'm just useful.

That hurts more than it should.

But I push the thought away and make myself *useful* right now, glancing at the closed door and listening for Xavier's voice.

I can't make out what he's saying, but his voice isn't changing like he's moving around. He sounds annoyed and distracted. He'll probably be busy for a few more minutes.

That's enough time.

I circle the office, scanning the bookshelves, looking for anything and everything that might look like a ledger, suspicious papers wedged in books.

I pry open an old wood chest. Nothing but pungent cigars lined up neatly in a row.

I rifle through the stacks of unopened mail in his inbox and outbox, but they're all from lawyers, investment firms, normal-looking business stuff.

Considering he was yelling about a boat, I check to see if I can find anything like a shipping manifest, but nope.

Nothing.

There are a few open envelopes on his desk. Only, when I take a careful peek at the contents, one is a tax form for charity donations and the other looks like a phone bill.

…oh, wait.

There are pages of call logs here.

I spread them across the desk with my heart slamming and dig out my phone. I take a quick snapshot of the lists of numbers, call times, inbound or outbound.

A few come out a little blurry with my hands trembling, but I get as much as I can before I stuff them in the envelope, leaving it where I found it.

His file cabinets are locked.

Dammit, of course they are.

But I try his desk drawers, opening one after the next. I don't know what I'm expecting to find.

A convenient plastic baggie of cocaine, right next to that silver dish he had before and a rolled-up hundred-dollar bill?

Way too easy.

It's just pens, letter openers, random odds and ends, and a couple photos of Xavier with his brothers. They're crumpled and stained like they were thrown away and then retrieved. Nothing at all incriminating—

Wait. No.

The bottom drawer.

I instantly regret it.

There's vintage smut. Old nudie magazines and what looks like a buckled leather strap just the right size around for—ahem. Well, I guess I know what he does in his free time here.

I really wish I didn't have that image, Xavier choking himself with that strap and masturbating furiously.

But tossed in there on top of what look like more ropes and chains and harnesses, there's something else.

A digital camera—just what Micah was looking for.

I try not to get too excited.

A lot of people still use digital cameras instead of their phones for photos. Maybe Xavier likes taking nature shots and it's got nothing to do with the dead hiker.

I should leave it.

I'll look really silly if I snatch it and it turns out it's full of Xavier's nudes while some supermodel leads him around on a leash, and then I'll have to figure out how to give it back to him without getting groped or something.

But there's also a strap attached to it.

Just inside the curve, I can make out a faded label.

PROPERTY OF BRI

. . .

Holy shit.

I can't see the rest.

But I know *Xavier* doesn't start with *B-R-I*.

Wasn't the hiker's name Brian?

My heart lurches.

My gut clenches.

I glance at the wall between the office and the conference room, then glance around quickly for something—anything —*the Kleenex dispenser on the desk*!

I hold the tissues like a shield so I can snag the camera by the strap without leaving any fingerprints. Gingerly, I lift it out.

It takes a few awkward fumbles, but I manage to flip my bag open and lower the camera inside without letting it touch my skin.

Just in time for the door latch to click.

My heart—oh my God, every organ in my body—leaps right out of my chest.

Good thing I have fast reflexes.

I knock the drawer shut with my knee before I freeze up.

The flap on my bag gives in to gravity and oh God, *oh God*, there's a little loop of the camera strap sticking out. I hope the flap covers it.

I don't dare look down and check because—

Here comes trouble.

Xavier Arrendell strides in with a scowl on his face, his lips drawn tight, his normally pale cheeks flushed with anger.

He doesn't look as sickly and tired as he normally does.

Those hard tracks of addiction aren't as deep today in the stark lines of his face and the shadows under his eyes.

I wonder if he lays off his habit when there's serious business? *Or maybe,* that little bit of human empathy I cling to whispers, *he's trying to kick it and go clean.*

There I go again, having too much sympathy for the monster.

And I feel like that devil can see my sins as he stops mid-stride in the middle of closing the door and gives me a piercing look.

"Planning to take over my office, Miss Grey?"

Yikes.

It must be obvious I was snooping around when I'm standing behind his desk for no good reason, unless—oh.

Oh, right.

I smile sheepishly, holding up the wad of tissues still crumpled in my hand.

"Sorry! These spring allergies are killing me." I make a big show of pressing the tissues to my nose and blowing until my eyes hurt.

"I see."

I can't read his expression as he watches me with that lizard-like stare.

Is he suspicious?

Did Joseph slip up and tell him anything?

I try not to let my nerves show as I pointedly blow my nose again, then look around until I find the wastebasket and toss the crumpled tissues in.

Surely, he wouldn't go digging around in the trash to make sure I actually used them, right?

I dust my hands off and circle around the desk, smiling brightly.

"Anyway, are you ready to go over the final details?" I ask brightly.

The way he looks at me makes me feel like I'm caged in with a tiger. But I hold on fast to my smile and wait, *wait*, just hoping he can't hear my heart pounding.

Xavier stares at me, then sighs.

"Of course. My apologies for keeping you waiting." He pulls the door open again and steps into the hall. "We'll discuss this in the tea room. I'm sure Joseph will be happy to bring you something for your affliction."

My affliction.

I just love how he makes it sound like something far worse than a little hay fever.

As I follow him into the hall, I just hope I can get back to Micah before Xavier realizes that camera is missing.

Ideally, before all hell breaks loose.

XVI: DARK CLOSET (MICAH)

The closet.

For some reason, my mind spins as I pore over Lucas' old folder of newspaper clippings, searching for clues about the Jacobins and Xavier. It's all old info Lucas gathered about Montero Arrendell's shady past during his obsession with his sister's death.

I'm back in time, remembering the closet in my childhood home.

That dingy, worn-down apartment. A two-room rathole that didn't even have a kitchen, just a mini-fridge and a foldout range top. The sink embedded in the wall had to double as a kitchen sink and the sink for the tiny telephone booth of a bathroom through the door just to one side of it.

Windows so grimy the whole world looked like mud. Bars over the glass.

Institutional as hell.

No curtains, so I'd tacked up blankets, tiny me standing on a wobbling, half-broken chair to reach.

Privacy was nonexistent.

My brother and I shared one little room, while our father

lived in the other. Ate, slept... drank. He was always half-fused to that stained sofa in front of the TV, either drunk off his ass or on his way there, surrounded by empty bottles.

It was always so fucking cold in that place, even in summer.

It's like the hopelessness of those dead grey walls sucked the life out of everything, especially me.

Maybe I was ruined long before Jet died and my life became one long vendetta.

Maybe I was ruined the moment our mother died and left us alone with that man, in that dead place, stealing more of our humanity into its awful walls every day until there was nothing left.

Except for the closet.

Barely taller than a coffin, just big enough to stand in.

No light inside at all.

Nothing on hangers or anything else, just a lot of old clothes piled up on the floor, like a standing junk drawer. For any other kid, it would've been a dingy nightmare.

For me, it was safety.

Because, weirdly, it locked from the inside *and* outside.

If our father was piss drunk enough, he couldn't fumble the outside latch and pry it open.

That's why I hid in that closet so many awful nights.

I'd make a nest in there with the rags and old clothes that still stank like sweat and God only knows what else. Sometimes Jet would hide with me, but most of the time not, and I think that was when I started to hate myself.

One of us had to be out there—visible—when our father came straggling home late at night after tearing it up at the bar down the street from the industrial building where he worked as a janitor.

As long as Jet was his punching bag, the monster wouldn't go rummaging around in the closet for me.

So I'd huddle in the dark and listen.

I'd listen to our father's slurring words, the banging, the clatter of bottles.

Listen to the meaty sounds of fists on flesh.

Listen to the sad, hurt noises Jet made as he tried not to scream or even cry.

Listen to my own deafening heartbeat as rage welled up inside me until I felt so full I could gag.

I could see it all happening, just from those sounds.

No comfort whatsoever, besides the old floppy stuffed crow crushed in the corner.

It was Jet's when he was a baby, a gift from our mom, chucked in here and forgotten ever since.

Those beady black button eyes would stare at me, even when I couldn't see them clearly. That's when I could always hear it whispering the loudest.

Look at you! Hiding away while your poor big brother takes the brunt of it. Is that what you wanna grow up to be, Mikey? A stinkin' coward?

You're just gonna stand around and listen?

That's what it feels like I'm doing now as I try to piece together this case against Xavier. Sitting on my ass, listening to the telltale cries, trying to form a complete picture that will let me *nail his dick to the fucking wall.*

I just need hard evidence and it's frustrating as hell.

My phone goes off in my breast pocket.

Blinking, I roll my shoulders.

I've been staring at these files without really seeing them for so long that the newspaper clippings have turned into an unfocused blur of black and white.

As my vision clears, I glance around the office.

Everyone's out except Mallory, manning—*womaning, whatever*—the dispatch desk. Really, she's playing with the

Korean boy toys in her game. I really wish I could un-hear the moaning coming from her phone.

But my phone needs attention, so I flip the file shut and swipe through a barrage of texts.

Talia: 911, 911, 911, 911

Talia: Well, wait, what's 911 for good things?

Talia: Maybe a good thing. I don't know yet but it could be. But it could also be big trouble and when can you come see me?

Talia: 411

Talia: That's it, I have the 411 on a thing!

Huh?

My dark memories implode in her jibber-jabber. Somehow, I'm smiling.

She does that a lot.

Calm down first, I send back. **Back up. What do you have?**

Talia: I can't say! Not here where it could be incriminating.

I snort with amusement.

Mallory stops tapping her screen and gives me a discerning look over the rims of her glasses.

I ignore her and type, **Stop watching dumb cop shows. I've got a lunch break in fifteen. Red Grounds? Or would you prefer somewhere not public?**

Talia: Grandpa's out right now. The Faircrosses need a new desk for their kid and he wanted to talk to them about dimensions. We can talk at the shop.

I'll be there as soon as I clock out. See you soon, I send back.

I set my phone down and look up.

Mallory's still watching me, sharp as a hawk.

"What?" I growl.

"You're smiling a lot lately," she points out. "Does it have anything to do with that nice young lady I see you out and about with?"

"No idea who you're talking about," I grumble, stuffing Lucas' folder into my desk as I stand. "But I think your 2D boyfriends are getting lonely. Those moans sound pretty impatient."

Mallory doesn't fluster easily.

She just gives me a flat look before turning her nose up and swiveling back to her desk.

No time to waste.

I straighten my uniform, resisting the urge to check my hair and my buttons in the station bathroom, and head out to meet Talia.

* * *

Ho.

Lee.

Shit.

I stare at the camera sitting in the middle of the kitchen table in Talia's loft.

It's a Nikon D3500. The black nylon camera strap with its woven green and yellow inner padding has the name BRIAN NEWCOMB stitched into it, plain as day.

In the silence, Talia fidgets with her hands, watching me nervously.

She looks like a doll today, wearing a knee-length off-the-shoulder dress in some sort of pale-lavender gauze with a flared skirt. Her red hair hangs down around her shoulders in a curtain of fire.

She must've changed and prettied up before I came over. I know damn well she wouldn't let Xavier see her with those bite marks blooming on her shoulders.

She's pale with uncertainty, too, moving back and forth from foot to foot, biting at her strawberry mouth until it's swollen.

"Don't worry. I used tissues to pick it up," she says uncertainly. "And gloves when I got home. So I wouldn't leave my prints on your evidence."

"We don't know if this is evidence just yet," I say, but my heart beats faster. "How did you get this?"

"Xavier—" Her voice cracks. She coughs anxiously, then tries again. "Xavier's office. I, um… I might have screwed things up with Joseph Peters. I was pretty direct, but he knew what I meant. He got all defensive and shut me down. But he left me alone in the office while his boss was on a call, so I did some sleuthing. Found that in his desk drawer. I also took photos of his phone records. He didn't even notice anything was messed with. He seemed really mad about some shipping issue, though, and he barely talked to me before sending me home."

Fuck.

I don't even know how to feel right now.

On one hand, this could be everything.

On the other, it could be bad goddamned news.

If Xavier realizes Talia took this, who knows what he'll do.

In my stunned silence, Talia's face falls.

"…I screwed up, didn't I? I thought just, y'know, with Xavier having the camera, that's incriminating, right?"

"No." I shake my head. "It's circumstantial. There are a million reasons why he could have a dead hiker's camera that have nothing to do with him being connected to Mr. Newcomb's death. A judge would toss out any accusations in a heartbeat." While that crestfallen look on her face deepens, I pull the nitrile gloves I always carry around on duty out of my pocket and snap them on. "Now, what's on this camera might be evidence. You did good. But you also took one hell of a risk, Talia. I don't want you going up to that house again and digging around. Not until this is sorted."

She'd started to brighten halfway through my speech, but then she frowns.

"But I have to. Won't it seem suspicious if I start avoiding him?"

"I don't care," I snap with a ferocity that surprises me. She recoils. I stop, sighing. "Sorry. Look, I just don't want him hurting you if he suspects you're snooping."

"I know how to run," she points out weakly, trying to smile.

I give her a hard look and pick up the camera, turning it over to look at the digital screen on the back and activating the interface.

It still has some battery life, and it only takes a few clicks to navigate to the gallery.

It's been completely cleared out.

"Fuck!" I drop the camera, letting it hang from my hands. "Somebody already emptied the archives. They deleted *everything*. It's been wiped. Digital forensics might be able to do something with this, but…" I hesitate.

But I'm not working this case for Redhaven or Raleigh PD.

For now, I'd rather keep them out of it.

"…but it might take too long," I finish lamely.

Talia rounds the table to lean against me, peering at the screen. She tugs on my wrist until I lift it again.

"What's that?" She points at something in the upper right corner.

I frown.

It looks like an account management icon, next to an email address. I read the address out loud, cocking my head.

"*SighinBrian*. Huh. It's an email." As I tap the icon, the account settings open, and I inhale, going stiff. "Looks like it was synched to the cloud."

Talia blinks at me, perking up a little.

"So the data was backed up? Oh, but we don't have access,

do we? Can you get like, I don't know, a warrant or a subpoena?"

"No need." My determination hardens. "Because I know who might be able to get us in."

* * *

IF WE'D BEEN an hour later, we might have missed Ariana Lewis.

When she opens the door to her room at The Rookery, it looks vastly different from last time. Restored to hotel condition, all her belongings—and his—packed up and piled next to the door, anything personal swept clean.

She's dressed plainly in jeans and a cardigan.

It's not hard to tell the grief has been taking its toll on her, judging from the creases under her eyes to the way she's shed weight. But she still finds a pale smile for me as her eyes warm with recognition.

"Officer Ainsley," she whispers, looking past me at Talia, who wouldn't even entertain staying behind. "And girlfriend?"

"Um, no, we're—" Talia makes a flustered sound.

"Yes," I cut her off. "Ariana Lewis, Talia Grey. Talia, Ariana." I can't explain our relationship to Talia, let alone to Ariana, and I'm not about to try.

This is easier.

That's why I say it.

That's the only damn reason.

Even as Talia goes silent, staring at me with her wide-eyed, delicate blush, I move on quickly, offering Ariana my practiced Officer Friendly smile.

"Sorry to bother you, but I'm glad we caught you. I know this is a hard subject, but you may be able to help us with

Brian's case." I stop short of saying *death*, a word the grieving never want to hear.

Ariana's smile fades, hurt flickering in her eyes, but she nods and steps back. "Come in. If I can help, it's my pleasure. I just need to make my flight in six hours."

I cock my head. "Your sister didn't make it?"

"Oh, she couldn't find anyone to watch the kids, so she's been yelling at me nonstop to come home ASAP." That weak smile flutters over her lips again.

She leads us inside, gesturing to the dining table. While Talia and I sit, Ariana starts making tea. She seems like the type who needs to keep her hands busy.

"So what's this about?" she asks.

I nod at Talia.

Right on cue, Talia flips open her messenger bag and retrieves the camera, now wrapped up in an evidence bag, and deposits it on the table. Ariana looks at it and freezes, dropping the teakettle she'd been setting down on the counter with a clatter.

"You... you found his camera?" she asks, sounding so lost, taking a step closer to the table.

"We did." I conveniently leave out how or why it's in an evidence bag. No point in hurting this poor girl with what-ifs without good reason. "However, it was damaged in the fall, and the data was corrupted." The lie works for now. "We're working on piecing together everything that happened before the incident, and being able to access those files would help fill in some gaps for the medical examiner's report. It looks like he had a cloud backup with his email address. You wouldn't happen to know the password, would you?"

"...I don't know. Is it his iCloud account?" she asks.

"I'm not sure. It seems like it might be Google, judging by the email address."

Ariana just stares at the camera like it might magically bring her dead boyfriend back.

Talia gives me a worried look, then says, "It's cool if you can't remember. I know it's hard for you right now."

See? I knew bringing her with me was the right idea.

Part of me *wants* to be the man Talia brings out, who was able to be so kind to Ariana the last time I was here.

Only, right now I smell blood.

I'm all sharp edges.

If I'm not careful, I'll be a spinning knife, cutting everyone around me.

Ariana looks at Talia for a few seconds, heavy with pain. She's a small woman, but her sadness takes up so much space.

"Talia, right?" Ariana asks. "Have... have you ever been in love?"

Talia makes a flustered sound.

There's a weird feeling as she looks down at the table. Her gaze darts over the smooth surface like she's looking for an answer. The only place she won't look is at me.

"Yes," she finally answers.

Fuck.

Does she mean me?

How *could* she, when I've been such a prick?

Ariana's gaze flicks to me before snapping back to Talia with a worn smile.

"Then you know," she says. "You know that when you're in love, you feel like your world revolves around them. Even things that don't have anything to do with them are just *like that*, in your head. All the little things. Noticing something your boyfriend would like in a store or thinking of something random and funny and wanting to share a laugh. Naming your pet after their childhood stuffed animal. Or... or..." She swallows, her throat working so

THE DARKEST CHASE

tightly it's easy to tell she's trying hard not to cry. "...or using their nicknames or birthdays as passwords. That kind of thing." Her smile widens, but it's trembling and heavy and hurt. "My email password is *MySighingBriBri-something*. How dumb is that?"

"No," Talia says, looking at Ariana with so much empathy in her eyes. "That's not stupid at all. It's the kind of thing you do when they're everything."

Why is it suddenly harder to breathe in this room?

Like there's just not enough air here anymore.

Not for the man I am and the specter of the man Talia wishes I could be, instead of this hollow shell who can't even give her a straight answer about whether or not we're truly together.

I hold still, though, letting them speak.

Letting Ariana say what she needs to.

She sniffles, wiping at her eyes, even though they're dry.

"Yeah. Brian was like that. He was my life and I'd like to think I was his, too. We were so ridiculous together, but it was great. I miss him." Her eyes sparkle with memories. "He used to call me 'Ariana Blondie.' You know, like the singer?" With a snort, she tweaks a strand of her wispy blonde hair and glances at me. "Anyway, yeah, I might have a few you can try. I'll write them down to make it easier, okay? And you can call me if none of them work and I'll try to think of something else."

I nod. "Thanks, Miss Lewis. That would help a lot."

She just stands there for a moment, though, staring at the camera like it's this talisman of grief.

"Any chance I can have it? When you're done with it, I mean," she asks.

"After we're done with the reports, absolutely," I say. "Once it's no longer considered evidence, I'll see if we can have the camera and any other belongings released to you, or to his next of kin. No doubt his family would want you to have it."

"Thank you, Officer Ainsley," she murmurs. "You've been great. And I'm really grateful for how kind you've been."

Kind?

You've got the wrong guy, I want to say.

Then again, it's not my place to deny the feelings of a grieving woman.

She jerks away then, moving on halting steps to rummage around in the kitchen drawer until she comes up with a notepad and pen and starts scribbling things down.

It's silent in the suite except for the scratch of her pen on paper.

Talia glances up at me, but I can't read what she's saying.

I feel like I'm goddamned Pinocchio turning back into a wooden boy, forgetting all the things I thought I'd learned about being human in situations like this.

It's the expectation of it, these two women looking at me like I'm something more than I am.

All I want them to see is the monster.

The man who's only here to kill Xavier Arrendell, and they're just a means to an end.

You don't mean that, idiot.

It's like I'm fighting with something inside myself. Like the monster has taken on a different face, a different will, and it wants to take me over and make me cruel, cold, remind me of my purpose.

Jet's face flashes in my mind, accusing and wagging a finger.

What's the matter, little Mikey? So busy chasing pussy you forgot I'm dead?

That's right, my dude.

I'm dead 'cause you couldn't stand up against Dad, so I had to do it for you.

I'm fucking dead, and you're over here getting your freak on with some girl who only likes you 'cause you're her kinky little albino doughnut.

Her pet freak.

And it looks like you let yourself be tamed.

No, goddammit.

That's not Jet's voice, even if it's Jet's corpse leering at me in my imagination. He has the same black button eyes as the crow in the closet.

That voice, that's our father's.

That ugly slurring voice I hated so much, constantly mocking and cruel.

I close my eyes, shaking my head sharply and pressing the heel of my palm against my temple, like I can force that voice out.

Shut it.

Shut the fuck up.

"Micah?" Talia's voice breaks the stillness. It's *insidious* how her softness gets into me, how she somehow wears down my barriers. Not with force, no, but more like the slow way a river carves a canyon a mile deep. "Are you okay?"

Yes.

Keep it the fuck together.

I open my eyes and pin on my Officer Friendly smile, even though I never use that smile with her.

"Yeah. Slight headache. Just a long day."

Hurt flashes in her eyes. She looks at me like I'm a stranger.

Damn.

I don't know how to tell her that the stranger is the *real me*.

Fortunately, Ariana saves me from having to say anything else.

She rips the top sheet off the notepad and offers it to me

with a trembling smile. "Here. I tried a lot of different combinations, but hopefully one of these will work."

"Thank you, Miss Lewis," I say, taking the note and standing quickly. I hold my smile like it's the only thing keeping me sane. "I'll be in touch if we need anything else or have any additional information to share. Have a good day." I nod to Talia, who's still watching me like she's trying to figure out what changed. "Miss Grey, let's head out."

"Ah, right. Sure." Talia stands with a confused smile for Ariana. "Thank you so much for talking to us. I'm sorry for your loss, again."

"Thank you." Ariana's eyes gleam briefly.

I turn and walk out.

I tell myself I'm giving Ariana space. No more people barging in and expecting shit from her or asking her to pretend she's okay, running from her feelings.

Really, I feel like I'm the one running now.

Running from this expectation to be human with the harsh gravity of Talia's hurt and confusion hot on my heels.

* * *

We barely make it to the parking lot before she stops me—reaching out for my hand, touching the back of my palm before I unlock my patrol car.

"Micah?" Talia asks. Her voice sounds so wounded it makes me want to drop everything and hold her until that wound stops bleeding. "What's wrong?"

I don't know.

Nothing and everything.

I shrug, glancing at her casually. "Nothing. I'm fine."

"That was *not* fine," she says with a firmness that surprises me. Her mouth tightens and her hand remains on mine. "Please tell me the truth. What happened to you in there?"

"I felt a little awkward, given the situation. That's all."

"Because you called me your girlfriend?"

There it is—the fucking can of worms I opened when she asked me what we really are, and I couldn't stop thinking about how much I'm going to hurt her.

When she finds out that's all I can do and realizes she deserves better.

So here I am, deflecting again.

"No. I'm not good with people. Especially people in a fragile state." I catch her hand, squeezing tight, but also free my keys so I can unlock my car and pull the door open. "I promise you I'm fine. I'm going to clock my time early and head home to see if I can get into his account. I'll drop you at the shop on the way."

Her fingers tangle with mine.

She's holding on desperately now. I wish like hell she could see it.

I'm already corrupting her.

I'm no fucking good.

Why can't she figure it out?

"Can I come with you?" she asks. "I guess I just need to see it with my own eyes. So I know."

I hesitate, but if I say no, she'll feel like I'm avoiding her.

"Sure," I say.

Guess that's not convincing enough. Her face falls and she pulls her hand away. "Don't say it if you don't mean it."

"I mean it," I promise, reaching for her hand again, pulling her in close and kissing her forehead. "C'mon. You went through all this trouble to steal that camera. Let's go find out what was on it."

For a moment, she leans into me, but the silence remains. It's just as troubled when she pulls away and walks to the passenger side of the car. I feel like I should say something, but I don't know where to begin.

Talia's finally figuring out I'm not her perfect dirty fantasy.

Not this wise fairy-tale beast who always knows what to say, how to thrill her, how to guard her heart.

I'm a broken man—a fucking imposter—and there's only one way this ends for anyone who gets too close.

It's silent as a grave on the drive back to my house. In the past, we enjoyed our easy silences that we didn't need to fill with mindless chatter, but now the quiet feels tense.

Empty.

It feels like the silence that falls over a forest when there's an apex predator moving through, everything small and frightened, waiting for the threat to pass by.

I hate it.

I also don't know what to do about it, so I hold my tongue.

When we pull up at my place, a loud bark echoes from inside. A second later, the curtains in the front windows bunch up as Rolf's head pops up under them.

He stares eagerly out the window, his big tongue rolling.

Talia laughs, some of her tension easing. "That dog really loves you."

"He's just hoping I brought some treats," I mutter.

It's just an offhand comment, but it makes her go still anyway.

She looks at me strangely. What did I say now?

"You really do see love as transactional, don't you?"

"I..." I freeze.

Fuck. Fuck, fuck, *fuck*.

I mean. Fucking maybe?

I had a brother once. I thought I loved him.

It's not like my father ever loved me, though there were times when if I was good enough, obedient enough, he'd give me little scraps of affection. Just enough to reel me in so I wouldn't be on my guard when he turned dark and violent again.

So maybe she's right.

Maybe I do think love involves keeping score, whatever people think they can take from each other. I think love is earned.

Even with Jet, it was always counting who took the most bruises, whose turn it was to hurt. Just as toxic and fucked up as it sounds.

Right on cue, I look up at the branch overhanging the corner of my roof. They're back again, three overstuffed crows staring down.

One of them throws back its head and lets out an angry squawk.

Goddamn you, enough.

Focus on the mission.

Focus on Jet.

I'm so close.

That's why I stuff those dark thoughts down, ignore the birds, and eye Talia.

"I just know my dog and what he'll do for a good chew." Keep it cool. I open the car door and step out. "Let's go."

She follows me quietly.

She's probably rethinking this, and I don't blame her.

It'll be easier if she starts pulling away from me now so it won't hurt so much later.

Maybe this is how it ends, like a flower wilting without water.

Why does my chest hurt like hell, then?

Cursing in my head, I unlock the door to the house.

We barely make it inside before Rolf comes barreling over, jumping up to lick my face.

"Hey, old man." I give him a quick squeeze—I'd never

admit it's comforting, giving me an anchor right now—before letting go so he can pounce on Talia next.

She catches him with a squeal, bursting into laughter as she buries her face in his thick ruff and scratches him all over. The two of them are practically in a wrestling contest.

And it makes that cramp in my chest worse, seeing them like that. My goddamned prickly, possessive dog fucking loves this woman.

I hate that I'm starting to wonder if I do, too.

I firmly push those thoughts away and pivot, leaving them in the entryway to enjoy their lovefest while I take a detour to the kitchen.

My laptop's on the breakfast island. I settle down on a chair and flip it open so I can pull up the cloud hosting service where Brian Newcomb kept his accounts, then I fish out the paper with the passwords Ariana gave me. I type in his email address from memory and try the first potential password.

No luck.

I'm on the third try by the time I hear Rolf's nails clicking and the soft clack of Talia's shoes against the kitchen tile.

She comes up behind me, peering over my shoulder, her soft vanilla-spice scent drifting over me. Rolf props his head on my thigh, looking up at me beseechingly. I let one hand fall, rubbing his head while I try number four.

"Anything yet?" Talia asks.

"No, still got three more…"

The next one comes up dead.

And the next, and the next, and the next after that.

I flop back, raking a frustrated hand through my hair.

"Fuck. Guess I'd better call Ariana Lewis."

"Maybe not." Talia leans over me. The soft curves of her breasts press against my arm, warm through the sheer layers of her breezy floral top.

She points at one of the passwords—*ArianaBlondieBabyI*.

I nod back.

"That one. That's a play on a song title about being in love," Talia whispers. Just like how Ariana said it was with Brian. "If they were really so gooey over each other, that might be the one. Try replacing the *I* with a one."

"You think that's all it takes?" I quirk a brow.

"I think it's the quickest way people change up their passwords to make them secure without forgetting," she says with a shrug. "It's what I do all the time."

"And if it doesn't work?"

She blinks at me innocently. "Then you use your big shot police resources to run a password cracker with these passwords as seeds to try every variant."

I stare at her.

"How the hell do you know about brute forcing passwords?"

"I spent my childhood as a shut-in." She shrugs. "I read a lot of dorky books."

"Apparently so." But it's worth a shot. I turn back to my laptop and try to log in again with *ArianaBlondieBaby1*.

No dice.

"Damn it," Talia hisses, and I hold a hand up.

"You gave me an idea. One number, one uppercase, one special character. That's how it goes these days, right?"

"On most sites, yes."

"Then…" I type in *ArianaB1ondieBaby!*

Bingo.

"What did you *do*?" Talia squeals with delight as the login screen pops up.

"I figured since one and the exclamation point are the most common substitutions, he'd swap the *L* or the uppercase *I* with one or the other, but not the lowercase *I* since it'd be harder to remember which one it was. So I made the *L* a one, and the uppercase *I* an exclamation." I smirk with satisfaction. "If that hadn't worked, I bet the other way would have."

"Okay, Mr. Smarty-pants, let's just see what he saved."

That's sobering. I'm almost hesitant to click.

The page opens up on dozens of thumbnail slides, all of them so dark it's hard to make out what's in the photos without expanding them to full size. My heart thumps hard.

If there's enough evidence in these pictures, I'm finally going to do what I came here for.

Swallowing hard to wet my dry mouth, I start the slideshow, clicking through quickly.

Nature shots. What else?

Pictures of the hills, the trees, the sky. Another shot with the sunset blazing past Redhaven seen from on high.

A fox coming out of its burrow to sniff leaves as the darkness settles.

The glade below the cliff.

The place where Brian Newcomb's body was found.

I'm clicking so fast now it's like I'm trying to keep up with my pulse.

A few shots clicked away, then back as headlights glow through the trees. Every shot after shows those headlights coming closer, so dim they're ghostly, so many successive shots it's almost like a moving film.

Then I see it.

The trucks.

That town car.

The usual swarm of people moving around, a thing I've seen so many times, but never anything incriminating enough for a search and seizure, except—

There.

Xavier fucking Arrendell.

Joseph Peters is behind the wheel and Xavier's stepping

out of the back, dressed to the nines like he's heading into a business meeting.

Only, the only person he's meeting is Eustace Jacobin.

I don't realize I've stopped breathing until my head goes light.

I suck in a mad breath while Talia exhales next to me. A quick glance shows her eyes wide, transfixed, while I click away.

There it is again.

Money changing hands.

A tight green roll passing from him to her, just distinct enough to be sure that's what it is, and then she passes a white-wrapped brick to him. Probably a product sample.

Oh, fuck.

It's perfect.

It's *enough* and even if there's no proof that brick is pure cocaine, it'll be plenty to convince a judge I have grounds for a full fucking raid on the Jacobins and the Arrendells. The smoking gun has arrived, all thanks to this dead hiker.

Finally.

I'm fucking *finally* going to put these bastards in handcuffs.

So many times I've wanted to go rogue, to get vengeance, damn the consequences. I'm still not sure I won't, but for now, there's a certain satisfaction in knowing that my patience paid off and I did this the right way.

All I need is a warrant and a SWAT team to make sure the pricks responsible for the deaths of my brother and so many others are finally arrested.

Justice at last.

The sheer excitement chokes me so hard I almost miss the significance of the next few photos.

Eustace, leaning to whisper to Xavier. A subtle turn of their heads, not quite toward the camera.

Then Eustace slipping off into the trees.

Brian clearly never figured out that he was spotted because he kept taking photos up until the point where the next photo goes blurry.

He's falling.

A few more shots auto-clicking, showing the night whizzing by.

Just pure sky.

And then the last shot.

An ominous, dark silhouette with a long skirt, standing at the edge of the cliff and looking down.

Talia's low gasp breaks my trance.

"Shit," I mutter, inhaling roughly and looking at her. She's staring at the screen, her blue eyes liquid with fear, one hand pressed over her mouth.

Rolf whines and noses at her thigh.

"Oh my God," Talia whispers. "She... she really pushed him."

"I'm afraid so. Not one word of what you saw here, Talia. I have a lot of legal channels to go through to put this to work. If they get wind that we know, even the slightest hint, they could just up and disappear. And I'll lose everything."

"What? I'd never do that to you!" She sounds a little hurt, but mostly just insistent. "I know how much you need this."

"I had to make sure." I look back at the screen and start downloading the files just in case they vanish from the cloud. "You should go home. I'm going to be wrapped up in this for a while. No reason for you to get tangled up deeper."

No reason for you to get hurt, I mean.

I've used her enough.

I never should have to start with, though without her I wouldn't have any of this.

I'm grateful.

More grateful than I know how to express.

Which is why I need to let her go before she gets in so deep she can't find her way out.

I turn slowly, swiveling the barstool—but my knee hits her bag and it slips off her shoulder. It tumbles to the floor, spilling folders and papers.

We both lunge for it, me cursing.

We almost bang heads as we hit the kitchen floor on our knees.

She grabs her portfolio while I sweep up the scattered papers and stop, frowning at what looks like a top sheet of legal jargon beneath the Arrendell letterhead.

"What's this?"

Talia blinks, then tugs it out of my hand and looks at it.

There's a guilty flush to her cheeks, but she's also smiling.

"Oh, the contract!" She fans the pages to the last one, where a monogrammed check is paper-clipped to the final signed page. "The first check." Her smile nearly breaks her face. I realize just what I'm about to do as she says, "Grandpa's going to be okay."

Fucking hell.

I'm about to rugpull every last hope she ever had from under her.

All so I can have my justice.

I've known.

I've always known.

Still, as long as it wasn't concrete, as long as it was this slow game of cat and mouse, I could pretend this day wouldn't come.

But it's here like a shooting star.

Come morning, this place might be swarming with Feds, if I make the right phone calls.

Then the money Talia needs to save Gerald Grey goes up in smoke as everything Xavier owns becomes either a seized federal asset or hot evidence.

I stare into her smile, missing my soul.

"Cash your check fast. Today, Talia."

It's like blotting out the sun.

Her lips go slack with confusion. Her eyes darken with worry, and she draws the papers with the check tucked inside close, as if she's worried someone might snatch them away.

"Why?"

"Because if—*when*—I move on Xavier, his assets will end up frozen and that check won't be worth the paper it's written on."

I stand, turning my back on her and pacing to my laptop.

I can't stand the stricken look on her face.

I also can't help pausing, glancing back, while Rolf dances around on his front paws between us, his confusion clear. He's always been sensitive to changes in the air, and the tension feels thick enough to choke me.

"I'll make sure you're labeled as an innocent bystander so the funds might not be seized when they chase the paper trail," I tell her. "I just can't guarantee anything. Also, I hope that check is enough. Go home. Get your affairs in order. I don't know how fast this is all going to go down."

I look away again, waiting for her to break the silence.

She's just standing there, so loud I can hear her.

A person makes noises that come with being alive. Quiet is never quiet as long as someone's breathing.

Everyone has their own special quiet made of restless motions and breathing rhythm, their pattern of sighs or subvocal murmurs, the way their clothing whispers with movement.

I hadn't realized I'd learned Talia's quiet by heart.

Not until it changes in the smallest ways.

Because her hurt and confusion change how she moves.

"Why, Micah? Why are you talking like this?" she asks. "Like... like we're strangers."

That's all we ever should've been.

I can't answer that, though.

So all I say is, "I said go, Talia."

Fuck, I'm itching for a cold shaker cup in my hand, biting my skin with the distraction of mixing a drink. My father turned to drinking to block out the world. I guess the apple doesn't fall far from the tree, even if for me it's the ritual rather than the booze clouding my mind.

Talia and I aren't the right mix.

"Get the check in your account. Look after your grandfather," I finish, fixing my gaze on my computer and not on her, watching the progress bar fill up as the files download rapidly.

It feels like once that bar hits one hundred, something ends forever.

"You've done incredible work, and I'm grateful. It's just that this case doesn't involve you anymore."

Talia's soft, choked sound hits my back like a bullet.

"You're dismissing me," she says. "Just like that, you're... you're..."

"I'm telling you to stay out of a very dangerous situation that doesn't need to worry you anymore. Thank you for your help, but I'll take it from here."

"Of *course* it concerns me! *You* concern me, you dick!"

"I shouldn't."

The silence after I say that rings like a death knell.

I don't know what I'm doing besides busting apart.

I don't know how to take it back.

Now that I started this, I have to finish it, instead of hurting her with weak deflections and weaker words.

I am a huge fucking dick.

That's why I have zero business with a girl like her.

Her quiet turns into a storm as my ears sting and she sweeps toward me.

"How can you not concern me?" she asks. There's so much emotion in her voice, it's like she's going to shatter when it overflows.

My heart shakes.

I don't have an answer. No combination of words will ever be good enough.

I close my eyes, gripping the edge of the breakfast bar.

Just before my eyelids turn everything dark, that progress bar hits 100%, just a little final marker that tells me this is over and I have to stop this now.

Fucking *now,* while I'm back in my dark closet, safe from her tiny hand reaching inside me and tearing my heart out.

I know that isn't it. I know she has more to say.

"You what, Talia?" I ask softly, and I know I'm going to crush her if she tells me, if she bares her heart to me that way. "What are you about to say?"

XVII: DARKEST SPACES (TALIA)

I can't believe he's doing this.

Making us complete strangers again.

No, maybe worse, because the man who revived me that day in the square was someone who smiled, someone who treated me gently, someone who—

Who definitely wasn't this cold.

He wasn't this strange, walled-off creature standing in front of me, feeling like he's a thousand miles away.

One silvery-blue eye watches me over his shoulder—icy, remote. No feeling at all.

And he's asking me to say the words that will crush me.

My heart is flipping pulp.

My lungs, collapsing sacks.

I breathe in and out slowly, counting one-two, one-two, until that awful tightness eases.

I don't even think it's an asthma attack.

It's just my heart breaking like a shattered iceberg.

"Micah, I..." I falter, digging my fingers into the straps of my bag. "What am I supposed to say? You're talking to me like I'm your employee. Like we never..."

Yeah, I can't say it.

"We never should have." He turns away from me again. His back is an impenetrable wall. "I'm not who you think I am, Talia."

I press my lips together.

I want to scream at him, but I'm trying to stay calm, stay rational.

"If this is about your past, your family, or even killing Xavier, I don't care! I know those things about you. I know. And I know there's a part of you that's afraid you really are capable of killing a man. And maybe you will. Maybe it wouldn't even be wrong after what Xavier and the Jacobins did to your brother, but... but that doesn't change *you*. I know you, and you're so convinced you'll ruin me that you don't even realize you're ruining yourself."

He doesn't say anything. Every second feels like a spike slowly piercing my skin.

His head bows.

His hand curls against the back of the barstool.

His grip is white-knuckled, bone and blue veins against ash skin, tendons standing out harshly.

Rolf flops down at his feet and looks up at his master with a pitiful whine, but for once Micah doesn't answer that plea.

Finally, his cold, emotionless voice emerges. "I'm with the DEA."

"You're—what?" I take a step backward. It doesn't make sense. I shake my head. "I don't understand. How are you Redhaven police and DEA?"

"Because I'm not really Redhaven PD. Not that anyone here knows it. Not even the chief, when he was under suspicion as well. I had to slip in completely unknown. Even my employment records in New York were replaced with falsified records with the NYPD." He delivers the news so flatly it's like he's briefing someone on a case, but every fact stomps on my heart. "I only came here on a mission. Now that I have what I need, the DEA will run a sting operation and I'll be leaving. I was never meant to stay here permanently."

"Oh."

It's the only thing that gets past my numb lips while my mind whirls so fast it makes me dizzy. At first, I'm just trying to take it in, to understand, to fit the pieces together.

It just feels like I've been looking through a window all this time, not realizing it was smudged and tinted, and what I thought I saw through it wasn't real.

But now the dirt is washed away, letting me see clearly.

What's on the other side looks completely alien.

And in that glass, I see my reflection.

I'm an idiot.

I'm a fool.

I'm in fucking love, and it's the dumbest thing I've ever done in my life.

"Y-you…" My voice chokes off. "You used me. You used me, you seduced me so I'd do what you want, and now that you've got what you wanted, you're tossing me aside. Because I'm not useful anymore. That's what it's been all this time. While I was so—"

I don't stop because I want to, but because a heaving sob rips up my throat and strangles me.

Clasping a hand over my mouth, I try to shove it back in.

Micah turns into a blur, this silent, untouchable ice prince who was never truly in my reach.

It's like he really isn't human after all, and our worlds were never meant to mingle.

Through the bleary haze, I can just make out his head turning toward me, watching me over his shoulder. I can't see his expression through the tears clouding my eyes, no matter how I try to blink and cling to some kind of dignity in front of him.

"You should take your grandfather," he says tonelessly. "Take your money and get out of town for a few days. Maybe head to Raleigh to discuss his treatment plans. I don't know how this will go down or how fast the DEA will move, but if Xavier figures out you took the camera before we have him in custody, I'm not certain I can protect you."

"Protect me?" I bite off. "What makes you think *Xavier's* the one I need protecting from? Xavier isn't the one who..."

Who shattered me.

Who made me realize how naïve I really am and then broke my innocence into a thousand cutting pieces.

Before Micah, I never believed people could be horrible.

Now, I know how wrong I was.

Trusting people, trusting men, trusting anything... it just gets you killed.

Again, he doesn't say anything. I'm reminded that I'm in his domain, an intruder, and he's waiting for me to show myself the door.

However I thought it would end between us, it wasn't like this.

I wipe at my eyes, dashing away the tears so I can see clearly—maybe for the first time in my life. So I can see the stranger in front of me, this stonehearted DEA agent who used me like a tissue. This man I thought I knew, when all I ever knew was his name—and even that might not be the truth.

"I love you." Somehow, I can say it, even though it tastes like acid. "*Loved.* I loved who I thought you were. I loved the time we spent together. I loved the way you kissed me. The way you listened, leaned on me, and the way I thought you needed me as much as I needed you. I loved that you didn't try to hold me back from opening up my world, from seeing new things, from standing on my own, but you were always there to hold me up whenever I started to tumble and fall." My throat closes.

My lips tremble.

I watch his chest heave like there's an explosion inside him trying to get out.

Good. He should hurt a little.

Everything inside me burns, but at least my lungs aren't failing, finding the breath to speak these words that break so much inside me.

"I fell in love with a lie. The way you'd watch me when I tried new things and how you'd smile like you were seeing it for the first time with me… It made me feel *special,* Micah. It made every first for me so much more. And now…"

Oh, no.

My voice breaks again. Another sob, but I won't let it out.

I stuff it back inside, taking a deep breath and stiffening my spine.

Micah's not looking at me. His head is turned over his shoulder, but his eyes are downcast, his face blank.

"Now I know it was an act," I force out. "While I was falling in love with you, you were playing me for everything I was worth." I know why they call it bitterness now. Because the tears in my mouth and the pain on my tongue all taste revolting. "I hope you had fun breaking the little small-town virgin girl. You'll never get another chance to do it again."

If I'm expecting an answer, it never comes.

Just Rolf's whine as he pads toward me with his tongue out and sad eyes. Like he's the one begging me to reconsider.

Micah just waits.

And I can't anymore.

I can't wait any longer for him to take it back, to make it better, when I know he won't and I don't know how he *can*.

So I turn away, staring at the sun streaming through the

tall windows of this cosmopolitan house that doesn't belong in Redhaven any more than he does.

I know what time it is—I *run*.

With all the strength I've built in my broken lungs and broken body, I run away from Micah Ainsley.

And I refuse to ever look back.

XVIII: DARK SILENCE (MICAH)

The Rum Martinez.

It's one of the most complex mixed drinks in the world. First created by Japanese bartender Takumi Watanabe, it's almost never served in the United States.

Back when I was bartending in NYC, it was my specialty.

A complicated process involving everything from maraschino liqueur and vermouth to smoke infusers and toasted wood chips, served on decorative dried tobacco leaves. It takes longer to make the drink than it does to consume it, though someone with a refined palate might linger over it longer.

For some, it's a delicacy.

For me?

It's a comfort ritual.

I started slinging drinks to pay my tuition and survive, but it gave me structure.

It gave me a ritual. If I just did everything in the right order with the right ingredients, I could make something magnificent.

I never had anything like that before in my life. It transformed alcohol from this poison that summoned my father's demons into a magical elixir I could use to comfort others.

I wish life was always that simple.

With the right recipe, maybe I could have made Talia happy.

Except I know that's not true.

Even as I calm my frantic mind and savaged heart with the focused process, infusing the heady tobacco smoke into the drink, standing over the wet bar in my dark house, her last words keep replaying in my mind.

She loves me.

No.

Loved.

I didn't miss that switch to past fucking tense.

And even though I tried to hide my reaction, tried like hell not to make it harder on her to walk out, it skinned me alive.

One little change in that word.

Something inside me broke.

Hell, probably something that needed to be broken.

Something that *deserves* it because I was a selfish asshole. I fell into this mess with her even while I knew I couldn't give her anything permanent.

I've lived a lie for so long that I dragged her into my own fantasy, and then I tore her to tatters.

That sweet, innocent woman, with her gorgeous blue eyes spilling tears and a bitterness I've never seen, erasing the fresh-faced way she'd look at everything with the wonder of someone seeing it for the first time.

"Goddamned jackass," I mutter to myself.

I close my eyes, blocking out *everything*, not even caring if I ruin the drink.

It doesn't help.

I can't erase the horrified look on her face.

I'm human scum.

I *hope* she hates me now.

Just so it'll be easier to get over me and leave me behind as the vampire fucking asshole I am, and not someone she genuinely cares about.

I open my eyes and shut off the infuser, staring down at the stubby wide glass coffee cup the drink is traditionally served in.

In the glow from the fireplace, it almost looks bloody.

Fuck, I had to do this.

Didn't I?

I have a duty.

The entire reason I came here.

It was already near impossible to pin the drugs to Xavier Arrendell and the Jacobins, working my way down the eastern seaboard one arrest at a time, until I finally found the thread leading back to this little town—idyllic and untouched by Xavier's cocaine empire when, like any sensible drug lord, he doesn't shit where he eats.

Years of work.

Years of agony, staked on my dead brother's life.

I couldn't let that go.

Not even to keep from ruining Talia.

Not even to love her.

It hits me then.

I dig my fingers into the edge of the bar until my bones hurt, fighting back a shout.

I love that goddamned woman, too.

That weird, sweet, anxious, brilliant splash of pink sunshine who looked at everything mangled inside me and touched my sharpness. She told me no matter how much I cut her, she wanted to bleed.

Well, I'm the asshole bleeding now.

Especially as I snap my eyes open, lift the drink, and toss it down, gasping from the burn.

I only wish it could drown more than my guts with fire.

Burn it all away, but it can't.

All it does is make me feel like I really could become the monster my father was, hiding from my failures in booze.

Snarling, I slam the empty glass on the counter, practically breathing fire.

A furious roar rips out of me before my arm jerks.

I hurl the glass at the fireplace.

It hits the stonework and shatters with a loud ringing.

Rolf, who was sleeping on the leather recliner, snaps up with a confused bark.

I slump forward, breathing hard, leaning my entire weight on the bar—then I drag myself over and wedge myself into the chair with the German Shepherd.

He lays his head on my chest, draping his body over me like he's trying to protect me from invisible bullets. I lay an arm over his warm, furry body and bury my face between his ears.

"Sorry. I know I fucked up, boy," I whisper. "That happy-go-lucky woman, she even made *you* love her. And I just went and shit the bed so bad she'll never trust me again."

Hindsight is twenty-fucking-twenty.

If I'd just told her from the start that I was DEA, here undercover, what's the worst that could've happened?

Maybe we could have come at this differently then.

Maybe I could've thought about taking her back to New York with me one day.

Too bad I've been so focused on finally getting my way that I only thought about myself.

I've wondered so long who I'll be when this is over, after I have my revenge.

A hollow shell?

Shit, if I walk away empty, it's because I made myself that way.

Sighing, I close my eyes, holding Rolf tight.

At least I can't ruin his love.

A dog's love is unconditional.

Unfortunately, I don't even know if I can protect Talia from the DEA snapping up every penny Xavier gave her.

They'll want to talk to her, and if they interrogate her enough, she'll slip.

She'll slip, and then they'll know she knew what he was and what I was doing when she took his money, and that will make it forfeit.

I can protect her from prosecution, yes, even if I have to pull a few strings, but it doesn't change the loss.

Her future, obliterated.

I can't let that happen.

Maybe I can't convince her to love me again.

But I can do right by her so she won't just be collateral damage as I take down Xavier Arrendell and the Jacobins.

There's a large reward for taking down large drug networks like this one. Even bigger if key information leads to the arrest of a high-profile kingpin. I can't think of a more high-profile figure than Xavier and his merry band of assholes.

It never would've happened without Talia.

All I have to do is report her as the person who tipped me off, leading to major arrests, and she'll be rolling in money. Not as much as Xavier's offer, but *enough.*

Enough to make sure she's safe.

Enough to make sure she can save Gerald Grey.

I fish out my phone, scrolling through my contacts until I land on a name I haven't looked at in over a year.

Jane Henway. My handler—the one I report to, the one who maintains my records and makes sure that anyone sniffing at my background doesn't trip over the fact that I'm not a big-city cop who just decided to migrate to creepy Mayberry and live the easy life.

She always tells me I never call.

Usually, there's no reason, and I've never liked the little reminders that I have so little to report on our check-ins.

I've got a hell of a lot to report now.

I tap Jane's contact and call, the burn of the liquor turning my guts hot with determination.

It's past time to kick things up a notch.

I'm going to make damned sure that even if Talia Grey regrets ever loving me, she'll never want for anything again.

XIX: DARKNESS PRESENT (TALIA)

When I was thirteen years old, I had my first and only crush.

I never really spent much time around kids my own age.

I just saw them from a distance when I was allowed out for walks around the playground, dragging my oxygen tank behind me like that girl in Bates Motel—I know, I know, there are a few too many parallels in my life, from the creepy murder town to the naïve girl with the oxygen tank who falls for men who turn out to be trouble.

My first brush with trouble was Red Harrow.

His name wasn't actually Red. I think it was Ryker, but everyone called him *Red* because his hair was an even louder crimson than mine. That's what grabbed my attention and made me feel an instant kinship with him. I'd watch him from the bench where I sat with my little tank propped against my thigh, a book open in my lap, pretending to read a fantasy novel.

Actually, I was watching Red.

He was two years older. Fifteen.

Tall and lean and strong, and he'd come to the playground after school to play basketball with other boys his age. He had sun-tanned skin and freckled shoulders that showed in his loose jersey, his muscles flexing every time he jumped.

Even now, I don't know if I really *liked* him.

I hardly knew him.

Was I just jealous with how gracefully he moved? With how he could break a sweat and get winded and run like mad for hours without dying?

How he could play and run. How effortless it was.

How he took it all for granted.

In my head, I dreamed he'd notice me and fall in love, and somehow his love would make me strong like him.

Vampirism again—go figure—only more like the Snow White kind where I'd borrow his strength from a kiss.

Even then, I wanted a hero to rescue me.

I wanted to be saved and transformed, never broken and weak again.

But Red Harrow didn't rescue me.

He never even noticed me until one fine day when the ball got away from his friends on the paved lot they used as a court.

It came bouncing over to me.

I put my book down and picked it up, wobbling to my feet.

I couldn't help staring.

I'd never held a basketball before, and the orange texture was interesting.

It was new and *wonderful*, and I was so absorbed in this simple experience that I didn't notice Red jogging over until his voice hit me like a hammer.

"Hey, kid. Give the ball back."

I froze. I couldn't even lift my head, but I raised my eyes, staring at him.

My crush, so close I could smell him and see the cocky twist to his smirk. His bright-red hair was sweaty.

My heart beat so hard.

I opened my mouth, trying to speak.

But all that fell out was a long wheeze, like someone trying to blow into a flute and failing. Just this godawful flapping sound around the prongs of the oxygen tank's hose, fitted in my nostrils.

First Red blinked.

Then he burst into the harshest laughter.

"The fuck? Are you deaf too? You sound like a donkey!"

My eyes burned.

I tried to protest—*no, no, I'm a girl! I'm just a girl who loves you*—but all that came out was another shrill wheeze.

Then a lot more of them, all loud, honking gasps.

An attack coming on so fast I barely felt it. I dropped the ball and I fumbled for my inhaler in my dress, my vision spinning.

Red didn't rescue me that day.

He just watched and *laughed*.

Before it was over, he was mimicking my honking, flapping his arms like a demented goose and calling his friends over to join in.

I could only half hear them over my wheezing breaking into sobs.

All while the boy I naively loved mocked me and called me a flipping *donkey*.

They were still doing it by the time I shoved the inhaler in my mouth and eased that killing tightness.

While I tried to breathe, I glared at them through the tears, tried to make my quivering lips work to speak, to shout, to tell them to go straight to hell.

But I couldn't.

I couldn't curse those rotten kids.

I couldn't do anything but *cry* while the boys cackled on.

That day taught me how cruel people can be.

It also taught me that no one was ever coming to save me.

But it turned out I didn't need Red Harrow or anyone else, not after I dragged myself home with my oxygen tank banging behind me.

I saved myself.

I learned to live with myself.

But I guess some small, wounded part of me still never stopped being that dumb little girl who falls for the worst men.

And it's that little girl inside me wailing now as I curl up in my room and unleash all the awful feelings building up inside me ever since I bolted away from Micah's house yesterday.

I haven't slept all night.

I've just been crying myself dry, slipping into a daze, then finding more tears from the darkest places.

I know it's past time to get up.

It's morning and Grandpa's already moving around, the smell of rich coffee permeating the loft, mingled with the sawdust scent from downstairs.

I can already hear the lathe going.

I need to get my butt moving and stop grieving.

Finalize some sketches. Help Grandpa with his latest furniture piece, then go right to the bank to cash Xavier's check.

Just like chronic asthma, life goes on with a broken heart when there's work to do.

At least this time, I didn't lose my words.

I told Micah how I felt before I ran.

I spoke up.

I stood up and I didn't back down.

And I didn't let him pull this crap without knowing exactly how much he hurt me.

There's some pride in that, and that's what gets me moving.

There's also enough coffee left in the pot when I drag myself into the kitchen. I pour myself a cup and snag one of the muffins left in a basket on the table.

I nibble at it while I go through the motions of getting cleaned up and changed into clean clothes.

Caffeine makes me functional enough by the time I head in to the workshop.

Through the door to the front of the shop, I think I see a flash of black and white go by, on the way to the station. Probably Micah's patrol car.

My stomach twists before I look at Grandpa.

He's at his lathe again, still working on those bedposts he's been shaping for the last week or more.

Nothing Gerald Grey makes is ever fast or easy. But everything is crafted with love and exquisite detail.

By the time he's finished, he's memorized every wood grain and tiny groove.

The expression on his face makes me smile.

Pure love, so utterly absorbed in his work as his fingers glide over the rotating wooden post and plies his tools with delicate care.

I adore my work.

I love working with *him*.

I just wish I could find that kind of love in everything I do.

Then maybe I'd never feel a need for another person's love again.

I don't know how he does it. Just sinks away from everything until there's nothing but the wood, his tools, and a creative spark flaring.

It's like existing in this sort of beautiful trance, and I settle on a stool with a fresh cup of coffee.

Instead of focusing on my own work or opening up the shop, I watch Grandpa work his magic.

It's soothing.

There's not a single sound except the spinning lathe as I focus on his hands.

They're wrinkled, wizened, but so very steady. Some days they shake, and other days they're so inflamed I can see the redness and swollen skin.

But today, they're as steady as a man who's twenty years younger.

I don't know how long I watch him.

Long enough to soothe my soul, maybe, washing away the hurt and losing myself in the familiar warmth of this space.

I learned everything I know and love right here at his knee.

That love... it's still enough for me, isn't it?

I realize he's breaking his trance when the lathe's rhythmic whirring slowly stops. He sets his tools aside on his workbench and touches the bedpost gently.

His eyes are twinkling. He glances up over the fresh, pale wood at me, his thin lips creasing in a smile.

"Lily," he whispers. My split second of morning peace dies in a single heartbeat. "How long have you been there?"

Normally, when he's lost in time, he calls me *Serena*.

My mother's name.

But Lily?

That's my grandmother's name.

Holy hell.

He's farther gone than usual.

My throat closes up.

Everything hurts so much when I desperately want to *stop* hurting.

"Honey?" He's up in an instant, crossing the room to pull me into his arms. "What's wrong? Why are you upset? Did Serena call?"

Oh, no.

I can't upset him.

But I'm struggling, my throat raw, and the tears are coming. I bury my face in his chest and sob wretchedly.

"No, no," I say. "Serena didn't call."

I can't tell him what's actually wrong.

I can't tell him my heart's turned inside out, and I don't know how I can ever trust anyone again. *Not even him.*

Not when the person I love most doesn't even see me.

Has anyone ever seen me beyond the basket case of illnesses?

Did Micah?

The sobs won't stop no matter how hard I try.

They just *won't*, and even if I can't tell Grandpa what's wrong when he won't understand his 'wife' talking about another man breaking her heart, there's still comfort in his embrace and in the way he holds me.

I need to believe that somewhere, under the dense clouds in his mind, he knows he's comforting the granddaughter he loves.

So I cling to him, and while I cry, he murmurs soft words.

The sound of his voice and his warmth are enough.

The knowledge that, even if he's not quite here, there's still someone in this world who loves me without conditions, without regrets.

Slowly, my tears fade.

Sniffling, I rub at one eye.

Grandpa lets out a gentle, crooning sound.

"There you are," he rumbles. "You just needed to let it out.

Do you remember what you always told me when things were hard, dearest?"

I smile faintly, still hiding my face against his chest. Even his scent is comforting. He always smells like fresh-cut timber and the rougher, piney smell of bark.

"Why don't you remind me?"

"That Francis Bacon quote you love so much." I can hear the smile in his voice. *"In order for the light to shine so brightly, the darkness must be present."* He gently pats my hair. "Whatever it is, dearest... if there's such darkness today, it only means your light will shine like the sun."

I wish I could believe that.

But it's enough to remind me that I can get past this.

I barely knew my grandmother, but by all accounts, she was a resilient woman.

I want to be her worthy granddaughter today.

So I pull back from him, finding a smile as I stand, brushing my hair back and leaning in to kiss his wrinkled cheek.

"You're right," I say. "And it's time to get started on the day, so I'd better go."

His smile glows fondly. "You never could sit still, Lily darling. Where are you off to now?"

"Errands," I say, smoothing down my shirt before picking up my bag from where I dropped it by my worktable yesterday. "Need to run by the bank, and I think we're out of paper towels."

He pats my cheek, then turns away.

"What did you want for dinner tonight?" he calls over his shoulder as he makes his way back to his lathe. "I thought I could make pierogis."

I watch him with that hollow ache I get every time I remember I'm having a conversation with a lovely man who thinks I'm someone else.

"Pierogis would be great," I tell him. "I'll pick up everything you need. Be back soon!"

He waves quickly, already sinking back into his work. I linger on him for a few seconds before I step into the morning sun that feels far too bright for the darkness of my mood.

I'm lucky Mrs. Brodsky will be by in the next hour or two to check up on him.

As I walk down the street, I can't shake the feeling of being watched.

For a second, I glance around, searching for the freaky scarecrow figure of Ephraim Jacobin or the black silhouette of his Iron Maiden wife.

But there's nothing, just familiar faces moving down the street, soccer moms chatting with each other or babysitters herding toddlers while they do the household shopping. Old folks out for their morning power walks. A couple kids skipping school and pointedly avoiding the small police precinct station so they won't get hauled back in for truancy.

I avoid it, too, turning one street sooner than I need to so I won't have to walk past and see a flash of ivory skin and quicksilver eyes through the window.

My heart couldn't take it today.

I'm trying to be steel.

But steel takes time to forge, and it's been less than a day since the man I love threw me into exile.

I distract myself by Googling what I'll need for pierogis as I make my way to the bank and step inside. The line's short, and I've already got a grocery list by the time the teller beckons me forward.

I've already signed the check—nine hundred thousand dollars just for the first installment.

Who said a deal with the devil doesn't pay well?

When I pass it over, though, the bank teller—a girl my age named Sarah—stares at the check with wide eyes.

I smile sheepishly.

"Um, it's a deposit for a big contract," I explain. "Mostly going to materials. I didn't win the lotto or anything."

I don't know why I feel the need to explain.

I guess it just feels like that kind of money isn't meant for me, especially with *their* name attached.

Once I'm done with this job—or Micah hauls Xavier Arrendell into custody, whatever comes first—I think I'll stay away from that house for the rest of my life.

I fiddle with my bag strap and look around idly while I wait for her to finish, but when she clears her throat nervously, I glance back at her.

The look on her face makes my heart sink before she says a single word.

"Miss Grey?" She clears her throat. "I'm sorry to tell you this, but the check just bounced."

XX: DARK MINDED (MICAH)

I'm about to murder someone.

Surprisingly, I don't mean the Arrendells or one of the hillfolk.

I can't believe it. After everything I've done, after everything *Talia* did, everything she put on the line to get that damned evidence...

I'm sorry, Micah, Jane told me. *This is still rather circumstantial. I might be able to get a judge to swing a warrant, yes, but it's far from guaranteed. I'll try, but... give me some time.*

We don't have time, I'd snarled. *Don't you understand? They're going to figure out they've been made, and you know what happens next. Everything goes underground. We might not get another lead for years. We have to move* now, *before it all goes to waste.*

I'll try, Micah. That's all I can promise you. I'll make something happen if I can.

I almost wonder if Arrendell money hasn't bought off the DEA.

Just enough for them to throw the investigation and muddy the waters. It's entirely possible, but it's just as likely that this is how things are. All because some fucks behind a desk needed to cross their *T*'s.

Bureaucratic red tape. A criminal's best friend.

It's one of the frustrating things about working with the law.

You fucking *know* what someone's doing, but until you get ironclad proof that will hold up in court and also preserve the chain of evidence without a single flaw, everything you know is useless.

Anyone you arrest will wind up back on the street in under twenty-four hours, now well-informed on your efforts so they can just hide that much better.

Also, well aware of who they should target to keep their secrets.

Which is why I'm creeping through the woods in the middle of the night again—only this time I've got a backpack full of surveillance equipment. I had to drive to Raleigh to get a few missing pieces, partly because Redhaven's small shops don't stock that kind of thing, and partly because I didn't want it getting back to anyone in town.

I have to make this work.

I have to do this.

I have to make *something* happen, no matter how much the paper pushers at the DEA sleep.

Because if I don't get Xavier behind bars?

There's no telling what he'll do if he figures out Talia took that camera from his desk.

I have to protect her, even if I can't shield her heart.

They're still at the last site I staked out. I've settled into a small hunting blind I built earlier today, building up brush to mask the blinking lights from the camera and audio devices.

Right now, it's only the Jacobins, and nothing I'm capturing is any good.

They're eerily silent, the patriarch and matriarch absent,

though their well-oiled machine needs no communication to swing into motion.

The DEA's not going to come down here for a thirty-second clip of some hillfolk making moonshine. They're going to tell me I'm crazy.

And maybe I am.

I'm doubting like I never have.

After screwing everything up with Talia, indulging my selfish whims and then breaking her just because I couldn't resist her, I don't know who the fuck I am anymore.

I don't know if this was worth it.

If *this* is even anything at all, when maybe I've been wrong this whole time, chasing down farmers in overalls for a few jars of two hundred proof rotgut that I'd swear is the cocaine that killed my brother.

No. I put the groundwork in.

Years of investigation, cornering every low-level drug mule I could find, pressing them for intel, cutting deals until someone finally pointed me to the tip of the spear and I convinced my department there was something worth pursuing.

Something that would justify a multi-year undercover surveillance op. The evidence is there.

I'm not psycho.

I'm just waiting for my moment.

And it comes when I catch the growl of a distant engine and faint glowing headlights on their lowest setting.

I know what I'm about to see even before the front fender breaches that break in the trees.

That town car with the valet Talia identified as Joseph Peters in the driver's seat.

I shift my weight, pointing both the camera and the listening device toward the car.

There's no doubt it's picking up audio clear as day when I

can hear the engine in my earpiece, growling just like I'm standing on top of the hood.

I make sure to get a clear shot of Joseph Peters' tight face.

I don't want to pressure a man under duress, but he could be a valuable witness in exchange for immunity. I'll play any angle to end this.

My attention shifts as the back door of the town car opens.

But it's not just Xavier Arrendell who steps out.

Chief Bowden is with him.

He's looking worse for wear, probably from sleeping in his office. Unshaven, wearing dark cargo pants and a flannel shirt that both look like they've seen better days. There's a sour look on his face, something dark and cold and heavy.

If I hadn't seen his face every week for years, I wouldn't even recognize him. It's like there's someone else pushing through his skin. Something creepy and animalistic wearing the face of the happy-go-lucky aging police chief as a mask.

I make sure the listener is recording.

"...have time for this," Xavier says irritably. "Thanks to the container delay, we have trouble."

Bowden hitches his belt up with a grunt. "Window's closing, that's for sure. But with a little extra security and a few more hands on deck, we might pull off a miracle. Push the timeline up."

"We have a two-hour window. *Two*," Xavier hisses. "Do you have any idea how much it costs to arrange a complete blackout on Customs and Border Protection for an entire day? A *day*. And thanks to these bloody *idiots*, we have two hours left to load up and make an entire ship disappear. A few hired mercenaries won't fix that."

Ship?

Wait.

THE DARKEST CHASE

Didn't Talia say she heard Xavier throwing a tantrum over something to do with a ship?

"So hire more than a few." That coldness is there in the chief's voice, too.

It's unnerving how much it reminds me of myself, whenever I shut down and focus on my obsession.

"Look," Bowden says. "Shit happens, man. We can't control the weather. Storm at sea means the boat's gonna be late. Load up as many of the hillfolk as you can, and I'll call in a few dozen guys. We'll make it work."

Xavier pins Bowden with a frosty look that's no doubt intimidated many—and if Bowden were the man he seems, he'd be wincing and wringing his hands. But he only meets Xavier's eyes, flat and unaffected.

For the first time, I think I'm seeing the real Chief Bowden.

"Be there by two a.m.," Xavier bites off, and turns back to the town car. "Take care of all of... all of *this*." He flicks a hand at the Jacobins.

"Uh-huh. Sure thing, Your Highness," Bowden sneers.

The only answer is the town car's door slamming shut.

Snarling, I check my watch.

Nine p.m.

That gives me five hours to figure out where the hell they're going and call in the cavalry. I don't have time to wait for the DEA to get off their asses and *do something* like, you know, enforcing drug protection laws.

Whether I like it or not, I need help.

And I know exactly where to find it.

* * *

THE LOBBY LIGHTS are still on at The Rookery when I pull up.

Janelle tends to keep it open late for the folks straggling

in at all hours of the night. I think it also helps her feel a little less lonely when her husband clearly isn't home as often as he should be.

The white columns of the massive building are tinted gold by the light spilling through the front windows and glass doors, reflecting off the glossy wood paneling inside.

Gerald Grey's work, I think.

I can see his touch now.

So very similar to Talia's.

The apple doesn't fall far from the tree.

Old Gerald must have been the one to consult with Janelle when she first bought this place and had it converted into a B&B, long before I ever came to Redhaven.

I wonder if anyone ever thought we'd wind up here.

I step out of my patrol car and stand at the foot of the walkway.

Janelle is a distant, lonely figure behind the reception desk.

When I step up the walk and open the doors, a soft jingle mixes with the low, pleasant piano music playing in the lobby.

Janelle's shoulders stiffen, but she doesn't look up. Her hair falls down around her face as she writes something in front of her.

I step up and lean against the counter, folding my arms. "Evening, Janelle."

She looks up with a guilty smile.

"Oh, Officer Ainsley! Micah. How can I help you this evening?"

I think she knows.

Deep down, some part of her knows why I'm here.

Doesn't make it any easier to say.

I wonder when I started to care.

Maybe when I found out exactly how it feels when a

woman realizes the man she trusted was the worst sort of asshole there is.

"I'm looking for the chief," I tell her. "He's not sleeping at the office tonight. I'm guessing he's not at home. Do you know where he is? Because we both know he's not here."

Her eyes close.

Her pen stills against the ledger, its soft scratch falling silent.

"I… I couldn't tell you," she whispers.

"That doesn't mean you don't know."

I hate pressing her.

It feels cruel, but fuck, I *have* to do this.

"I can't play around, Janelle. I have one chance to catch him," I tell her. "Him, and a lot of others. We've looked the other way for years. Pretended it was just moonshining up in those hills because we couldn't prove anything else. But you know it's not moonshine, don't you? And you know your husband is in deep."

Her hands tremble.

She swallows hard.

"What do you want from me?" Her voice shakes.

"To know where the hell he goes when he disappears." I hesitate before reaching across the counter to rest a hand on her shoulder. "Look, I know whatever he's involved in, it's not your fault. But if you're willing to speak up, you could help a whole lot of folks tonight."

"I… I…"

"Janelle, what are you afraid of?"

"*Him!*" she flares, her open eyes brimming with tears as she looks up at me. "Clarence, he's… he's not the man I married. Or maybe the man I married was a lie, but it's like there's a stranger behind his eyes. God, I thought he was having an affair for years, but…"

Carefully, I squeeze her shoulder, trying to be reassuring.

"But what?" I prompt softly. My heart drums, and I don't want to make this harder for her by pressing her too cruelly. "Janelle, please. I won't let him hurt you. I just need to know where he goes, if you have any clue."

She presses her quivering lips together, just staring at me for a long time.

I can feel her pain hanging in the balance, this painful decision to betray the man she thought she loved. To admit he was never who she thought he was out loud.

If this were me and Talia, I'd want her to give me up in a heartbeat, as long as it meant doing what was right.

She'd have a better chance at happiness by moving on.

And I hope, when this is over, Janelle can find happiness, too.

After several rough breaths, she jerks her head away, lowering her eyes.

"Mariposa Cove," she whispers. "When I thought he was having an affair, I snuck a tracker app on his phone. He had no idea. About once a week, sometimes more, he goes to Mariposa Cove. I don't know what he does there, but I don't think he's meeting other women."

Mariposa Cove.

I know the name.

It's a tiny waterfront town about an hour and a half away from here on the Atlantic Coast. Hell, it's barely a town, just a dock and a terminal with a few buildings clustered around it.

A shipping dock favored by people running all sorts of clandestine operations.

If a ship's coming in tonight as part of the Arrendell/Jacobin drug ring, that's a mighty good place for it to land.

"Thank you," I say breathlessly. If there wasn't a counter between us, I'd hug her. "*Thank you.* You did the right thing, Janelle. Let me find out what's happening and end it."

THE DARKEST CHASE

She lifts her head, looking at me mournfully, hot tears gathered in her eyes.

"Go," she whispers. "Don't make me regret this. I'm so sick of living a lie. I'm tired of all the secrets in this town, all the heartbreak… and tired being part of them. Fix it, Micah. *Please*."

"I will, ma'am," I promise.

I may not be able to fix breaking Talia's heart, but I can still manage this.

Not alone, though.

It's time to call in reinforcements.

* * *

I'M stunned at how fast the Redhaven PD assembles at the station when I call them for a late-night meeting, no questions asked.

I never thought of myself as someone who's built that kind of trust.

Aside from Mallory, there they are, all lined up in the back room with Henri still buttoning up his uniform shirt and Lucas bleary-eyed from being up with their baby and Grant still sporting bedhead from hell—and bed beard, which I didn't even know was possible.

"What's this about, Micah?" Grant folds his arms across his burly chest, hazel eyes watching me keenly.

"I don't have time to explain," I say. "And we have even less time to move. I need you guys to trust me and believe every word I'm about to say."

"Hell of an intro. Now I'm curious." Lucas rubs his thick black scruff, his green eyes sharpening.

"I'll answer questions later. For now, this is all you need to know." I glance around.

Though I've told myself many times that all the relationships I've built here are temporary and surface deep, something in me knots up at the thought of this team I've worked with for years hating me for the lie, rejecting me.

I draw a deep breath before I speak.

"I'm not who you think I am. I'm undercover DEA, and I was sent to Redhaven to root out a drug operation that's been poisoning the entire East Coast for years. That operation is the reason my brother died. Xavier Arrendell runs that op with the Jacobins, while Chief Bowden runs interference so no one ever thinks of them as anything more than harmless moonshiners." I look from one stunned face to the next. "I have evidence. Clearly. Wouldn't dream of standing here right now if I didn't. They killed that hiker, Brian Newcomb, and if we can get to Mariposa Cove in the next two hours, we might just get a hell of a lot more than that and take them all down."

I'm breathing hard when I finish.

My crew just stares at me.

Tension prickles up my spine.

Fuck, time is running thin.

I don't have time for a thousand questions and even less for disbelief.

If they won't trust me, I'll have to do this on my own. I can't let it slip through my fingers after laying the groundwork for years. It has to happen *now*, or—

Grant cuts off my rabbiting thoughts with a long, deep sigh.

"You albino dumbass," he growls before breaking into a smile, fierce and carnivorous. "Why the hell didn't you fess up sooner? We could've helped you, you stubborn goddamn mule."

I can't help a shaky smile of my own. "Better late than never. I'm telling you now and hoping you'll help me anyway."

Lucas answers with a dark smirk.

There's blood in that look.

Even after finally getting his answers, that need for revenge against the Arrendells still rides him so roughly I can practically see it clinging to his back.

"I'm game," he says. "Just let me call the wife and tell her it'll be a late night."

Henri hesitates, an odd look in his eyes, before he lets out an easygoing chuckle and rakes his brown hair back. "Who needs sleep when we have hunting?"

"Then it's settled," Grant says darkly.

My heart jumps with hope as I realize the guys are truly with me.

They're with me, they *trust* me, and we might just pull this off.

"Let's gear up and get moving," Grant rumbles again. "Time for a little late-night fishing."

XXI: DARKNESS IMMORTAL
(TALIA)

I hate that when my phone rings, my heart still leaps with hope that it's Micah.

It's only been... what? A day or two?

Too soon for me to be over him, but I'm still telling myself I should be.

I've always been my own harshest critic. Always feeling like everyone else forgave me *too much*, and while my family and friends and doctors told me it was okay I wasn't like the other kids, okay that I couldn't do the things they did...

Really, I was the only one telling myself it wasn't.

I was the one pushing for *more*.

I pushed myself to have a life, and that life isn't over just because I'm missing my heart.

I just need a little time to heal.

Preferably without late-night calls ripping at the same wounds all over again.

As I lift my head from my worktable, I realize it's been hours since Grandpa went to bed. I've been lost in fine-tuning details, working them into proper drafting plans with measurements and materials, then picking out just the right piece of lumber to start shaving away. I carve out the basic shape, curls of pale pine wood littered across my drafting table, my familiar tools resting in the velvet bed of their wooden case.

But it's almost midnight and my phone is ringing.

Why the hell would Xavier Arrendell be calling?

I haven't had the energy to confront him about the bounced check yet.

Maybe it's a mistake.

Maybe a million other things I wouldn't know because I'm not from a world where that kind of money changes hands easily.

I should ignore it.

Let him leave a message, and I'll call back during normal business hours.

I really should go to bed.

But if I do, I'll just wind up staring at the ceiling, wondering what Xavier wanted and trying not to think about Micah.

So, with an annoyed sigh, I pick up my phone.

"Mr. Arrendell," I say, brushing sawdust and shavings off my shirt. At this time of night, I don't have anything left in me to be soft and polite. "It's pretty late. What can I do for you?"

"First, accept my humblest apologies," he says smoothly, completely immune to my coldness. "I understand you had some trouble at the bank today. I'm deeply sorry for that, Miss Grey. I'm so accustomed to doing everything digitally that I must have picked up an old checkbook. My bank said a check of that size so dated triggered a hold for fraud."

"So that's what happened…" Relief floods my veins. "Apology accepted. We can sort it out in the morning, I guess."

"I'm afraid we can't," he says quickly. "I'll be out of town, handling an urgent business merger in Riyadh for the next two weeks. I've drawn up a cashier's check—no risk of that bouncing. My flight leaves at the crack of dawn, I'm afraid, so I need to be out the door shortly. Would you mind dropping by since you're still up? I'll have Joseph leave the front light on for you."

There's a touch of teasing, familiar humor in the last comment, but it falls into an empty pit in my soul.

Holy hell, I can't just say no.

But I don't exactly want to do this.

"...couldn't you just leave the check with Mr. Peters?" I glance idly at the darkness outside, barely lit by a crescent moon through the clouds. "I can come by and grab it first thing tomorrow morning."

Xavier's response sounds pained.

"Forgive me. Please don't think me snobbish, Miss Grey. However, a cashier's check is as good as cash, and I *never* leave that much cash with the help. You understand, yes?"

Yikes.

If you don't want me to think you're a giant snob, maybe don't be such a sneering prick, I think glumly.

"All right. Give me half an hour. I'll be there."

"Lovely, Miss Grey. We'll see you then."

He doesn't sound like he's trying to be slimy, but it still sounds unclean.

I wrinkle my nose, then slide off my stool, stretching and rubbing my aching neck.

I head upstairs to change into something presentable—an instinct now, to cover myself as much as possible around Xavier—and leave a quick note for Grandpa on the kitchen table.

I glance into his room before I leave.

He's folded up, sleeping with that little whistling snore

he's always had, a tiny squeaking whisper that used to make me giggle.

But his hands are bandaged.

The prescription bottle of anti-inflammatories on the nightstand looks nearly empty, when he shouldn't run out for another week or two. That tells me it's bad, and if he keeps going this way, he might accidentally overdose.

Oh, Grandpa...

Sneaking in, I kiss his wrinkled forehead, then ease the keys off his nightstand, folding them tight in my palm so they don't jingle.

It's moonless when I step outside, the clouds low in the sky.

Even the streetlamps feel dimmer, turning the night into grey mud—or maybe it's just my mood.

I hate seeing Xavier Arrendell this late.

Even worse, I hate the messy feelings about taking his dirty money, considering the source.

But it's for my grandfather.

When it comes to family, I'm no better than anybody else. I guess my morals bend.

Only for Grandpa?

Wasn't your moral compass spinning like a ballerina the second you joined Micah's little schemes?

Oh my God, I can't.

Not right now.

I still can't process the whole DEA thing, and that takes a back seat to the bone-crushing way he ended things. I don't need to show up at the big house upset and vulnerable.

Just the thought of what Xavier might do with that makes my gut lurch.

If that creep tries to hug me, I swear only one of us is leaving that house alive.

The truck does a lot of lurching of its own as I drive up the hill. It might just die on me again, but I wasn't walking out there alone this late at night.

Still, the old girl makes it. *Barely.*

When I pull up, I see Joseph Peters has, in fact, left the light on for me. Just a lonely lantern next to the tall double doors, a gold beacon guiding me toward his slim, wary figure as I park the car and climb the steps.

He looks tired tonight. Troubled.

Maybe his conscience is starting to drag him down.

"Mr. Peters." I smile.

"You're welcome to call me Joseph." I wonder if he's defrosting a bit. But he reaches for the door to open it, then stops, and suddenly his arm is a barrier as he gives me a long look. "You really shouldn't be here tonight, Miss Grey. If I told you to turn around and go home, would you listen?"

My heart stops.

"What? Why? Do you know something I don't?" I search his face.

"No," he says, shaking his head. "I simply know there are people here tonight who prefer not to be seen—and it would be unwise for you to see them, Miss Grey."

What people?

The Jacobins?

That rips at my heart, but I mask it behind a numb smile.

"If I'm going to call you Joseph, you should call me Talia. Look, I promise I'll be in and out. Less than five minutes. I'm just picking up a check before Xavier leaves the country."

He gives me a long, heavy look that makes me realize I would never be one of the final girls in those movies—you know, the ones who survive because they listen when the creepy, seemingly crazy old man with the bulging eyes warns them before they head into the woods where their friends will be murdered.

I mean, Joseph doesn't really fit the crazy old man bill, but…

I'll be fine. He'll be close by.

What could happen just by sneaking in to grab a check?

Joseph's look lingers a little longer.

I check to make sure my phone is in my bag and that app Micah had me install is on the main screen. Even if we're strangers again, I still think he'd come running if I needed him.

"I promise," I repeat with a smile that's braver than I feel. Everything in me screams to turn around and go home, forget the check. But I can't forget my grandfather's bandaged hands and that nearly empty pill bottle. "Five minutes. Go ahead and count. I'll keep my head down and avoid eye contact with anyone else. And you'll be there, won't you?"

The look he gives leaves me so uneasy.

"Hurry. He should be in his office." Silently, he pulls one of the double doors open and waits for me to enter.

For once, I lead the way with Joseph close behind me like a shadow—guardian angel or stalking demon, I don't know. My back suddenly feels too exposed and it's a little harder to breathe.

Stop it.

You let him get inside your head.

You let him scare you.

My chest aches by the time I stop outside Xavier's partly cracked door.

The halls are a little dimmer, making the golden light falling through that slit brighter. I rest my hand on the door and turn back to Joseph with a smile and a wink.

"Start the timer," I tease.

He doesn't answer.

He just stares like this is the last time he's ever going to see me.

A cold lump settles in my stomach.

I hold my breath and knock on Xavier's door.

"Mr. Arrendell?" I call. "It's Talia Grey."

"Of course. Come." Past the door, his voice is icy and eerily calm.

Stealing one last glance at Joseph for reassurance, I find nothing there except blank withdrawal, save the silent warning in his eyes.

It's like he's still telling me not to go in there.

I hold his eyes for another second, then push the office door open and step inside.

Xavier looks more casual than I've ever seen him.

His suit coat is draped over his chair, the sleeves of his pale blue dress shirt rolled up to his elbows, the collar unbuttoned.

His blond hair seems disarrayed. He leans back in his high-backed leather swivel chair with one leg crossed, his elbow propped on the arm and his gaze fixed on his laptop screen.

A paperweight on the front corner of the desk pins down a slip of paper that looks very much like the infamous check I desperately need.

How bad would it look if I just grabbed it and ran out the door?

But he looks up, his dead green eyes piercing me as he gestures to the empty chair across his desk. "Come, sit. I have something I'd like to show you."

Oh, no.

He really wants to talk about the project *now*?

So much for in and out in five minutes.

But Grandpa's treatment is riding on keeping Xavier

Arrendell happy, so I force a fake smile and pull up one of the desk chairs.

"Sure. What do you want me to see?"

He says nothing, just gives me a measured look.

Then he slowly turns the laptop around so I can see it.

I'm expecting something normal.

A Pinterest mood board with new designs, a home tour video, an Instagram home show that screams we need a whole new direction, suited to his rich, finicky attitude. Instead, I see—

Me.

Caught on video.

First, slipping Micah's number into Joseph's pocket, my lips moving soundlessly.

Then I'm rifling through Xavier's desk, taking photos of his phone bill before I'm pawing through the drawers like a hungry bear chasing honey. I know what's next.

Taking the camera from his desk drawer.

My vision goes white for a second.

I can *feel* him glaring, but I can't take my eyes off the screen.

Every passing second steals more air from my lungs. I can't seem to make the simple act of breathing work anymore.

I am a flipping idiot.

Of course there was a hidden camera.

Of course someone as paranoid as Xavier would have cameras *everywhere.*

And now, he knows.

I'm gasping, making a strained, wheezing sound.

"Problem, Miss Grey?" he bites off.

I jerk my head up, my heart hammering, my lips working as I meet his eyes.

Except nothing comes out.

I don't have air for words. Not with my entire body imploding while I'm trapped in those inhuman jade eyes.

Sometimes, I thought Micah's eyes were hollow when he'd shut me away.

But they're nothing like this.

Nothing like the arctic green void of Xavier's as he tries to decide how to kill me.

"Mr. Arrendell, um..."

A tired, angry sigh boils out of him.

"I suppose I have you to blame for the fact that my domestic bank accounts have all been frozen by the federal government. You really should have minded your own goddamned business, little girl. Now that idiot cop you've been fucking is going to make himself a problem, too—or perhaps not, once he realizes you're such a desperate little jezebel that you'd flirt with my *valet* for information."

Flirt?

Oh. Without the sound on the camera, he must have thought I was—

Yeah, it doesn't matter.

There's a second of surreal relief knowing that Joseph Peters won't be implicated by my stupidity.

But then Xavier's gaze flicks past me with a weariness, like he's done this a hundred times.

"Take her," he growls.

I don't understand the flick of his hand.

Not until a shadow falls over me from behind.

It's hard to move, but I whirl around, half expecting to see Joseph Peters, complicit and doing his master's bidding.

Oh, if only I was that lucky.

Eustace Jacobin stands over me, this hideous witch in black.

She leers like a nightmare, reaching bony hands out, aiming for my throat.

She doesn't get a chance to strangle me.

Panic detonates in my brain until I'm spinning.

The lights go out as I fall down a black vortex of fear, screaming silently into total oblivion.

XXII: OH DARK HUNDRED (MICAH)

The very last thing I need to be thinking about right now is Talia Grey.

Yet as I strap myself into protective Kevlar, she's it.

The only thing on my mind.

I can't tell if what I'm feeling is anticipation, grim determination, or the urgency of the ticking clock. Every second it takes us to prep is another second closer to our window slamming shut, Xavier and the Jacobins slipping through my fingers yet again.

I'd definitely breathe easier if I could see her, feel her soft fingers against my face and have those bright-blue eyes looking at me with the same innocence that saw a better man than I actually am.

I've tried.

I've tried like hell to tell myself our breakup was for the best.

That it wasn't real.

I was living a lie, and she was steeped in this fantasy with a man who doesn't truly exist.

Too bad the heartache tells me that's the furthest fucking thing from the truth.

Talia saw me.

She *accepted* me.

And maybe, just maybe, she saw me in a better light than I ever saw myself.

Then I went and fucked it all up.

Hell, once this is over, maybe I can try to undo the damage.

I throw on my tactical gloves and check the spare clips strapped to my bulletproof vest. We're hoping to get through this without a firefight, but the Jacobins can get a little trigger-happy.

If they're going to be down at the docks, they'll probably be packing a little more than old shotguns chock-full of buckshot, too.

Grant clears his throat to get my attention and passes me a Colt M4. "You certified on this thing, Mr. DEA?"

"Very funny. I recertify at the firing range once a year, which is more than you small-town cops do." I grab the Colt and put it away.

Lucas, looking like a goddamned assassin in his own black tactical gear, flashes me a feral grin. "Watch it, Mikey. We small-timers can outshoot you city boys any day."

"Let's hope we don't have a reason to find out," Grant says sharply.

"What's the plan?" Henri asks sharply.

"For now, play it by ear," the captain responds, adjusting his Kevlar vest. "I've called in to Raleigh for backup, but we'll get there first. We go in quiet, get the lay of the land, see what we're up against. Then we figure out the rest." He turns a sardonic hazel eye on me. "If that's okay with the Feds, of course."

"You guys are never going to let me live that down, are you?"

Henri smirks. "Not in a million years, mon ami."

"You know your French accent sucks, right?" I snort.

"Hey!" He jabs a gloved finger at me. "It's *Creole*. Technically, the bastard cousin of French, and completely foreign to anyone outside the Atchafalaya Basin."

"That thing you just said was not a word. I refuse to believe it was," I retort.

"All right, all right, time's wasting," Grant says. "Let's move, you clowns."

I'm jonesing to get this shit show over with.

Even if I left broken hearts and damage in my wake, I've been waiting for this day for too long.

Finally.

I'm finally going to get to see blue sky again, instead of the endless dark clouds of purgatory, my home since Jet died.

As I stand up with one last tug to check the fit of my gear, my phone goes off from inside the vest pocket.

Fuck.

I almost ignore it.

I don't have time for anything now but the mission, and it's annoying as hell to fish my phone out in this bulky mess. There's no ignoring that hot prick of warning, though.

Something that says anyone calling me this late shouldn't be ignored.

Everyone stops, eyes on me, as I pluck my phone out and look at the screen.

Unknown number?

What the hell? If this is some clown calling to ask if I'm happy with my long-distance carrier, I'll bite their goddamned face off.

"Hello?" I answer the call.

"Officer Micah Ainsley?" It's an unfamiliar male voice.

Breathless, urgent. A slight New England accent. Probably around my age, but I have no idea who the fuck this is, calling me by name. "You have to hurry. He took her."

If I had ears like Rolf, they'd be standing up like spears.

"…who is this? Who fucking took who?"

"Please, I can't," he answers quickly. He's whispering, I realize. "I couldn't even call 9-1-1—you know they pay the phone bills. But he took *Miss Grey*. He knows, Officer Ainsley. He knows she took the camera."

Shit, shit.

It all clicks together instantly like a gruesome puzzle.

It's *him*.

The valet Talia told me about.

Joseph Peters.

And Xavier found out Talia took the camera, and he took *her*.

I'll fucking kill him.

He already took my brother, and now he's taking the woman I love?

"Where?" I demand. "Where has he gone? Is she hurt?"

"I don't believe she's injured," Peters answers swiftly. "She seems to have passed out from fright. He didn't tell me where he was going, no. He has me drive him locally, but when he goes on his endeavors, out of town, he never takes me along."

"No point creating a witness," I mutter grimly. "What direction did he go? Dammit, give me something."

"North," Peters hisses. "I'm sorry—someone's coming, if anyone overhears—"

"You'll disappear next."

"Or end up like Cora." There's grief in his whisper. "Please, Officer Ainsley. *Please*, hurry."

He hangs up before I can thank him.

I stare down at my blank screen.

Cold sweat slicks my brow.

My heart feels like someone's drilling screws into it.

There's no doubt in my mind that he aims to kill Talia.

I just have to hope he's more focused on making his shipping window first, to buy us some time.

I want to fucking call her.

I want to hear her voice, to know she's alive. Only, if she's in a delicate situation and her phone rings, if she can't silence it, if I endanger her—

No, I can't take the risk.

"Micah?" Grant growls. "What's wrong?"

I snap up from zoning out, looking at the three men who stare back resolutely.

"Bad news. Xavier and the Jacobins have a hostage," I snarl.

"Talia Grey?" Henri whispers.

I can only nod.

Lucas and Henri both wince, dissolving into curses.

Grant's stormy expression hardens into death.

"He's taking her to Mariposa Cove, I assume?"

"Maybe," I say, but there's doubt eating me. "Can we risk it if he's not? What if he dumps her off somewhere along the way, and we miss our chance to stop him because we're chasing him to the docks?"

It takes a second for the raw desperation in my own voice to sink in.

My throat's tight, scratchy, hurting.

I feel like I've caught Talia's asthma.

But I can't be wrong.

I can't let him hurt her.

I love her too goddamned much and she doesn't even know it.

"Hey." Grant steps closer and claps one big hand to my shoulder, his steady gaze locking on me and holding me firm. "Trust your instincts, man. What are they telling you?"

My jaw clenches.

I stop as my phone buzzes again in my palm.

This time, no ringtone.

It's the safety app I made Talia install.

It lights up, blinking with a GPS location pinpointing an emergency signal, somewhere east of Raleigh and speeding up the coast.

It's not just urgency erupting inside me now.

It's *hope*.

My fingers clutch the phone until they burn.

"My instincts say we're damned lucky Talia Grey is a fucking genius," I say breathlessly. "Load up. We'll cut them off at Mariposa Cove."

XXIII: SHOT IN THE DARK (TALIA)

Minutes Earlier

I don't think I'm dead.
But everything is black.
Pitch-black.

So black that if I couldn't feel my eyelids moving, I wouldn't know my eyes were open at all. This is what death must feel like, this lightless darkness that swallows everything.

But if I'm dead, I don't think my head would hurt so much.

I don't think it would rattle my bones every time I'm jolted around.

My arms and legs definitely wouldn't be this sore.

Plus, I don't think being *dead* involves getting locked in the trunk of someone's *car*.

I can hear the engine, the shift in tone as it changes speed, the whizzing of tires over asphalt.

There's a faint whiff of gasoline and oil, too, that subtle hint that clings to even the cleanest car.

I think there's carpet under me.

When the momentum throws me around, I touch round things that feel like wheel caps. My arms and legs are tied behind my back.

Nope, I'm not dead.

But if Xavier Arrendell has me tied up in his trunk, that's going to change pretty fast.

Okay.

Don't panic.

If I panic, I'll just trigger an asthma attack, and passing out earlier killed any chance I had to run. If I get a second chance, I can't miss it.

I close my eyes—not that it makes much difference—and focus on counting. Measuring my breaths. Controlling my fear.

It's more than just fending off an attack at this point.

It's a calming ritual. It's—

I freeze as my fingertips brush something against my back.

Something with a textured weave, something that feels like—

The nylon strap of my bag?

Oh.

Oh, crap, if Xavier didn't take my phone out, if he didn't mess with it...

I might be able to signal Micah.

Hope blooms in my chest.

Grunting with exertion, I wiggle backward, fighting the way the car bounces me around and trying to dig my feet in to brace myself.

I fumble blindly. My wrists are tied but my fingers can

still move. I manage to snag a fold of fabric, dragging the bag closer.

With my teeth clenched, I feel around until I find the zipper, then tug, lose my grip, swear, catch it, tug, lose it again, nearly scream, try again and then—

There!

The zipper opens.

Just enough for me to plunge my fists inside.

No time for finesse.

I don't know how long I have before Mr. Congeniality decides to stop and take care of his annoying Talia Grey problem.

My pulse kicks up as I rummage around, feeling for the edge of my phone.

Got it!

I'm not someone who prays, but you'd better believe I do it right now.

Pray that the app screen stays active for situations like this.

Pray that Xavier didn't do anything to shut it down.

I mash my fingertips against the screen, begging, pleading —*oh, thank God!*

A low beep.

Barely there, the sound purposefully muted so it won't alert whoever might be listening to someone seeking help.

But it's *there*.

If I'm lucky, maybe that's enough.

Maybe Micah will save me one last time.

Even if he doesn't love me, I know he'd never leave me to die.

I just hope there's time.

Who knows how much longer this drive is.

Time doesn't have much meaning in this blind killing darkness. My head throbs with adrenaline.

And I feel every movement when the bouncy road changes, like we're moving over a different kind of pavement now.

It slows, turns, then stops.

I brace myself, biting the inside of my cheek, assessing my pathetic options.

What can I do? Headbutt whoever opens the trunk?

But nobody does.

My chest tightens.

I hear voices, other engines in the distance, but no one even bangs on the trunk, let alone opens it.

What's happening? What's he doing?

Is it even Xavier who brought me here or just some minion doing his dirty work?

My mind runs away with me, wondering if someone can suffocate to death in a car trunk. Is that what they're going to do? Use my asthma against me, so that even if a healthy person might survive a long time in a car trunk, I'll asphyxiate and die?

Or did Xavier hand me over to the Jacobins to finish the job?

Ugh.

Vicious images flash through my head, all the horrific things they could do to me. I don't even want to think about what Culver Jacobin almost did to Delilah Graves.

But I can't help myself.

Especially when there are worse things a gang of men can do to a woman while she's still alive…

No! No, that's not going to happen.

Micah's going to show up and put a stop to this any second.

And if he doesn't… well, I'll find a way out.

I'll save myself.

Even if I have to use my *teeth*, I'll give them a fight.

Right now, though, I need my arms and legs free.

Curling my fingers, I stretch them as far as I can, feeling at the ropes around my wrists. Feels like nylon, like the kind of emergency cords you find in car kits.

Not good.

That kind of nylon knots tight, and even two free hands would have trouble getting it untied.

Oh, but I try.

Even though my knuckles hurt and it aches to reach, pulling on the tendons in my wrists and making the rope bite my skin, I feel along the wrapped cords until I find the knot.

Crap!

There goes my manicure.

I'm picking at the closest knot with my fingernails and getting nowhere.

I just can't pull it free, but I can feel something else.

Oh.

Subtle fraying.

That happens with nylon sometimes, doesn't it?

You can pick and pick until the fibers come loose.

If they're going to ignore me, maybe I can use this precious time to tear the cord apart.

Still counting under my breath, I work frantically, fuzzy threads brushing against my wrists and tickling the sides of my palms.

Slowly, one fiber at a time, I tease one bit free.

Then another, making a mess of the weave.

I don't think I'll be able to fully unravel the cord, but I don't need to.

I just need to unravel it so the knots aren't so tight, and I can work them loose.

I work at it for what feels like an eternity.

Until my fingers are nothing but pain.

Until my fingertips burn and I can feel the blisters forming.

Until my arms and wrists are so sore I could sob, but I won't.

Until I sink my teeth into my bottom lip to bite back the pain, knowing if they hear me, it's over.

Bit by bit, I rip that cord apart until my fingernails are ragged, and then I use *that* to snag even more of the nylon weave and pull a few more threads free.

Pain is nothing.

I've known it my entire life.

Just like I knew the pain of Micah's touch, teaching me that sometimes pain can be a beautiful thing.

And sometimes pain has purpose.

Pain gets my adrenaline going, makes me breathe, pushes me to try harder, *fight on.* And just as I test the knots and think maybe I've found a little slack, there's a *ker-CHUNK* of the trunk popping open.

I'm paralyzed.

I almost yell out *No*! I was so close—so close, if I'd just had my hands free I could've—

It doesn't matter.

The trunk swings open.

After a breathless moment of pure terror, I'm blinded by dim starlight and a few distant red and orange running lights.

There's no mistaking Xavier Arrendell, looking down at me with cold contempt, the faint ocean-scented breeze ruffling his hair in blond arcs.

"You really are a clueless bitch," he says flatly.

Then he grabs me by the arm, hauling me up with a brute strength that nearly dislocates my arm.

I refuse to scream.

And as he drags me up to kneel on the edge of the trunk with the metal biting into my calves?

I draw back and spit right in his face.

He remains unmoved.

Glacial stone.

If I hoped to catch him off guard and run or something, my hopes are dashed.

"Feeling better now?" Xavier snarls. "Do it again, if you'd like. I won't deny a woman her dying wish."

I take half a second to catch my breath and look around.

It's bleak, almost desolate here.

A broad concrete loading dock with a couple piers spearing out into the flat black expanse of ocean, the rocky gravel beach stretching to either side, a lonely lane sloping up to the empty highway.

The Jacobins' trucks are lined up along the dock, and there's a massive black-painted freighter dotted with orange and red lights at port. Dozens of people are busy off-loading crates from the trucks onto the crane that lifts the cargo onto the deck. There are tall area lights up on poles, but they're off, leaving the place gloomy and black.

Off to one side, Eustace and Ephraim Jacobin supervise, standing with Chief Bowden.

Jesus, it's all true.

Not that I ever had much doubt.

Everything was true, and it's the most awful sinking feeling.

What's worse?

Even if I got loose from Xavier, somebody else would tackle me before I got far.

Crap.

"What's the point of killing me?" I ask. "It won't change anything. The police have the camera. They have *everything* and all you're going to do is add to the charges against you. So you might as well just let me go."

Xavier's smile is frigid. Cruel. Nasty. Knowing.

"And how will they charge me with the murder of a woman who's simply disappeared?" he whispers. "Once you've been stuffed into a barrel, darling, you'll sink fast. If you're lucky, maybe I'll shoot you first." He jerks me closer, into a face full of teeth. "Or maybe I'll simply seal you in so you can find out what happens faster—suffocation or drowning as the water slowly seeps in."

I stare back in frozen horror.

"…Micah was right about you," I whisper. "You're sick. Everyone in your family. I can't believe I ever pitied you!"

"When did I ask for your pity? If anything," he sneers, "I pity *you*. Falling in love with that pathetic cop?" He smirks. "Oh, you thought I didn't notice?"

"I don't care if you did."

"So *defiant*." Icy, amused words. "Your little love affair is why you're going to die, Miss Grey. Do you really think Officer Ainsley cares now that he got what he used you for? Love is always a mistake. Never make yourself vulnerable. They'll only use it to hurt you."

That hits a little too close to home.

So close I can only stare at him with my entire body feeling hollowed out.

Is he right?

I don't know.

But I *know* Micah's coming.

The sick doubt running through me feels like nothing compared to the revulsion as Xavier leers. "People are only good for money or pleasure, when you take love out of the equation," he says, fingers digging into my arm. "I thought, perhaps, before I dispose of you, I could use you. And since you are rather short on money…"

His meaning sinks in as he grips my chin with harsh fingers, tilting my face up to his. I bare my teeth.

Holy hell, I'll bite his nose off before I let him touch me. I'll—

Xavier jerks back then.

There's a thundering boom, metallic and echoing over the night.

Everyone on the dock freezes in place.

I lift my head sharply, turning toward the sound. Past a group of shipping containers, I think—I hope—I catch a glimpse of white.

Micah.

Hope leaps in my heart.

Xavier hisses through his teeth.

"We'll finish this later. After I paint your white knight red," he snarls—then catches me by my hair.

This time, I can't hold back my scream as he drags me out of the car fully by my roots, slamming me to the pavement as he raises his voice in a ringing shout.

"Come out, come out, little white wolf!" he roars. "Come the hell out or little red riding dick won't last much longer."

XXIV: DARK HUNGER (MICAH)

"Grant," I whisper through clenched teeth, "let me fucking go."

Grant only grabs my arms harder, forcing them behind my back and restraining me with all his might.

"Not till you cool down," he whispers. "Charge in now, you'll just get her killed."

If I *don't*, she might get killed anyway.

And it'll be my goddamned fault.

All because I wasn't quick enough.

We took one hell of a risk, hightailing it out here in unmarked cars, breaking God only knows how many speed limits. Better to get pulled over and flash our badges than to have Xavier and the Jacobins catch a glimpse of flashers on their bumpers and blowing the whole operation.

I didn't have anyone to leave Rolf with, so I stuffed him in the back of Grant's truck and brought him along for the ride.

We couldn't afford another wasted minute.

There was barely time to park about half a mile away and make the rest of the trip on foot, leaving Rolf leashed to the truck while we assess the situation.

Pretty standard black market operation by the looks of it.

The silent loading and unloading, the dark, unmarked ship, the remote location.

The entire time, I've been scanning around for Talia. Until we knew we wouldn't endanger her with friendly fire, we couldn't move.

Grant and I took up positions behind several large freight containers, while Lucas and Henri split up to circle around to the other side.

We're outnumbered as hell, judging by the Jacobins and their associates swarming around like pissed off ants.

Who the fuck knows when Raleigh PD will show up.

When Xavier pulled Talia out of the trunk, I almost lost my shit and charged the gap between the shipping containers.

Only for Grant to rip me back, kicking and twisting and fighting me. Only to freeze as one of my boots hits the shipping container with a resounding *boom*.

Shit!

So much for keeping a cool head, but if that miserable fuck touches her, if he touches her at *all*—

Talia's scream splits the night.

A frigid, murderous rage lashes my blood.

I can taste death on the air.

I go stock-still, save for my clenched fists.

"Grant?" I snarl.

"Yeah?"

"You're going to want to let me go before I make you," I bite off, right before Xavier's voice carries over the dock.

"Come out, come out, little white wolf!"

Grant swears softly, his grip easing off.

"Don't think I have much choice," he mutters. "Think our cover's fucking blown."

Yeah, I'd agree.

The silent dock clatters alive with noise and activity—Jacobins, Bowden, people I don't recognize diving for their guns.

I catch a glimpse of carbines, shotguns, and pistols before I hunker down behind the freight container and sling out my M4.

"Look," I whisper. "They're sitting ducks, out there in plain sight. We've got cover. We can take them while they're confused."

"And Talia?" Grant peeks around the corner of the freight container, hefting his own weapon.

"Don't risk it." I shake my head. "Pick off the assholes around Xavier first. Don't engage him. She might take a stray bullet, and we wouldn't be able to get to her in time."

Grant nods tightly, pressing the headset clipped to his ear and muttering into it. "Boys, we're going sniper. Use the freight containers. Duck and dodge like hell. Never step in the same place twice. Go for the hostiles, avoid Xavier Arrendell and the hostage. Understood?"

Lucas' voice crackles in both our earpieces. "Suicide run, got it, Cap."

"Like hell I'm dyin' here!" Henri joins in. "I'm too good a shot for that. Let's fuck some shit up, my friends."

Grant just sighs, rolling his eyes. "Fucking children, acting like it's a video game. Move on my mark."

"If you don't show yourselves," Xavier calls out, "I'll kill her now! Right here in front of you."

Talia's pained cry follows, and my heart shatters again, each sliver furious and cutting.

I close my eyes, shaking, forcing myself to *wait, wait.*

Fuck, if I can't control myself, I'll just make it worse.

The three seconds until Grant snaps are the longest of my life.

"Now!" he roars.

Then he darts away and I'm free.

I charge in the opposite direction, glancing between freight containers. The Jacobins and their hired mercs fan out defensively.

Ephraim and Eustace hang back with Bowden, his service pistol clenched in both hands.

Xavier clutches Talia, holding her close by the throat.

His fingers dig at her skin, her face red yet defiant with anger, her blue eyes bright.

Of course, he's using her as a human shield.

That sick, cowardly piece of shit.

When I get my hands on him—

But my thoughts snap and I duck.

A shot pings off the corner of the freight container shielding me.

Shit, shit, *shit*.

More shots—coming from all directions this time.

I dive for cover behind another bulky container just as I notice several Jacobins going down howling.

My turn.

I hit the ground, roll, come up on one knee, and fire off three rounds.

Two hit targets before I'm moving again, weaving between containers.

It's like a nightmare maze, and our best bet is to bait them into it.

Fewer bodies shielding Xavier.

Fewer targets close to Talia.

Easier to isolate and pick them off.

I scuttle to another quick vantage point, aim, pick off one more, then duck and head in the opposite direction. I deliberately let myself be seen, slowing in the crevice between two containers, waiting, watching as several more peel off from the main group and give chase.

THE DARKEST CHASE

Before they can catch sight of me again, I double back, breathing hard, flattening myself against the back of another container. Right as three men go charging down the corridor of space I just abandoned.

I count out three seconds, then slip behind them.

Aim.

Fire.

One, two, three, blown down like leaves.

Xavier wants to call me a white wolf?

Little pig, little pig, let me in.

Again.

Again, and there's still no fucking end to it.

Screaming bullets piercing flesh, men crying out, the sharp ricochet of bullets flying off steel.

One thing I don't hear is Talia now, and every time I duck down, I risk exposing myself for another glimpse of her.

I need to know she's safe, dammit.

Xavier's backed himself up to Bowden, Eustace, and Ephraim, screaming something desperate, probably about a getaway plan.

There's still too fucking many of their men, and now the strategy to scatter them turns against us as we lose them in the containers.

My arms ache from the rifle's recoil. I slide into a dark crevice to catch my breath, tapping my earpiece.

"We good?" I gasp.

"Low on ammo," Grant barks back.

"Took a graze to the thigh, but still livin'," Henri replies a little too cheerfully.

Lucas is quiet, making me fear he's one of the bodies littering the docks, until he whispers, "...I have a clear shot at Xavier, but if he moves..."

"*Don't*." Panic leaps in my chest. "We *can't* risk a hostage like that."

"What you mean," Lucas says gravely—no pun intended, "is your albino ass can't risk the woman you love."

"I'd say the same for any civilian," I snap and then sigh. "And yeah. I fucking love her, so let's try not to shoot her, okay?"

"What's the plan?" Henri asks.

"One option," Grant growls. "We *Braveheart* it."

I frown. "What? You think one last rush will catch them so off guard they think we're completely fucking insane?"

"I hope so," Grant says—followed by the sound of his M4 going off in a quick burst.

"If you get me killed with this shit," I say, "I will *haunt* your gigantic ass."

"Then don't die on me, DEA," Grant snorts. "Okay, on my mark. One... two... *three!*"

That's all I need.

I grip my M4 like it's keeping me alive and *charge.*

You can feel the air over the docks change.

Suddenly, we're no longer angry ghosts sniping from the shadows, but roaring madmen coming in from all sides, spilling down the throat of chaos.

With everyone scattered, there's no united front as Xavier's men fall back.

Easy targets.

But we've got our backs exposed, and there are still too damned many of them left.

The four of us link up, crowding in tight, until we're a phalanx cutting Xavier and Bowden and the Jacobin heads off from their men.

We make ourselves vulnerable to them.

It's not good.

Not at all when we're crunched together, firing like madmen, looking over our shoulders, taking more shots, picking off a few more.

There's something deathly cold in Bowden's eyes as he lifts his service pistol and—

Another sound splits the night.

Sirens?

Everyone freezes.

Us, the Jacobins, the mercenaries, Xavier, Chief Bowden.

I risk another glance at Talia.

Her blue eyes have never left me the whole time.

I can feel her telling me, *Do what you need to do. We'll come out the other side, I know it.*

Reinforcements then.

Finally.

Close—so close, we've got under a minute and they're already scattering in a mad run. Best of all, the ringleaders can't when we've got them boxed in, and now it's our advantage. Grant, Lucas, Henri, and I swing around to face Xavier, Bowden, and the Jacobins.

Grant takes aim.

"Four against four, and you've lost your minions," he grinds out. "One more minute and this place will be crawling with Raleigh police. You're done. Let the girl go."

"Like hell," Xavier spits and glances over his shoulder —*fuck*.

I see what he's planning.

He wants to make a break for the ship.

If he can get there using Talia as a hostage, he can vanish into the open sea.

An angry cry explodes through the chaos.

Not from Talia.

From Eustace Jacobin, just as Chief Bowden snags her arm and yanks her in close. A long bowie knife materializes in his hand, pressed to her throat.

He stares at me with his dead, soulless eyes.

The mask is truly off now.

For the first time, I see the old chief for the demon he is.

A darkness deeper than anything I ever fathomed.

"The problem," Bowden says almost merrily, "is that you boys need evidence for a case. Information. Testimonials. And since our darling Eustace here kept everything in her pretty little skull as insurance..." She's white-faced but stone-cold, refusing to show fear, her wizened face curled in pure disgust as Bowden taps the knife against her throat. "... slit her throat, and I ruin all your hard work. So if you want her alive, you'd best back the hell off."

"Where does that get you?" I demand. "Kill her with four cops as witnesses, and you'll still be arrested. You're not getting off that easy, *Chief*."

He smiles, a sickly thing. "Maybe I just want to kill her, then I'll—oof!"

Fucking Eustace.

Not going down without a fight.

She rams her elbow into his ample gut.

"Hands off my fucking wife!" Ephraim swings his gun up toward Bowden.

Bowden tightens his grip on Eustace. It's a messy tangle and I swing the muzzle of my M4, trying to find a clean shot until—

Until Rolf strikes first.

I must not have tied his leash tight enough, because suddenly there's a furious bark.

He comes flying over the hill, just ahead of the Raleigh SWAT team swarming out of their boxy vehicles. He moves like a pup half his age, launching himself into Chief Bowden.

The dog's teeth clamp down viciously on Bowden's calf.

Bowden shrieks, flails—and drags the knife right across Eustace's throat.

Shit.

Everything happens at once.

Talia yells in terror.

Eustace collapses in a pool of blood.

Ephraim lets out a guttural howl and turns on us, swinging his shotgun, only for his scream to turn into a shout of pain as Grant lines up a shot and clips him hard in the thigh.

Down goes the grizzled old man.

Bowden shakes Rolf off with a sharp blow to the head, making my dog whimper in a way that spikes my rage as much as Talia's screams. Before I can move, Bowden flops back and disappears over the edge of the dock with a loud splash.

Xavier turns, dragging Talia, and bolts for the ship's loading ramp.

Fuck. Fuck, fuck, fuck, fuck, fuck.

I lunge forward, bracing my back foot, and take aim.

His shoulder.

He's got Talia clutched against one side, but the other shoulder's vulnerable.

If I get a clean shot, it'll go right through and pass over her.

I know it.

I know I can save her.

I wouldn't trust anyone else with this shot but myself.

Breathe in.

Breathe out.

Aim.

Fire!

The trigger jerks.

The recoil slams through me.

The bullet stabs the night.

It feels like time slows down, watching and hoping I didn't just kill the woman I love.

Not until I see it.

A red blossom against the back of Xavier's shirt.

He drops Talia and she tumbles away, bound and rolling, but unharmed.

Xavier falls forward slowly, struggling against the ground.

He still tries to lunge at Talia—and that's when the white-hot fury takes over, hurling me forward.

Not again.

He won't take anyone else from me *ever again*.

I drop my M4 and tackle him in a bloody heap away, sending us both skidding across the pavement, away from her.

On top of him, I'm snarling, pinning his ugly ass down by the throat.

My fist crashes into his face again and again.

"I'll kill you," I hiss. "I'll fucking *kill* you for what you've done!"

Even bleeding with a bullet embedded in his shoulder, even with his face pulped, he sneers, daring me to do it again, blood streaking his perfect white teeth.

"For what, you asshole? For messing with your whore?"

I nearly rip his throat out with my bare hands.

I swear to God, there's a murder of crows in the distance going wild with amusement. I think all that racket brings me back into myself as I rear back and stare at him.

He doesn't know.

That's the worst part.

He doesn't fucking know what he's *done*, what I've lost, *who*, and he doesn't care.

Finish him, Mikey, Jet whispers through the chaos. *Put this asshole out of his misery and I'll never bother you again.*

I swallow hard.

I hate the dumb blank look on Xavier's face more than anything.

He knows what it's like to lose his brothers just like I lost mine, and he doesn't care at all. Right now, I feel like I could be every bit the monster Xavier is if it helps Jet's ghost rest in peace.

Yet if I kill him now, he'll die without understanding why, and it won't mean shit.

I think I'll do it anyway.

The dark thing inside me uncoils, murderous and hot, desperate for the blood of the man who destroyed the only family I had.

I've craved this for too long.

I won't be denied a second longer, not while I hear those mad birds shrieking in my ear.

Gritting my teeth, I clamp my hands down on his throat and press *hard*.

"M-Micaaah..."

The crows go silent.

There's just Talia's voice. Weak, raspy, calling to me, but I don't want to listen.

"Mi...cah. Th-this isn't who you are... *Stop...*"

Doesn't she get it?

This *is* who I am!

It's the moment I've lived for, watching Xavier suffer the way he deserves, struggling under me, the satisfaction of watching his life drain away and his face turning purple, then blue. *Yes*.

"...*Micah*."

Fuck.

I jerk my head up, looking at her, and my heart stops.

She's blue in the face, wheezing, on the verge of passing out. Her inhaler's nowhere in sight, her hands and feet bound so she couldn't reach it even if she had it.

Damn.

I have to make a choice.

The man I hate, or the woman I love.

Really, it's no choice at all.

I fling myself off Xavier and tumble over to Talia, slipping my arms under her and lifting her up.

"Talia? Talia—Shortcake—hold on for me. Breathe. Count. You remember how? Fucking *breathe* for me, woman!"

She looks up through wet eyes, her crimson hair spilling over me like she's bleeding out.

She smiles.

Her eyes close.

And then she stops breathing completely.

Anguish erupts out of me like a gunshot wound.

I frantically press my fingers to her pulse.

It's there, it's there, but weaker by the second.

I forget to breathe myself as I lay her down, as I rip the ropes off her, get her prone, then tilt her head back, pinch her nose, bend over her, and seal my mouth to those beautiful lips I don't deserve.

Breathe!

Forcing air into her lungs, pushing hard, pleading.

Please breathe. Please don't leave me.

Take my breath.

Take my heart.

Take my life.

Always and forever.

Deep breaths.

Check her pulse.

Keep her alive until—

She inhales sharply, coughing like a swimmer coming up from drowning.

Her eyes snap open with streaming tears, turning them into twin blue nights of shining stars.

"M-Micah?" she rasps.

I barely notice the hot trails cutting down my cheeks as I wrap my arms around her so very tight, clutching her close.

"Right here," I whisper, listening to her labored breaths. "I'm here for you, Talia, and I'm never leaving again."

XXV: LIGHT IN THE DARK (TALIA)

Talk about déjà vu.

Somehow both beginnings and endings with Micah involve him reviving me with mouth-to-mouth after I pass out from an asthma attack.

I'd have to say this has been the most stressful attack of my *life*, though.

If it wasn't for him breathing into me, I think I'd have given up and told the EMTs to leave me alone and let my lungs collapse.

I'm *tired*.

And even more worn out later, sitting in the back of an ambulance with a mask over my face, forcing oxygen into my lungs to compensate until the meds the emergency techs gave me kick in and my lungs no longer feel like deflated footballs someone's been kicking around for hours.

I can barely sit up.

Good thing I don't need to.

Micah sits next to me with his arm around my shoulders, holding me up, keeping me warm and…

And confusing me so much.

He should be with the rest of the Redhaven PD and the Raleigh people.

They've got their hands full with arrests, reading rights, identifying bodies, arresting *and* treating the injured. I've never seen so much blood before, and if not for Micah, I might be panicking at freaking everything.

I almost died tonight.

But I was right.

Micah came for me.

He came, and he stopped himself before he did something awful he could never take back.

I glance up at him uncertainly. Only to recoil when I realize he's still watching me with those arctic eyes, yet they no longer seem so cold.

Bowing my head, I brush my hair back and touch the mask with a weak smile.

"Bet I look super sexy right now."

"Ravishing." He doesn't miss a beat, pressing a kiss to my hair. My heart leaps with hope. "Just a little longer and I can take you home. *Both* of you," he says, leaning over the bumper, where Rolf rests cheerfully at our feet. The dog looks almost smug for playing his part in my rescue. Micah looks at me with concern. "Unless you need the hospital. You really should go. You almost flatlined, Talia."

It's a little easier to smile now.

"But I didn't. You brought me back! You saved my life and you didn't even need to kill Xavier to do it."

Micah looks stricken before he glances away.

"I wanted to kill that fuck," he clips. "So badly I can still feel his pulse in my fingertips. I wasn't thinking about the fact that technically, we need him alive for his testimony. I just wanted him dead. Your life was more important, though. Hands down."

Tentatively, I risk resting one hand on his chest.

He looks so dangerous in his tactical gear, but it's only a small part of his allure tonight.

"I told you," I whisper. "That's not who you are."

"Yeah. Guess you know it better than I do." He covers my hand with his. "Talia, I—fuck. I said a lot of shitty things I didn't mean. None of it. It was never about using you or convenience. I never should have let you think that. I never should have used that to hurt you. I wasn't faking. I never was. Just because I faked my identity a little, no. With you, woman, it was as real as it gets."

Holy hell.

I'm so stunned I don't know what to say.

After the way he sledgehammered my heart, those words can't just pick it up and piece it back together like there are no cracks at all.

But sometimes a broken thing shines brighter when every fragment catches the light, doesn't it? Just like a diamond.

When I don't respond, Micah's brows pinch together.

"Are you okay? You're not having another attack from the shock, are you?"

"What shock?" I ask faintly.

"...me being honest for once?"

I giggle.

"Um, I think that might kill you more than me," I point out dryly, leaning into the curve of his arm. "I think I get why you said the things you did. Why you ran. Why you hurt me. But I never stopped having feelings for you even with that, Micah. I trusted you to come for me today."

"I *never* would have left you with him. I couldn't."

He takes a shaky breath.

Maybe he's right and I do know him better than he knows himself, because I know his patterns.

I know how he looks away, looks down, then finally looks back at me with his lips tight and nervous when he wants to say something from the heart, pulling it out slowly like a knife lodged in his ribs.

"I never learned how to love. Not really," Micah says. The wind teases his arctic fox hair, making it stand wild and rakish. "The only person in my life I ever truly loved was my brother, and that…" He shakes his head. "He died. No warning and no goodbye. Jet was the only person I knew how to love, and he *died* on me."

"That doesn't mean everyone you love will always die."

"But it means the part of me that *can* love died with him," Micah growls. "All I had left was hate after that. Think I even hated myself, because of how Jet protected me. When we were kids, he took the abuse while I hid from our father and I *let* him, when it should have been me. When all you have is hate so deep you don't know how to stop, you forget how to love anything at all."

I just smile, nudging the big German Shepherd lightly with my toe and getting a warm, wet lick to my calf.

"Nope," I say. "Rolf says you're a liar."

"Rolf talks, huh? Guess he's a bigger hero tonight than I thought." Micah arches a skeptical brow.

"Micah Ainsley," I proclaim, pulling the mask down around my neck. "You love that goofy dog more than you love yourself. You dote on him. You saved him from being retired and bored to death. You know all his little habits, his moods, everything about him—and you know he'd do anything for you, even charging into battle." I laugh. It's getting easier to breathe now. "They say you never trust a person who doesn't like animals. And as much as you love Rolf, I trust you're still able to love things with two legs, too." My fingers curl against his chest. "Maybe you need to start over. Start with you. *Forgive* yourself for all the things you couldn't control."

"With Xavier in custody, I might be able to work on

forgiveness, but I'm not sure loving myself will ever be possible." Micah's lips twist.

I love you, so it must be, I want to scream.

But I'm afraid to. There's a new fear that I'm misreading what he's trying to say, what he's implying. Fear that he's about to break me all over again.

I only duck my head and whisper, "...yes, it is."

"Talia?"

"I'm sorry." I avert my eyes. "I won't say it. I know it's uncomfortable for you, I..."

"*Say it.*" I'm stunned when he grabs my face in his palms, turning me toward him, leaning in until our foreheads touch. "I need to hear it tonight. I need to know I haven't broken it."

My heart rises in my throat.

It's so intense I almost can't do it.

But ever since I took my life into my own hands, I've never turned away from risks. So I take a new one now.

"I love you, Micah Ainsley," I whisper.

I never expect the way he smiles.

Soft, sweet, a little in awe, piercing my heart and breaking me in a new, beautiful way.

"I was always so worried my darkness would scare you away," he rumbles. "Or break you. Somehow, all it did was bring you closer, and I love you for it, Talia. I love you for *you*. For everything you are. Your courage, your kindness, your wisdom, your sweetness. I fucking love you. I want to beg for your forgiveness, but even without it, I won't stop. You shine so bright it burns, and I need the pain. I know I don't deserve you, no, but it doesn't change the truth. I need *you*."

My breaths are soft and shallow. I don't need them right now.

Not when Micah is better than the air I breathe.

I lean into him, ghosting my lips on his, aching for how it feels like new after he broke us and welded us together again.

I remember that night with my grandfather, when he thought I was my grandmother and yet still found a way to ease my hurting heart.

"Francis Bacon," I whisper into the stillness between us. "He said, *In order for the light to shine so brightly, the darkness must be present.*" I smile. "If I'm too bright, it's only because you're the darkness—and you make me shine."

"My light," Micah whispers, holding me closer. "My redemption."

There goes my heart.

Basically forever.

The last time his lips touched mine, Micah gave me life.

This time, when his mouth claims mine, he makes me feel *alive.*

A hot rush pours through me, filling me until I'm dizzy.

His kiss comes slow, tender, his mouth tracing mine with a reverence that makes me feel cherished. That lets me savor every last sensation of skin until I'm tingling and gasping by the time his tongue dips in to taste me.

His kiss draws me up to meet him until we're twined tongues, slick pressure, lingering and sweet.

God, I could live this kiss forever.

This is how he transforms my night in hell.

Ending it in heaven.

The man I love loves me back.

Truly. Darkly. Gloriously.

Yes, he made a mistake.

He was scared, and he ran.

I get that more than anything.

I spent the first half of my life letting fear make me timid, before I learned life needs risks, no matter the outcome.

Micah took so many for me.

He saved my life.

And now he's showing me how he truly feels.

Proving my faith in him wasn't misplaced and that he's every bit the bold, strong, honorable man I thought he was.

No matter what happens after this, we'll find our way home.

His teeth tease my lips, a shivering promise of more—later, when we're not hovering on the edge of an active crime scene with bodies disappearing into coroner vans.

When we don't have an audience, apparently.

An amused clearing of a throat breaks us apart. We give each other sheepish looks of silent laughter before we glance at the EMT who first put me in the oxygen mask.

"That works better *on* your face, just so you're aware," she says with a dry look at the mask hanging around my neck. "At least you're breathing easier. You feeling okay?"

"I am." I nod, breaking into a smile that feels like it takes over my entire face. "Thank you. I really am okay. I can tell when it's going to last, and I think I'm in the clear to go home."

"All right, but keep your local doctor on speed dial for a few days. The stress after incidents like this can catch up with you in surprising ways long after they're over." She gives me a long look, then glances at Micah. "You good?"

"Bruised knees, a few cuts on my hands. That's about it," he answers.

"Then I'm going to go do my job." She lifts a hand in a mock salute, then jogs off to join her coworkers, tending to the wounded—including an older woman in an EMT jacket who seems very, very interested in the wound staining Henri Fontenot's thigh.

Meanwhile, Grant Faircross growls at the technician fussing over a scrape on his forearm, and Lucas Graves patiently endures getting a cut on his shoulder stitched up.

Micah watches the rest of Redhaven PD for a minute or two, and I'd swear those cool eyes are almost *fond*.

Yeah, I think Micah's been lying to himself about his capacity to love for a long time when it's so clear in his eyes.

He loves his friends on the Redhaven police team.

He turns back to me, though, looking down at my hand that's still flat against his chest. Gently, he separates my fingers, stroking their length.

I wince, though I can only feel a minor twinge past the meds the EMTs gave me. They look like my grandfather's hands, or worse.

Swollen, my fingertips raw, my knuckles inflamed from the ropes against my skin. I probably should've had the medic take a look, but…

That means being apart from Micah longer.

"What happened to your fingers?" He frowns, turning my hand over with a gentle touch.

I smile weakly. "The princess tried to save herself. I tried to pick the rope apart and I was going to use it to strangle them."

"Brave girl." With an approving rumble, Micah kisses the center of my palm almost reverently. "You didn't even need me. You'd have gotten out of there just fine on your own. You're too stubborn not to."

"I *did* need you," I promise, leaning into him hard. I needed—*I need*—him for so much more than just this. "The odds were one in a million. Maybe I'd have found a way to escape on my own, but with you there, I *knew* I'd be safe."

"I'll never give you a reason to feel unsafe." Silvery ocean eyes capture me, bathing me in his love. "Let's go home, Talia, so I can look after you."

* * *

It's still over an hour before we can leave.

I end up tucked into the back of Grant's truck with Rolf and a pile of blankets, dozing contentedly with a pile of sleepy German Shepherd who clings to me like I've been gone for years. Micah takes care of business with statements, evidence, and discussions with Raleigh PD.

I overhear something about how the Feds wouldn't move and how typical that was, but they'll sweep in at the eleventh hour to take all the credit.

And then a hastily cleared throat, a glance at Micah, a "Not you, I mean."

Micah just laughs it off and joins me in the back of the truck.

We stay there for the drive back to Redhaven, Grant in the driver's seat and Lucas and Henri's vehicles trailing after us.

Micah holds me tight in his arms.

I don't even feel the chill night wind whipping over us when our blanket nest feels so warm. There's just the starry night above, his body wrapped around me, and his lips pressed against my hair as he holds me so tight.

That's when I know he's true to his word.

After tonight, he'll never let me go again.

* * *

I don't remember dozing off.

Soon, I'm waking up in Micah's arms. He carries me gently as he steps off the tailgate of the truck and lands on the sidewalk outside his house, so lightly I barely feel the jolt.

I open my eyes with a sleepy murmur, catching Grant's voice as he leans out of the driver's side window.

"Take good care of her," he rumbles.

"I can't do anything else, Captain." Micah's grip tightens.

Flushing, I hide my face in his chest.

I can feel his laughter, vibrating softly as he nuzzles my hair and turns to carry me up the walk. The click of Rolf's nails and his jingling collar follow us.

"I see someone's awake," he says.

"Mm-hmm." Curled up in the blanket still wrapped around me, I snuggle into him. "Sorry I fell asleep."

"Don't apologize. You've had one hell of a night. Let me get your hands taken care of, and then you can go to bed."

I don't want to go to bed, I think. *Not unless it's with you.*

It's an embarrassing thought, but I can't help it.

Feeling his arms around me now as the rush of adrenaline fades ignites something hungry inside me.

I've missed him.

Yes, it's barely been a few days, but I feel like he hasn't touched me in years. I'm exhausted, hurting bone-deep, and sore everywhere.

Yet all I truly want is Micah's touch.

I hold my tongue as he lets us into the house and carries me through the dark living room to the sofa. He tucks me gently into the corner, smoothing a hand over my hair.

"Wait here. I'll grab the first aid kit."

He starts to turn away from me, so tall and strong in the moonlight drifting through the windows, this striking white knight in black armor.

But I frown, reaching for Rolf as the dog jumps up on the sofa with me. He drapes himself halfway over my lap while I scratch his ears.

"Take care of Rolf first?" I can't stand to see it, this patch of blood dried on his jaws from where he bit Bowden. For some reason, that upsets me more than anything, this innocent animal stained in red.

Thank God he wasn't hurt.

Micah glances back at me, then comes back and kisses my forehead. "I'll get him cleaned up, then you."

I smile gratefully and touch his cheek, then watch as he turns away, flicking on the lights at their lowest setting to illuminate the cozy living room before he ducks into the kitchen and comes back with a wet rag.

He settles in with me and Rolf, hooking an arm over the dog's ruff and getting his face licked. He laughs loudly.

Is it just my imagination, or is he laughing easier now?

Like a crushing weight's been lifted off his shoulders.

I watch as Micah carefully wipes Rolf's muzzle clean. He pauses in the middle of the cleanup and looks at me.

"...what? Don't tell me I have blood on me, too?"

"No." I shake my head quickly. Well, there's a little on his bruised knuckles, but that's not the point. "It's just... you're different now. You seem lighter."

Micah freezes, except for the hand steadily scratching behind Rolf's ears, and tilts his head. He's wearing a puzzled look.

"I don't know. I thought I'd feel empty after this shit went down, with nothing left to live for. Actually, I feel relieved. Like I can finally breathe again, and the air tastes different."

"Does it taste good?" I bite my lip, holding back my smile.

"Yeah." He gives me a warm, lingering smile.

And he finishes cleaning up Rolf, then stands and slips away with one more kiss to my head. If I had any inkling of loneliness, that disappears when I end up with my arms full of German Shepherd.

I can't believe this beast used to hate me.

Giggling, I bury my face in his clean-smelling fur.

That's how Micah finds me, when he returns with a first aid kit tucked under his arm and one of his button-down shirts folded on top of it. He's traded his tactical gear for a pair of dark-grey pajama pants and nothing else.

As the lamplight paints his white skin gold, that lingering desire in me becomes a slow simmer. My gaze roams his sculpted chest, the narrow dip of his waist, the way his pelvis arrows past the line of the pajama pants.

With an almost shy smile, Micah holds up his shirt as he settles down on the sofa with Rolf between us.

"In case you wanted to change for bed. If you want to stay here tonight, I mean. I can take you back home. I shouldn't have—"

"*Micah.*" I touch his lips, but pull back when I realize my fingers are still bloody and scraped. "Let me stay with you tonight. I need to."

There's something reverent about the way he looks at me, this new man peeking past the storm clouds.

"I'm glad as hell to hear you say that," he whispers. "Because you belong here, Shortcake. I need you, too."

His confession leaves me dizzy.

We only lock eyes for a moment, my heart trembling in the silence, before he ducks his head and pops the first aid kit open.

He picks through it and finds a gauze pad and a small bottle of alcohol.

"This will sting a bit," he says. "I'm sorry."

Understatement of the century.

I think I'd have a better time juggling angry scorpions.

I grit my teeth, hissing as he wipes my fingers, sterilizing the abrasions and blisters before soothing them with some amber cream in an unmarked tin.

By the time he wraps each fingertip in a little cap of gauze, the pain fades with the sweet-smelling cream easing it away.

In a weird way, the hurt feels worth it.

Having Micah caring for me so tenderly makes my heart wobble.

He really does love me.

Part of me can't quite believe it's true.

The rest of me desperately needs to.

He finishes with my left pinky and lifts my hand to kiss my knuckles.

"There," he says softly. "The salve should stop any infection. You need anything else? Something warm to drink? I think I have some pills if you need help sleepi—"

He doesn't get to finish.

Because the need building inside me erupts, this explosive thing that can't help wanting this wonderful man who shows me his vulnerabilities, his kindness, the way he *cares* so flipping much no matter how hard he tries to hide it.

Seeing Micah Ainsley as he truly is, unburdened...

I can't help but kiss him like a crazy woman.

I lean over Rolf, seizing Micah's mouth quickly, hotly.

I catch his lips like I could devour his love—only to be devoured in turn.

For a second, there's this sweet, frozen stillness before his arm drags me in, crushing us together.

The motion sends Rolf scampering off the sofa with an offended grunt as he heads for the dog bed in the corner.

Micah kisses back with a ferocity like wildfire, this frantic heatwave that pricks me everywhere with burning pleasure.

That fire starts in my toes and leaves me burning every time his tongue teases my lips, delves inside me, opens my mouth until he steals my gasps.

"I need you," I whisper harshly. "You're *all* I need."

"*Fuck*, Talia," he groans. His fingers bunch up my shirt, dragging it up my back. "I need you out of these damn clothes."

I never thought I could be so bold.

But I'm the one standing, letting the blanket fall away as I take his hands, nearly tripping over Rolf as I lead him to the bedroom.

Halfway there, we're kissing again, under a spell, stumbling and pulling at my clothes and tossing them around until they litter the house.

I don't care.

Not when I'm addicted to his *mouth*, those sharp teeth driving me crazy.

His tongue plunges in, chasing mine until it feels like he's fucking me already.

Somehow, I'm naked and he's still wearing those pajama pants I can't stand when I need *skin*.

But when I reach for the waist of his pants, he catches my wrists, slamming me against the wall with just enough force to make my pussy throb.

"Naughty girl. Patience," he growls, pinning my wrists over my head with one hand. With the other, he skims down my naked body, teasing my breasts, flicking my nipples until I clench my teeth and exhale sharply.

Oh. My. God.

"When did you get so brazen?" He smiles slowly.

I'm writhing in his grip, pressed against the wall, straining toward him—then crying out as he catches my nipple and pinches deliciously.

Just right.

So right.

God, he always knows how to tease and how to make the pleasure feel ten times better, amplifying it with that sizzle until I'm panting as he toys with it over and over again, my eyes squeezing shut. I jerk at my wrists.

"Micah!" I plead.

I can't stand it anymore—and apparently neither can he.

A second later, he's not just pinning me with his grip but with his body, pressed against me from head to toe and letting me feel every muscular inch of him against my bare skin, his cock hard and straining through the cotton of his pants to nudge my belly.

His mouth storms over my neck, my shoulders—all bites and kisses, raw and wonderful, urgent and needy, pushing me to breaking point.

When his rough hand slips down and shoves my legs apart, I nearly lose it.

Of course, he finds me soaked.

He gently pinches my clit, locking eyes before he plunges two fingers inside me, giving me a savage taste of his desire.

Then, it's so on.

He plays.

He torments.

He claims everything I am.

He steals my breath until I'm sagging from his grip. My knees go weaker with every commanding thrust of his fingers, every roll of his thumb over the aching bud of my clit.

He bites down on my neck a little harder, a promise as he growls, "...how do you want me, Talia?"

I tremble as I realize what he's asking.

If—after everything I've been through—I can take him as he is.

Love him like he needs, no matter how rough he might be tonight.

"As hard as you want," I whisper, holding his silvery-blue eyes and arching until my thigh rubs his cock, begging to have him inside me. "As yourself."

Hellfire ignites in his eyes.

An inferno that tells me he's missed me just like I've missed him.

Fire, everlasting, proving he craves me with the same crazy energy as I crave him.

I'm so tuned in to his touch that it's like we've been apart for years, not days—and the absence makes everything so much more intense.

That's why I feel it in my bones when he takes me.

No gentleness.

No hesitation.

He lets his pants fall and his fingers dig into my ass, lifting me against him.

A groan boils out of him when I wrap my legs around his waist, spreading myself open for him, all so he can hold me in place with his hips.

His fingers fist my wrists, making me his willing captive as he drags his cock against my wetness and leaves me whimpering, squirming, aching inside.

Holy hell.

I'm one second away from outright *begging* when he gives me what I want.

Micah plunges inside me mercilessly, filling me with a single rough stroke.

We both gasp.

It's like being torn in the best way.

Pierced so deep, stretched open, touched in those intimate places that scream for his heat and his powerful, raw thrusts.

Our frantic breaths come in tandem as he *takes* me, fast and hard, slamming me into the wall over and over.

It's so animalistic I shudder.

The force of his thrusts stroke me until I'm screaming.

He answers with low growls—suddenly muffled as he buries his face against my throat, and his teeth sink in.

The sweetness is instant, fiery and almost bruising, exploding over me and turning every new thrust into a firestorm of obscene pleasure.

He's *marking* me again.

Etching himself on my body so there's no doubt who I belong to, this time forever.

He brands me inside and out, this wild thing, the two of us crashing together until I can't tell up from down.

I barely realize it when he lets go of my wrists.

Only that I'm free to cling to him now, to rake my nails down his back, to pull him in tighter and harder when I want him so deep, so *deep*, until I feel him inside me every time I move.

Sheer insanity.

That's what this connection is.

And I want *more*.

But we're both so tight-strung that we can't last forever—and when he bites me again, when he strokes my belly and pinches my breasts with a feverish grip like he's trying to consume me with his hands, when he surges up inside me and marks new places he's never reached before—

I am gone.

And it's so good I'm not coming back.

So hot.

So *feral*.

I come like fireworks, screaming his name and leaving marks down his back as I grind myself into him.

My pussy convulses on his cock.

My pulse beats like a drum.

Hard, throbbing, fluxing.

My body becomes this violent machine, and he becomes my master.

And he's right there with me, every blinding second.

"Don't fucking stop," he orders roughly. "Not before I come inside you."

Holy shit!

Fusing our bodies together, straining to reach even

deeper inside me, I watch his head snap back and his eyes pinch shut.

He bares his teeth as his whole body tightens like a cord.

Then he's pulsing, jerking hot inside me, cursing his pleasure through shining teeth.

The instant he comes, he takes my soul.

I feel his come as his princely face becomes savage, as his hands bite my ass hard enough to hurt, as he marks me in the deepest way possible, flooding me with sin so sweet it must be divine.

I could never, ever be this way with anyone but Micah Ainsley.

Together, we're too perfect.

And after tonight, I'm certain we'll never let each other go.

* * *

So, it turns out I didn't need that shirt after all.

I'm quite content to snuggle up in Micah's arms as we collapse into bed together, tangled up and sated and breathless. It's wordlessly comforting to be held like this, to be reassured.

This is real.

It's not some fever dream caused by oxygen deprivation while I slowly suffocate to death in a barrel sinking to the bottom of the ocean.

Just the thought of what Xavier almost did—what he *threatened* to do—makes me shudder and huddle closer to Micah. His hand glides down my back, gathering me closer, like he *knows*.

"Shh," he whispers. "You're safe with me."

I let out a contented sigh.

And I burrow into him, breathing in his scent. But the

relief is short-lived as his phone buzzes on the nightstand.

I open one eye, looking at it over his shoulder. He twists to glance back at it, then groans and buries his face in my hair, ignoring the call.

The name on the caller ID says *Jane Henway*.

I arch a brow. This better not be an eleventh-hour reveal with a secret wife back in New York or something.

"Shouldn't you get that?" I ask.

"Nah. That's my DEA handler. The one who told me I had to wait for the paperwork to go through before I could hit Xavier and save your life." His hold on me tightens. "They can wait until tomorrow to yell at me before I tell them to fuck off. They'll have to deal with me staying in Redhaven."

My heart nearly stops.

"You're staying...?" I pull back, just enough so I can see his face.

He opens his eyes, looking at me quietly, and pushes himself up to brush his lips over mine.

"There's nothing waiting for me in New York. Somehow, while I was busy faking fitting in here, I found my calling." He hesitates, his eyes lowering. "I made a real home here in Redhaven. I care about the people. The guys. Everyone." Those stark silvery-blue eyes meet mine again. "*You.* Obviously."

He's doing it again.

He's nearly tearing me apart with his honesty.

"I want to stay with you, Talia. Zero doubt." His lips quirk. "Though my ego's going to have to get over having a rich girlfriend."

"Huh?" I shake my head. "I'm broke, Micah. Xavier's check bounced. He said the Feds froze his accounts. He just used a cashier's check to lure me up to the house to ambush me."

"Wrong." Micah drags it out a little too long, a little too

casually, before he grins. He falls back against the pillows, looking up at me smugly. "There's a one-point-five million dollar reward for information that leads to the arrest of the heads of the East Coast drug ring." His grin widens, and he reaches up to tap the tip of my nose. "I made sure my DEA handlers know I couldn't have pulled this off without you. You'll have a check in the next month."

My eyes widen.

Shock rips through me and comes out in a startled laugh.

"Wait. Wait, you're serious?"

"Never would've moved on Xavier without making sure you could take care of your grandfather first. Even if it means giving up my pay."

"I… You… Oh my God, *thank you*!" I tackle him in a flurry of blankets, hugging him and burying my face against his chest. "Thank you for caring about my grandfather."

"How can I not? He matters to you."

"But destroying Xavier was all you've ever wanted… and you'd have given that up?"

"I would. Because I was wrong." Micah kisses my hair over and over again, holding me against him like he never wants us apart. "Taking Xavier down was always second to what I truly wanted. That's you."

Oh, I don't know how my heart can get any fuller.

I definitely don't know what to say.

I can't fathom how to express how much I love this man —his good, his bad, his darkness, his light. His bravery, his strength, his secret kindness, and his brash sense of honor. The way he challenges me to take risks and cushions me when I fall.

I push myself up to meet those eyes that hold the entire universe.

"And I've been waiting my entire life to find you," I whisper, leaning down to kiss him.

XXVI: DARKNESS LIFTED (MICAH)

I think I need a new prescription for my glasses.

I sit behind the wheel of my car, waiting outside the Raleigh clinic, and wipe a few smudges off my lenses with a microfiber cloth. I had to ditch the contacts today because lately they've been giving me halos when I drive at night, and it'll be dark by the time I pick up Gerald and make it back to Redhaven.

It's my turn to shuttle back home this week.

He stays at the cognitive therapy clinic for about a week every month before coming home brighter and clearer, armed with new exercises and meds to help restore his mind.

Normally, Talia and I make the drive together.

Only this time, the shop had a massive order come in for custom furniture for a wedding present placed by some wealthy couple from Virginia. The Bridezilla's been driving Talia so batshit that she's been shut up in the workshop for days.

I didn't dare interrupt her flow.

Then again, I may also have an ulterior motive for

wanting to see Gerald alone today, but I'll cross that bridge soon enough.

I finish wiping my glasses, put them back on, and squint across the parking lot. It's turning brassy from the heavy rays of sunset.

Yep.

Still a little bit blurry by the time my line of sight hits the far edge of the parking lot. A minor adjustment should fix it, though I should probably go in for another round of Lasik. For some people, it's a permanent solution, and for others it has to be redone every decade.

Guess which one I am.

I'm lucky that I can, though.

I've never really thought about that shit before.

I've spent my whole life with a chip on my shoulder over my condition because it made me a target. Never thought about the fact that I'm lucky to live in a time where minor defects can be treated, and I can have a life as normal as anybody else's.

Damn.

Maybe my outlook on life *has* changed lately.

I chuckle to myself, leaning against the steering wheel.

Considering I'm playing chauffeur to my girlfriend's grandfather and fussing over mundane crap like my *glasses* instead of plotting how to catch and murder a billionaire, I'd say my outlook has changed a lot.

All credit goes to Talia Grey.

I won't say the last few months with her have been easy and effortless.

I'm still struggling with bad habits.

To remember to be open.

To give back the same trust she gives me every day.

It's a long goddamned process, unlearning the bullshit my

abusive father and my brother's death beat into me. I'm learning how to be human again.

She holds my hands and guides me every step of the way with the patience of a saint.

No, maybe it hasn't been easy.

But in its own way, it's been perfect.

Just like her.

The way she lights up when I stop by the shop after I get off my shift.

The way she's just as happy to coax me to stay for dinner with her and Gerald as she is to let me spirit her away, whether it's back to my place or wandering off into the woods for the weekend to camp, sight see, and scare the animals with the racket we make when we really get going.

For her, every camping trip feels like she's seeing everything new.

I love her sense of wonder.

I love *her*.

Last weekend, it was a snap date night at the movies.

Our camping trip got rained out, early autumn squalls soaking the forest and sending us running back home early. Rather than give up and stay in, we headed over to Redhaven's tiny theatre and bought tickets for every showing until closing time.

That's when I found out my girl hides during horror movies, clinging to me and peeking past her fingers when the psycho starts swinging his knife.

She found out I doze off during documentaries.

The kids working at the theatre found out the easiest way to wake me up is by Talia kissing me, only for the seventeen-year-old usher to catch us making out and chase us out, laughing, so they could lock up.

You already know the rest of it.

We finished what we started in my bed.

Even the trip where we booked a little bed and breakfast in Greensboro had fresh surprises. I loved every damned minute.

Technically, it was a business trip for Talia. She was looking for a new supplier for a special type of red cedar, but there was no mistaking her pleasure in dragging me along to tour the lumberyard, chattering away about wood grain, cuts, and finishes.

Her love for the family craft shined through in every enthusiastic word and touch, even if most of it flew over my head.

I listened anyway, learning as much as I could.

If it matters to her, it's important to me.

Sure, I could pay a little more attention sometimes when I can't pry my eyes off her high-necked sweater—a staple of her wardrobe in the cooler months, along with turtlenecks—when I know what's underneath it.

Her addiction to saucy pink lingerie is now complemented by the roses I add to her skin, dragging my mouth over her and making her bloom so sweetly for me.

She is my garden.

I still burn, too, remembering how I marked her up the night before when we almost broke the B&B's bed, getting so sweaty we had to change the sheets before we could sleep.

She still blushes like it's the first time.

Especially every time I give her that *look*.

And I fucking love that, too, along with a million other things.

Now is not the best time to be thinking about the fact that I can't keep my mind off her legs, her peach of an ass. Fuck, that curve of her waist as it dips just below the full swell of her breasts, the way she always wears pastel-pink bras that turn her nipples into dark shadows of temptation—

A voice cuts in again.

The only man I'll ever share her with calls my name, his voice distant through the car window.

I glance up as Gerald Grey waves to a nurse through the glass doors of the clinic, then turns to stroll down the walk toward me. The man looks like he's aged backward ten years —spry, alert, energetic, his blue eyes calm and clear.

He hasn't had more than one or two spells where he slips into the past in the last few months.

It's made Talia so happy.

And anything that makes Talia happy makes me happy, too.

Gerald pulls the passenger door open and climbs into the Jeep. "Just you today, son?"

Son.

It always gives me pause when he calls me that.

I know it's a thing with older folks. They call any man younger than them *son*, but lately I've grown so fond of Gerald Grey it doesn't bother me.

I've never known a man who cares so much for his family. It's a new experience, and for him to offer that same kindness to me the way he does my Talia strikes deep.

It shakes me.

I'd never turn away from it, though.

Hell, I crave it.

Especially when Gerald shows me, in his own way, the kind of man I want to be as I make a new life with Talia.

While he buckles up, I smile.

"Just me today. Talia's still struggling with the Bridezilla job. I think she's on her twenty-seventh revision."

"Goddamn! They keep at it like that, there's no way the real work will start before the wedding." His eyes gleam. "You think she'll need some help?"

"I think she'll remind you that you're retired, argue with you out of obligation, and then gratefully accept another miracle from Gerald Grey," I point out dryly as I start the engine and head for the street.

"That still sits weird with me, Micah. *Retired.*" Gerald props his hand against his chin, elbow against the base of the window, and looks out with a smile. "Almost feels like a waste. Tally-girl put all that money into surgery for my hands, and now all I do is diddle around making things for fun."

"Talia wouldn't call it a waste. It makes her happy to see you working for your own pleasure. It makes her happy to see *you* happy."

"Yeah, that's her, all right. My Tally's always been a softie." His smile warms with fondness. "The girl always feels so much for other folks. I did the right thing, putting the shop in her hands, didn't I?"

"Absolutely," I answer. "She'll save your legacy and make you proud."

"*Hey*." With a snort, Gerald lightly smacks my arm. His age-spotted fingers are bony and strong, free from the painful swelling that plagued them before. "Don't be talking like I'm gonna check out anytime soon. I'll be around to watch over her and my own damn legacy just fine—and to help her as long as she needs."

I grin. "I know, Gerald. You're too stubborn for much else."

"Mm-hmm." He eyes me sternly. "Remember that when y'all are locking that bedroom door every time you stay over."

For a second, I sputter.

Gerald just grins like the old smartass he is and turns his gaze right back out the window as we pull out onto the highway, driving into the sunset home.

I can't help how my mind lingers, though.

The dynamic that's evolved between the three of us is better than anything I imagined.

Something I want to make permanent.

As the mile markers tell us we're getting closer to Redhaven just as the sky descends into twilight, I clear my throat.

"There's something I need to ask you about," I say. "I thought we could talk about it now."

"Aw, hell." Gerald glances at me slowly, knowing as he smirks. "You don't need my permission, son."

"How did you—" I blink, my grip tightening on the steering wheel.

Gerald scoffs. "Hmph. You really wonder when you go and pay hundreds of thousands for treatment and then act surprised when I'm sharp as a tack?"

"That's not what I meant." Shit, I can feel my face turning red, and I never fucking blush, but this is *serious*. "Have I been that obvious?"

"Not at first," Gerald muses. He scratches at his stubbly chin. "But over the last few months, you've really grown into yourself. You're not so wooden anymore, son." He looks at me long and hard, then reaches over to squeeze my forearm. "Anyone can see how much you love my granddaughter—and how much she loves you. I'd be a fool to stand in the way of your happiness."

Amazing how a few words can make me grin like a madman.

"That's *if* she says yes," I point out, earning a rough laugh.

"What, you nervous?"

"*Yes*," I throw back.

"Well, good," Gerald retorts. "Every woman needs to keep her man just a little stirred up. That's what my wife used to say."

I don't miss the break in his voice when he says *my wife* or the way his eyes mist up.

I glance over, watching him for a moment before returning my eyes to the road.

"You still miss her, don't you?"

"You never stop. Sometimes, I think my mind started slipping just because I was chasing her into the past, desperate to be with her again. I'll always miss my Lily." He sighs. "I still love her, too. That's something that will never die, even if I lose myself again."

"I know the feeling," I mutter, my chest tight as that resonates like mad.

It's an odd kinship, this unspeakable thing we both know.

I suddenly wonder if Janelle Bowden ever felt that with her asshole husband, and what it must have broken in her when she realized it was all a lie.

No, there's been no sign of Chief Bowden all these months. Raleigh PD concluded he must have drowned or bled out when he jumped in the water and crawled away, and they're just waiting for his remains to surface in the next year.

I have my doubts.

The pure evil looking out at me from the chief's face when he finally came unmasked doesn't die that easy.

There's a sixth sense like a blade running over my neck, telling me the day will come when we'll have to deal with this shit, and next time we'll finish the job.

Janelle's been soldiering on as best she can, but it's been torture, realizing the man she married, the man she loved, was a criminal stranger.

I hope like hell I'll never hurt Talia with any dark surprises, even if mine would never scratch Bowden's fuckery.

She's taught me how to be honest with her—and with myself.

It's a lesson I won't forget.

"Gerald?"

"Hm?"

"Thank you."

"For what, son?" His wrinkled brow furrows.

I chuckle. "For being you."

Gerald's only answer is a thoughtful look and a slow smile.

Yeah.

He gets it.

We drive the rest of the way in happy silence, making our way home.

* * *

When we get back to Redhaven, I drop Gerald at the shop without going in just yet.

I have a few things to throw together first. I don't think Talia even realizes I'm outside. Through the window and half-open workshop door, I can just make her out, bowed over her drafting table and focused.

I wave Gerald off, waiting until I'm sure he's safely inside, then pull away to go do a little shopping.

It's well past sunset and I'm dirty and sweaty by the time I'm done.

I stop by my place, shower, change, pack a camping bag, and head back to the shop. The front lights are out and the door's locked, but there's still that telltale golden cone of light through the door, the lamp over Talia's desk shining off her autumn-fire hair.

I head to the side door and knock.

Gerald tromps down to let me in, already smirking. "So you're gonna do it tonight or what?"

"Shhh," I hiss as I step inside.

"She's not gonna hear you, son. She's in another world. Seems like *somebody* needs to give her a good reason to take a break."

"Yeah, I'm working on it." I take a deep breath. "Wish me luck."

"Fine, but you won't need it."

I hope like hell he's right as I duck into the workshop.

Talia looks so breathtaking it fucking hurts in the low light, like she just stepped right out of a fairy painting with her hair spilling out of its messy bun.

Still totally absorbed in her work, just like Gerald said.

I almost hate to interrupt her—only, she's got that crease between her brows that says she's been stressing, too.

As I walk in, Rolf perks up from his spot by her feet.

I've started leaving him with her during the day for company while I'm working. I think he might love her more than I do sometimes, and he's even becoming an unofficial Touch of Grey mascot. The customers adore him. He gets plenty of extra affection during the day with the way they all spoil him.

He'll be keeping Gerald company tonight, I hope.

"Hey, Shortcake." I clear my throat, stepping closer.

She doesn't even look up.

I laugh to myself.

When my woman's in the zone, she's fucking *there*.

I wait until she's not sketching anymore, lifting her stylus from her tablet before I touch her shoulder lightly. She jumps, blinking her wide blue eyes rapidly with a small gasp.

"Oh! Micah, when did you get here?"

"I've been and gone. Did you even notice your grandfather was back?"

"He is?" She cranes her head toward the stairs. "...oh. Whoops."

I lean over, peering at the delicate linework sketched on her tablet screen. "Project's making you that crazy, huh?"

"Ugh, you have no clue." She sighs. "I'm about to tell them to take their money and find someone else. Half the stuff she wants isn't even feasible, and if I try to tell her that she gets all snotty and I...." She stops and shakes her fists, the stylus twitching between her fingers. "I'm tempted to do what she wants and then ask the wedding photographer to send me the pictures when it all breaks and dumps her on her ass."

"Careful. Someone's getting my vindictive streak." I reach over and pry the stylus from her fingers, setting it aside. "Break time. You're taking the rest of the night off."

"But the deadline—"

"Will get even tighter if you work yourself to death." Catching her hands, I tug at her gently, coaxing her off her seat. "C'mon. Get your gear. We're going camping."

"On a weeknight?" Talia frowns, her pink lips pouting.

"Yes. One nice night under the stars so you can de-stress and start fresh in the morning."

She hesitates, but then smiles and squeezes my hands.

"Okay, deal. Give me five minutes."

"I'm timing you."

"You're so *not*." Laughing, she bounces to her feet and leans in to kiss my cheek, giving me a whiff of that lovely vanilla scent mixed with the warmth of fresh sawdust. Then she's off, pattering up the stairs and leaving me alone with Rolf, who strains after her with a low whine.

"Whose dog are you anymore?" I kneel down to ruffle his fur, chuckling.

The enthusiastic lick to my cheek says he's still mine.

True to her word, Talia's back in five minutes.

As she comes tumbling down the stairs in her cute little pink flannel, I straighten and lightly slap Rolf's rump.

"Find Gerald, old man. Keep him company."

Talia gives me a puzzled look, adjusting the straps of her camping rucksack. "We're not taking Rolf?"

"Not tonight. Let the two old guys keep each other company." I hold my hand out to her.

She smiles.

She knows this isn't normal.

I can tell she wants to ask what's up my sleeve, when normally Rolf comes along almost everywhere. Still, even though she's bristling with curiosity, she seems to know better.

Talia takes my hand and follows me to the Jeep without question.

It's insane how well she knows me by now.

Press me about it, and I'll just tease her and draw out the suspense.

The inside of the Jeep feels warmer with her in it.

Hell, *I* feel warmer with her in the passenger seat.

We head for the roadside parking area where we usually leave the vehicle and move out on foot.

Couldn't have picked a better night. The sky is overflowing with stars.

The full moon, a silvery disc that shines down like a blessing, lights our way so clearly that we don't even need flashlights.

Hand in hand, we take the familiar paths branching into the woods and up the hills. The night glows, all pale moonlight shining off the foliage and branches, leaving Talia looking around with wide, glimmering eyes that take everything in with wonder.

And her wonder turns into genuine surprise when, after

less than an hour of hiking, I take a small detour and lead her down a narrow trail.

Soon, we break into a clearing overlooking the town.

It's the same clearing where we stopped to take in Redhaven before, back when we were staking out the Jacobins.

That trip was where I started falling in love with her.

Later, over the photograph from this vantage, too.

Finding out she'd saved me as a damned vampire in her phone.

Laughing over so many messy ways we collided.

Sharing our stories, our fears, our dreams.

Discovering how thoughtful, how brave, how determined she is.

Maybe it's the small things.

Or maybe I've just decided I *like* the small things an awful lot.

Which is why, there's a thick plaid blanket laid across the grass and a wooden square serving as a table, already prepped with candles just waiting to be lit.

The insulated nylon bag next to it keeps the food inside warm—and thankfully safe from nosy animals until we showed up.

While Talia stares with bewildered delight, I pull away, dropping my backpack and then pulling out my lighter for the candles.

One by one, they illuminate the table, and what's resting in the middle.

"Micah, what is all of—"

When she sees it, she stops cold.

Talia goes completely still, staring down at the dark-grey velvet box in the center of the table, painted in flicking shadows by golden candlelight. I can't quite read the stunned expression on her face.

My heart starts pounding as she brings her hands to her mouth.

"Micah?" Her voice sounds muffled behind her fingers.

Damn.

Even though my nerves are about to snap like twigs, I smile.

"Thought we'd have a romantic dinner under the stars. We can still eat, even if you say no."

"I—you—" Her eyes fly from the box, to me, and back to the box again. "Are… are you really asking me to…?"

"I am. And I should do this right, or Gerald will skin me alive." Her shocked smile gives me courage. I dip down to retrieve the little box and sink down on one knee in front of her—my beautiful girl, my perfect light, my pink doe.

Yeah, I'm feeling cheesy as hell.

No, I don't give a damn as I pop the box open for her.

It's a delicate band in rose gold, set with a diamond twined in golden branches.

When I saw it in the store, I knew it was perfect, especially when she spends her life shaping wood into beautiful things.

Her eyes widen as she stares at the ring.

I clear my throat and get on with it. "Talia Grey, will you do me the honor of becoming my wife?"

"…ohGodwhere'smyinhaler…"

"Shit. Are you okay, I—"

"*Yes!*" Breathless and bursting into laughter, Talia flings herself at me, her bag falling away and thudding to the ground as she tumbles on her knees and throws herself into my arms.

I realize then she's not having an asthma attack.

She's just *that excited*.

"Yes, I'm fine. Yes, I'll marry you!"

"Jesus Christ, don't scare me like that." I'm grinning from

ear to ear, though, and I hug her tight, clutching the ring against her back. "You just made me a very happy man, Miss Grey."

"*Talia*," she insists playfully before bumping her nose to mine. Her eyes glisten. "And it won't be 'Miss Grey' for much longer, will it?"

"Mrs. Ainsley," I say.

Heavy words.

She goes crimson, blushing so prettily.

"Soon," she whispers. "But kiss me like it's already true."

"Gladly," I growl, claiming her mouth.

My Talia.

My fiancée, who brought me out of the darkness and into the light.

My salvation, my everything, and soon to be my forever.

XXVII: DARK DELIGHT (TALIA)

Months Later

A winter wedding.

It's everything I never knew I wanted, and everything I've always dreamed of.

I don't even feel the cold as I stare at my reflection in the mirror in the small boathouse on Still Lake's shore.

It's been converted into a makeshift dressing room for tonight. It's so busy, and I'm surrounded by people.

Janelle Bowden, adjusting her lavender off-the-shoulder matron of honor dress. Delilah Graves and Ophelia Faircross, both fussing with the sash of my dress. I've only known them for a few months but they've treated me like a bestie from day one.

I almost don't even know what to do with this crowd.

I've never had actual *friends.*

Not counting Grandpa, of course.

He's easily been my best friend my whole life.

But the last few weeks, getting my wedding together after Micah told me the guys at Redhaven PD would be his groomsmen...

I never expected their wives to step up and throw themselves into being my bridesmaids.

And I wasn't expecting how much *fun* I'd have with Delilah, Ophelia, and Janelle, even if Janelle's been a little subdued. Who can blame her?

The poor woman still looks at me like she wants to apologize. The best way I could tell her that I don't blame her for what her husband did was to invite her to stand in for my deceased mother in my wedding.

I can tell she's felt alive again, and it makes me crazy happy that I could do something to help ease her pain and the nagging mystery of what happened to Chief Bowden.

I know all too well how being *part* of something can take the edge off old wounds.

And it feels like I'm catching up on a lifetime of being the weird, unpopular kid in just a span of a couple months as the four of us gossiped over fabrics, flowers, and the ceremony.

Micah has been pretty hands off the entire time, claiming he didn't know the first thing about weddings and he'd just screw it up. Though he gave me a *look* when I told him what I had planned—and what the girls were wholeheartedly on board with.

Micah indulgently accepted it, but I could tell what he was thinking.

You're the only reason I'll ever embarrass myself like this.

I mean, if your man doesn't love you enough to wear breeches and riding boots to your wedding, is it really love?

Besides, even if I've let go of my girlish fantasies about vampires, loving my soon-to-be husband for who he really is, I do have strong opinions.

Like the fact that every girl should get to live out her fairy tale just once.

And I feel like a fairy-tale princess now as I take a final spin in the mirror.

My dress looks like it was spun from pure silk, all gorgeous gossamer layers with a high empress waist and a trailing skirt. The small puffed-up sleeves leave my arms bare, save for the spirals of white gossamer wrapped around them, streaming from my wrists to the floor.

My hair is piled up in ringlets and dotted with white flowers. The same flowers circle my wrists and throat in a fragile collar and delicately woven bracelets.

For my makeup, I went with a subtle and dewy look.

I feel like I'm just waiting for my prince to sweep me away into the meadows.

The subtle shimmer of silver and white dusted against my skin fits the winter wedding theme. A snow bride, surrounded by sparkling frost on the shores of this frozen lake.

How fitting.

It's like everything started here, camping that night.

So I guess it's the place where our lives should turn over a new chapter, too.

A fresh beginning as husband and wife.

Breathlessly, I try to smile at my nervous reflection.

"Don't look so scared," Delilah teases. "He's not going to run away, girl. And if he does, we'll send the whole Redhaven crew after him."

She clasps my arms, looking at me over my shoulder in the mirror with a warm smile. Her dark hair tumbles down over us both, her lilac bridesmaid dress swirling gently against her.

"He might eat her," Ophelia teases from my other side. "The big bad wolf coming for Little Red."

I blush wildly, and I can't help looking at my throat in my reflection.

My pale, smooth throat, completely unblemished today.

Yeah, he's been forbidden from biting me for *weeks* now—anywhere that might show in my wedding dress, at least.

He grumped. He growled. He sulked a lot.

But he listened.

Even if he's been busy marking up my inner thigh.

They throb with a hot twinge, a deliciously dark memory of everything he's done to me.

Big bad wolf, indeed.

"He's not going to eat me," I say, my voice shaky. "And I *know* he won't run. He's way too proud for that."

Janelle looks up from fussing with her hair and her flowers and steps closer to clasp my hand warmly.

"Then what are you so worried about, dear? You're practically shaking."

"I just..." I swallow. "I don't want him to go through with this and regret anything."

Janelle smiles reassuringly.

"Oh, I had a peek a few minutes ago," she says with a smile. "He looks elated. I've never seen that boy so fired up since he came to Redhaven. Before you, his smiles were always missing a little something. I know what it is now." Her thumb strokes my knuckles. "Talia, he was missing you. You've brought him back to life. I can't see how he could ever regret that."

Laughing, warmth spreads through my chest.

"God, I hope you're right."

"She is!" Delilah nudges me gently. "*You* aren't the one getting cold feet, are you?"

"No way!" I promise. "I really want this. I'm just worried I'm going to trip or have an asthma attack. You all worked so hard, and I'm going to ruin the whole thing."

"You are not." Ophelia drapes her arms around my neck from behind, leaning into me, grinning at our reflections. That's another thing I'm getting used to—having girlfriends who just want to hug and be *close*. It's nice. "If you start losing your breath, I've got your inhaler on me."

I stare at her reflection.

"Where? Your dress doesn't have pockets."

"No, but I've got plenty of cleavage." She grins wickedly. "So don't make me go fishing down my bra in front of the whole wedding party."

I blink and then laugh, releasing the tension that's been building up in one big rush of giggles. Janelle, Ophelia, and Delilah laugh too, until we're just a *mess* and I'm in danger of ruining my makeup with the tears of laughter building up on my lashes.

But I needed that.

I needed this.

I needed *them*, these newfound friends who already mean so much.

Delilah playfully pinches my cheek.

"There we go," she says. "You good now?"

"Ready as I'll ever be." I grin.

Just then, there's a polite knock at the door.

"Everyone decent in there?" Grandpa calls through.

Ophelia leans away.

"All good, Mr. Grey," she calls back.

To my surprise, Janelle turns flustered, letting go of my hand to pat at her hair and dress with a soft sound. Her cheeks are pink.

They turn even pinker as my grandfather pushes the boathouse door open, peeking in with a proud smile.

He's the sterling image of dapper in his tailored steel-grey suit.

"We're ready when you are," he says.

Delilah snaps her fingers. "That's our cue! Let's get out there and pave the way for the blushing bride."

Suddenly, I'm buried in hugs. More affection than I know what to do with before the girls file out while Grandpa steps inside the cluttered room.

As he and Janelle pass by, there's a lingering glance, an almost secret smile between them.

Did I miss something while I was so wrapped up in wedding planning?

But then it's just me and Grandpa again, while everyone else bustles out to get the whole wedding procession started.

He just stands across the room, watching me.

Then he steps closer, clasping my hands and looking up at me with tears in his eyes and his face shining.

"If your parents could see you now," he murmurs. "They'd be so proud. You've come so far, Tally-girl. You fought your way here."

Oh God, I'm going to start crying.

Delilah will shit a brick after she worked so hard on my makeup.

I sniff, trying to hold it in. "Well, somebody raised me to be as stubborn as a mule."

"Damn right. And I'd do it again. Being headstrong, that's one of your best traits." His eyes twinkle. "You really do get that from me."

I laugh. "At least I didn't get your arrogance."

"It's not arrogance if it's truth, girl." He grins. "Hope that man of yours is ready."

"How'd he look?"

"Like a little boy on Christmas morning," Grandpa reassures me. "You found yourself a good one, my darling. Hope he has the good sense to never let you go."

Me too.

More than anything, I want Micah forever.

But the tenor of the music floating in from outside changes, dashing my thoughts.

It's time.

My heart flips over.

Grandpa offers me his arm with wordless approval.

I slip my hand into the crook of his elbow and pick up my pretty little bouquet of white roses and lilac rosebuds.

Together, we step outside into the glittering evening.

There's snow everywhere.

People bundled up in warm coats over their fine outfits, sitting in the chairs flanking the flower-strewn aisle.

Silver and glitter and pale flowers everywhere.

Still Lake, partly frozen over behind the altar, snow shimmering along the icy sheets. It's a winter wonderland just for me, so I can feel like the delicate winter princess gliding down the aisle.

And waiting for me at the end, my prince.

Micah may have spoiled me with his wedding outfit, but he looks so stunning it was worth it.

Cream-colored breeches hug his narrow hips and muscular thighs. Dashing black thigh-high leather riding boots. A matching cream-colored waistcoat over a billowing, stark white linen shirt, the waistcoat caging the linen against his broad shoulders and trim waist. The only color is the lilac rose corsage pinned to him and the subtle blue tint to his eyes.

Plus, the scarlet joy in his cheeks.

With his white hair slicked back, he looks rakish and unreal, this ice prince who's warmed his heart enough to let me in.

Only, there's nothing icy about the silver-blue eyes that land on me as I step into the moonlight.

There's nothing but warmth as our gazes find each other and never let go.

I'm barely aware of walking down the aisle.

I feel like I'm floating on the love in his eyes, wrapped up in the sudden realization that this is *happening*.

The man I love waits for me right in front of a patiently smiling priest. In a few more minutes, we'll be hitched.

I want to laugh.

I want to cry.

I'm definitely doing both by the time Grandpa leads me to the altar and kisses my cheek before letting me go.

As he passes by to take up his place with the groomsmen, all of Redhaven PD handsome in their tuxedos, he grabs Micah's hand with an approving squeeze that means so much to me.

There's nothing better than knowing the two most important men in my life respect each other so deeply.

Especially when Micah squeezes his hand back with a smile and a murmur.

"Gerald," he says warmly.

For a second, there's a loud commotion in the trees overhead. A huge flock of crows takes off with deafening caws, launching into the sky like spinning shadows.

Micah stares at them until the noise disappears, and I wonder why there's such a bright starry smile in his eyes.

Then he looks at me again and it's just us, standing across from each other.

I can see his heart pounding in his throat, his pulse wild against pale skin, matching my own. Micah takes a quick breath and lets it out in a laugh.

"Remind me again how you make yourself breathe when you're this excited?"

The last of my jitters melt away.

My smile lights me up from the inside out.

"I count," I whisper. "I count and pace my breathing."

Micah reaches for my free hand, watching me with those luminous eyes that hold me spellbound.

"Maybe we should count backward then," he says. "To the moment when we'll be husband and wife."

"In your head," I tease. "I don't think the priest would like it very much."

Micah's eyes glitter. "I'll count if you will."

"Every second is a second too long," I promise.

"Shall we?" The priest clears his throat.

I nod shyly, and Micah nods more boldly.

In my head, I'm already counting down backward.

With every word from the priest, another second slips by.

Another second closer.

Another instant narrowing the end of my life as Talia Grey, and the beginning of my life as Talia Ainsley.

Another tick closer to eternity with Micah.

The entire time, we never look away from each other.

Micah's lips move silently and I realize he's really doing it —counting backward. I fight the urge to grin with everyone watching, squeezing his fingers playfully and getting a wink in return.

I took a wild guess on how long it would take the priest to recite the wedding vows, and I'm not far off.

I'm down to ten by the time he gets to *In sickness and in health, for richer or poorer, for better or for worse, 'til death do you part*.

Nine.

"Do you, Micah Ainsley, take this woman to be your lawfully wedded wife?"

Eight.

"I do," Micah answers firmly.

Seven.

I'm fizzing to bits, nearly bouncing on my toes.

"And do you, Talia Grey, take this man to be your lawfully wedded husband?"

Six.

"I *do*," I say, more emphatically than I've ever said anything in my life.

Five.

And then Rolf is there, trotting down the aisle, looking very pleased with himself that he's doing his trick right. Micah spent a month teaching him as he jogs up to us with his tags jingling against the ring box hooked to his collar.

Four.

"Good boy." Micah tugs the box free, scratching behind Rolf's ears.

Three.

The box open.

The rings are waiting.

Two.

Sliding onto each other's fingers, cool gold bands that quickly warm with shared love, affection, and trust.

One.

The priest looks into our smiling faces and says the magic words. "Then by the power vested in me, I now pronounce you man and wife. You may now kiss the bride."

Zero!

An ending.

A beginning.

A forever.

Our new life starts with Micah sweeping me into his arms with our ring-bound fingers pressed together.

His mouth captures mine, kissing me so deeply, so passionately.

I wonder how I ever thought this man was cold.

He gives me every emotion now with crushing lips and

delving tongue, with a possessive hold and a whisper that gives me chills.

"Talia," he growls against my lips. Like I'm a cherished thing he wants to taste and hold and keep.

And I kiss him back just as deeply, ignoring the people around us breaking into celebratory shouts.

It's so distant when everything I need is right in front of me, here in my arms.

His lips taste like a promise—and a little like the salt of my tears, spilling down my cheeks.

Yeah, I don't care if I ruin my makeup anymore.

I don't care, because this is perfect.

I took a risk.

I jumped.

And I fell headfirst in love.

I am Mrs. Talia Ainsley.

I am cherished.

I am his.

The darkest chase ends, and I'm giddy for the many happy years ahead.

Only the rest of our lives.

FLASH FORWARD: DARKNESS DIVINE (MICAH)

I wasn't made for the southwestern sun.

Honestly, I think I'd need SPF 10,000 to survive the blinding Nevada daylight. I'm sweating through my clothes, I can barely see, my fingers are slippery as hell inside my climbing gloves.

The drop below me looks so dizzying it'd give Spider-Man an aneurysm.

Like hell I'm going to slow it down, though.

Not when I'm having the time of my life chasing my wife up this cliff.

Fuck me, my wife.

It's been almost a week and I still can't get over those two words.

A week of camping at Pyramid Lake, just north of Lake Tahoe, soaking up the sun that's a far cry from snowy North Carolina.

A week of rock-climbing on sheer cliff faces, fighting our way to the top one finger and toe-hold at a time.

A week of admiring just how brave Talia Ainsley is.

She throws herself at fresh challenges with such enthusiasm, determined not to let anything defeat her.

Of course, we're playing it safe, using every harness and rope known to man. I also triple checked her climbing kits to make sure we had extra inhalers.

With the wedding in her hands, the honeymoon was on me—and I took a risk and surprised her with this trip.

At first, I was worried it wouldn't be special enough, considering we went camping all the time in Redhaven. It was pretty much our default date night.

Yet, Redhaven has hills and a few sharp drop-offs, but it doesn't have these imposing arid rocks, spearing up into a hard blue sky as bright and brilliant as the shimmering waters below.

The risk paid off.

I've never seen Talia so excited to try something new.

We did our first week of climbs with a climbing instructor, learning the ropes—literally—and getting safety precautions hammered into our heads. This is our first solo climb, the campsite at the peak of this cliff waiting to reward us with a quiet evening underneath one of the most amazing skies I've ever seen.

The Milky Way glints like diamonds, offering a pathway of stars over the austere landscape every night.

Right now, though, my view isn't the stars.

It's a cloudless, shimmering azure sky.

Plus, my wife's delectable ass in a pair of fuchsia leggings, flexing and curving and pulling her muscles tight to show off *every* detail.

The unexpected show conjures up the most inappropriate fucking erection of my life, thousands of feet above ground and held in place only by the sheer persistence of my own fingers stuffed into a crevice.

My feet are braced on a small ledge, waiting and watching

while Talia edges slowly along another ledge to seek out the next good grip for her hands.

She pauses, glancing down at me over her shoulder.

A few wisps of her brilliant hair escape from its tight bun, sticking in scarlet-wet sweaty lines to her cheek. She grins breathlessly.

Her inhaler dangles against her chest, nearly falling down the plunging neckline of her sleeveless shirt and into her cleavage. She hasn't needed it yet, thank God, but we were right to keep it in easy reach for both of us just in case.

The last few months have been amazing, no question.

The way she's blossomed after taking over A Touch of Grey, dealing with clients not just as Gerald's apprentice but as a master carpenter and woodworker herself.

It's been awesome to witness.

Even if I'm sure she'll always have those sweet, shy mannerisms, she's a confident woman now. Fully confident to face challenges head-on, and as her confidence has grown her anxiety has lessened, and that means fewer asthma attacks.

No, her asthma will never be totally cured any more than my eyesight—which currently hates me, contact lenses discarded for the climb so I could get the full effect of sweat running and stinging my naked eyes behind the glasses clipped into my hair—or the way I bruise so easily, but just like me, she's standing.

She's found a way to live the life she wants.

And I'm proud as hell of her for that.

Just like I'm proud of her for laughing as she calls, "We're halfway there, lazybones! Think you can keep up?"

"Woman, when I catch you," I growl playfully, "I'm going to remind you what happens when the wolf catches Little Red."

"So you're a wolf now, and not a vampire?" she teases. "I

guess you'd have to be, to keep surviving in this sun. But if you remember, the huntsman killed the wolf and ran off with Little Red."

"No damned huntsman here." I inch myself up closer, grinning fiercely. "There's just a man who's high on adrenaline, desperate to rip off his wife's clothes."

With a laughing shriek, Talia turns away, catching the next handhold and pulling herself up.

That's how we pass the hours.

Hours of climbing only inches at a time, teasing, pretending to chase her at a snail's pace, laughing and throwing ourselves against nature and realizing we can win.

It's goddamned exhilarating, being so *high* and having our lives in our hands this way, having to trust our bodies to carry us to the top.

It's almost sunset by the time we reach the peak.

My arms and legs—hell, my entire body—are on fire from the strain, and I love it.

It's that feeling of pushing yourself to the limits and your body answering the call, discovering you can do more than you ever thought you were capable of.

I watch Talia pull herself over the slightly overhanging edge of the cliff peak.

Her cute, chunky sneakers with their cleated soles vanish over the ledge of the mesa, before I dig my toes in and grind my way up those last few feet.

I reach up for the rocky ledge—and instead find her taking my hand, soft even through the thick climbing gloves.

Talia kneels over me, framed by a halo of fading sunlight, grinning as she gives me the last heft up to pull me over the ledge.

Then we both collapse on our sides, drenched in sweat and winded, both of us grinning like fucking loons.

"You good?" I grind out.

She laughs, rolling onto her back and spreading her arms and legs, gazing up at the sky.

"I feel *amazing,* Micah." She turns her head to look at me. "I think I'm getting addicted to this climbing stuff."

"I've created a rock monster."

Chuckling, I shift onto my back, catching the straps and buckles of my pack to let it fall free so I can lie flat. She does the same, and together we stretch out to catch our breath.

Our hands drift over to find each other—we always seem to need to be *touching* each other—while we watch the sunset, turning the sky into a mosaic of purple streaks and orange and gold, this brilliant sky-fire that's too breathtaking to be real.

Only, it is.

There's something about seeing the world like this after conquering a good climb.

It makes you realize how much larger it is than all the petty, hateful things we hold on to. How there's something greater out there than old pains and ugly scars, deep grudges and wounds we keep picking at until they never stop bleeding.

There's something healing, something wonderful, about being under a sky like this.

Especially when I'm with the woman I love, her fingers tangled in mine.

I turn my head from the sunset to her—only to find her watching me right back. She's as beautiful as ever.

I don't give a damn if she's streaked in dirt, her hair sweaty, disarrayed crimson that looks like it declared war against her hair tie.

She'll never *not* be gorgeous to me, especially with the slow, warm way she smiles, the way it lights her blue eyes and turns them violet and gold in the evening light.

"Hi, husband," Talia whispers, her fingers tightening on mine.

"...hello, wife." I smile slowly.

A giddiness I never thought I could feel whips through me.

It's insane how you can lose so much time in someone else's eyes.

I don't know how long we stay like that, completely absorbed in each other, rapt and lost, feeling like my heart is swimming in some deep red pool of warmth, but it's twilight by the time we're interrupted.

Mostly by my stomach snarling like a wolverine.

My gut lets out the most unholy gurgle, and I blink. So does Talia, before bursting into loud laughter as she rolls over to push up on one elbow, leaning over me with a wry grin.

"...we should probably set up camp and eat more than protein bars crammed down our throats at three thousand feet."

"Shit, you're right. I think I could handle that." Groaning, I roll to sit up and kiss the tip of her nose. "Good thing we didn't pick a campsite where we'd have to fish for our dinner before we could even eat."

"*That* is one thing you will never get me into. Fishing, sure. But if we caught anything?" She points at me teasingly. "*You're* dealing with the smelly fish guts, mister."

Chuckling, I haul myself to my feet. "*If* we're ever in that situation, I'll gladly take on that responsibility. C'mon. Let's get a fire going."

We fall into familiar routine.

We've gone camping so many times now that it's practically instinct as we break down our packs for supplies and get everything set up.

We packed light, knowing we'd have to haul it up the sheer cliff face and any extra weight could drag us down.

We have a paper-thin pop-up tent only in case of inclement weather. Thankfully, we won't even need it with the night so clear, our compact but well-padded double sleeping bag laid out in a comfortable spot with some leaves and grass underneath for a little extra insulation against the rocky slope.

We start a fire with dry brush in the stone-circled fire pit left behind by other travelers passing through.

Dinner is a freeze-dried beef stew reconstituted with canteen water and reheated over a portable unit.

Dessert? Janelle Bowden's homemade brownies, chewy and thick with a crispy, flaky top. After a few minutes warming near the fire, they're as fresh as if they just came out of the oven.

It's simple enough, roughing it up here, and as long as we're together, it's all we really need.

Talia's taught me more than ever how to appreciate the simple things in life.

And we're content to be quiet, lingering on our inner thoughts after we're done eating and the dishes are wiped clean.

We lean against each other, watching the fire, half-dozing in that kind of pleasant exhaustion that can only come from a long day of pushing yourself in all the best ways.

Talia turns her head and nuzzles my shoulder. "...Rolf would love this."

"Yeah, he would." But Rolf is safe at home with Gerald right now. He's too old to handle the flight from North Carolina to Nevada in cargo, and definitely too heavy to carry up the cliff in a harness. I kiss the top of her head. "Don't worry, Shortcake. Your grandfather's probably spoiling him silly right now. We'll get home and find him ten pounds heavier because Gerald kept sneaking him treats all day."

Talia laughs. "…Grandpa, too. If I don't watch him, he eats nothing but muffins and bear claws from the bakery all the time. That man's got the worst sweet tooth."

"Just him?" I ask dryly, and she snorts and flicks my arm.

"You're still mad about the last brownie, huh?"

"Not *mad*, but…"

That gets another delighted laugh out of her. "Oh, hush. I'll make you brownies when we get home. *After* Rolf climbs all over both of us."

"You know, looking back, I think Rolf knew it before I did."

Blinking, Talia tilts her head, looking up at me.

The golden firelight turns her skin into soft velvet, and dwells in small, glimmering suns inside her eyes. "Knew…?"

"That I'd fall madly in love with you." I lean into her, resting my forehead on hers. "That dog never warmed up to anyone else in all the years I've had him. But he rolled right over for you with barely a token protest."

Talia blushes.

Goddamn, I love it when she blushes, the way it lights up her face. With a teasing smile, she brushes her lips to mine.

"Rolf was easier to win over than you."

"Rolf doesn't have three decades of daddy issues and trauma turning him into a raging asshole working through denial."

"Aw, you weren't a *raging* asshole. Just a temperamental one." My lovely wife steals a kiss, then pulls back, giving me a playful shove. "Now get off me, hubby. I *stink*. I know that look in your eyes, and nothing's happening until I get cleaned up."

I feel like I'm pouting.

I've got to be pouting.

"Would it help if I said I like the way you taste when you've been sweating all day?"

"Micah!" Talia swats my arm and rises to her feet, laughing, then glances at the far end of the sloping mesa top. There's a small natural spring there, just barely a liquid gleam in the darkness. "Would *I* be an asshole if I took a bath in the pond? People drink out of it, don't they?"

"Most folks bring water filters for that reason. You never know what someone or something has been doing in the water. *But.*" I stand, reaching for my pack. "I brought a surprise."

Talia watches curiously as I pull out a flat-packed zipper bag that has what looks like a tarp inside.

It's not a tarp.

It's a snap-open collapsible tub with a little pump and a small heating element, powered by a rechargeable battery pack. I hold it up with a grin.

"Give me twenty minutes to get this set up and we can both have a hot bath."

Her eyes round with wonder. "...my aching thighs and I *both* love you, Micah Ainsley."

"The things I do for my wife."

With a teasing salute, I head down the gentle incline to the spring and shake out the folded square of grey nylon.

The thin wires inside snap into place, turning it into a bowl-shaped little tub that will barely fit one of us, let alone two. Still, that's not going to stop me from getting wet and naked with my wife.

It makes me think of shows with backwooded hillbillies, bathing in steel basins and thumping banjos.

I'd settle for those kinds of hillfolk than the ones back in Redhaven any day.

Not that anyone's seen hide or hair of the Jacobins in months. Their farms are deserted, most of them in jail and either awaiting trial or already sentenced. The few left ran away only God knows where.

Xavier Arrendell rolled over the minute the cocaine withdrawals started kicking in. He realized he wasn't getting medical treatment for his addiction without a plea deal, and in the end he almost seemed relieved to let it all go and get it off his chest, no longer stuck in a life of cocaine and money and family corruption.

Everything came falling out—the entire dealer network, how they ran their operation, foreign contacts. Basically an encyclopedia worth of damning information in the DEA's hands, leading to sweeping busts.

And I want no part of it.

I'm not a DEA agent anymore.

Just a small-town cop who loves his dog and his wife.

Xavier Arrendell, Ephraim Jacobin, everyone connected to them, they're getting the justice they deserve.

Nobody ever found a body to close out Bowden's fate, but I'm sure he'll turn up sooner or later. If he shows up alive, that's a problem for another day.

For now, I have the closure I needed.

I don't have talking crows leering over my life anymore, taunting me with dead voices.

Wherever my brother is, I hope he's finally resting easy.

I look up at the sky, searching the stars while I put the pump hose in the spring and let it fill the tub.

Maybe Jet's up there watching me, right now, nodding in approval.

I hope he's happy for me.

I hope he's saying, *Good on you, Mikey. You finally grew a heart and got yourself a good life after all. Don't you dare let it go.*

The little pump fills the tub surprisingly fast.

I make sure the heating element is fastened safely into its housing where it can't burn through the nylon, then leave the water to warm up and climb back up the incline, my calves straining.

I watch as Talia pulls the chain with her inhaler over her head, fighting her hair tie loose and shaking that gorgeous cloud of fire down.

Slipping up behind her, I wrap my arms around her waist and rest my chin on her shoulder.

"Since you're so sore," I mutter, running my fingers along the zipper of her top, "I would be a terrible husband if I didn't help you out of these clothes."

Laughing, she turns in my arms and grabs my neck, leaning into me. "That was a pathetic excuse, even for you."

"Fine," I admit shamelessly. "I want to strip my wife naked, get her wet in every possible way, and ravish her until I have to carry her back to our hotel tomorrow."

God, I love making her blush, making her breaths catch like that, making her lashes tremble as her eyes dilate, smoky and needy. Her body goes just a little softer against mine, her curves molding to me.

"You like saying that a lot," she whispers. "'My wife.'"

I smooth my hands down her back before I cup her ass, overflowing my palms with soft flesh, and then jerk her closer so she can feel just how much I want her.

"Don't pretend you don't like hearing it," I growl.

Her voice hitches, but she doesn't pull away.

If anything, she moves closer, a silent invitation.

"I like hearing it very much." Stretching up on her toes, she nips my lower lip. "Say it again."

That one little bite is all it takes to ignite my blood.

With another rough growl, I lean down to kiss her, bite her back, tease her mouth with punishing nips until she tastes the way I love.

Bruised and ripe, her tongue wet and submissive as I take control.

"You're pressing your luck, *wife*," I whisper.

She smiles against my lips.

"I'm not. I'm getting exactly what I want."

Little *minx*.

And entirely mine, turning me on and setting me on fire. She makes me want her in ways I've never wanted anyone before.

We crash together with a kiss so feral it could light the sky, hands everywhere, ripping at each other's clothing.

Somehow, we back down the slope without tripping, falling, shedding our shoes and our climbing gear until we're naked under the stars and falling into the steamy bath without ever parting our lips from that all-consuming kiss.

The water splashes. The snap-up sides of the tub nearly collapse as we stumble into it.

It's a tight fit for sure, especially when we're a tangled mess together.

Fuck, I can't help touching her *everywhere*, sliding over her smooth skin to feel her warmth, soaking her body heat into my palms.

Soon, we wind up on our knees—me kneeling in the bottom of the tub, Talia straddling me.

And we're already gliding together in a hot rhythm that tortures me as her wetness slides over my cock, all molten flesh teasing and making me want to be inside her *now*.

Her entire body is covered with love bites—her shoulders, her breasts, her stomach, her thighs, her neck—and I find every last one.

Touching, kissing, savoring my handiwork, making her gasp and writhe as I suck at the marks I've made.

Over and over again, I bite over her shoulders.

I toy with her nipples, pushing her into a frenzy, making her thighs grip me until she's shuddering, moaning, throwing her head back.

Fuck, fuck she's ready.

Oh so ready as I dig my fingers into her ass, lift her up, position her over me, and then slam her *down*.

Her heat plunges over me in a wild rush.

She screams rough pleasure into the night—then chokes off as I sink my teeth into her throat.

We're frantic.

Wild.

Two unhinged animals out here in the dark, under the stars, rutting and giving over to our baser urges without shame.

She rocks her hips, her powerful inner muscles convulsing around me, locking tight as she rides me. I drag her in deeper to meet my every thrust.

We've been crazy like this since the day we said *I do*.

Insatiable.

Manic.

I can't get enough of devouring her, the feel of her, burying myself deeper and deeper like I can mark her permanently from within.

My balls churn with fire, aching to breed this woman.

Yeah, I said it.

I'm ready for a kid, and soon enough, she'll be too.

That's blazing in my mind as Talia's pussy shudders and clenches around me.

As my pubic bone finds her clit, pushing her further, *harder*, needing to feel her clasped around me, needing that sweet moment when she loses herself, falls apart.

And when she comes, she's fucking perfect.

This pale sculpture arched over me, glistening in the desert moonlight, her expression transfixed as she throws her head back and gives her screams to the sky.

I almost don't need the violent pressure of her inner walls fluxing around me, tormenting my cock with pleasure.

I could just come from seeing her alone.

She's everything.

Everything.

And as my nerves short-circuit and my eyes roll back and I fill her to the brim, as I join my voice to hers, as I tear my teeth from her throat and take her lips, grinding her name into her mouth, branding her with a kiss, I know.

I will never let this woman go.

In darkness and in light, we are one.

In darkness, we're divine.

In darkness, we renew our love, no matter where the years ahead may lead.

ABOUT NICOLE SNOW

Nicole Snow is a *Wall Street Journal* and *USA Today* bestselling author. She found her love of writing by hashing out love scenes on lunch breaks and plotting her great escape from boardrooms. Her work roared onto the indie romance scene in 2014 with her Grizzlies MC series.

Since then Snow aims for the very best in growly, heart-of-gold alpha heroes, unbelievable suspense, and swoon storms aplenty.

Already hooked on her stuff? Visit nicolesnowbooks.com to sign up for her newsletter and connect on social media.

Got a question or comment on her work? Reach her anytime at nicole@nicolesnowbooks.com

Thanks for reading. And please remember to leave an honest review! Nothing helps an author more.

MORE BOOKS BY NICOLE

Dark Hearts of Redhaven

The Broken Protector
The Sweetest Obsession
The Darkest Chase

Rory Brothers

Two Truths And A Marriage

Knights of Dallas

The Romeo Arrangement
The Best Friend Zone
The Hero I Need
The Worst Best Friend
Accidental Knight (Companion book)*

Bossy Seattle Suits

One Bossy Proposal
One Bossy Dare
One Bossy Date
One Bossy Offer
One Bossy Disaster

Bad Chicago Bosses

Office Grump
Bossy Grump
Perfect Grump
Damaged Grump

Heroes of Heart's Edge

No Perfect Hero
No Good Doctor
No Broken Beast
No Damaged Goods
No Fair Lady
No White Knight
No Gentle Giant

Marriage Mistake Standalone Books

Accidental Hero
Accidental Protector
Accidental Romeo
Accidental Knight
Accidental Rebel
Accidental Shield

Stand Alone Novels

The Perfect Wrong
Cinderella Undone
Man Enough
Surprise Daddy
Prince With Benefits
Marry Me Again

Love Scars

Recklessly His

Enguard Protectors Books

Still Not Over You

Still Not Into You

Still Not Yours

Still Not Love

Baby Fever Books

Baby Fever Bride

Baby Fever Promise

Baby Fever Secrets

Only Pretend Books

Fiance on Paper

One Night Bride

Grizzlies MC Books

Outlaw's Kiss

Outlaw's Obsession

Outlaw's Bride

Outlaw's Vow

Deadly Pistols MC Books

Never Love an Outlaw

Never Kiss an Outlaw

Never Have an Outlaw's Baby

Never Wed an Outlaw

Prairie Devils MC Books

Outlaw Kind of Love

Nomad Kind of Love

Savage Kind of Love

Wicked Kind of Love

Bitter Kind of Love

Printed in Great Britain
by Amazon